2017 January 19
Melanie —
Enjoy the ride
All the best
Mark Berman

Substance of Abuse

Mark Berman

authorHOUSE®

AuthorHouse™
1663 Liberty Drive
Bloomington, IN 47403
www.authorhouse.com
Phone: 1-800-839-8640

This is a work of fiction. All of the characters, names, incidents, organizations, and dialogue in this novel are either the products of the author's imagination or are used fictitiously.

Published by AuthorHouse   9/12/2012

ISBN: 978-1-4772-6745-5 (sc)
ISBN: 978-1-4772-6743-1 (hc)
ISBN: 978-1-4772-6744-8 (e)

Library of Congress Control Number: 2012916649

Any people depicted in stock imagery provided by Thinkstock are models, and such images are being used for illustrative purposes only. Certain stock imagery © Thinkstock.

This book is printed on acid-free paper.

Because of the dynamic nature of the Internet, any web addresses or links contained in this book may have changed since publication and may no longer be valid. The views expressed in this work are solely those of the author and do not necessarily reflect the views of the publisher, and the publisher hereby disclaims any responsibility for them.

Prologue

The Near Future...
Friday, March 11

Heroin.

James Ralston opened the paper bag and withdrew the brown vial. Damn, it was easy, he thought as he headed for the exit. He didn't notice the man in a tan sports coat who had just entered the building, bumping into him and causing the bag to drop, with its contents scattering across the floor. The man proceeded to help him retrieve the new possessions, all the while apologizing for the mishap. Ralston couldn't get over how life had changed now that it was legal to buy drugs in Santa Barbara. He put everything back in the bag and simply smiled and nodded, indicating no harm done. The man walked on and Ralston continued out the door.

Only minutes earlier he had waited patiently in line as the crowd at the Drug Procurement Center (DPC) thickened with Friday night approaching. At the counter, he had handed his authorized request and magnetic-stripped identification card to an attendant behind bulletproof windows. She had given him a bill, which he then presented to a cashier, along with his Mastercard, for payment. In exchange, he received a duplicate receipt with a purchase number on it. Ralston then sat in the waiting area and read a magazine to pass the

1

time. He didn't wait long. Looking up, he saw his number on the "ready for pick-up" screen. Ralston presented his receipt and ID to an attendant, who stamped the receipts, kept one, and returned the other, along with a paper bag and two pamphlets. One pamphlet described the risks of taking drugs. The other listed local Alcoholics Anonymous meetings and the various treatment facilities for acute and chronic drug disorders. The paper bag contained a small vial with heroin premixed in a sterile saline solution, two new syringes and needles, alcohol wipes, and instructions for intravenous administration. The bag was labeled, in large red print, "FOR PERSONAL USE ONLY." Another warning label reminded the user that it was a felony to sell this product, give it to a minor, operate a motor vehicle, or commit any misdemeanor while under its influence. The label added: "Recommended to be used only in your private residence."

The last two months had been a blessing. James Ralston, a shoe salesman, used to have a much more difficult time getting his heroin. No one knew about his habit. He insisted it was not an addiction — weeks would go by without any heroin. Nonetheless, he enjoyed it, perhaps too much. Over time it had become more costly and much riskier. It was always the same scenario. Late at night, with a pocket full of cash, he walked through the seediest section of town or in a dark and isolated park, hoping his contact would show up and treat him fairly. In his mid-fifties and diminutive in stature, Ralston knew he was lucky never to have been injured and to have been cheated by dealers on only a couple of occasions.

When the drug legalization pilot program had been announced in Santa Barbara County, Ralston's first instinct had been that it wasn't for him. He feared losing the anonymity he got in exchange for the risks of the street. That didn't happen. DPCs were scattered widely, so users could easily go outside their own neighborhoods. More important, the drugs were extremely inexpensive compared to their street equivalents. Anyone interested in recreational drugs could now get quality product at one-tenth the old street price. Although the street vendors would tout the purity of their product, Ralston knew from experience that street heroin varied widely in how it was cut. He figured it would be safer to trust the government pharmaceutical companies to deliver a controlled substance. It didn't take long for him to give up the corner junkies in favor of the government-regulated DPCs.

In the mere two months since the pilot program had started, Ralston noticed he actually used considerably less heroin. Perhaps because it wasn't illicit, it may have lost some of its excitement. Ultimately, though, it was probably the sheer availability that helped limit his usage. Before the program started, he would seek out the drug whenever he heard it was available. The price would creep up little by little, but somehow the drugs were always available. He wouldn't describe himself as an addict, but when he ran short on his supply a couple of times, he experienced the worst flu-like symptoms he could remember. Each time his supplier somehow came through. Ralston was savvy enough to know he was purposely being strung out. Still, he made it a point to make a purchase whenever he could.

James Ralston was no thief. In fact, he had become quite a hustler in shoe sales. If a customer wanted to see a particular style of shoe, he made certain she tried on other colors and similar styles as well. He told the other salespeople he enjoyed the competition of selling, but in truth he had felt a degree of panic setting in as his monthly drug bills began to escalate. He paid his mortgage on time, but his recreational habit had started to eat into his food money. When the DPCs opened, it took Ralston less than a week to abandon his worries about loss of privacy. Instead he proceeded to shed his worries about loss of income.

Ralston got into his car, looking forward to the weekend. He was a simple man who enjoyed eating at home, listening to classical music, reading novels and occasionally taking a little heroin to take him into his fantasy world. As he turned onto the street, a blue Firebird parked near the entrance to the DPC lot turned on its headlights. Ralston laughed to himself as he remembered having to look for a blue Firebird at Pine Crest Park. He would drive a half-block past it, park his own car, and then drift between the trees into complete darkness. He'd be located by his connection, make his transaction, and head for home, hoping he hadn't been cheated, his heart pounding from the excitement he really didn't need. He was glad those times were behind him. Still, by habit, he watched as the blue Firebird pulled behind him at the traffic light. The light turned green, and Ralston continued straight ahead as the Firebird turned right. He let out a sigh and laughed to relieve the tension associated with old habits and concerns.

He cooked lavishly that evening, preparing himself a Tuscany treat to Pavarotti's tenor arias on the stereo. He thought about saving his heroin for another night, but instead he eased into his favorite chair and immersed himself in La Traviata.

He took out his new purchase, drawing up 1 cc of the clear liquid into one of the syringes. It was so easy now, he thought, as he fastened the Velcro tourniquet on his left arm. He took an alcohol wipe and prepped a spot on the forearm near a good-sized vein. He eased the needle into his skin, trying to imagine it was not his arm. He barely felt the fresh needle. What a relief, as its silicone-coated body slid smoothly through his skin and entered the vein. He drew back just enough that a tiny drop of blood came into the syringe, affirming its proper position, then released the tourniquet before slowly plunging the contents into his vein.

He sat back as the music grew more intense. His eyes remained open but not focused on anything in particular. He could taste the subtle changes as they permeated his mouth and spread through his head, enveloping him in a rapture that seemed to heighten the intensity and flavor of the opera. His eyes closed, and he could see the colors of the opera dancing and lightly parading through the scenes in his head. He smiled as Joan Sutherland reached a note too high for a mere mortal, and the opera continued to enchant him. He felt himself drifting steadily with the music, deeper as the tenor sang, floating serenely as a velvet warmth caressed his brow like a gentle tropical breeze and effortlessly laid him in the downy meadows of his dreams.

Frascati's buzzed with the usual Friday night crowd. Good food and a warm family feeling mixed with a light party atmosphere were the trademarks of the restaurant. You could find plenty of friends, particularly at the bar, yet it also felt cozy and intimate to sit in the deep leather booths with the soft lighting one seldom found in the trendier restaurants. This destination would be the site of a mini-celebration for the Masons.

Although they had been married for only two years, Robert and Stephanie

Mason had been eating there since they met nearly six years ago. They had just made their first legal purchase of marijuana. Although it was legal, they still felt as if they were committing an illicit act.

As Rob and Stephie got into their BMW to head toward Frascati's, for the first time Rob didn't resent the sobriety device he had installed. All people who wanted to participate in the drug legalization program, or even purchase alcohol, now had to have such a device in their cars. For most people, it was like fastening their seat belts. You simply got into the car, put in the key, punched a six-digit identification code, blew into a breath analyzer, and performed a quick reflex test. Within thirty seconds you were on the road. The device was equipped with a valet service drive, which allowed the car to be driven no faster than thirty miles an hour for a maximum of five miles. Rob was actually relieved to have the device. Not only did it relieve him of the danger of being on the road legally drunk, but it would prevent him from being hit with a DUI, the punishment for which had been greatly expanded with the advent of the experimental program. In fact, any passenger or "buddy" found to have taken and passed the sobriety test to allow access for a drunk driver would receive a minimum five-year prison sentence.

With their newly purchased marijuana from the DPC, Rob and Stephie stopped at a park on the way to Frascati's for a few hits. They reminisced about the first times they had tried the stuff — well after high school and college, when all of their friends were heavily into it. For them it was a sexual drug, for it always seemed to heighten their lovemaking. It was also a major appetite stimulant, for which they would be well rewarded at dinner. At the DPC they had been impressed with how the product was sold. Marijuana from several farms was available. Each farm provided a leaflet with a short description of its crop, clearly taking a lesson from the wine industry on how to sell one's wares. Words like bold, sensuous, uncomplicated, mellow, or tantalizing added personality to the product. The marijuana itself came processed and ready for rolling, piping, or cooking. You were allowed a maximum of twenty grams — enough for ten normal-sized cigarettes. The Masons bought eight grams and took just two hits each at the park before leaving for the restaurant.

Inside Frascati's they began to get that tingly sexual feeling. They also felt a bit giddy — and hungry to boot. (It was not unusual these days to see customers a little bit hungrier than usual.) The linguine di mare was delightful, and though Rob was not a big mussel enthusiast, tonight they went down easily. They enjoyed a glass of Valpolicella before heading home for fun and games.

Feeling like a man on top of the world, Rob handed the parking valet a five-dollar bill as he got into the car. Stephie looked on expectantly as Rob passed the sobriety device's check without any problem. Ascending the winding road up the hills toward Mission Ridge, Rob thought the steering felt a little stiff and told Stephie they ought to take the car in to check the power steering. But the BMW rapidly became more difficult to maneuver. In fact, Rob was just about to stop when he came upon a curve at Las Alturas that he could not handle. The steering locked. He braked hard and tried to make the turn, but it all happened too quickly. The BMW swerved right, caught the curb at an angle, and launched over the embankment. More amazed and perplexed than frightened, Rob held the wheel tightly, as though he could still maneuver his vehicle. Stephie screamed as their airborne car plunged helplessly into the dark ravine.

The small crowd finally began to thin, leaving the Weldings' party in ones and twos. Gordon and Catherine Welding had put on an intimate affair for just thirty guests. No attendee was any more prominent than U.S. Congresswoman Leslie Phillips, and none was having any more fun or looking any better than she. Resplendent in her deep purple Versace dress with its plunging neckline, she represented the sexiest Capitol Hill had to offer.

She had been escorted to the party by the pride of Hollywood, director Randal J. Weissman. R.J., as he was affectionately known, had just come off one of the most successful weekend film openings in the last two years. He was living a fairy-tale life, and now, dining among the Santa Barbara nobility, he was only too happy to be seen with the glamorous congresswoman.

After a memorable evening, R.J. led the way to the awaiting limo. He had a little surprise waiting for Congresswoman Phillips. As he had told Leslie when they arrived at the party, "If only the high school kids who voted me 'Most Pathetic' could see me now..."

Leslie stepped through the back door of the limo while R.J. shook hands with Gordon Welding, then slid next to her, pulling the door shut.

Waiting inside was a gorgeous young woman named Sherie. Longer and leaner than the curvaceous Phillips, but with full lips and slender hands, she cut a sexy figure in her short, black Gucci dress. Sherie had opened a bottle of Cristal and was now offering the elegant champagne to the congresswoman and the director. Leslie smiled and clinked glasses as the car left on the short trip from the Weldings' Montecito mansion to Weissman's estate.

Sherie raised the privacy window in the limo and lit a joint. She took a deep hit before passing it on to R.J. He took a hit and offered it to Phillips. She seemed content to sip her champagne, but he offered again.

"Oh, don't tell me. Aren't you the congresswoman who got drugs legalized? I guess you're not allowed to imbibe."

There was enough challenge in the question to make Phillips grab the joint and inhale deeply. Sherie reached for the grass and slid across the car and onto the seat next to Phillips. The buzz was strong now. R.J. leaned over to Phillips and began to kiss her passionately with slow, soft kisses, caressing her lips and gently probing her mouth. Her eyes half-closed, Leslie could feel the tingle flow through her body as she held her mouth open, inviting his kiss. Another sensation flooded her senses as Sherie began to massage, then caress her neck and shoulders. Sherie's long fingers glided softly over her skin, just under the front of her neck, to her shoulders and then down the length of her arms until their fingers met and gently entwined. Phillips lifted her head as R.J. began to kiss down the front of her neck and then between her breasts. Sherie shifted so that her leg was now alongside Phillips, and as Phillips leaned back, she put her hand high on Sherie's thigh.

Before much more could happen, the car pulled into the driveway of Weissman's estate. Inside, with the house lights dimly lit, they could see the scattered twinkling of the homes below and perhaps one or two boat lights shining from their moorings on the Pacific, far beyond the panoramic windows.

The trio's heightened sexual responses continued as they drank the rest of the champagne and smoked more grass. Clothes began to shed. Sherie stood in her high heels and panties and proceeded to unzip the congresswoman's dress. Phillips at that moment was undoing the belt of the shirtless R.J. and putting her right hand into his pants. Sherie slid her long silky fingers into the sides of Phillips' dress, softly touching her sides and allowing her fingers to slide down and tease along the band of her panties.

In R.J.'s bedroom, the tryst continued. Sometime during the activity, unbeknownst to Phillips, R.J. activated a remote video unit enabling him to record what would surely be his most memorable evening. Leslie writhed ecstatically as his tongue tasted between her legs and Sherie caressed her breasts. She had never had sex with another woman before, but under the circumstances it seemed natural. She became even more aroused as she saw R.J. voyeuristically mesmerized by the two women sharing passions. She could not remember a time when she had felt such a wondrous sexuality.

She giggled aloud and turned to R.J., saying, "No wonder this stuff was illegal. It makes you feel too good."

Chapter 1

11:30 p.m., Friday, March 11, 2011

THE REVOLVING LIGHTS OF the police and fire engines cast a red glow on the emergency personnel gathered at the accident scene on Las Alturas. Detective Jimmy McVee, who had been a Santa Barbara police veteran since moving there from Boston with his wife ten years ago, now served as the liaison for the experimental drug program. As such, any crime that may have involved drug use was his beat.

He walked up the hill where a group of firemen was working. A man sat on the curb with an ice pack held to his nose while a couple of paramedics checked his vital signs. At the ravine's edge, emergency lights had been set up to illuminate a car lying upside down against a boulder maybe sixty yards below the level of the road. Beyond that boulder lay nothing but steep jagged hillside. As a winch whined, a cradle began to rise with a victim in it and a fireman alongside.

"Hey, McVee, ever seen two luckier people?"

Frank Ramsey at six-two, towered over the stout senior detective. Ramsey, at forty-six, was twelve years McVee's junior. Ramsey still looked young and athletic for his age, so instead of two cops, they could have passed for the coach and his player.

9

"What do we know about this so far?"

McVee ran his hand over his gray crew-cut.

"Two kids, a young married couple," said Ramsey looking at his notes. "Robert and Stephanie Mason. They purchased some grass at the DPC, smoked some of it, went to dinner, had some wine, were driving home, and then drove their car off the road. What's amazing is they didn't get killed. The car landed up against that boulder. They were both strapped in their seat belts with the airbags deployed. They're bringing up the wife now."

"No injuries?"

Ramsey gestured at Rob Mason, "Well, he smacked his nose pretty well, but not much else."

"Is this a DUI?"

"We're going to run blood and urine tests, but the kid actually did all right with his field sobriety test and claims he passed his car's breath check and kinetic reflex test."

"His wife could have done the test for him."

"That's why we'll run all the tests, but he swears he passed the tests himself. Also, there seems to be a discrepancy about the amount of marijuana they smoked."

Rob Mason dropped his ice pack to join the emergency cradle that had finally arrived safely at the street level. Released from the emergency basket, Stephie rose and clung to Rob.

"What type of discrepancy are you talking about?"

Ramsey lifted a small plastic bag containing marijuana. "Mason had this in his jacket. It's the stuff he bought at the DPC. I've already been on the phone with them. They bought eight grams. He says he and his wife rolled one joint and only took a couple of hits. Look at this bag. I'd be willing to bet there's less than four grams. What happened to the rest?"

"We can see if he's positive for marijuana, but we already know he is. If his field sobriety is negative, you got no case."

McVee joined the couple. He didn't want to get in the way as the paramedics examined Mrs. Mason, but he wanted a few words himself with her husband.

"Excuse me, Rob. I'm Detective Jimmy McVee." He gave the mandatory flash of the badge. "Can you tell me what happened?"

"Am I being arrested?"

"No, son, but we will have to take you in for a breath, blood or urine test and get a statement from the two of you. You will be detained for a while, but based on the little I've heard, I don't believe we're ready to arrest you." McVee saw Mason relax at that. "So what the hell happened?"

"I don't know. I wasn't drunk or high. We were on the way home. There was nothing in the road. As I got near this curve, the steering completely gave out. I tried to pull the car to the left, I even slammed on the brakes, but it was too late. We went over the side. The car flipped to the left and skidded on the roof and then bam. I guess we landed up against a boulder. I thought we were dead for sure. I can't believe we didn't even get hurt."

"I'm not so sure about that. Have you seen your nose yet?"

"Is it bad?"

Stephie moved around to face Rob and took a look. "It's really swollen on the left. It looks like it's broken."

McVee shrugged. He'd seen worse — twice — on his own face. He pulled out his wallet and handed a card to Mason. "Give this guy a call on Monday. Let him check your nose. If it needs fixing, Dr. Ryan's the best. He straightened mine out a couple of times already."

Rob took the card. "Thanks."

McVee sensed he had put the kid at ease and removed some of the natural antagonism that accompanied such situations.

"Is this the same Dr. Ryan who's in charge of the legal drug program?" Rob asked.

"Yeah, but most of us think it's just a temporary job." McVee winked and turned to watch a tow truck pull the Mason car up over the curb. It made a screeching sound as it slid on its roof, and McVee winced like he'd heard nails on a chalkboard.

"BMW might want to consider making a commercial with your car. Just look at it."

As smashed up as it was, the passenger compartment was largely intact.

"What's next?" Stephanie asked.

11

"Detective Ramsey will finish a little more paperwork, and then he'll take you down to the station to complete the investigation. Your car, what's left of it, is off to the station for forensics. It shouldn't be too long before you're home."

McVee looked at his watch. It was after midnight, and he had put in a long day. Being the liaison for the drug program had been a non-job until today. He'd get little sleep before his morning meeting at the DPC with FBI Special Agent Roger Felton and Jeffrey Buchman, the assistant director of the program. Two sudden heroin overdoses already had government agents crashing the party. The Mason case would surely add to the festivities.

Chapter 2

9:00 a.m., Saturday, March 12

"You can take your time, Tony. I'm going down to the lobby to meet Spencer and Lynn for some coffee. The way the snow's blowing down here, it's got to be miserable up on top."

Tony looked up from his laptop as Montana emerged from the bedroom. Ten years into their marriage, her brown eyes and full, pouty lips still sparked his desire. In her ski gear, she looked like a model out of *Ski* magazine.

"Go ahead. I'll catch up with you. I'm just going to check some of my e-mail. We can give it some time to see if it clears up. If not, we can hang around town." Tony said the magic words, but he sensed Montana wasn't buying it.

"You hang around town? When there's fresh powder on the hill? Are you running a temperature?" She didn't wait around for an answer, and when Tony looked up again, all he saw was the door closing behind her.

From their suite at the Little Nell Hotel, Montana and Tony Ryan had a view of the base of Aspen Mountain and the Silver Queen Gondola. A few hearty skiers still climbed the stairs to the gondola bundled in all their bad-weather gear, already dusted white with the Colorado powder coming down.

13

Tony had seen worse. But he knew better than to challenge Montana about the weather. They had skied four days since Tuesday, so it wouldn't hurt to sit out their last day.

Tony resumed with his laptop and opened his e-mail. While most people relied on their phones these days, Tony still preferred his laptop for sending and retrieving messages. He clicked through the usual advertisements and offers to the main menu and "You have mail." He opened his e-mail to find three letters waiting.

The first, from Joanna Kane, his office manager, provided his schedule and outlined his week ahead. Although she was only a couple of years older than his forty-five, Joanna felt like a mother hen caring for her eldest son. Responsible to a fault, she had been organizing Tony's life for nearly seven years.

Under the header "Anthony Ryan, M.D., F.A.C.S.," Monday morning's schedule showed a breast augmentation followed by a rhinoplasty, with an afternoon filled with post-op follow-ups and new-patient consultations. Tony audibly exhaled. It was clear that the saying "Work hard, play hard" should be "Work hard, play hard, go back and work harder."

Aside from his day job as a cosmetic surgeon, Tony served as the director of the government's legal drug program in Santa Barbara County. During the first two months of the program, he presided over an endless string of meetings. Now, with the program practically running on auto-pilot, he was happy to let Jeffrey Buchman, the assistant director, capably run the day-to-day operations as his own role became more titular. Nonetheless, ever since he had gone to Washington, D.C., more than two years ago to testify before Congress, the "experiment," as he referred to it, had consumed more hours than he thought possible. It was the one remaining reason he and Montana had put off having kids.

Mentally he added another item to his agenda. When they got home, they'd barely have time to change clothes before a cocktail party/silent auction at the home of Gordon and Catherine Welding. The annual fund-raiser benefited the Children's Hospital, and Tony had been talked into donating his cosmetic surgery services. Last year, someone had donated six thousand dollars, and Tony got to suck fat for three hours.

Next he opened an e-mail from Leslie Phillips. Until he had traveled to D.C. to testify, Tony had assiduously managed to avoid politicians. He certainly had not intended to become friendly with Congresswoman Phillips. She had all but spanked him verbally during his initial testimony before her subcommittee, but he held his ground and eventually won her respect. That very evening, at a cocktail party given for the invited witnesses, it was Montana who had found common ground with Leslie Phillips and ushered her over to Tony for a more personal introduction.

Leslie Phillips had an attribute unusual in Washington — an open mind. She was one of the first members of Congress to lighten her stance against drug legalization. In fact, she had volunteered her district of Santa Barbara as the proving ground. Tony's inclusion in the establishment of the program, not to mention his presidential appointment as director of the legal drug program, had brought Leslie Phillips and the Ryans even closer.

Tony clicked on the heading "Friday, March 11, 2011, Leslie Phillips, message." A video e-mail came to the screen. Unlike Joanna, who preferred to write her messages, many people preferred to record a video message on e-mail. With the cameras built into the computer and the available compression chips for video, real-time audio/video transmission was replacing the answering machine.

Leslie sat in the backyard of someone's house in Santa Barbara. It looked like she was wearing a bathing suit, at least a top, which showed off her well-endowed congressional assets. She had on sunglasses, with her raven hair pulled back into a ponytail. Behind her stood an expansive wall of windows that partly reflected a swimming pool and, in the distance, a small knoll with two palm trees, one bent low at an angle, before the Pacific Ocean.

"Hi, Tony. As you can see, I'm not dressed for skiing. I hope you and Montana are having a lovely time. Let me congratulate you on a fine start with the experiment. Although the official stats won't be published until the end of the first quarter, I spoke with our liaison, Detective McVee, and he tells me that the crime rates have fallen precipitously. Of course Jimmy thinks we're just in a kind of honeymoon period. But wait until Congress gets the update next month. A lot of people are going to wake up.

"I'm sorry I couldn't free up the time to join you two, but I've been all over the map. I'm finally at home now — well, not exactly my home — and must attend an intimate dinner at the Weldings tonight. R.J. Weissman, the director, is my date."

Leslie leaned forward in a conspiratorial whisper. "I think he's cute. He's a few years my junior, but what's age? You're the one who says, 'Look in the mirror and see how you feel. That's how old you are.'

"Anyway, give my best to Montana. I hope you make it to the Weldings' fund-raiser Sunday. I'll see you there."

Last came a note from Buchman, also a video, called "3/11/11 - note - J. Buchman." When Tony clicked on the e-mail, he saw the baby-faced Jeffrey Buchman trying to look professorial with his horn-rimmed glasses in his office at the DPC.

"Dr. Ryan, I'm afraid there were two heroin overdoses this week. I don't have any details about the circumstances, but Jimmy McVee has been here with an FBI agent, Roger Felton. Felton wants to go over our lab records. Apparently he has the authority to do so. I'll be here straight through the weekend, and I'll keep you posted."

So much for vacation. Such was the magic of technology. Already he felt like he had returned to work. Certainly the honeymoon with the drug program had ended. As far as he was concerned, this political hot potato didn't need to get any hotter.

He shut down his computer, walked over to the desk by the window and placed a call to Leslie Phillips. Phillips could keep this under control. No use letting a couple of overdoses smolder into a political brush fire. He looked out the window, impatiently drumming his fingers while the phone rang. Her voice mail picked up the call, and he left a simple message ending with "See you at the fund-raiser." He wondered if she already knew about the heroin overdoses.

He held the phone ready to call Buchman. Outside, the sun started to win the battle as the clouds dispersed. The snow looked great, and several skiers started lining up to get on the gondola. Tony put the phone back in the cradle before placing the call. There was nothing Tony could do from Colorado.

It had been midmorning when the clouds cleared, and though Montana complained about the cold, even she admitted that the snow conditions were perfect, and she never skied better. Tony knew that once he had gotten them on the slopes, Mother Nature would delight her company.

When he walked into his room that afternoon, having joyously survived in one piece, a message from Jeffrey Buchman waited.

"What's up, Jeffrey?" Tony asked, the phone cradled between his head and shoulder as he used his free hands to get out of his ski gear.

"Did you get my e-mail?" Buchman asked.

"Yeah. Any update?"

"They're doing an autopsy on the victims today, so I should know more by early tomorrow. Also, I forgot to tell you that there was a marijuana-involved DUI late last night. A young couple went over the edge way up on Las Alturas."

"Oh, my god."

Buchman jumped in and quickly added, "Amazingly, they survived without any significant injury. The car luckily slid up against a boulder."

"I guess you've been busy."

"Agent Felton just left a few minutes ago. He's tearing this place apart. He's not only going over computer records, but he's been in the lab and stockroom."

"Don't worry about it. There's nothing to hide. Maybe it will do them good to check out the program. Have you heard from Leslie Phillips? I left her a message."

"No, and I've called her a couple times myself. I just wanted to check in with you before I left," Buchman offered.

"Offhand it doesn't sound like much. I know there are plenty of boys in Washington who'd like any excuse to terminate the program, but I wouldn't worry about it yet. I'll stop by tomorrow."

That evening Tony stepped downstairs to the Little Nell lounge. He relaxed in one of the deep leather sofas, watching the courtyard fill with a fresh dusting of snow.

He was amazed how quickly this first week in March had flown by. Five days in Aspen weren't enough. Sipping a Mexican hot chocolate, Tony surveyed the Saturday evening scene. From the crowd he saw Montana and their good pals from Washington, D.C., emerge and join him.

Across from Tony sat Rick Santiago. Rick, roughly Tony's age, was a lucky man. Tall and good-looking, he had his mother's raven hair and father's deep blue eyes. He had a Treasury Department position working with the FDIC. It provided him with a close-up and in-depth look into America's financial institutions. It was Rick's ultimate dream to be the President of the United States — the first of Mexican descent. By the grace of God, Rick worked in Washington, D.C., and not in a rural town outside of Jalisco. For this, he considered himself lucky indeed.

"I don't know. I'd say there's a good chance they'll pull the plug on the program if more incidents start rolling in," Rick said to Tony and Spencer as he sipped his beer.

Spencer McCade looked like a teddy bear with his feet propped up on an ottoman while he sipped something that left a dollop of whipped cream on his nose. The image made Tony chuckle in spite of the conversation.

"Do you really think they'll raise a ruckus over a couple of ODs and a DUI?" Spencer asked as he wiped his nose.

"I can tell you," Tony replied, "from the time I spent in Washington, there's a lot of people looking for any excuse to pull the plug."

"Tony's right. I can name dozens of senators and congressmen, not to mention your own Senator Winston, who oppose it. They think it's the second coming of the plague," Rick added.

"At least you have Congresswoman Phillips on your side. What's she say?" Spencer asked, sipping from his mug.

"Actually, I haven't gotten a hold of her yet. I think she's been partying with a new boyfriend this weekend. I hope to see her tomorrow."

"No offense," Rick directed to Tony, "but personally, I've never been very supportive of your experiment — legalizing drugs, maybe, but not the experiment."

"Why's that?" Tony asked.

"It's too localized. You know how the former Mexican attorney general argued that the American drug trade was the cause for so much corruption."

Spencer interrupted, "That's one of the reasons why legalizing drugs is necessary."

"Sure," Rick jumped back in, "in the long run. But for the rest of the country, drugs are still illegal, so you've still got these organized distribution networks in full swing. Don't you think they're going to invest in your failure?"

"That's definitely a good point," Tony admitted, "but we had to accept this compromise or we'd never get a foot in the door at all."

In an effort to relax and enjoy the rest of the evening, Tony turned the conversation back to the college basketball playoffs about to get under way.

Five minutes later the conversation went from basketball to hockey then soccer, and Rick and Spencer had a new argument.

As Tony watched them argue, he remembered the day Montana had invited Rick to their home. Rick had actually tried to pick her up during a 10K run in Santa Barbara. Tony's and Rick's interests could hardly have differed more, but still they managed to find a decent amount of common ground.

When Montana and Tony went to Washington for his congressional testimony, it was Rick who introduced them to Spencer McCade. Spencer arranged private tours for Tony and Montana, getting them into every place from the FBI to the White House. After he had spent his younger years in the Navy as a public relations officer, it was a natural transition for Spencer to serve as the Pentagon correspondent and bureau chief for the newest major network, Satellite News Service. Spencer was so well connected that it came as a shock to Tony when there was someone he didn't know.

Tony looked over at Montana, while she entertained Lynn, who was now Mrs. McCade; and Rick's girlfriend, Carolyn, who wanted to be Mrs. Santiago. Had it not been for the recent incidents involving the drug program, he would have been savoring the height of contentment. Instead, he found himself anxious to get back to Santa Barbara, talk with Phillips and do some quick damage control.

7:30 a.m., Sunday, March 13

At the Aspen airport a light snow continued to fall. It didn't threaten the Ryans' pending flight, as their plane was already on the ground and had plenty of visibility for takeoff. In all the years they'd been coming to Aspen, Tony had been rather lucky in terms of flights in and out. Nonetheless, the unpredictability of nature should have taught Tony long ago not to schedule surgery on the day after the planned arrival home. Although it had happened only twice, it was an unpleasant task for Joanna to call patients scheduled for surgery to inform them that their doctor had been snowed in at Aspen. Patients paying fifteen thousand dollars for face-lift surgery do not like to hear that they need to be rescheduled.

Whether the flights were on time or not, hanging around the airport waiting to leave while the new passengers arrived always felt slightly depressing. It didn't make matters any better that Tony could only make contact with Phillips' voice mail before leaving the hotel. He also left an e-mail message for her this time. Oh, well, at least he'd see her in the afternoon.

While waiting for the boarding call, Tony sat at a table sipping orange juice while Montana browsed the magazine stand. Tony watched as she conversed with a friend she recognized. The vivaciously outgoing woman he'd married was a strange contrast to the little girl from whom she had grown. Predominantly of Italian background, she was a beautiful woman who never gave importance to her appearance. She had been an adorable little girl with big brown eyes and full pouty lips, but shy. So shy her mother thought it might be a good idea to enroll her in drama class. For most of the other children and their parents, the West Los Angeles Drama School held the dream of future stardom. For Angela Martin (formerly Martinelli) it was a way to help her daughter become more comfortable in public. Meanwhile, with each performance, another new agent approached Montana Martin. The other kids dreamed about the offers that Montana would repeatedly turn down. Her looks only improved with maturity as her big brown eyes became graced with a perfect body and legs shaped by good genes and several years of ballet.

Meanwhile, Mrs. Ryan had certainly come out of her childhood shyness shell. She was still not one to initiate conversation, but she didn't have to. Always a few steps ahead of the latest trends, her friends and sharp acquaintances picked up plenty of ideas from her. People always sought her out. Men especially. Her single girlfriends, glad that Montana was married, loved to hang out with her to use her for bait. Then they'd get upset when the men that they met were usually interested in Montana or were married. She was never flirtatious, but her outgoing and inquisitive nature turned many disappointed men into friends. Such was the case with Rick Santiago.

As Tony and Montana prepared to stand and walk through security, Tony heard a familiar voice.

"Well, if it isn't Doctor Ryan, Santa Barbara's finest cosmetic surgeon. Or do you prefer going by your new title, director of the drug program?"

Tony looked over his shoulder to see Dr. Burton Wesley and his wife.

"Damn," Tony said under his breath.

Wesley proceeded straight toward them, with his wife, Natasha or something — Tony couldn't remember her name and didn't really care; he just remembered she was from Eastern Europe — walking along in her sporty fox with her arm locked around her husband's. Wesley wore her on his sleeve like the trophy she was to him. Tony recognized his arrogance as a shield for his lack of self-esteem. Everyone else just thought Wesley was nasty.

Tony remained seated and tried to show no emotion. Wesley's large frame towered over them. Normally he tended to glare at Tony, but this time he appeared to be smiling.

"What, no hello? How was the skiing?" asked Wesley.

"Do you ski?" Tony asked with condescending overtones.

Wesley ignored the barb. "What a coincidence. We must be leaving on the same flight. I suppose you'll be at the Children's Hospital fund-raiser this afternoon. Donating some more liposuction. Or maybe it'll be a little marijuana this year,"

God, he was annoying, thought Tony.

Wesley turned to his wife and, in a comfortably patronizing tone, exhaled, "Nadia, do you remember Dr. and Mrs. Ryan?"

Montana politely offered her hand. "Montana Ryan. Nice to meet you."

Wesley pulled a current copy of USA Today from the side pouch of his carry-on piece and dropped it on the table in front of Tony. It unfolded so that the front page and its glaring headline, "ODs in Drugtown," stared straight up at Tony.

"Here, enjoy this. Go ahead, take it. I've already read the thing. I'm sure you'll be real proud of yourself."

"You know better than most that there were many more overdoses before the program."

Wesley was still smiling. "But this time the heroin overdoses are being caused by the DPC, not the user."

"What are you talking about?" Tony asked, picking up the paper.

"You won't find it there. Didn't Buchman tell you? The FBI found super-concentrated heroin in the vials of the dead men. Someone sabotaged the vials. Hell, the user was safer buying from the black market. You'll no doubt be meeting Special Agent Felton in a few hours."

"Since I'm only the director of the program, how is it you know so much more than I do?" Tony asked.

"I still run my rehab centers. The word gets out awfully quick when someone ODs. And Roger Felton is a long-time acquaintance. He called me before he left for Santa Barbara."

"And I'm sure you provided him with just the right orientation."

"Something like that."

Tony could feel his temper starting to rise. He had to neutralize the hostility. "Well, I guess we'll see you at the fund-raiser," he said.

He looked in the direction of Mrs. Wesley in a meager gesture of civility.

Thankfully, Wesley took the cue and left for the boarding gate.

Once Wesley and his wife were far enough away, Montana asked, "Why do you give him the pleasure of letting him bother you?"

"What do you mean? I kept my composure. I barely showed him any concern at all."

Tony knew Montana was right. It wasn't worth it to keep up pretenses with his wife. She just looked at him, waiting for a straight answer.

"Okay," he said, "I can't stand the guy. Privately, I've always known he was a real snake, long before we considered the drug decriminalization program."

"Really? Did you really dislike him before the congressional hearings?" She challenged him to come up with a reasonable explanation.

Before Tony could respond, the speaker announced the departure of their flight. They gathered their things and headed toward the gate.

"I remember when Burt Wesley was starting out. He didn't always have such a fancy house, big boat, and huge —"

"And I remember when you were starting out, we didn't have anything," Montana interrupted. "So what's the point?"

"Burt Wesley started as a simple family physician. But after he built up a large group practice, he got heavy HMO contracts and started buying nursing homes and converting them into so-called 'psychiatric institutes.' Basically, drug rehab centers. You know how they work. They advertise on the radio, 'Recovery West, the most important step is the first.' They even have a special incentive program for referring physicians. If you have private insurance, they get you into the program. The day your insurance runs out is the day that you're cured. Great program, huh —?"

"If that's the case, why doesn't the state medical board go after him?" Montana asked.

"Guess which California Medical Association delegate is also a member of the state medical board?"

"Are you kidding?" Montana replied as she put her purse on the x-ray belt, walked through the metal detector, and waited for Tony.

Tony picked up the cue after he passed through the metal detector. "Look, I don't like anything Burton Wesley stands for, but he's bright when it comes to politics and, apparently, business. If it wasn't for his opposition, I'm sure he would have been running the drug program, even if it were a conflict of interest. Whatever he's doing with his rehab centers is probably just within the guidelines — nothing more, nothing less."

Montana stated her case. "Still, I don't see why he has any complaint with you. You'd think he'd love the program — more drug addicts, more money, no?"

Tony replied with a small grin, "Well, not exactly. You see, his weren't among the rehab centers chosen to participate in the program."

"What did you have to do with that?" Montana now suspected Tony had had a more significant role in Wesley's disenfranchisement from the program.

"Actually, nothing. He brought it on himself. If you recall, he spoke the morning of the same day I addressed Congress. He pleaded that drug legalization was a miserable idea. He was certain that the change in attitude would flood his clinics. There simply would not be enough facilities available to deal with new addicts. He cited some dumb-ass survey they performed indicating sixty-three percent of the 'cured addicts' would not return to drug use because it was illegal. Do you know how the questions were actually posed? Try this: 'I won't return to drug use because, number one, next time I might get caught and serve time,' or number two, which accounted for a mere fifteen percent, 'I don't want to cause more hurt to myself, my family or my friends.'"

"Sounds fairly reasonable to me."

"Montana, do you know who Wesley has in those rehab centers? Mostly young unmarried males. All of their answers are going to be skewed. Like I said, he brought it on. The organizing committee — "

Montana quickly interjected, "Which you were on."

"Okay. There was a consensus that sources outside the county and a university program would have less conflict of interest involved, and it would be a better way of gathering unbiased data. It also gives an opportunity to compare costs through the government-run program and the privately insured, who seem to be getting ripped off."

Ahead of them, Nadia and Burt handed over their boarding passes and exited the terminal on their way to the plane.

Montana looked up at Tony and said, "Nonetheless, it appears that directly or indirectly you epitomize the guy trying to put Wesley out of business."

They entered the light snow on their way to the boarding ramp. Tony took the paper from under his arm and held it up. "Only a dirt-ball like Wesley would gloat over something like this."

Chapter 3

12 noon, Sunday, March 13

THE FLIGHT HAD ARRIVED on time, so the Ryans, in their convertible Jaguar XK8, drove up the Coast Highway to Santa Barbara just after noon. Having left their skis at the Little Nell allowed them to enjoy the warm Southern California day with the top down. The black cat purred along the highway. Instead of turning off the road to head to their hillside home, Tony proceeded directly to the DPC. He had phoned Jeffrey Buchman from L.A. to make certain he would be there to meet him.

The Ryans walked into the DPC, passing only a modest number of people. Tony withdrew his identification badge and entered his code numbers at the door to the inner offices. Once inside, he and Montana were greeted by a guard where signed in. The two hurried down the hall to the director's office.

Tony opened the door, entered and found his assistant director, Jeffrey Buchman, standing behind a man who occupied a keyboard connecting him to the DPC computer system. From Buchman's message, Tony assumed it had to be Felton, the FBI agent. The crevices etched into Buchman's brow made it clear they weren't playing computer games. Compared to the slightly built

Buchman, Felton, though twenty years his senior, had a hulking appearance. Of course, Buchman made Tony look fairly imposing.

"Dr. Ryan, I'm so glad you're here. We've got some problems." Tony suspected that Buchman didn't overstate the dilemma. "Oh, hi, Mrs. Ryan."

"Hello, Jeffrey," Montana said, almost maternally.

The man at the keyboard looked up for the first time. He was reasonably youthful-looking in spite of his full head of gray hair. He took the initiative and introduced himself: "Roger Felton, FBI, special agent to this narcotics program."

Tony didn't like his salutation. "Tony Ryan, M.D., director of this narcotics program. Oh, and this is Montana Ryan, wife of the director of this narcotics program."

Felton eased off the pedal just a bit. "Excuse my curt introduction. I could stand a little polishing of my social graces. Nonetheless, Dr. Ryan, Mr. Buchman here is right. There are some serious problems with the supplies at this DPC. We've determined four recent deaths were from an apparent heroin overdose."

"Four? Didn't you tell me two on your message?" Tony directed his inquiry to Buchman.

"Yes, I did," said Buchman, biting his lower lip. Then he added, "but two more cases were reported late yesterday. A young woman, apparently a first-time user, and a shoe salesman, a known habitual user, were both discovered by relatives. By the way, we got a call from Senator Winston's office. He's wondering if it might be a good idea to shut down operations for a while until we complete our investigations."

Tony turned momentarily and looked at Montana, then asked, "What about Leslie Phillips? Has she talked with Winston yet?"

"I've put a call through to her office — twice, in fact — but we haven't heard from her yet," Buchman offered.

"Damn, I'm sure she could cool his jets. Winston's never supported this program. He doesn't need any extra ammunition. Not now, anyway. He'd pull the plug and it'll just open the black market again. I don't get it," added Tony. "There hasn't been a heroin overdose since the program started. I'm not surprised we finally had one or two, but four all around the same time. What are you looking for?"

"I was about to tell you." Felton looked only slightly annoyed about being interrupted. "We were able to sample the vials from the users. All four had ten times the stated concentration. They would have never seen it coming. So we're, Mr. Buchman and I, going through the computer files so you can do a recall and check any outstanding vials before someone else dies."

"Excuse me for asking, but how did you get the authority to investigate the program?" Tony didn't like the smug attitude he'd been sensing.

"Do you doubt Mr. Buchman's ability to check my credentials?" Felton challenged.

"Hardly. I just know that when we organized this program, there was a federal task force established as an advisory board. There were FBI agents involved, but I don't remember your name on the list."

Buchman interceded. "It had been updated just after you left, Dr. Ryan. Mr. Felton and another agent, I believe Mark Hansen, were added to the advisory panel."

"Maybe you'd like to call the Bureau," Felton chided.

Check, Tony thought. "Is an internal investigation really necessary?"

"Let's put it this way. There's a good possibility that someone in your DPC, or along the supply route, is dangerously altering the drugs you're doling out."

"You're fishing. Everyone in this program has been screened by the FBI, the CIA and the Secret Service. You know damn well it's not an internal problem. Where else are you looking?" As his tone grew harsher and his voice a little louder, Montana reached for his arm, as though she could externally control her husband's volume.

Felton stood up, pushing his chair back and forcing Buchman to retreat a few steps to the side. "Look, Ryan. I don't know what your problem is. Maybe you have something to hide. Maybe you've been conveniently out of town. You've got four dead people as a result of this asinine program you call your 'experiment.' We're not looking for someone to sweep the dirt under the carpet. We want some answers. You have any?"

"You don't get answers until you find the problem," Tony said, moving a couple of steps closer to Felton, remaining eye to eye. "Part of the experiment established built-in problem-solving mechanisms to deal with unfavorable and unexpected outcomes. Don't you get it? We organized this program knowing there would be problems. We have to see if 'we' can deal with them. While Senator Winston may want you here, Congresswoman Phillips is the liaison to the feds. I think you've jumped the gun."

"I'm an employee of the federal government. I was sent here by the authority of a United States senator. Senator Winston, if you weren't listening, would just as soon shut down the program while we investigate. And I'll be around until I conclude this investigation. At this point, my authority supersedes yours, so if you don't shut your mouth and start cooperating, you'll be cited for obstruction of justice. Do you really want to spend the next few days behind bars?"

Felton placed his hands on his hips, purposely opening his jacket enough to reveal the weapon in his shoulder harness.

Tony got the message.

Just in case he hadn't, Montana gladly stepped in on his behalf. Moving quickly in front of her husband, she explained, "Mr. Felton, I'm sure there's no need for threats." Looking back at her husband, so that he got the message, too, she added, "Since you're both on the same side, I'm sure you'll be able to conduct a meaningful investigation together. This may prove to be an enlightening experience all around."

The two men stood there scowling at each other, trying to maintain their macho postures.

Montana forcibly grabbed Tony by the arm. "Come on, Tony. We've still got a full schedule."

Tony looked down at his watch, acknowledging the time, then offered, "Okay, Felton. Do your investigation. We'll be most cooperative, but I expect a full accounting of your findings on a regular basis." Tony turned for the door with what he thought was the last word.

Felton made sure to add, before the Ryans were out the door, "Don't worry, Doc. I plan to keep you in the loop."

As they left the building, Montana said to her fuming husband, "There's still smoke coming out of your ears."

"The whole thing stinks. I need to speak with Leslie. Maybe she can pull the reins in on Felton. I don't think it's a coincidence that Wesley knew this guy was here. And they both have the same arrogant manner."

"I think you matched his arrogance. The two of you looked awfully silly putting on that macho show. Was that for me or Jeffrey?"

Tony shrugged, saying, "I don't think Felton and I are going to be very good friends."

Minutes later, they drove up the winding road to their hilltop home. The heavier-than-usual rains had left the hillsides a brilliant green, which blended well under the vibrant blue sky. It was a Santa Barbara postcard day.

As Tony maneuvered his car through the curves, Montana leaned over and cautioned him, "Hey, if you're going to drive like this, at least keep your eyes on the road."

After all these years, he still loved to glance out at the ocean as it peeked through the lush shrubbery around each curve. He couldn't explain it, but on those picture-perfect days it simply drew his attention because it felt good. It also felt good gliding through the turns in the Jag.

"Tony, please. You're not on the slopes of Aspen, or are we letting off a little steam?"

Tony slowed down to a comfortable pace. "Sorry. We do need to get moving if we're going to show up at the fund-raiser, though."

"I'd like to get there in one piece."

Changing the subject, Tony asked, "Are you looking forward to going to Rome?"

"I don't mind, but it would be a lot more fun if you could meet me there."

"I'd sure like to, but with this investigation and the schedule Joanna has for me, I don't see how I can."

"Don't you think it would be beneficial if you showed up for part of the conference? After all, this is your implant company." A glance to his right and Tony saw the brow furrowed of a visibly annoyed Montana.

"<u>Our</u> implant company," Tony managed to add.

"Oh, right." Montana indignant at the suggestion chimed back, "It's your company when you develop a product and my company when we have to sell it."

"That's what I said — 'our' company," Tony repeated.

"Well, I wish you were going. Doctor Della Torrini's a nice guy, but you should be presenting your own paper."

"He'll do fine. You just need to make sure you have a lot of samples of the new nasal implant. I'm telling you, there should be a lot of Asian doctors there, and they'll love it. Are you staying at the Hassler?"

"Actually, since you're not going, I've made plans to stay with Gina at her apartment."

"And save all of that money?"

"This way I'll have more left over for shopping."

Tony shot her a glance then added, "Look, I know you're doing me a favor by going. I appreciate it. Really I do. At least you'll be able to hang out with Gina. That ought to be fun."

"You're such a putz. I'm going to one of the most romantic cities in the world to cover 'our' implant company, and you tell me I'll have a good time because I can hang out with Gina."

"That's not what I meant." Tony wished she'd let up. "I think you know I'd rather be going with you than sending you off for a week with Gina."

Tony hated to argue with her. He also knew she'd been looking forward to going to Rome with Tony, one of their favorite cities. Since she had been responsible for running the distribution network for Medform, Inc., an implant company of which Tony was one of the primary owners and designers, it was actually more important for her than Tony to be in Rome. The International Society of Plastic and Reconstructive Surgery would be fairly well represented by the European and Asian community. This would be a good opportunity for Medform to pick up an expanded base.

Tony pulled into the driveway, wound his way up a short incline, and parked in front of the house. It felt good to be home. Drug problems aside, he would have gladly stayed in Aspen, but now that he was back home, he was happy. Montana, for that matter, would be just as happy if she picked up a few things and took off again without even stopping. She loved traveling, and leaving the next day didn't bother her, even if primarily for business.

Their Connecticut-style farmhouse, awash in spring flowers in full bloom against its white siding, looked ready for the cover of Architectural Digest. Their house wasn't as big as some of the mansions around them, but they found it cozy, and they loved the layout. The grounds were fairly large, with lots of room in the back. The house basically sprawled around the grounds, with the Pacific serving as a backdrop for most of the rooms. There was plenty of space for entertaining, and the backyard flowed harmoniously with the house. One of their favorite spots, their lap pool built with a horizon edge looked as if it blended in with the ocean. On a relaxing Sunday morning they would sit out back with the paper and savor the view. Everyone had their own version of "God's country," but this was reminiscent of their "piece of heaven" in the South of France. Tony started unloading the car as Montana went into the house.

With the front door open, Tony could hear the excitement of two barking creatures. Their dogs started barking, certainly glad to see them. Sunny, their three-year-old golden retriever came flying out of the house and nearly knocked him over as he came walking in with the luggage. He kept jumping up trying to kiss Tony. Tony had no choice but to put everything down and give him a big hug. Sunny might not have missed them more, but he certainly acted a lot happier to see them than Critter.

Critter was a ten-year-old fourteen-pound all-American with a lot of terrier in him. This little black dog with a patch of white on his chest displayed the feistiest character. At first glance, the unsuspecting thought they would have to reckon with Sunny, but make the wrong move and Critter would eat you alive. Over the years he had become accustomed to their vacations. When they walked in, he came out and acknowledged them, but then turned and acted as if he had more important business. His payback for their leaving him was to ignore them for a while. Nonetheless, come bedtime, he would undoubtedly cause a scene, jump up on their bed and snap at Sunny to get out of his way so he could have a closer spot next to Tony or Montana. Sunny, good-natured and not one to fight, didn't care. In fact, he, like everybody else, gladly got out of Critter's way.

Critter had actually been Montana's dog before they got married. He may have been one of the reasons she married Tony — Critter really liked him.

31

"Well, Critter, did you miss us?" Tony bent down with Sunny still jumping on him, and Critter slowly sashayed over and licked him on the face.

Montana shook her head. "I don't think anybody at the fund-raiser this afternoon is going to treat you this well."

Across from East Beach Park, at Milpas Street, Michael Cirrelo occupied a public phone booth. The wind picked up a little, and the traffic outside made it a little difficult to hear clearly. The lean Cirrelo, just under six feet tall, with gaunt angular features wore his receding dark-brown hair pulled back into a pony tail. Although only thirty-eight, he looked like he had been thirty-eight for twenty years. He had clearly been marked by street time. Through a dark pair of Ray-Bans he gazed at the ocean across the street while he concentrated on the call.

"Listen, pal. I'm ready to leave Dodge. I've fulfilled my contract. Anything else is gonna cost double."

The voice on the other end of the line gave the instructions.

"Are you crazy? You want me to go to the zoo?"

He looked straight ahead, out toward the water. On the sand, a few volleyballers tuned up their game. A nanny pushed a stroller with a little pink-outfitted infant. Cirrelo smiled briefly. He didn't like hanging around in one place too long, but this had been an unusual situation. He was not unaware of the importance of his role. The careful execution of his job could swing the balance of power back to his bosses. Ultimately, he'd be in line for more than a simple commission.

"Sure I can find it. I'll make like a tourist and blend in."

He hung up the phone. He turned and walked back up Cabrillo for nearly a block until he got to his parked car, a blue Firebird. He then drove down the street, turning off in the direction of the zoo. He parked in the lot and purchased a ticket at the window. He was used to elaborate pick-up locations, but this was a new one for him. He felt a little silly.

He sensed the serenity of the area. He hiked up the hill to an area near the elephants. He had been directed to a location behind a beverage cart. There in the thick brush lay a brown plastic bag, neatly hidden from view. He reached into the bush, wondering how stupid it would look if anyone noticed, and pulled out the bag but didn't open it until he sat back in his car.

In the privacy of his car he thumbed through forty thousand dollars in one- hundred-dollar bills. He smiled at the first half of his installment. He wrapped the money back up and stuck it under the car seat. He laughed to himself as he left the parking lot. All of this fuss because of some drugs he thought. He appreciated his good fortune. He never took drugs. Certainly beer didn't count. How ironic that he could make so much money dealing with someone else's problem.

Chapter 4

2:00 p.m., Sunday, March 13

THEY LEFT MOST OF their stuff in their bags, cleaned up a bit and changed into casual cocktail attire. After nearly a week in Aspen, it felt a little strange transitioning back to more cosmopolitan dressing.

Tony and Montana made fairly good time and were only fashionably late as they drove up the curves on Buena Vista in Montecito.

Gordon and Catherine Welding had an estate set back in the hills of Montecito. Security guards and valet parking attendants blocked the front entrance. Tony brought the car to a stop. Montana was escorted from her side, and Tony set the car on valet parking mode before he got a claim check from the parking attendant. After they cleared security, they were ushered onto the property through the main gates.

Two or three small trams provided a shuttle service driving people the quarter of a mile to the house. They chose to walk instead, enjoying the beautiful day and savoring the luscious property. The asphalt driveway wound its way up to a large circular courtyard capable of holding a half-dozen buses. A path cut through the grass between the towering pine trees leading to the house. A variety of flowers had been planted along the path, adding brilliant colors to their walk. The pines pulsed with birds and squirrels rustling overhead.

As they approached the house, they could see the marble fountain in the courtyard where two-dozen people gathered, exchanging salutations. Tony cringed as he saw Burton Wesley among them. He slowed his pace to avoid another encounter with him. Eventually, the crowd slowly made its way through the side corridor to the back. The way the house was built, its south side came right to the edge of the hill, affording it a maximum view of the Pacific below and leaving maximum exposure to the land behind the structure. Tony glanced up at the second story and admired the sweeping balcony that jutted over the ravine to the right. The house had definitely been set up to provide a mix of the practical and the dramatic. Montana and Tony followed the throng until they were upon the immaculately landscaped grassy knolls, which lent a Gatsby flavor to the occasion.

A casual chic crowd meandered around dozens of tables set up with articles for a silent auction. As they browsed, Tony kept his eyes open for his cosmetic surgery donation, curious to see what kind of response it would draw. Meanwhile, Montana kept busy exploring the potential of the tables.

"Did you enjoy that La Costa trip we took last year?" asked Montana, monetarily looking up from the brochure detailing the auction item.

"Sure, why?"

Without lifting her head, she said, "Here's a three-night trip to La Costa. I think we should bid on it."

"If you really want it, you should probably wait until the end to place your bid." Then sarcastically he added, "On the other hand, it is a charity. Maybe you can run up the price."

Then from behind her back, a familiar Italian-accented voice announced, "There are far lovelier trips available for a woman such as yourself."

As Montana turned around, Emilio Frascati flashed his charming Roman smile and directed her to another item on the table.

"You should have that plastic surgeon husband of yours purchase this trip to the Ventana Inn. That is far more romantic for a princess such as yourself."

Montana smiled broadly and received a warm hug from Emilio. He

35

was a young-looking fifty-year-old with thick, wavy salt-and-pepper hair straight out of an Italian fashion magazine. He could have been an actor. At any rate, he had the suave and sophisticated demeanor that comes with an Italian accent. His restaurant, Frascati's, had become part of the core of Santa Barbara, making him a local celebrity.

Tony, for his part, greeted Emilio with a handshake and commented, "Sounds nice to me. Not quite as romantic as Italy, though."

Montana shot Tony a glance, letting him know he was on thin ice. Without missing a beat, she turned to Emilio. "How have you been, Emilio?" Now the three of them stood a few feet away from the table, allowing others to walk by.

"I've been just fine, thanks. So you're going to Italy?" Emilio inquired.

"I'm representing Tony's implant company next week at the Rome meeting for aesthetic surgery." Emilio looked at her, waiting to hear the rest, and Montana knew it. "Yes, I'll be seeing Gina. I think she's the one you shouldn't have let get away."

Looking up to the sky, Emilio slowly shook his head in agreement. "Yes, I think you are right. Who knows? Something was missing for Gina. I think she was a little jealous of all the activity around me. It got to be too much of a problem with us. But you're right. She's the one who took my heart."

A waiter walked by with a tray of hors d'oeuvres. Tony took a small cannelloni and popped it into his mouth. "Hmm. Tastes like a Frascati. Are you catering this party?"

"Of course. You can tell my cannelloni, no?" Emilio responded, proud that Tony recognized his preparation.

"Delicious." Tony licked his fingers while Montana gave him a disapproving glance. "So what kind of a guy is Gordon Welding? Is he easy to work with?"

Emilio didn't appear too interested in Tony's small talk, but politely noted, "Actually, I dealt with Mrs. Welding. She set up this whole affair. You know Catherine? She's a charming lady. Bright, energetic. Runs this whole charity, puts on the show, easy to work with. The Weldings are also good customers. Gordon, he's an interesting gentleman. Well-established businessman, you know — president of the bank, First Montecito. If there's a deal going on, he seems to know about it. The rich, they get richer, no?"

Having spent enough time with Tony, Emilio turned his attention back to Montana. "By the way, did I tell you how lovely you look today? You and Gina were always the two most attractive women at the restaurant. I wish I could join the two of you in Rome. I could have in the old days, no? My family's still mostly there. I wouldn't need much of an excuse to go."

Catherine Welding came over looking for Emilio. "Emilio, do help me. It seems there's a problem with the cappuccino machine." She reached over and took him by the hand.

"Catherine, I'd be delighted to help. First, let me introduce you to Montana and Tony Ryan."

Catherine Welding, tall and blonde, and young enough that she wasn't quite ready for Tony's services, smiled warmly and offered her hand first to Tony. "Of course, the illustrious Dr. Ryan. Thank you so much for your donation. I just passed by, and it looks like a feeding frenzy for cosmetic surgery." Then, turning to Montana, she offered with gracious faux charm, "Being so attractive, you must get asked all the time what your husband has done for you."

Montana didn't let it slide. "Actually, I'm much like the shoe cobbler's daughter. I assure you, your husband has done far more for you. Pleased to meet you."

Politely Emilio turned and said, "Please, excuse me." He then proceeded to follow Mrs. Welding back toward the kitchen.

"Isn't she a delight?" Montana softly said to Tony when Mrs. Welding was sufficiently out of range. "How about a glass of wine?"

Tony surveyed the area. There was a bar on the other side of the pool. "Okay, let's go."

"Why don't I keep up with the auction items while you get us something to drink?"

"Leaving you alone? This can be a costly glass of wine."

Montana gave him "the look." "You're so cheap."

Tony shrugged. "Fine. I'll be right back." He strolled through the crowd with an eye out for Leslie Phillips, stopping momentarily to offer an occasional hello. He chuckled lightly to himself as he saw a few patients who recognized him and headed in another direction. Tony was either praised by former patients or avoided by those who were worried that they would be found out for having had cosmetic surgery. It bothered him in that he hoped over the years people wouldn't feel so secretive about surgery.

He finally pulled into the crowded area around the bar. After a few minutes he was able to retrieve a couple of glasses of Chardonnay. As he spun around back toward Montana, he was greeted, though he felt accosted, by Burton Wesley.

"Well, twice in one day. What do you know?" Wesley had an annoying way of gloating over insignificant issues.

"Hello, Burt. Long time no see." Tony kept it simple and polite, mostly out of respect for the two gentlemen standing next to Wesley.

Explaining to his gathering, Wesley announced, "We both came back from Aspen today. What a coincidence."

Then, turning to the men next to him, he said, "Gordon, George, this is Dr. Tony Ryan. He's the guy responsible for beautifying much of the scenery around here today."

While Wesley stunned Tony with the compliment, the feeling didn't last long.

"Did you know our do-gooder here was not only one of the strong proactive supporters of our maniacal legal drug program, but he's also its director?"

Tony awkwardly positioned the two wine glasses into his left hand, accidentally spilling a little on Wesley's pants and causing him to jump like it was hot oil. "Oh, sorry. Good thing it's only Chardonnay."

Gordon Welding politely held out his hand to Tony.

"Gordon Welding. Burt's just a sore loser. And this is George Hearst, of course."

No doubt Tony was well aware of the legacy of the Hearst family.

Welding continued, "That program must keep you fairly busy, especially these days."

Welding, though not as tall as Wesley, struck an imposing figure, wide at the shoulder, with thick strong hands. Tony thought he could have been a construction worker at one time. His gray hair had long ago lost any traces of color, but it was full and straight, and were it not for the wide jaw and somewhat craggy features, it would have lent him a more boyish appearance.

George Hearst, in his seventies, tall and stately, stood dressed casually in jeans and boots. His ranch was well known to the locals, and clearly he enjoyed the time he spent on it.

"I just met your wife a few minutes ago. This is an incredible place you have here," Tony politely and genuinely offered. "It's very generous of you to hold the party on your grounds."

"Thank you. Really, it's something we looked forward to doing. A really nice cause. We got blessed with a perfect day, too. So, Dr. Ryan, do you think the program stands much chance of succeeding?"

So much for simple pleasantries. "I would have thought so until this morning," Tony said. "I've read that there already are members of Congress calling for its termination. We got a call from Senator Winston's office asking if we would consider shutting it down for a while. It doesn't seem too terrible to let the program run its course, does it? I'm kind of an old-fashioned doctor. I like to see what the problem is and establish a diagnosis before I offer treatment and a prognosis." Tony looked at Wesley, who seemed to be waiting for a confrontation. Tony promised himself he would remain cool-headed and neutral in tone. He then turned his gaze back to Welding, waiting for his response.

"I'm afraid I'd have to go along with Burt, maybe for different reasons. I have no financial stake in this matter. But I am concerned about my personal safety. I assume by the ring on your finger you're married."

Tony nodded affirmatively.

Welding continued. "Aren't you a little more worried about what might happen when your wife gets on the road? Oh, sure, we've got these new breath checkers and reflex devices, but they're mostly useful for the responsible drivers. I'm sure others will find it an amusing inconvenience. Eventually, with more drug users, there's going to be less concern about responsibility. I believe there will be an increased sense of permissiveness, further eroding the fabric of our so-called civilization. I know I'm a bit more concerned when

Catherine is out driving. I fear it's simply a matter of time. People don't know their limitations, especially on drugs."

"I think your points are quite valid," Tony conceded, "but if you're really concerned about your wife's safety, let me remind you that with the present laws, nearly forty percent of the prison population is serving time for nonviolent drug-related crimes. Because of this, the jails are overcrowded, and violent criminals are frequently released early. I know I don't have to recount any of the recent horror stories for you."

"I can't help but think you've taken a rather surprising position for a man who prides himself as a rational thinker," said Wesley, slipping in another derogatory remark for good measure.

Welding, in a conciliatory way, turned to Wesley, rested his hand on his shoulder and said, "Rational thinkers have a way of working through the problem. History, I fear, has gone largely unheeded. Didn't Emerson say you should learn from others' mistakes because there's not enough time to make them all yourself?"

"Twain, Mr. Welding," Tony politely corrected him. "Mark Twain said that. I couldn't agree more."

If being caught at that slight mistake ruffled him, he didn't show it. "Yes, you're right," Welding smoothly continued. "Perhaps I might do better with a line from Shakespeare that you might consider — 'He lives in fame that died in virtue's cause.' Maybe you should reconsider your stand."

If Tony hadn't known better, he would have thought it sounded like a command.

Then, before Tony could make a simple retreat with his two glasses of wine, George Hearst asked, "Being a doctor, don't you feel rather strange providing marijuana and such?"

"Funny you should mention that. Your family still runs a very large publishing company. What if you could reduce your paper costs by well over sixty percent? What would that do for your business?"

"Obviously, that would be a tremendous cost savings." Hearst gave a simple nod of the head, prompting Tony to continue.

"Well, sir, I believe you would have been just a toddler, so I doubt you remember any of this, but in 1930 there was actually a patent awarded for perfecting a method of making paper from hemp. This occurred the same time that the Bureau of Narcotics was formed. Hemp became one of the prized targets for the head of the department, Harry Anslinger, and of course, he got help from the evangelical movement. But they could never have made hemp illegal without the help of the press. I believe your very family had a little notoriety as a source of 'yellow' journalism at one time."

"Excuse me, doctor. I'm not sure where you're going with this story, but my family were pioneers in American capitalism. They fed a lot of people."

Hearst appeared rather indignant, and Tony knew he wasn't winning any friends here.

"That's quite true, and I respect that, but no one ever accused big business of always playing fair. Your grandfather owned huge forests which he used in large part to make paper which he not only used but sold all around the country. In fact, in those same years, he had teamed with du Pont, which provided the chemicals to make wood pulp into paper. Do you think it was a coincidence that his newspapers became known for publishing stories about the notorious killer weed, marijuana – the latest scourge of the earth? It was, in large part, those fairy tales that helped the government, under Harry Anslinger, eventually make hemp illegal."

"Speaking of fairy tales, where do you come up with these stories?" Wesley interrupted.

"I mean no disrespect, sir, but this is a matter of public record. Dr. Wesley, like myself, was in Washington when a lot of these issues were discussed. Look, the original Declaration of Independence was drafted on hemp paper. Nobody even called the stuff marijuana until the 'papers' started using the pejorative based on the image of some Mexican bracero out in the fields getting stoned."

"You seem to know a lot about my family, but I'm certain your facts are taken out of context."

"You might want to check out a recent IPO that's emerged as a result of our little experiment. HIP, Inc., is the first major company born out of the recent Industrial Rights Act."

Welding chimed in, saying, "Our CFO turned the bank on to this IPO, and I believe we purchased several thousand shares. It's doing quite well, too."

"Mr. Welding, congratulations. You are benefiting from the legalization of marijuana. HIP, Inc., is Hemp Industrial Products, and they manufacture paper, clothes, fuel, cosmetics, food supplements — you name it — made from the hemp plant."

There was a momentary silence. Welding looked like he'd been slapped in the face, George Hearst looked at Welding like he was an idiot, and Burt Wesley gloated as usual. This seemed a good time to exit.

"By the way, has Congresswoman Phillips arrived yet?"

"If she has, my people haven't informed me," Welding replied.

"Well, then, I'm afraid if I don't bring this wine to my wife soon, my consideration of this issue will be the least of my problems. It was very nice meeting you, Mr. Welding and Mr. Hearst," said Tony. He then nodded at Wesley and simply said, "Burt."

When he finally got back to Montana, she was well into the silent auction process. "Tony, where have you been? There are some wonderful items. I've bid on only a few, so don't worry. Nothing outrageous."

She accepted her wine from Tony. "Well?"

Tony lifted his glass to hers. "I had another encounter with Burt Wesley. This time he was with the host of this party, Gordon Welding, and George Hearst from the publishing company of the same name. I'm sure he's been hounding Welding on the drug project. A guy like Welding has got to be very influential. Anyway, he was polite, but of course opinionated against the drug program. The way that whining jerk Wesley lobbies everyone about the drug program by scapegoating me is getting a bit old. I think it borders on slander."

Montana didn't seem to think it was much of an issue. "Tony, let it go. You always knew you'd have enemies from the start. That's the nature of politics. Let's get back to the business at hand."

An hour later, Montana and Tony had been all over the tables. They had made several bids, though Tony wasn't sure on what. Montana excused herself and made her way indoors in search of the powder room.

Ten minutes later she found Tony walking away from a couple of people he had encountered. "Are you having a good time?" she asked.

"Sure. Why?"

"Because I overheard Gordon Welding complaining to Emilio as I walked back from the powder room. He said this affair wasn't handled the way he expected. It should have been taken care of properly. He said it was much too sloppy. Emilio stayed rather quiet, but then I heard him say that he had taken care of all of the details. Seems to me the party's gone well enough. Maybe there could have been a few more people coming around with drinks and such. I don't know."

"There could have been more food, I suppose, but all in all, I'd say everything's just fine. Who can figure with people? Welding must be very meticulous. Maybe that's why he's a rich man. In fact, I was thinking we should go over to Frascati's for dinner later." Tony looked at Montana for a response.

"Fine with me."

An hour later, Tony and Montana traced their path back to the car. They managed to walk away with a few items. Tony, the high bidder on a magnum of wine, an '82 Haut Brion, carried it along tucked under his arm. He read from a brochure and a letter describing the terms of a trip to the Ventana Inn they had also purchased. Montana had a large decorative floral vase from Bertolini's under her arm, a Beach Boys anthology, and a certificate for a facial, a massage and a loofah treatment at the Genesis Spa.

After getting their car from the valet attendant, Tony placed the bounty in the trunk, cushioning the vase and wine with a couple of sweat shirts he kept in his ever-ready gym bag. Within seconds Tony passed the car's sobriety check, and as he buckled his seat belt, Montana suggested, "Let's go into town. I'd like to get a cup of coffee and stop by Bertolini's. I want to get another vase to match the one we just got. I think a pair of them would look great in our entrance."

"What did we end up paying for the vase?" Tony was not enthusiastic, but kept his tone neutral while he drove off heading down the hill.

"It's a charity. Anyway, we spent less than three hundred on it."

"Three hundred dollars for a vase?" Tony lost his neutrality.

"Just under. The bidding started at two hundred. I'm sure it's worth much more."

"How much more?"

"I'm not sure. I forgot to check." Tony knew by her tone she was getting annoyed with his questioning.

"Great deal, Montana. It's such a great deal, now you get to buy another one for full price."

"What a grouch."

Tony had been called worse. Certainly, there were some choice comments being made about him after he left the little gathering with Welding and company.

"You know, I never saw Leslie Phillips. Did you see her there?"

"I saw Senator Winston. He had the usual crowd around him, but I didn't see Leslie at all, although I must admit I really wasn't looking for her. There were a lot of people there. It would have been real easy to miss her."

Something bothered Tony about that. "She said she would be there in her e-mail. I assumed it was obligatory, so I'm surprised we didn't connect. I've worked with her a lot setting up this project. She's one of the most compulsive people I've ever met when it comes to appointments."

"Leslie's a big girl. I'm sure something else came up."

They drove into Santa Barbara and parked off Anacapa Street. They walked over to State Street, down to El Paseo and into one of the busy local coffeehouses. There were two or three of them on every block now. Tony figured they were the original legal drug stores. Caffeine to go. A few minutes later, Montana emerged with her cappuccino and Tony his decaf.

"How about walking over to Bertolini's to check out the vase?" Montana wasn't interested in a reply. Tony took a sip from his cup as they headed toward the well-known ceramic store.

As they turned down Ortega Street, Montana pointed out the patina sign of Bertolini's. The downtown streets were filled with the weekend shopping crowds. The store was open and a few of the weekend shoppers meandered in and out as the Ryans approached.

Inside the store they found a cornucopia of ceramics and imports. "Who buys this stuff?" Tony asked quietly to Montana. He picked up a place setting of dishes, and Montana looked at them with him.

She pointed out the label on the dishes. "Pinto, VSM. It must be the manufacturer. That's the same as on the vase we bought."

"Look at the price. Two hundred per setting. Isn't that an awful lot?"

Just then a store clerk walked over. "May I help you?" she asked courteously.

Tony was quick to reply, "We're just browsing, thank you."

But Montana asked, "What is this label?" pointing to the bottom of the dish. "Is it the manufacturer or the style?"

"Oh, isn't it beautiful? That's the shop where it's made, I believe. I don't know for sure. They're shipped in directly from Rome." She spotted another customer standing near the register. "Excuse me, please."

"Thank you." Montana continued walking through the store and then called to Tony, "Oh, good, there's another vase like the one we bought."

"Aren't we the lucky couple?" Tony walked over and looked at the vase. He picked it up and turned it over.

Montana read from the base, at first smiling. "Pinto, VSM, just like the other one." Then she paused and added, "Uh oh."

Tony acknowledged the price. "Fifteen hundred dollars. Are they serious? For this ceramic vase?"

"I told you we got a great deal at the fund-raiser. We've got to get another one. It'll really look great in the entrance if we have a pair," Montana pleaded.

Tony looked at the pottery and kept thinking he could get similar pieces in Mexico for under a hundred dollars. What in the world did Montana see in this stuff? Was this a woman thing? But this was not a time to salute "la difference."

"Look, I'll tell you what," he said. "Let's discuss it over dinner. At that price I'm sure it will be here for a while. You're leaving tomorrow anyway, so why don't we at least wait until you get back? Maybe I can surprise you."

"You're right. It would be a surprise if you bought it. And I sure wouldn't bet on it."

"You're such a cynic. I could buy it, but maybe I can work something out, you know, get a better deal."

"You'd end up paying double before you'd haggle out a good price."

Tony gave in. "Maybe you're right, but it can still wait. Aren't you getting hungry?" Change the subject, he thought. Go for the stomach and just maybe…

"I'm starving. I need a caesar salad and some pasta at Frascati's. Let's go. It'll make you happy and we can get the vase later."

"Good idea."

Relieved for the moment, Tony tossed his empty cup into a corner trash can, and they crossed the street and headed for Frascati's. It was still early, not quite six o'clock, but when they walked into Frascati's, there were few unoccupied tables. They thought this was the way an Italian restaurant should be, and they loved the place. The bar up front bustled with activity as a dozen stools were occupied and several people stood in between. This was one of the cherished watering holes in town.

It surprised Tony when he spotted Emilio Frascati from across the room. He must have come straight from the Weldings'. This guy was definitely the Wolfgang Puck of Santa Barbara, except he preferred to wear regular clothes and spend more time with his feminine clientele than his kitchen crew. Catering parties for the high-brow likes of Gordon Welding might not have been his choice activity. He looked much more comfortable in his own surroundings. Tony couldn't imagine Welding bawling him out as Montana had described earlier. Looking at him now, Tony saw that Emilio was relaxed, smiling, and clearly enjoying entertaining his guests.

As Montana and Tony were led toward their table, Emilio spotted them coming, and true to form, he politely excused himself and jumped to his feet as soon as Montana neared. He wrapped his arm around her shoulder as though he had happened on to one of his best buddies. Tony went unreceived as Emilio escorted her past the booth where he had been sitting. He didn't stop to introduce them to his friends, who were now both looking at Montana, inquisitively trying to figure out why Emilio was so attracted to her. Tony, odd man out, at least temporarily, found himself standing alone in front of Emilio's vacated table. He smiled politely and gave a shrug as the three of them faced each other in this mildly awkward situation. One of them, with a low-cut top and lots of cleavage, smiled back directly at Tony.

"Hi, Dr. Ryan. Admiring your work?" she asked.

Oh, great. How Tony hated when this happened. Quick, he thought, go through the alphabet. A, B, C — what was her name? H, I, J, K, L, M. Yes M, Melinda. "Excuse me, Melinda. I didn't mean to stare, though I suppose if anyone had the right to, I should." He decided he'd better move on.

He thought the other woman looked familiar, but she turned away, avoiding eye contact. She revealed much less except for a gaudy cross with amber-colored stones. She seemed annoyed by the intrusion and the sudden loss of their host to Montana. Tony assumed she was just another jealous hanger-on for Emilio's pleasure. Oh, well, even Dr. Ryan can't expect everyone to like him, he thought, and so he marched on to his table.

Although Emilio always had pretty women around him, Tony could remember but one distinctly: Gina. Emilio had not had a steady girlfriend since Gina had left him not quite two years ago.

It was more than fondness that drew Emilio to Montana. In part it was Montana's connection with Gina. Montana and Gina had hit it off from the start, as if they were soul mates. They were both Italian, though Gina had just moved to California from Rome, while Montana had only visited the land of her heritage. They were both beautiful women - Montana with sophisticated good looks and Gina with sultry peasant charms. They both had a clean, almost innocent appearance. Neither wore much make-up, but no one would confuse them for plain. Although they both turned a lot of heads, they never seemed to notice. They were too busy having a good time and were not at all flirtatious.

While Montana and Gina were close, Emilio and Tony were congenial but superficial. The men got along fine and certainly enjoyed each other's company, but neither of them took the time to cultivate more than a warm cordiality. The women had a chemistry, and their friendship persisted even after Gina left Emilio and went home to Rome. Montana even arranged for Gina to become a distributor for their implant company.

They sat down in a booth with Montana in the middle. Tony smiled politely and looked at a menu while the two chatterboxes finished their tête à tête. Emilio then turned to Tony and politely said, "Well, Tony, what did you think of that carnival this afternoon? That's some spread that Welding has, no?"

"Pretty impressive," Tony casually replied while reaching for a bread stick. "That must have been a difficult job to cater."

"No, not really. You know Welding's type," responding just as casually. He's a big banker but still likes to count those pennies. Knows his business, no?"

Tony decided to mind his own business.

Emilio seemed intent on avoiding any comment about Welding's displeasure. After all, it probably went largely unnoticed. "So how's your practice holding up these days? Keeping busy?" Then, pouring on the charm, he said, "I'll have to come in for an overhaul soon."

"I've practically been able to resume my normal surgery schedule, and luckily the patients haven't yet forgotten me. You're still looking too good for my services. Save your money."

"Montana, don't you ever get jealous of Tony? With all these good-looking women coming in, just wanting to get a little bit better. I bet a lot of them come on to him. Rough life, Dottoré?"

Montana shot back, "No rougher than all of the attention you seem to be getting here. Are you playing doctor, too?"

"You're right, Montana. I guess that's why Gina couldn't take it anymore. She's not like you. She forgot this is just business for me, too."

As Emilio said this, Montana furrowed her brow slightly, just enough to show she wasn't buying his line.

Emilio bounced back and changed the subject. "So what did you buy at the silent auction?"

Montana, only too happy to list her conquests, shot back, "Well, Tony took your advice and bought that stay at the Ventana Inn."

Tony nodded to Emilio, half smiled and said, "Thanks, Casanova."

"My pleasure," Emilio nodded back politely.

Montana continued, "A full day at the Genesis Spa, Tony got a bottle of wine…"

"A magnum of '82 Haut Brion," Tony injected.

"Excuse me," Montana said with mock consternation, "an '82 Haut Brion and a vase from Bertolini's."

"That beautiful vase from Bertolini? I know the one. Che bella." Emilio smiled. "My family, they own the Frascati Terrecotte in Roma. They sell directly to Bertolini. It's a small world, no?"

"There's a matching one I want to get so I can have one on both sides of the entry," Montana declared. "Of course, el dottoré here, he no wanna spend the money," she said in her best Italian accent.

"When are you leaving for Roma?"

"Tomorrow."

"So soon. You are a very busy woman, no?" Emilio got a sparkle in his eyes. "Hey, I've got an idea. Give me a couple of minutes. I want to make a call." He excused himself and retreated to his office.

Montana picked up her menu. "Do you believe that crap about Gina being jealous?"

"I thought you once said Gina left Emilio because he seemed to be jealous of her, or something like that."

"Oh, you do listen now and then. Actually, Gina felt like he was suffocating her. He kept her under tight wraps. It certainly sounds like a 'jealousy' thing. Meanwhile, it's obvious he still has a thing for her. He should have gone after her."

A waiter came by and took their order. A moment later Emilio reappeared.

"I've got good news. I talked to Alfredo. He runs the shop, Bertolini. They're going to send that vase over to the house later this week," Emilio announced with a wide smile.

Tony looked on perplexed, and Montana dropped her jaw waiting for Emilio to explain.

Emilio picked up on their expressions. "I know you were going to buy it, but this way I give it to you as a present. Alfredo doesn't mind. It's all in the family."

Montana was aghast, saying, "You're kidding. No, you're not. Oh, god, that's so sweet of you. I can't believe it."

"Believe it. I've got to go back to work." He raised his eyebrows a couple of times. "You make sure you say hello to Gina, and take this card."

Montana reached across the table and took a business card from Emilio. Emilio continued, "When you get a chance, stop by. Gina knows the place. My cousin Ernesto will definitely want to take you two to dinner. He'll take care of you and show you a nice time. I guarantee it."

"My god, Emilio. That is so nice of you. I can't thank you enough. We'll definitely stop by."

"Great, ciao. And, Tony, you come on in for dinner while she's gone. We'll make sure you eat well."

"Thanks, Emilio. Thanks a lot." Tony responded with gratitude flattered by his graciousness.

After Emilio left, Montana turned to Tony, saying, "Can you believe my luck? Ha. I knew something good would come up."

Tony, a bit cynical in spite of their good fortune, tried to figure out the motivation and replied, "I think that's his way of holding on to Gina. At least with you going to Rome, he'll be able to have some contact with her. You can tell her how wonderful he was to get you the vase and how much he misses her."

Not fazed by the concept, she simply responded, "Who knows? They certainly seemed like a good couple, but what do we know? It'll be interesting to talk with Gina."

"Like you said, what do we know? Maybe you should mind your own business."

Montana, content with her additional acquisition, decided to drop the subject. "Yes, sir. Whatever you say."

Satiated from Frascati's Italian cuisine, Tony drove the Jaguar unhurriedly, gliding gently through the turns to their house. Although still standard time, the days lasted longer, and a soft light with pink hues shown through their windows as they walked into their house. It had been a long day, and Tony felt relieved to walk into his study, look over some of his personal correspondence and play back their phone messages. Montana seemed satisfied, too, to sit down with Tony and the dogs and enjoy a few quiet moments.

Montana looked up at Tony and asked, "Any word from Leslie Phillips on the machine?"

"No, nothing. I don't get it."

"Why don't you give her a call?"

Tony looked up her number and dialed it. The phone rang four times and then the message machine clicked on. He hung up without leaving a message.

"If she's not home, she would have gone to the fund-raiser. She's meticulous about that stuff," he said, visibly concerned.

Montana then added, "Well, maybe she left you another note on your computer. Didn't you tell me she loves that e-mail stuff?"

"Maybe she did. Let's check." Tony plugged in his computer, booted it up and went online. There were no new messages, but he had saved the old ones.

Montana looked over his shoulder and saw Phillips' message, not recognizing it had already been played. "Look, isn't that a message from Leslie?" She reached over Tony's shoulder, and before he knew it, she had clicked it on.

"I've already played that message. It's from Friday," Tony said while the audio/video e-mail repeated itself. Not having seen it before, Montana watched it play.

"Wow. Nice backyard."

"I know. She sent this from Weissman's house, only I don't have his number or know where he lives."

"Hey, look. You see that knoll and those palm trees reflected in the windows?" Montana made a keen observation, but Tony still didn't clue in.

"So?"

"I know where that house is. It sits up on West Ridge Road right across from that knoll. I'm sure that's Weissman's house. I heard a Hollywood film-maker bought it several months ago. Maybe a year, but I know exactly where that is. Maybe we should swing by and make sure things are okay."

Tony couldn't believe his wife. He just wanted to relax. He had a full schedule starting with surgery early in the morning.

"Let's try information first and make a call."

But there was no listing.

"Come on. It's only ten minutes from here. She'd probably check on you if things were reversed." Montana had hit Tony's weak spot, for he was ultimately very responsible and, more than that, would feel guilty if he didn't check it out.

"Okay. Let's go."

Tony drove down the road and over to the next canyon and then wound his way up to West Ridge, coming to the spot with the two palm trees that they recognized from the e-mail. He continued past the knoll, winding sharply around to his right and then slowing down in front of a driveway that led to the wide one-story structure with the panoramic windows in back. It was now completely dark, but when he pulled his car into the driveway, he saw Phillips' white Corvette parked in the carport.

"Jeez, you ought to be a detective. That's her car. Let's go home." Tony started to put the car in reverse.

"Why don't we just stop and ring the bell as long as we're here?" There were no lights on in the house nor around the driveway.

"Are you sure? You're the one who never wants to just drop in unannounced. They're probably having a wild time."

"Look, we came over here. We might as well just check."

Tony parked the car in the driveway and got out while Montana remained seated. He walked by Phillips' car and pulled on the door handle, and it opened. Nothing amiss. He walked over to the front door and rang the bell. A loud chime erupted enough that it startled Tony. There was no answer. He waited a few seconds and rang it again. He heard the bell resonate within the house, placed his head to the door and heard no other sounds. It was completely quiet.

He walked back to the car and reached into his middle compartment, where he pulled out a small flashlight. He turned it on and it lit up.

"Maybe we should go," Montana suggested, looking up at Tony, who had started back toward the house. She decided she'd better join him, so she got out of the car and scurried up to his side.

Continuing on his path, Tony added, "Her car's here and the door's unlocked. If she left with Weissman, you'd think she'd lock the door."

"Then maybe they're home and don't want to be disturbed."

"I didn't hear a sound in there."

"She probably took off with this Weissman guy or went out to dinner with him. Hell, they probably take a limo everywhere." Then Montana noted, "A lot of people don't lock their cars around here."

"Then a quick look around couldn't hurt."

There were a few windows in the front of the house, but they were covered with closed plantation shutters. Tony followed the light to the right side of the house, where a narrow side entry led to the backyard. Montana followed close behind. A slightly rusted gate with a "beware of dog" sign opened with a slight creak. They waited a moment, listened for barking or the sound of a rushing animal, but nothing happened. They walked along silently into the backyard.

Tony shone his light over the backyard, getting an overview of the layout. A few chaises framed a lighted pool. There were no lights coming from the inside of the house, but farther down they could see the long, maybe fifty- or sixty-foot, expanse of windows. Tony aimed the beam toward the house through a group of bay windows. They looked inside and could see the kitchen – neat and clean, more decorative than used, with lots of granite counters and a large preparation area in the center. Nothing appeared out of place.

They crept quietly along, flashing the light into the house. Its reflection made it difficult to see inside, so they had to cup their hands around their faces as they pressed them to the glass. Shades of white filled the house with a number of murals framed and hanging on the walls. The fireplace mantle bore a couple of statuettes, probably awards. The furniture, mostly cushy rattan couches and chairs, were spaced around the room.

Sure enough, in the middle of the floor of the living room, not far from a fireplace, they saw the first signs of human activity. Clothes had been scattered about on the floor, most likely leaving a trail down to the bedroom.

"Maybe we better leave. It looks like they're probably having a private moment. That's why no one's answering the door. They'll arrest us for trespassing." Montana turned to Tony, hoping he would listen, but he continued to explore with his little flashlight. Montana, reluctantly now, walked along with him.

Tony aimed the light outside, and they moved farther along until they came up behind the chaise where Phillips had recorded her e-mail. Again he aimed the beam toward the window, only to have it reflect back at them, momentarily blocking their vision with bright spots — night blindness — that took a moment to blink away. Again they pressed their faces up to the window, trying to make out anything in the room. The light shone over a couple of other articles of clothing, now in another room, maybe a den, with a large-screen television screen up against the left wall – nothing out of place, no music, no noise. Tony swung the light to the right, and before he could stop to focus, Montana let out a scream and jumped straight back, then grabbed on to Tony.

"Oh, my God, oh, my God." Her body started shaking as she buried her head against his chest. Tony quickly moved the beam back, and he saw it. A man sat naked in a rattan chair, frozen in position, nearly white, drained of any life, with his head grotesquely torqued backward and to the side. His mouth gaped open, with dried blood streaked down one side and a larger amount of dried brown blood and scalp caked on the back of the chair and pooled onto the floor. If Montana hadn't been holding on to him, he would have jumped ten feet himself.

"Hang on, Montana; hang on." He moved the light around the room. It was still. He did see what appeared to be an opened vial on a counter not far from the dead man.

"Please, Tony, please. Let's go. We have to call the police."

Tony went into a kind of investigative doctor mode. Something clicked inside of him. He pulled Montana along with him, now urgently. He quickly looked into the remainder of the house, now fairly certain what he would find. At the end of the house, behind the expansive windows, he saw a bedroom, clean, untouched, except for the bed, where he could make out the figures of two women, face down, also naked, motionless, with a dried pool of blood around their heads. The woman closer to them was Leslie Phillips.

Chapter 5

9:00 p.m., Sunday, March 13

JIMMY MCVEE STOOD BY the side of the bed, staring at the nude bodies. He tucked a yellow pad under his left arm while he chewed on the end of his pen. Two formerly gorgeous women lay dead, face down on the bed, with their wrists handcuffed to an outer brass rail and together between themselves. They each had a single bullet wound to the back of the head. The small amount of blood caked around the back of their heads belied the terrible damage the bullet had done to their brains.

Suddenly a camera flashed and caught him squarely in the eyes. "Damn, can't you give me a warning when you take those shots?"

The criminalist with the camera wasn't interested in a confrontation at nine o'clock on Sunday evening, and he politely offered, "Sorry, sir."

Not much compensation. McVee knew he would end up with a migraine. He rubbed the bridge of his twice-broken nose with his fingers and then opened his eyes and shook his head lightly while he refocused on Ramsey. "Hey, Frank, check this out."

"What have you got?" Ramsey stood in front of the lifeless nude body of Randy Weissman, looking it over. He had just finished noting the opened vial of cocaine near Weissman's feet. The stench of blood and death was thick in the air, and McVee waited while Ramsey stuck a little Vicks in his nose to camouflage its effect. He moved across the room toward the bedside.

McVee picked up an undisturbed purse, opened it and retrieved a wallet and identification.

Ramsey looked over his shoulder. "Holy shit. That's Congresswoman Phillips. When you said we had a VIP, I thought you meant Weissman."

"I told you Leslie Phillips. Dr. Ryan phoned it in."

"I guess I just wasn't thinking it could really be a congresswoman. Don't we have to call the FBI?"

"I called Roger Felton a few minutes ago. He and his little entourage are on their way. We'll gather evidence and investigate with them. Let them have carte blanche. Don't let Cooper get in their way." He shook his head, looking at the carnage. "What do you think happened?"

Ramsey rubbed the back of his head and surveyed the room. "Well, first of all, there's no sign of forced entry. There's no apparent sign of robbery. I mean, nothing's disturbed. There's not even any sign of a struggle. Look at that wallet you're holding. I can see money and credit cards. The women are obviously restrained. There's an open vial of cocaine near Weissman, and there's a murder weapon next to him as well. I think they were having a party, but he started to freak out on cocaine. The women were probably scared to death and yelling at him to let them go. He probably went into a rage and shot them. You know how crazy and guilt-ridden these guys get when they're high. He goes to his chair and, pow, it's over. Bad night on drugs."

"Any other possibilities?" McVee questioned.

"I don't see how. You got anything in mind?"

"Not yet. Where's Cooper?" McVee then turned and headed across the room toward a paneled wall. The photographer took another picture. The flash caught the mirrored wardrobe and McVee's face almost at the same time that a hidden paneled door opened directly into McVee's pathway and nose.

"Ah, shit, is this a bad joke or what?" He held his nose, pinching it at the tip and sniffing in, anticipating a bleed that thankfully didn't occur.

Cooper emerged with his briefcase and a DVD disk. "Oh, hey, sorry, McVee. Hey, man, is it bleeding? I don't see anything. You want some ice or something?"

McVee was not having a good night. He looked up at the hollow-cheeked detective with the dark straight hair and dark sunken eyes. Although the same age as Ramsey, Cooper reminded him of a burnt-out hippie who had become a born-again conservative. McVee was more annoyed than hurt. He dabbed at his nose a couple of times, but still no blood. He'd survive.

"Anyway, I found this in the machine," said Cooper, wearing latex gloves, as he held up a disk. "Tons of video equipment back in there. You should see what he's got. It's quite a setup — real fancy stuff, well hidden. Did you see the remote control on the dresser over there? We'll wrap this as evidence. Who knows? Maybe he was filming during the escapade. Let's log it and take it back to the lab." One of the criminalists placed the disk in a plastic bag.

McVee stuck his head into the small room. It seemed to be a sophisticated video entertainment center. It housed a veritable library of DVDs and tapes. The only obvious opening was an inconspicuous receptor spot for the remote signal and a spot where a camera pointed into the room. McVee nodded his head a couple of times as though in appreciation of the ingenious setup.

Ramsey came and looked in on McVee. "Two chicks and a remote control — I know I'd have it on tape."

"If you were planning a murder, you'd tape it?" McVee asked.

"This sure doesn't look planned. I bet Cooper pulled out a porno. I'm sure there'll be a few late-night viewers back at the department tonight. Say, why don't you call it a night? Felton's on the way, and the coroner should be here soon. I'll wait until Felton gets here; then Cooper's got this covered."

"Okay, I'll see you guys at the morning briefing." McVee filed his notes into his leather satchel and headed for the door.

Tony waited in the car with Montana. She still trembled from the horror while Tony sat stoically, lost in his own thoughts, but when he saw McVee emerge from the front door, he jumped out of the car and walked up to him.

"So what do you think happened?"

McVee shook his head, "That was one of the most gruesome scenes I've seen in a long time. Of course we've got to finish the investigation. I left

Ramsey and Cooper in there, but the FBI will add their two cents. Still, it looks like a double murder followed by a suicide."

Tony looked aghast. "You think Weissman did this himself?"

"For right now, that's the way it looks. No forced entry, nothing disturbed – well, nothing not human – and there's a weapon. Oh, and there's drugs. Some grass and an open vial of cocaine. Maybe this is a case of 'live by the sword, die by the sword' for our congresswoman."

"I can't believe it. I knew Weissman. Not well, I admit, but I knew him. He frequently played tennis at the club. I just don't get it. Why in the world would he even consider doing something like this?"

"That's the whole problem with drugs. No one would ever consider doing such a thing in his right mind. But if we give them this shit, who knows what they'll do?"

"There is going to be screaming for the termination of the program. It just doesn't make sense, does it?"

"You can't take this personally."

"I wasn't," Tony shot back. "Believe me, I may be the director of this program, but I know it's an experiment."

"Look, Tony. I'm not your enemy. If this thing works, it's fine by me. I just don't see it. Hell, I'm just a simple guy. I see things in black and white. Meanwhile, it's not the only drug-related incident we've had lately."

"I know about the heroin overdoses. The FBI's already crashing the party to figure that one out."

"Well, they'll certainly be joining the party here. Do you know about the couple that drove their car off of Las Alturas after smoking dope?" Tony thought McVee seemed a little anxious to rub it in, or maybe Tony just felt overwhelmed.

"What else happened while I was away? Don't tell me we spiked the grass. I suppose I'm going to be arrested for murder." This weekend had become a bad joke, but for a moment Tony almost saw the humor in the ridiculous.

"Amazingly, they both survived. We're not sure why it happened, but it's pretty clear that the driver had consumed some quantity of cannabis. By the way, things aren't all that bleak for you. He did smack his nose against the steering wheel or the side window. I gave him your card and told him how you fixed my nose. After seeing how gorgeous I am, I'm sure he's anxious for you to take a look at it. You are planning on keeping your day job, aren't you?"

Tony, numb with the horror that had transpired and the uncertainty of the problems he would face, nodded his head in affirmation. "Thanks, Jimmy. Please keep me posted. The first-quarter report will no longer be boring. If we even last to the first quarter, we'll surely have plenty of quality assurance issues."

During the drive home, Tony described McVee's findings to Montana. It was an eerie drive, where around each turn the images of Weissman or Phillips would flash in front of their eyes as though it was burnt into their brains and activated by transitions between dark and light. They walked into their house before eleven. In spite of their long and eventful day, neither Tony nor Montana was tired. It would take a while before their adrenaline would wear down enough and allow them to get some rest. They sat down in their library, the dogs curled around their feet. Tony didn't want to believe what appeared to be obvious, and it was starting to get on Montana's nerves.

"Can't you just let it go? We all know drugs are bad for you. That's always been part of your premise. Don't be such a hypocrite," she scolded him.

Tony looked at her inquisitively.

Montana continued, "Don't you get it? If this happened to someone in a trailer park, you would have shrugged, maybe even pompously proclaimed that everyone knows better or has been warned or something sanctimonious. Why should it be any different with celebrities? Maybe this will be a stronger lesson to others about the dangers of drugs."

"The problem with these celebrities is that one is from Congress and helped set up the program here in Santa Barbara. She's been too close to the situation to simply be dismissed as a statistical malady."

"What are you going to do? Do you think you'll have to shut it down?"

Tony rubbed his brow, not wanting to face what might be the inevitable. He and many others had worked so hard to establish the checks and balances, anticipating so many possible potential downsides, that the program was considered a slam dunk.

"We might have to shut down the program. God knows there will be a lot of pressure, but until the President or Congress pulls the plug, we'll run business as usual. We have to be willing to wait and examine the results of the investigations."

"Right now I'd say your program doesn't have a prayer."

"Oh, it's my program now. Dr. Ryan's Drug Procurement Center. Are you abandoning the ship so soon?"

"I think you're the only one that doesn't see the iceberg. Anyway, you know what I mean. Look, it's late. I've got to pack if I'm going to Rome tomorrow. Otherwise, if you prefer, I can just take a toothbrush and an American Express card. I'm sure I won't have any trouble finding the necessary items there."

"Go pack. You're still okay about going?"

"When I sat in the car at Weissman's I figured there's no way I would be going, but on the ride home, especially when you said what was involved in the investigation, I figured I might as well. God knows when they'll have a funeral for Leslie or where it will be. I might as well go, unless you want me to stay for support. You're going to need it."

"You'll probably be back before the investigation's through. There's just nothing we can do or say until then. It's definitely better for us if you go to the conference." Tony watched as Montana got up, blew him a kiss and walked out with two four-legged fuzzy friends following behind.

After a moment, Tony got up and walked over to the television console. A multitude of framed photographs stood scattered among the books on the shelves. Tony scanned over several – Montana in Paris outside the Hotel Bristol; Spencer and Lynn outdoors in Telluride; Montana, Tony and Leslie Phillips in Washington, D.C. during the organizing segment of the legal drug program; and then Tony and Paul.

He picked up the picture of himself and his brother Paul. An old photo taken of the two of them during their fraternity days showed a couple of good-looking boys whose resemblance was definitely genetic. Paul, a couple of years younger, a couple of inches shorter, but just as competitive, if not more so, frequently teamed-up with his big brother. His fierce and feisty attitude, and a shock of blond hair that must have come from the milkman, earned him the nickname "Viking." They had just won a case of beer for their victorious efforts in a fraternity two-on-two basketball tournament. Tony replaced the photograph, then sifted through his video files and pulled out a DVD titled "January 2009, Joint Congressional Meeting for the Evaluation of Narcotics Prohibition." He put it in the player, grabbed the remote and clicked on the DVD.

He walked over to the bar, grabbed a handful of ice cubes and poured a little scotch. This might be a good time for a little nightcap, he thought as he plopped down in his chair.

He thought of his brother. Had it not been for a series of circumstances involving Paul, he wouldn't be sitting here tonight thinking about the fate of a legal drug program. He closed his eyes for a moment, and instead of the winning basket, all he could hear was a loud slam. Only it wasn't a slam; it was a shot. There remained a place in his head where it forever reverberated in spite of the finality it had brought to his life.

He looked on as the DVD played. The chyron for C-SPAN January 17, 2009 appeared on the corner of the screen, and so began the disk recounting the great drug war debate. The leader of the panel, Senator Warren Obermeyer, a portly Republican from Minnesota, introduced the various senators and congressmen. First he presented Michael Delgado, a Texas congressman, a couple of others and then Leslie Phillips. The camera seemed to linger on Phillips a bit longer than the others. Tony smiled. He knew Leslie behind her reading glasses, a congresswoman with glamour, and the camera crew and directors must have enjoyed it. She utilized her powers to the fullest extent.

The camera panned the room, and Tony was surprised to see that he and Montana were actually sitting next to Burt Wesley. How that seating arrangement had happened Tony couldn't recall. It made him uncomfortable to watch, and he clicked on the fast forward.

He passed right through most of the testimony, wanting to see his own and particularly remembering the initial conflicts he had had with Leslie Phillips. The speakers paraded in rapid fire in front of him. He went quickly past Stanley Feingold, the noted economist, delivering a tedious litany of statistical analysis while turning more charts than Ross Perot. The cost of the drug wars had been in the hundreds of billions, starting with the Pentagon, the prosecution and imprisonment of drug criminals, loss of property from thefts for drug money, injuries and healthcare expenses related to drug crimes and drug use, and finally lost tax revenue because of the huge underground economy. Tony remembered that if the numbers themselves hadn't been so staggering, the gathering would have been lulled into a somnambulistic trance.

There had been a speaker from Holland who reviewed the successful open policy of the Netherlands. There were others who argued that it wasn't so wonderful.

Speakers presented arguments as to why marijuana should be legalized and decried the failure of the federal government to recognize states' rights when it came to medicinal use of marijuana. Others warned about protecting children and not setting more bad examples. Still others declared that if drugs were legalized, then more of the law enforcement efforts could be directed at preventing experimentation and usage by non-consenting participants — the children.

Tony zipped by Burt Wesley's speech. Wesley tried to convince the panel that the rehab centers, already bursting with patients and with extensive waiting lists to get in, would never be able to keep up with the sure-to-follow boom in new addicts. Tony knew it was self-serving, but at the time it was still a good argument.

There she was again. Tony switched to "play" and listened to Leslie Phillips.

"Excuse me, Judge Reynolds," she said as she looked over the top of her reading glasses down at the petite Southern California judge. "If you believe we're letting violent criminals out of prison because they're overcrowded, particularly with, as you say, nonviolent drug offenders, maybe the problem is with the parole boards. Maybe they need to be tougher."

Reynolds responded, "These are valid points, and I agree. I think we have made a mockery out of our parole boards, but we've been forced to use them to limit the crowding in our jails. The laws bind them in their determinations as to whom they can send back on the streets. But if you want to get tougher, what will you do? The jails will be even more overcrowded, and there will be a greater tax burden to pay for more jails and prisoners. Nonviolent drug users, in large part, already backlog the courts. And what happens in jail? People who shouldn't be there are enrolled in the university of crime. They may go in naive, but they come out entrepreneurial criminals."

Senator Obermeyer chimed in, "So legal drugs, which can be purchased by anyone — okay, anyone of age — will not contribute to more crime? Is that what you believe?"

Reynolds remained tenacious. "At the very least, the decriminalization of drugs would decrease the court cases by half and drastically relieve prison overcrowding. Also, we must ask whom we are trying to protect. Now, all law-abiding citizens are victims. They pay higher taxes to jail more inmates. They are at increased risk of being robbed or maimed by those in pursuit of money for drugs. The responsible citizen doesn't take drugs now, and there is no reason to believe that will change. Like some of the earlier speakers said, we can put most of our resources into protecting our children. And we must take tougher stands against real crimes committed while under the influence."

"All well and good, Judge Reynolds, but how do you know it will work?" the pragmatic Phillips asked.

Tony wondered if this was where Leslie started to change her mind about her opposition to legalization.

"Maybe it's time, Congresswoman, that we consider a new social experiment, perhaps on a county level, legalizing drugs."

Tony fast-forwarded through Dennis Gaylord's testimony regarding drunk-driving issues and how it related to the problem of drugs. He was the one who had come up with the idea of mandatory breath analyses and reflex tests in cars.

Tony finally got to his segment on the tape. There he was, with Montana sitting by his side. He remembered how she had protested before he finally convinced her to sit with him at the table while he testified. She not only provided moral support, she helped him appear more human and even classier. Her presence had a way of doing that.

After Senator Obermeyer's introduction, Congresswoman Phillips questioned abruptly, "How in the world does a cosmetic surgeon come to be an expert testifying before this panel? Did we send out open invitations or something?"

There it was, that Phillips glare. Tony was tempted to freeze-frame that look. She hid no glamour behind those eyes, only a challenge not to waste their time. He swirled the drink in his hands and let the disk continue.

Senator Obermeyer responded, interrupting Tony's prepared speech. "Actually, Congresswoman, there was a summary bio prepared for all of our speakers. While Dr. Ryan's C.V. is included, the descriptive bio was unfortunately omitted." Turning back to Tony, the senator then continued, "Perhaps you might take a few minutes and explain how you became involved with this issue."

Tony held his prepared speech in his hands, ready to deliver his sermon, but now they had asked him to dredge up old, painful memories to satisfy the panel. He turned to Montana, and she simply gave him a nod to just get on with it.

"Okay, that's a fair question, especially in light of the previous speakers and their considerable expert backgrounds." He stalled a moment, took a deep breath and pushed his papers aside, choosing to focus his reply on Leslie Phillips. Since she had asked the question, she would be his audience.

"I grew up with a younger brother, two years my junior. And though he humiliated the family name by going into law, we still remained very close." Tony smiled and added, "On a personal, not professional, basis, in case you're wondering.

"Since he was old enough to walk, he was always tagging along, hanging out with me and my friends, playing sports with us. He became a hell of an athlete. Of course, I was always the big brother. Funny how that is, you know. You always feel responsible for your younger brother, even if he can do things better than you."

Phillips looked inquisitively over to Obermeyer, then back at Tony. Tony held his gaze steady and continued in a casual manner. "We used to play a lot of basketball. Paul played a scrappy, aggressive game. You know, the kind of kid who could pester the devil out of you. It was much better having him on my team." Tony smiled to himself, remembering that Paul always drove the other team nuts.

"Anyway, we had a regular Saturday morning game on the outdoor courts in Santa Barbara. Talk about bad timing. On this one particular Saturday, Paul was supposed to pick up a wedding ring from our jeweler, Sam

Kellerman. He had an appointment with Sam for ten-thirty but insisted we could still get in a game or two. It wasn't my wedding ring."

Tony stole a quick glance at Montana, who chose not to acknowledge the remark. "So I dragged myself over to the courts where we played. Our team was hot. We kept winning, so we kept playing. It was creeping up on ten-thirty, and we really needed to leave. Maybe it was cold feet, maybe just fate, but Paul insisted on one more. One more game. Only this time, midway into the game, he took a sharp elbow to his brow. His aggressiveness got to someone, I think. Ever see the way a brow bleeds from a blunt laceration?" Tony gestured with his left hand, pulling his fingers away from his brow, indicating how it burst open.

The camera turned back to Phillips. "Please, Dr. Ryan, I don't follow where you're going."

Watching this segment made Tony smile, but only momentarily — he shook his head at the tragic reality and sipped his drink while the disk continued.

Not addressing her concern, Tony continued in his subdued manner, looking directly up at her. "So we slapped a towel on this wound, and I drove him over to my office, where I stitched him up. Sam said he'd wait for us. By the time I got done and over to Sam's, it was nearly noon, his Saturday closing time. You should have seen the ring Sam had for Paul, or actually for Paul's fiancée, Cynthia. It was quite a rock. We all figured Cynthia earned it by having to put up with my brother the last five years and now planning their wedding."

As Tony watched the video, he started to well up, just as he had during the testimony, where he had paused, not visibly crying, but glassy-eyed nonetheless.

"I barely noticed the customer that Sam buzzed into the store. He came up alongside Paul, and while the two of us were ogling the ring, this guy pulls out a gun and announces his plans. 'This is a hold-up,' he says. We just stood there looking at the stone, not really hearing what this guy said, or at least not believing this was actually happening to us. It happens to other people, doesn't it? You know, on the five o'clock news, but not to you. Anyway, the guy sees

65

the diamond and grabs for it. Paul pulls his hand back. I don't remember any words, just a loud slam."

Tony grabbed a book and slapped it down hard on the table. "Like that. I never really saw the man's face as he turned and fled almost immediately. I figured he took the stone. I froze, not sure if we should chase him, call the cops or what. For an instant, I felt relief as Paul opened his hand and still had the ring. In the next second, Paul slumped back into my arms, his weight catching me off balance and taking me to the floor underneath him. He was only thirty-one when he died that day from a single gunshot wound."

Tony leaned forward in his chair, reliving the emotions. He wiped back a tear at nearly the same time he was doing it on the video. He heard his tone harshen slightly as his sorrow changed to anger.

"It turns out the police eventually found the killer. They recognized him right away. A well-known drug dealer, he had been too elusive for his own good. If the cops had caught him, with our present justice system, he'd be in jail getting three square meals. Instead, because he had fallen way behind on some heavy drug payments, the dealers' association meted out a much swifter and more definitive sentence. That's why they found him dead in a dumpster.

"Paul was my brother. He would have been a wonderful husband and a great father. He died because of someone else's money problems with illegal drugs. He died because some clown was more afraid of his own business partners than our police force. It made me completely rethink my position on drugs until I was satisfied that I understood what the real problem was and what needed to be done. Not to belabor the obvious, but it became my crusade to discuss the drug war and its most reasonable solution — legalization. I'm sorry if I'm not well known to you, but over the last ten years I've spoken to well over a hundred various groups and associations about this issue."

Obermeyer shot a glance to Phillips. She responded bluntly, "Thank you for that explanation, Dr. Ryan. Please proceed." For a moment it appeared that her steely gaze might have softened.

Tony picked up his papers, grabbed a quick sip of water and continued with his prepared testimony.

"Our country has been referred to as the Great Experiment. It is truly a society in evolution. If we are here because God so gave us the opportunity, we have been given the tools to either improve or destroy this land that we cherish. In particular, we are here at the very least to exist and be happy. More eloquently, Jefferson wrote in our Declaration of Independence that we were endowed with 'certain unalienable Rights, that among these are Life, Liberty and the pursuit of Happiness.' We are in a situation where this pursuit has become increasingly threatened and even nonexistent for many innocent people. It is time for us to evaluate one segment of our societal problems and to explore how we can improve our pursuit of happiness."

Tony found himself mouthing the words as they came out of the TV.

"It's not unusual that when trying to prevent a problem, we often create more troubles than the original problem ever imposed. In medicine, we have many examples. Thalidomide comes to mind. In trying to reduce the nausea of pregnancy, we developed a drug that caused devastating birth defects. Every industry has its examples of how attempts to solve problems have actually unleashed a Pandora's box of new disasters. When this happens in private enterprise, we act to correct the situation. If nothing else, we can generally identify cost factors to limit our continuous wasteful trends. The lesson to learn is to identify the problem and find cures without inducing worse problems. Indeed, the problems of fighting a drug war might be worse than the problem caused by the drugs themselves. This has largely gone unquestioned for so long because we forgot our history, how drugs actually became illegal, and because of our tainted concepts of political correctness, which force our representatives to politic without truly leading."

Yeah, who'd want the risk of being a leader? Tony thought. He shook the ice in the glass before finishing it off.

"Under the auspices of the Department of Justice, we refer to our court system as the justice system. In reality it is a legal system! We have been lost in a quagmire of legalities which barely approximate justice. What system of justice would allow a first-time seller or user of cocaine to be incarcerated for life? I will tell you. It is the same system of justice which allows celebrities to get away with years of substance abuse, seek refuge at the Betty Ford Center and emerge with best-selling books and screenplays. If someone were to commit murder or rob a bank and later confess to it on Good Morning

America, how long would it take for our criminal justice system to find and prosecute these individuals? Yet you could spend all morning on the same show talking about your drug habits. There is no justice in handling the 'crime of drug abuse,' rather a blasphemous hypocrisy that captures so few users and dealers only to make a mockery of the laws that were so poorly conceived. In order for justice to exist, it must potentially exist for everyone. Since I do not see any way in which we are going to lock up everyone who has ever taken 'illegal substances,' why are we so tough on those who have taken or sold even the smallest of quantities? In the sense of true justice, are they any guiltier than the others? Would you argue there is a deterrent factor from the fear of getting caught? Well, not only is the money so great an incentive for selling drugs, but the cartels spread much more fear and deterrence to the sellers than the state could ever approximate. My brother's story is a tragically common example. The cartels certainly have much more interest in getting new buyers or addicts who ultimately become sellers. It's a classic pyramid system.

"While I may sound rather philosophical, I come here as a physician as well. While it has been the duty of physicians to support good health, we have never been able to do it through prohibition. If that were the case, I would suggest we start by eliminating tobacco and saturated fat. Based on the incidence of heart disease and cancer, these two legal substances are far more harmful than anything else we could imagine. We already learned the mistakes of prohibition with alcohol. As physicians, it is our duty to learn about the foods and substances we may consume and to educate the public as to the risks or benefits. This is a process in evolution. There are always going to be people trying things that may turn out to be detrimental. They may even turn out to be beneficial. There will also be people doing detrimental things that we will not know about until trends develop from which we can learn. Post-World War II America became the beef-eating capital of the world, and cardiovascular disease crept up on us at an alarming rate. Through medical education, consumption of fat is dropping, and at least people are better informed about their choices. In no way would I prohibit fat. I would only suggest that people limit their quantities for their own sake and perhaps so they could enjoy their occasional steak and ice cream more.

"The same precautions should be applied to drugs. As a physician, I would like to see the public well educated about the drugs that are potentially available. As Judge Reynolds pointed out, we need to prosecute people for their harmful behavior and not excuse it as being 'under the influence.' The naturally produced drugs of rage — chemicals produced right within our bodies — are as devastating as most synthetic substances. These drugs are beyond regulation, but a protective society should recognize when a crime occurs and remove the perpetrator for the protection of the victim and society. Taking a drug does not necessarily predict criminal behavior. In fact, based on the tremendous numbers of drug-taking individuals already, one would think the numbers of harmful crimes would be much greater. There is no reason to believe that we shouldn't be allowed to independently screen people intimately entrusted with the care of others, such as airline pilots. Certainly, there are many details to look into in plotting a course of action. Judge Reynolds had the positive idea of considering an experimental county to help us evaluate potential changes in our present drug policies. It is time we re-evaluate our present beleaguered legal system."

Tony sat upright and pushed the microphone away, showing the senators he had completed his testimony. Montana said a few congratulatory words.

The camera turned to Leslie Phillips. "Dr. Ryan, how can a physician support something as harmful as drugs? Doesn't your Hippocratic oath say something about 'do no harm'?"

Tony nodded his head in agreement, saying, "It is not only my job to protect the individual but society as well. If an individual came to me with a drug problem, I would be compelled to educate him and get him into a rehab program. On the other hand, the vast majority of society has little desire to become involved in serious drug habits. They are mostly affected by the crime associated with drugs. Somehow we have perpetuated the notion that people on drugs become crazed criminals. This is not the case. It is the organized criminals who cause the most harm. It is such a scary proposition to owe money to a gangster that committing a crime against an innocent victim is not that terribly difficult. You, the government, have been telling us that you want to protect the drug user. Why? This has been the person who has been the main accomplice inflicting the most harm on our society. If someone absolutely chooses to harm themselves, it is largely unpreventable.

What should be prevented is the harm that can be done to innocent victims. If you can allow people to smoke or drink, it is purely hypocritical to pick what substance you choose to prevent them from taking."

Tony fixed his attention on Leslie Phillips. The camera caught Phillips staring back, her scornful glare replaced perceptibly with a hint of a smile. The camera's view lasted only a moment, a moment Tony remembered as significantly longer, before switching back to Senator Obermeyer.

Tony stopped the video and played it back a bit. He paused it on Phillips. There was a smile — almost affectionate. He stared for a few seconds before letting the video resume.

Obermeyer gave Tony a stern look as he tapped his pencil on a pad of paper. He cleared his throat as if getting ready to scold him and then responded, "Doctor, I'll tell you what's hypocritical and blasphemous — for you and the other panelists to sit there and be so smugly narrow-sighted. What do you say when entire families are ruined by this curse of narcotics? Yes, our country is a social experiment, but may I remind you its purpose is also to 'form a more perfect union.' As an elected official it is my duty to help this government achieve that goal. So how in the world can we allow drugs to freely invade our treasured communities, which they most certainly will, should they become decriminalized?" His face turned beet red as he made his politically correct grandstand at Tony's expense. There was some background applause as the camera turned back to Tony.

Montana whispered in Tony's ear, and then he spoke. "Then, Senator, I must submit to you that the only faction that is more against the decriminalization of drugs than you, sir, is organized crime. Do you think the organized network of drug dealers is at all anxious to give up such a profitable business?"

Tony remembered the bloated senator looking horrified, but the camera stayed on Tony, then Montana, as the hearing room erupted in a cheer of affirmation.

He stopped the video and ran it back to Leslie Phillips again. He played it slowly and he looked at her face, frame by frame.

While the disk played in slow motion, he sat back in his chair, staring into the monitor, and he remembered. He remembered how she had been indispensable in the establishment of the program. At their first personal encounter at the Hay-Adams Hotel, when Montana brought her over to meet Tony, she was warm and enthusiastic. "Dr. Ryan, your wife tells me she wrote your entire speech. You make a terrific puppet."

"Oh, did my strings show, or did Montana move her lips? Now that you've found me out, are you going to sell the story to the Enquirer?"

"Heavens, no. Now I think we can force you to help set up the legal distribution program I'm going to propose."

Tony couldn't believe he heard that from someone in Congress. And then weeks later, he had indeed found himself immersed in several organizational meetings back in Washington. During a break from one of the committee meetings, he sat with Montana and Senator Sheffield from New Jersey in the lounge of the Ritz-Carlton discussing the morning's meeting with representatives for the marijuana farmers. The farmers had voiced their concerns about the vulnerable position they'd be in if the program failed.

Montana had seen the obvious. "Listen, if hemp is such a wonderful plant, why don't you pass a law — you're good at that, Senator — so that even if the program fails, hemp can still be farmed for industrial use, maybe even as a controlled medicinal substance, too. The farmers would have nothing to lose. In fact, it would stimulate peripheral industries as well."

Allan Sheffield looked at her and shook his head. "Your wife's not only beautiful; she's a genius. I'd love to give you a position on my staff!"

"Excuse me, Senator. I'm not that kind of woman." Montana looked right at him. It took him a moment to figure the double entendre. Then he rolled his eyes, and they all had a nice chuckle.

The logistics, though somewhat nightmarish, were not that difficult to work out. The federal government sponsored the construction of the local centers. They invited open participation in drug sales, but through the quality-controlled management of major pharmaceutical companies.

The technological wizardry of the twenty-first century was essential to the fundamental organization. Remembering one of the meetings in late fall, Leslie Phillips struggled with a problem. "How do we keep Santa Barbara from being a weekend drug resort? I can just see the new ads: 'The Biltmore. It's more than a natural high.' Or what about people passing through who want to buy drugs and take them outside of Santa Barbara, where they're still illegal?"

Tony addressed the issue. "Luckily we've got the technology now to handle that. I figure we should provide new drivers' licenses or resident IDs with a smart chip. This will identify the person when they go to the DPC. It will be issued only to legal residents of the county. When they hand over the card to place an order, their picture will appear on a computer screen along with other important identifiers and essential health information. It should be reasonably easy to prevent non-locals from intruding. I suppose if someone sneaks in with their own grass, they would be able to smoke it without repercussion during a stay in Santa Barbara, but they would still have to follow the same guidelines of the new tort system we've set up. Of course, you should sell limited quantities so that you don't encourage anyone to start selling their purchases down in Los Angeles. I'm sure people leaving Santa Barbara are bound to be more carefully scrutinized, if not simply harassed, during the course of this experiment."

"Smart chips would work. You don't think a lot of people will be put off by such an intimate relationship with Big Brother?" Phillips inquired, knowing that the DPC computers would have a lot of information about the buyers.

"Probably, but that's the trade-off for having legal, and much cheaper, access to drugs."

Then Phillips announced at the same meeting, "During a closed session with the President and the congressional leaders on this committee, we have elected Dr. Tony Ryan to be the first director of the legal drug program. We hope he'll accept the position. It has only a one-year tenure because that is the length we've determined necessary for the phase one evaluation of the experiment. At the end of phase one, the evaluation process will be scrutinized, and subsequent plans will then be laid out."

Having spent so much time on the organizational process, Tony was well suited to manage the program as its director. He was honored to accept, commenting, "I hope I'm not the last director."

Still, he was apprehensive about how this would affect his professional life. Ultimately, he appointed a former hospital administrator, Jeffrey Buchman, as the assistant director and hoped that would allow him the opportunity to eventually re-establish the normal pace of his practice, assuming his image wasn't tarnished by his position at the DPC.

At another meeting they wrestled with which drugs could be sold.

"I think we should limit the sales to marijuana, "suggested Michael Delgado from Texas. "It's probably the most popular and the least harmful."

"Why not all drugs?" one of the committee members asked.

"Let's limit it to so-called recreational, nonprescription drugs," said Tony. "I think we should provide anything that the underground would otherwise produce, with the exception of less-popular aggression-producing drugs such as PCP. If someone wants to sell it, we might have to give them a spot in the DPC. But if someone commits a crime while they're high on it, then they'll get a very long lock-up." Tony then looked over to Phillips for her input.

She was one hot, sexy woman and perhaps even more alluring because of her status. Tony's mind started to wander as he watched her suck on the end of her pen, contemplating the issue before the committee. Her teeth, her tongue, her soft, full lips caressed the top of her Mont Blanc pen. She had no idea what she was doing, but for a moment Tony knew every man in that committee had forgotten the issue, had succumbed to a testosterone induced lascivious fantasy.

Thankfully, she quit playing with her pen and announced, "I think you're right. Let's head in that direction."

Tony froze the video on her image. That ever-present Mont Blanc pen rested seductively between her lips.

He shut down the TV and VCR, shaken at the loss, angry and determined that her death would not be marked by the legacy of a failed experiment.

Tony walked into the bedroom and found Montana in bed, not yet asleep.

"What have you been doing?" Montana asked.

"Thinking. Looking at those C-SPAN videos." Tony then knelt down by Montana's side and stroked the side of her cheek. "Are you packed already?"

"Already? I just about fell asleep before you walked in. You've been out there nearly an hour. You sure it's right for me to go tomorrow?" Montana looked up at Tony, holding his gaze and then lifting her hand to his wrist.

With his other hand he wiped the vestige of a tear from his cheek and then bent down and kissed her on the forehead. He straightened back up and replied, "There's nothing that you need to do here, other than take care of me." He smiled softly.

She reached her hand up along his arm. It felt small against his triceps, where she lightly pulled, coaxing him closer to her. "I'm sure you'll survive my absence very well."

Tony leaned forward, still kneeling by her side, and this time kissed her on the lips. He closed his eyes as he enveloped her soft, full lips. They parted slightly, inviting him on. Her lips parted further, and he felt the warmth of her tongue barely caressing him until he sank deeper into her mouth with his own. He slid his hands along the back of her head, holding her close to him while she wrapped both arms around his back and embraced him.

They kissed. Sweet, languid, long, caring kisses. These were the kind of kisses reserved for survivors. They had witnessed their mortality in the loss of their friend and now clung to their own vitality with passion.

Without parting lips, Montana grappled with his shirt, tugging it free from his pants, and then slid her hands along Tony's back and sides. Her touch magnified his desire, and he straightened, risking the moment to quickly pull off his shirt. Barely skipping a beat, he wrapped his arms around her and resumed their kiss as he slid his hand under her nightgown, down along her leg, up to the small of her back and up under her shoulders.

If they could fuse as one, it would happen now. Well aware of the excitement of the moment, perhaps heightened by the fatalistic darkness of the occasion, Montana pulled on Tony's belt, freeing it, and hastily unfastened his pants with his eager assistance. Tony stood and stripped in seconds before placing his naked body on top of hers. Her smooth body felt like silk against his broad frame. Her lips and eyes, wanting and devilish, yet fragile and vulnerable, heightened his arousal. They continued kissing, full, deep and sensuous, while Montana slipped her hands alongside his belly and reached down, grasping him firmly and guiding him into her.

They were one. As he slid inside her, slow and deep, she urged him on as her passion became increasingly frantic. Their kisses were deeper, in step with the mounting pressure between their legs. Yet for all of the sensations flooding his body, the thoughts between his ears enraptured him, taking him to an orgasmic brink. When Montana parted her lips, barely gasping, he looked at the most sexually charged creature he had ever seen.

"I love you," he said, soft and low, as he embraced her moments before he climaxed.

Chapter 6

5:45 a.m., Monday morning, March 14

THE NEXT THING TONY knew, the alarm went off at a quarter to six in the morning. As he walked off to shower, he left three dozing bodies, two of them quite furry, completely undisturbed. By six forty-five he was in the office. His office was truly his home away from home. The building itself, Spanish style, blended nicely with the architecture of downtown Santa Barbara and did not look like a traditional glass-and-steel medical office building. On good days, Tony thought it was charming. On days when the air conditioning didn't work or the elevator wasn't functioning, he thought it should be converted into a mission for the homeless. But once he got to the third floor and opened his door, he was at home. Although he had a private entrance just down the hall, he preferred to come in through the front. He still enjoyed the ocean view that he could see as he entered through the secretarial area. The decor was comfortable, light and stylish without being overbearing. There were no dark woods and leathers, but instead rather pale, muted tones that worked well with the light off the ocean.

As he walked past the reception desk and entered his office, he was surprised to encounter Joanna. "You don't usually come in so early," he said to her.

"It's good to see you, too. We've got a very full day today."

"Anyone miss me?"

She had the Saturday mail piled in her arms and handed it over to him. "Yeah, the mailman."

The stack of debris on his desk dimmed some of his excitement at returning. Although it could easily wait, he quickly flipped through some of the mail, put it down and then made his way down the hall to the office surgical suite. There, already on the operating table, Cynthia Franklin waited to have a breast augmentation. Ron Matsuda, the anesthetist, started the intravenous line while Tony's surgical assistant, Brenda Williams, secured the EKG leads and blood-pressure monitor. Tony considered himself very fortunate to have these people working with him.

Tony considered Brenda more than a surgical technician. She was also a good friend. They had worked together for more than eight years, ever since she'd left Los Angeles for Santa Barbara. Though only a few years younger than Tony she had been working in the field of cosmetic plastic surgery since the early days of office surgery. Indeed, she had worked for two surgeons who were commonly credited with starting the concept of outpatient office-based cosmetic surgery. Her experience was valuable, but more important, she was flexible and innovative. Tony always looked for ways to improve his operating techniques, and it was nice to have someone else share the creative effort, whether it be to solve new problems or improve approaches to old ones.

When Brenda first called about a job, she genuinely impressed Tony with her phone presentation. She had the eloquence of an East Coast aristocrat. Her mother, a schoolteacher, insisted she speak with perfect diction. When Tony first met her, he was surprised to greet a café au lait colored woman from South Central Los Angeles. Black or African-American, Brenda was a good-looking lady with impeccable speech. Tony knew he was lucky to get her.

Ron Matsuda was dependable. He had worked exclusively with Tony over the last three years. "Mats" had worked for one of his colleagues, Dr. Joseph Segal, in the Beverly Hills area during the '80s. Tony had gotten to know him during his occasional visits to the "Mecca." When Segal decided to retire and sell cosmetics, Tony coaxed Mats to Santa Barbara. He did a first-rate job with his patients, keeping them safe and comfortable.

"Konishi-wa, Ronaldsan," Tony said. He felt himself forcing his words through a veneer to hide his feelings. He wondered if the others knew about last night's discovery. It was too soon for the newspaper.

"Looks like our honorable patient is nice and relaxed."

Then, with a slightly sinister laugh to mock the likes of a Dr. Frankenstein, he said, "Pass me the scalpel, Miss Williams, and I shall begin." Tony figured he had a fifty-fifty chance that his patient, who was wide awake, would catch the humor meant to break the tension of the operating room. Just in case his sardonic wit was not perceived, he walked around the operating table to face his patient and smile directly at her. He gave her a gentle squeeze on the arm and asked how she felt.

"Ask me in a couple of hours, Dr. Ryan. I see you got some color on your ski trip."

"What ski trip? I was at an important medical meeting," he said with another sheepish grin. "We're going to take real good care of you. This will be a very easy experience for you. You're going to be very comfortable, and I will do my very best work." It was time to be positive and reassuring.

Cindy Franklin was anxious and excited at the prospect of her pending breast augmentation. While Tony teased her, Mats started to give her some Compazine through the intravenous line. The Versed and Demerol followed, and soon she was drifting off to a nice sleep. Tony made the appropriate marks on her chest and then injected the local anesthetic around her breasts. He easily settled back into his normal routine. It didn't seem as if he had been away at all.

The patient's chest was cleaned thoroughly with a betadine scrub, and then Tony scrubbed his hands. Sterile drapes were then placed over the patient, exposing only her chest. Tony looked on as the patient was reduced to the parts on which they were to operate. Consciously, he knew there was a person attached to those breasts, but during the procedure he was simply focused on the task at hand. His friends would often tease him about the sexiness and glamour of operating on breasts. One visit to the operating room would end their fantasies.

He was helped on with his sterile gown and then his gloves. Positioned over the right side of the patient, he made a three-centimeter incision in the lower part of the left areola. Brenda dabbed a gauze pad at the bleeding. As she retracted the tissues, he proceeded with the dissection of the pocket necessary to accommodate the saline-filled silicone rubber implant.

Although they sedated Cindy to the tune of Bach, Mats switched the radio to Howard Stern once they were working. Not only did Tony find Stern an enjoyable diversion during surgery, but he personally enjoyed listening to his commentary on the daily news. Stern's disdain for hypocrisy was so refreshing that they forgave some of the crasser elements of his broadcast. Nonetheless, they found themselves laughing quite a bit more than one would expect of a surgical team. The levity was good for his seasoned team and never interfered with their work. Besides, operating was the fun part of surgery, and this was the part of the day that Tony enjoyed the most.

"Not today, Mats. I think Bach's better for now, if you don't mind."

Mats and Brenda stared at each other. Then Mats interjected, "What gives, Tony? You seem a little off kilter today. Since when do you not feel like listening to Howard?"

In his greatest effort to remain professional and give the patient his earnest effort, he simply replied, "I just want to stay focused while I get back into the swing of things." He promised himself he would tell them after he had seen his surgical patients.

As he completed Cindy's operation, they sat her up temporarily, secured a bra and an elastic bandage around her chest, and then laid her back down. Over the next several minutes, Mats began slowly raising her back up in order to stabilize her blood pressure. Essentially, she had been recovering during the course of the operation, so a long wait in the recovery area wouldn't be necessary. It wasn't long before Cindy was on her way home and the next patient was on the table being prepared for her operation.

Tony had one post-op patient from the previous Monday to check while they were getting the next patient ready.

He quickly walked down to the first exam room and picked up the chart for Jennifer Isaacs. There she sat in the exam chair, sporting a tidy plaster splint on her nose. There was a small dot of red in the conjunctiva of her right eye, and just barely a little yellow discoloration remained on her lower eyelids.

"Hi, Jennifer." Tony got right to work loosening the splint from her nose.

"Nice tan. How was your ski trip?" she asked.

"You mean my medical conference?" he smiled.

"Yeah, the one in Aspen. Must be rough. Ooh, that's sore. Be careful."

"Sorry, this thing is really glued on. Here it comes. Now there will be some swelling on the sides, at the tip and near the forehead, though the area under the splint will be tight. You can expect it to swell a bit the next day or so, and then it will all gradually subside." After he removed the splint, he gently cleaned the adhesive residue from her nose.

"So, Dr. Ryan, how does it look?" She was anxious to know that it looked good.

He didn't like to prejudice any patient's reaction unless he'd seen something negative and needed to warn them. "Here's a mirror. Why don't you let me know what you think?"

"Oh, doc. Oh, doc. I mean, oh, Dr. Ryan. This really does it. God, I like it. Even with the swelling, this is really good. Thanks, Dr. Ryan. I was so nervous. I was afraid I would be disappointed, but this is even better than you showed me on the computer."

"It's my perception," Tony said, " that it takes about five minutes to forget your old nose. This is you now. Don't be too critical during the healing period. Your nose will still be quite sensitive for another week or two. If you bump it, you'll see stars, but it won't fall apart. After a while you'll get used to it feeling like a piece of wood on your face, and one morning, maybe five or six weeks from now, you'll wake up and it will feel normal again. You can expect the swelling to mostly be gone in six months. In the meantime, I'd like to check you again in about two weeks."

Tony shook her hand and left the room with her chart. He made a few notations and then gave her chart to Joanna and told her he'd like to see Jennifer back in two weeks.

"The boss lady's here. She's in your office. I can't believe you're letting her go to Italy alone," said Joanna, clearly admonishing Tony.

"I better check on her."

Montana sat behind his desk with the back of the chair facing him so she could be looking out to the ocean view. Tony usually did the same thing, looking out past the palm trees to the Pacific. The serenity of the ocean view was a contrast compared with the welcoming pile of correspondence and patient charts cluttered on his desk. Light and location. Tony had both with his State Street office, and with a 180-degree swivel of his chair he had instant calm. He'd occasionally remind himself not to take it for granted.

Montana rocked in Tony's chair with the phone pressed to her ear. She sounded excited and seemed to be laughing intermittently. Tony walked in and came around to face her. She made a sophisticated appearance in her Donna Karan outfit. She had appeared more innocent and vulnerable last night. She needed to be held. So did Tony, for that matter. Having witnessed such horror had a similar effect on the two of them, ultimately making them aware of their need for one another. With the morning, it was back to business as usual — at least it appeared as such. Now Montana made her last-minute calls before leaving in the awaiting limo. They had taken separate trips before for short periods, though rarely. It had never bothered him until just before it was time to go, regardless of who was going. He didn't mind being alone; he just didn't like having her away. It reminded him of the Greek tales about love. God, as a punishment to man, divided him into two halves so that he was left without his other half. Finding the other half, or the love, was what made him whole. Montana clearly made him feel whole.

As he caught her eye, she winked back at him. Then he could tell she was talking to Gina. Whatever they had been talking about was now replaced with "I'm really looking forward to seeing you, too. See you in the morning, ciao."

Tony stood in the doorway of his private bathroom, hanging on to a chin-up bar that was mounted there. "I'm glad you stopped by. I didn't really get much chance to say a proper goodbye."

"I just needed to pick up some of the implant samples and your slides for the conference. We said a pretty decent goodbye last night." She smiled slyly.

"It's so good to know I'll be missed."

"You know, that bar really looks silly there. You ought to take it down."

"Are you kidding? That's half of my exercise program. That and liposuction keep this boy in shape." Tony leaned over and gave her a peck on the lips.

"By the way, do you have any special instructions regarding the implants we're showing at the meeting?"

"I'd emphasize that we're strongly recommending extended malar and temporal implants for repair of the aging face. Mention the work we've done with the new breast implant. Make sure you focus on the tissue interaction with our implants, especially the nasal implant. Otherwise, you know what to do."

"You sure you can't meet me there for a few days?"

"I'm booked, but maybe something can work out. Actually, I've been meaning to get to Nice. I've wanted to watch Dr. Serra do his fat transplantation procedure. Maybe I could meet you in Rome and stop over in Cap Ferrat for a few days."

"Do you think you can? That would be great. I love Cap Ferrat. Then we could swing through Paris on the way home."

Tony lifted her up by the shoulders and kissed her on the lips. "I love your enthusiasm for traveling. Too bad one of us has to make a living, or I swear I'd be on the plane with you. Let's see what happens. I'll talk to you tomorrow."

Joanna popped her head into the office. "I've got all the things you need," she said. She handed Montana the implants and slides she'd come to pick up. "I hate to break things up, but they're ready in the OR for your next case."

Having said his goodbyes, Tony walked into the OR just before nine o'clock. Cheryl Waksberg was there for a rhinoplasty. Tony found nasal surgery more enjoyable work than breast surgery. It was technically more challenging, but required considerably less physical effort.

With a mallet and a chisel, or osteotome, as doctors called it, Tony had just finished narrowing her nose when Mats switched on the radio to the all-news station.

"… with the most serious news of Leslie Phillips' death just being announced, is there really any life left in the program?" a reporter asked.

"Look, Michael, this is a tragedy of greatest proportions," said a voice. Tony recognized the voice of Texas Congressman Michael Delgado, "but we have rumor and speculation as to her death. We need a fully detailed investigation. Most of the noise is coming from the same members who were opposed to this experiment in the first place."

Brenda looked up at Tony, handing him a needle holder with a suture. "Did they say Leslie Phillips' death? Your Leslie Phillips, the congresswoman?" She looked at Tony incredulously.

"Unfortunately, Montana and I were the ones who discovered the bodies," he said. He remained focused on suturing the tip cartilages in place.

"Are you serious?" Mats chimed in.

"I was waiting until after surgery to tell you. We spent a couple of hours at Weissman's house while the cops ran their investigation. It wasn't pleasant."

"Weissman? The director?" Mats asked. "Was he involved?"

Tony shook his head. "Apparently, very. They found Phillips and another woman shot to death at his house."

Brenda gasped, "Oh, lord."

"He was there, too, dead, with a self-inflicted head wound."

"Hey, so you saw it? Oh, man, I can't imagine." Mats waited for details.

"It was eerie. Very macabre, like something out of a wax museum. I was glad I didn't have to go into the house." Tony just shook his head.

Mats then asked, "Did you know Weissman very well? He belonged to the tennis club."

"I met him a few times but never really talked with him much. Played doubles with him once or twice."

Mats then jumped in again. "Well, I played with him quite a few times, and let me tell you, there's no way that guy would shoot anyone. He was the most passive, nonaggressive guy I ever played with."

Brenda looked over, adding, "I know lots of passive guys who own guns. One thing doesn't have anything to do with the other."

"Maybe so," Mats replied, "but he wasn't just easygoing and passive. He talked about guns and gun control and issues of that nature. He was involved with those animal rights groups like PETA. He didn't even believe in hunting. We were having a beer one day, and he got into it big with Rex Horston. You know Horston, big white hunter. Anyway, they agreed to disagree. Horston teased him because he said he'd never own a gun. R.J. thought if you wanted

83

to own a gun, then you should at least keep it at a rifle range or a club," Mats stated emphatically.

"You're sure about this, I mean this conversation?" Tony asked.

"I'm telling you, I'm shocked by the story. Maybe the guy went nuts. Even that's far-fetched, but even if he flipped out on drugs, I'd have an easier time believing the story if he killed someone with his tennis racket."

"Well, he didn't use a tennis racket," Tony noted. "He had a gun which was registered to him."

"Maybe your hunting buddy talked him into it," Brenda conjectured. "Weissman was a big shot. He probably bought it for protection. Obviously, he didn't know what he was doing with it."

Tony finished sewing the tip cartilages in place and started to suture the skin back together. They both had valid points, but clearly Mats had some kind of inside information about Weissman. "It'll be interesting to see what the cops or the FBI finds out about him. I'm sure someone's going to propose that this is a right-wing conspiracy."

Chapter 7

9:00 a.m., Monday morning, March 14

McVee took another look at his watch. He stood by the podium of the Santa Barbara Police Department's conference room. Although it was lined with desks and chairs, some money had been put toward interior design, establishing a more sophisticated environment than a mere classroom. McVee took another sip of his coffee. It was nearly nine-thirty before Cooper finally walked into the briefing room. "Okay, let's get started. A.T., why don't you bring us up to date on the Phillips/Weissman case? Then Frank can discuss the Mason case." A mix of officers and detectives sat in the room.

"Sorry I'm late, Jimmy," Cooper stated. "I just got back from the lab. I wanted to check on the ballistics of the Weissman case. I might as well start with that. At approximately nine-fifteen Sunday evening, we were summoned to 875 West Ridge Road, the home of Randal Jeffrey Weissman, thirty-seven years old. The call was placed by Dr. and Mrs. Tony Ryan after they discovered the bodies. Three victims were found within the residence, all dead from apparent gunshot wounds to the head." Cooper then paused for a moment to dim the lights and turn on the slide projector from the podium.

"In the master bedroom, two women were found face down and handcuffed, as you see. The victims have been identified as Sherie Powers, twenty-seven years old, from Abilene, Texas, and on the right is Leslie Phillips, forty-eight-year-old congresswoman from Santa Barbara. Each woman had a single gunshot wound to the back of the head. Toxicology reveals the presence of alcohol, marijuana, cocaine and PCP within their blood. Cocaine and PCP residue was recovered from areas around their labia. There was no sign of forced sexual penetration. There was no semen present in or on either woman."

The next slide, of Weissman grotesquely positioned in the blood-splattered chair, brought a few groans and shivers from the group. Cooper seemed to enjoy the reaction and proceeded. "Weissman was found with a Beretta 92FS in his lap. It had his prints. He had a single gunshot wound through the mouth, exiting his occipital area. Blood serum analysis revealed the presence of alcohol, marijuana, cocaine and PCP. Cocaine/PCP residue was present on the nasal mucosa and around his penis."

"What about the urine?" McVee asked.

Cooper lost his rhythm and seemed to stumble a moment. "Oh, we don't have the final coroner's report on that yet. I'm sure it will test positive. Meanwhile, I do have ballistics and registration information."

"How are you so sure?" McVee still wanted the routine information.

Cooper, a bit annoyed, said, "Excuse me, Jimmy, how am I so sure about what?"

"About the urine." McVee was now using Cooper as an example to the other officers. He had always taught to gather all your information before you speculate. Now Cooper was clearly jumping to conclusions that were probably correct, but would be revealed with a simple lab test, not a lazy speculation.

To his credit, Cooper recognized his error in presentation and admitted it. "Sorry, Jimmy. When I get the urine analysis, I'll file it in the final report." He paused and looked at McVee, who simply nodded, signaling him to proceed. "First, the bullets were all fired from the recovered weapon. Second, the weapon was indeed registered to Weissman. It was purchased a couple of weeks ago. Paid for in cash, but his record has been checked and his fingerprints are a match. Speaking of prints, his were the only ones on the cocaine vial. The vial has been handed over to the FBI. The house was dusted for prints, but aside from the victims', it was clear. No signs of forced entry, and there do not appear to be any witnesses. A video room was set up and a DVD was found in the video recorder. Weissman had quite a set-up that even included a remote-controlled hidden camera. We hoped there might have been revealing footage on that tape." Then Cooper smiled and added, "Well, it turned out to be revealing footage, not of the crime scene, just some porno tape. Nothing homemade.

"The present speculation, based on the information available," Cooper continued, looking toward McVee, "leads us to conclude that Weissman committed a double murder and then suicide. The motive is not completely clear, but may have been for a couple of reasons. Most likely, he experienced a cocaine/PCP psychosis during their romp and became panicky. He may have experienced some kind of personal humiliation. The women may have threatened him in some way. He may have been embarrassed. With cocaine and PCP present all over their genitalia and no semen present, it's possible he was not able to perform, and this may have further fueled the cocaine/PCP psychosis. Of course the feds are extremely interested in how PCP got into the cocaine vial purchased at the DPC."

"Does there appear to be any premeditation?" McVee asked.

"Who knows?" Cooper shrugged. "There's obviously the handcuffs to suggest he had something kinky in mind. Any way you look at it, though, he was playing with dynamite. We've all known it was only a matter of time before someone really flipped out and did some damage."

"Thanks for the editorial," McVee offered. "By the way, were there any calls from the neighbors? Any witnesses or anyone reporting gunshots?" McVee looked at Cooper, waiting for an answer.

Cooper paused and appeared either tired or indignant at being questioned by his senior partner. "If there had been any other reports or witnesses, I would have included that in my report."

"Hmm," McVee added, nonchalantly pulling at his chin, "seems strange that no one heard any gunshots. I saw the gun that night, too. No silencer. You'd think there'd have been someone reporting gunshots." McVee let him off the hook and asked, "How about the Ralston case? Weren't you covering that one, too?"

"Give me a second," said Cooper as he rearranged his files. "Okay, this is a case involving James Ralston, a local shoe salesman. He was victim number four this week from an apparent heroin overdose. A 911 call was registered by the decedent's sister, Mrs. Jean Colton, on Sunday morning from his home. She apparently went to check on him, as he had not responded to her phone calls and was expected for a Sunday morning brunch. She called the paramedics, but the coroner believes he had been dead since late Friday night. High levels of heroin in his blood stream indicate an overdose. No signs of forced entry, and according to his sister, he barely had any friends, let alone possible enemies."

"Do we know how high the blood heroin levels were? Doesn't it seem odd that a heroin addict should overdose on the stuff out of the DPC?" McVee questioned Cooper.

"Well, heroin addicts overdose all the time. According to lab findings, the purchased heroin measured more than ten times the normal concentration. At this point, I'd like to introduce Roger Felton, FBI special agent. He'll be our liaison with the feds during these investigations."

Felton rose in the back and made his way to the podium. "As you've heard, we've got some preliminary information indicating some major contamination of DPC-delivered drugs. I've shipped off several samples to Mark Hansen, FBI agent in Washington, D.C. It's been confirmed that there was PCP contaminating the cocaine, and heroin concentrations were over ten times that labeled. Meanwhile, I don't plan on stepping on too many toes. The majority of our investigational efforts will be around the DPC." Felton then stepped back and turned the podium back over to Cooper.

"Thank you, Mr. Felton. I think that wraps it up for now," Cooper said as he gathered his files together.

McVee commented, "Okay, we'll go over your cases again when your investigation is complete. Not bad for a weekend, Cooper."

"Yeah, for New York, maybe. I think I prefer our usual sleepy Santa Barbara weekends." Cooper, with files in hand, took a seat.

McVee walked toward the podium and then stopped and turned toward Cooper. "Where did Weissman buy his gun? Did you get a chance to interview the guy who sold it to him?"

Cooper looked a little annoyed, as if it were a dumb question. "Same place most of the folks around here get their guns. Western Rifles and Guns. The salesman's name is in the computer, but we haven't interviewed him yet. I'll take care of it."

McVee mumbled, "Very good," in a conciliatory manner and then turned to Ramsey. "Frank," he said, signaling Ramsey to come up to the podium.

Ramsey brought his file up and began his review. "On Friday evening at approximately 10:25 p.m., a '98 BMW 535i driven by Robert Mason went over the edge of Las Alturas and rolled down the side of the hill. The driver and his passenger, wife Stephanie, were freed from the wreck and lifted up the hill to the street by the fire department. Search of the car revealed marijuana present in the glove compartment. The couple admitted they had smoked some prior to the accident. Detective McVee was notified, as this appeared to be an investigation into an apparent narcotic-involved felony. Frankly, I was amazed no one was killed. The car flipped over but landed hard against a large boulder, that prevented it from falling further. Mrs. Mason was uninjured, and Mr. Mason sustained an apparent blunt injury to the nose. On initial questioning, Mason stated he was driving up the hill toward his home when he felt a sudden loss of control in the steering mechanism. He was unable to pull the car out of a turn, and before he could adequately brake, the car went over the edge. As the car tumbled, he struck his nose against the steering wheel or the window, he wasn't sure which, before the air bags deployed. They landed upside down, but were both strapped in their seat belts and cushioned by the airbags. A curbside sobriety test was performed on both occupants. Mr. Mason passed, but the results were slightly ambiguous for Mrs. Mason. She stated she was simply too shaken to steady herself for the test. They stated that they had purchased eight grams of marijuana and admitted they had smoked a small amount prior to dinner. However, only three-and-a-half grams of marijuana were recovered at the scene. They were booked on suspicion of felony reckless driving under narcotic influence. Legal levels of alcohol were found in the blood, as well as evidence of marijuana. The car was impounded, and it's definitely well mangled. We're waiting for the mechanic check it out — and determine whether there was any truth to Mason's conjecture of malfunction. Mason contacted an attorney. There were no priors, and the

Masons were insistent about their story. The magistrate allowed them to be remanded to the custody of their attorney."

"Lucky kids. What's your plan for follow-up?" McVee simply prompted the next response.

"I've just corroborated the quantity of the marijuana purchase with the DPC. They definitely were unable to account for over four grams. That would indicate they consumed quite a bit more than they admit to. However, they've got a tough attorney, Denise Taylor, and she's firm that her clients are innocent. Mason passed his sobriety test, he blew a .02, way below the .08 limit, and she says there's still no absolute setting for marijuana limits. Therefore we must base our findings on the actual occurrence. She contends her client rolled his car, but since he was clinically sober, his account is reasonable." Ramsey looked back to McVee for further prompting.

"And the missing marijuana. How does Miss Taylor account for that?" McVee asked the obvious.

"She doesn't. Apparently, she thinks it's ultimately irrelevant. Based on the assessment of the Masons, she feels there's no proof that they were under the influence of drugs. She contends it's possible one of the parking attendants from the restaurant could have removed some of the marijuana for themselves."

McVee nodded his head affirmatively. "Good point. You might have a difficult conviction."

"I've sent someone to investigate the parking attendants. It might dead-end on us, but it looks like he's facing a possible reckless driving, but that might not even stick. If they get her to back down, which she won't, the kid could get cited for a first-time marijuana DUI. It's just a misdemeanor, but he'd get a five-month suspension with the usual DUI classes and AA program stuff." Ramsey seemed content with his conclusions.

"Okay, so for now we've got three new cases under investigation. Ralston and the three other heroin ODs with tampered heroin. Weissman with contaminated cocaine. And the Masons with a possible DUI involving marijuana. The conclusions are apparent, but I don't think we should respond to the press until the investigations are thoroughly wrapped up and signed off. What do you think, Leonard?" McVee now turned the meeting over to the chief of police, Leonard Callison. The serious matters of the investigation were conducted by McVee, but the symbolic leadership was left to Callison. Leonard Callison, a stout man in his fifties, had served the community well for more than thirty years, working his way up the ranks from a beat cop. He was a good man, but very much used to the cozy, quiet community of Santa Barbara, where petty crime, burglary, and, previously, drug infractions were the main concerns of law enforcement.

"Thank you, Jimmy," Callison responded in a friendly manner, unconcerned with perceptions. "I've already spoken with Senator Winston's office. You can only imagine the commotion this has stirred in Washington. Anyway, his senior advisor, Morton or something, says the senator's really worried that this whole program is going to blow sky high. The fellow thought he was real funny, says to me, 'sky high' again, like I'm supposed to start laughing at his stupid pun. Anyway, they're anxious to know exactly what happened. They think if there's more of these drug problems and they don't go public to pull the plug on the whole experiment, they'll be out of luck next election time."

Cooper took advantage of a momentary pause in the chief's explanation and inserted, "It's only going to get worse. I'd say Winston's safely covering his butt."

Callison nodded, but then added, "You might be right, Cooper. Nonetheless, I think we should do as McVee suggests, finish the investigations, and not make any statements until we're signed off on the investigation. Here's what I told this Morton fellow. I told him, 'You boys can take any position you like — you're politicians. Meanwhile, we have a simple job. We investigate and work with the DA to get the appropriate convictions. We're not the judge; we don't interpret the law or pull the strings. We do what we've been asked to do.' I did offer him this, though: 'If you're asking, I can tell you that the last two months have been nearly free from drug crime. Burglary is way down. We haven't had a single armed robbery reported. We used to get two or three a week. No drug-related homicides in two months.' So let's not jump the gun. Public opinion is already being formed based on this weekend's events. Maybe it's gonna hit the fan. We'll see. What do you think, Jimmy?"

McVee got up from his seat and sat on the edge of the desk, saying, "I don't really know what to expect. Cooper may be right, This program may erupt on us. On the other hand, I always expected that if there were going to be problems, we'd see them right off the bat. You know, with the excitement and newness, I figured there would be a rush on drugs. At least, I expected a rash of traffic accidents or more domestic violence cases. Haven't seen it. Maybe Santa Barbara's very sophisticated. Maybe people started out wary of the program and were being very cautious. The DPCs are doing a brisk business, so somebody's buying the stuff. So far, the university rehab center has been treating former addicts, but maybe they're in for an overflow crowd soon. Or maybe the program's working."

Ramsey responded, directing it back to Callison. "I don't know, chief. I've been talking to folks on the street. Seems like folks started out being rather cautious. I think they're a little concerned about Big Brother knowing about their private lives. Now that the cat's out of the bag, so to speak, there's more opportunity for people to use drugs who would never have used them before. Maybe the last group of people who didn't use drugs because they were illegal will also fall into the fray. These folks are not prepared to deal with this stuff."

Callison wanted to end the meeting. "Maybe you're right," he said. "Let's get these investigations wrapped up. In the meantime, stay out of the press. I don't want the SBPD editorializing this situation. Understood?"

Michael Cirrelo walked into the motel room and found his partner, Arthur Salinski, screwdriver in hand, making some careful adjustments to a metallic device.

"You got that thing ready yet?" Cirrelo demanded.

"Hold your horses, chief. This is touchy business. Gotta be done precisely."

"Yeah, well, I've gotta get moving before the cat takes off."

"Hey, that's funny. Get it? Cat takes off." Salinski laughed to himself while Cirrelo paced the floor, waiting for the device. "Oh, man, that cat'll be taking off, all right."

When Salinski finished, he carefully placed the device in a cushioned compartment and handed it to Cirrelo. "Kiss him for me," he laughed. "You still planning to meet him personally, or are you over that nonsense?"

Cirrelo cradled his prize and smirked at Salinski. "There's a little more excitement to the sport if you come eye to eye, don't you think?"

"I could give a rat's ass. Just get it done. I don't want to hang around here one day longer than we have to."

Chapter 8

10:00 a.m., Monday, March 14

Tony molded the plaster splint to Cheryl's nose.

"How'd it come out, Dr. Ryan?" Cheryl uttered, still groggy from the sedation.

"I think you'll like it. It looks like the nose that belonged there in the first place."

Relieved to be through with her operation, yet still quite sleepy, she still managed to say "thank you," then drift off again.

After thanking his O.R. crew, Tony emerged from the operating room and discarded his gown and gloves. He stood by the sink and washed his hands to remove the powder lift from his gloves as Joanna came up to him.

"You've got a half-hour if you want to make any calls or go over any mail. Then you've got a full load of patients." When Joanna spoke, Tony felt like he worked for her.

Already on his desk lay several faxes from local clergy who suggested Tony consider shutting down the experiment. A few congressional members had called wanting an updated status report.

Tony proceeded to muddle through his correspondence. He couldn't really concentrate on any of it and found himself flinging the mail into more piles – bills over here, sales pitches in the trash, future conferences in a pile over there. He'd get to it later. Especially with Montana out of town, what else did he need to do?

He had barely made a dent in the stack when Joanna called over the intercom. "Dr. Ryan, you've got patients in the rooms waiting."

Tony looked down at his watch. That was the quickest thirty minutes, he thought. Where did it go?

Tony stared at the phone momentarily and then grabbed his long white coat from the closet and slipped it on over his scrubs. He marched down the hall and managed to button his coat before he got to the first consultation.

He sat down and made notes on the chart of Alice Dwyer, a forty-eight-year-old woman interested in liposuction surgery.

"I agree. You could certainly benefit from liposuction, but you're telling me you weighed 125 last year and didn't have a problem with your figure until now. I think maybe some of the stress from your divorce has shown up in the form of a few too many Big Macs."

"I just want to get rid of the belly. Then I know I can get the rest off."

Tony still wasn't sure she was very well motivated. "I've got an idea, and it should save you a lot of money. Why don't you be fair and give yourself six months and make a good effort at weight reduction with diet and exercise? If you lose a pound a week, you'll be back to your fighting weight and you'll have all that extra money for a trip or something special."

"Yeah, like more attorney fees. Okay, how about three months? Really, Dr. Ryan, I just need a little jump start, but I'm willing to give it a try."

"Good. Then I'll see you in three months, and maybe you won't need anything done."

"I'll try, but I think this tummy will be here when I come back."

In the next room, a twenty-six-year-old man, Charles Rosenfeld, wanted a rhinoplasty.

He pulled out a half-dozen pictures of different model and celebrity noses. All of them had high cheekbones and strong chins, two things that Charles Rosenfeld definitely lacked. "You see, Dr. Ryan, if you just shave a little off the hump and raise the tip a bit, don't you think that would look so much better?"

"Check this out." Tony had his picture on the computer and made some changes to strengthen the chin. It put his face into balance. "Look at your nose now," he explained. "It looks fine; it fits with the rest of your face. All you need to do is lengthen your chin and maybe your cheeks."

"What if you just smooth down that hump and raise the tip a little?" Rosenfeld remained insistent about his nose.

After making the alterations, Tony looked at him askew, saying, "Now it looks like a fellow who has had a nose job."

"Yeah, that's it."

Tony wasn't making his point. "Sometimes it's a good idea to get a second or third opinion."

"Ah, you can do it. You've operated on my friends. This should be an easy operation for you."

This patient seemed like gum stuck to the bottom of Tony's shoe. He couldn't get rid of this guy politely. He finally apologized, saying, "I'm sorry, but I just can't see myself doing the surgery the way you want it. I really don't think it would be in your best interest. I'll ask Joanna to give you a couple of referrals on your way out."

Tony walked back down the hall, where he saw Brenda coming toward him. "How's it going, Doc?" Brenda inquired.

"0 for two," Tony stated. "But the day's still young."

"I was just talking with your next patient. I'm not sure he's going to do anything to change your streak."

"Why's that?"

"It's the young man who went over Las Alturas Friday night. The one Jimmy McVee sent in. He's got a nasty bump on his nose, but I bet it's all swelling." Brenda was usually very good in her assessments.

"Maybe I ought to say hello," Tony conceded.

Rob Mason sat in the exam chair sifting through People magazine as Tony walked in. Rob dressed neatly but casually, with an open-collar white shirt, tan slacks and Gucci loafers. His face appeared distorted by a nose slightly shifted to the left and wide from swelling. He had the expected purplish bruising in the lower eyelid skin found with forceful nasal trauma.

Tony offered his hand. "How are you feeling, Rob? I'm Dr. Ryan."

"Lucky. Although I'm sure I used most of it up."

"I suspect you did. I know that area where your car went over."

"Yeah, quite a testimony to seat belts, airbags and roll bars. What do you think of my nose, Dr. Ryan? Detective McVee referred me and said you'd fix it. Told me you fixed him up once or twice."

Tony smiled softly, thinking of the time he had operated on Jimmy McVee. About five years ago, McVee, in spite of his karate background, couldn't avoid an elbow to his nose while investigating a heroin network. After Tony straightened his nose, they remained friendly, occasionally meeting for a game of racquetball. The stocky fifty-something McVee could kill a shot from anywhere on the floor, and Tony was the only one getting exercise when they played.

McVee knew Tony's position on drug legalization. God knows they'd argued it often enough. McVee opposed it, but so did everyone else in the police department. Still, Tony suggested McVee for the position as police liaison to the program, which McVee accepted reluctantly out of a sense of friendship or obligation.

Now, as he considered Rob's nose, he knew there was too much swelling to fix it at this time. Tony took a look inside his nose using a headlight and a nasal speculum that he held in his left hand.

"How's your breathing?" Tony asked.

"Stuffy, not normal yet, but better today than a couple of days ago."

"We've got to make sure you can breathe through your nose," Tony said while he looked inside Rob's nose. "I saved McVee's marriage. His wife was going nuts from his snoring. After I fixed his nose he slept like a baby."

Tony saw a lot of internal swelling, some dried blood, but fortunately no signs of a septal hematoma. He tried to wiggle the bridge of the nose and Rob winced.

"Sorry. Actually, the bones feel like they're intact. We'll have to give it until next week and let the swelling subside. Maybe we won't have to operate. It's too difficult to tell if your septum will need to be straightened as well. The swelling will go down and we'll decide what to do next week."

"What if it doesn't straighten out? What do you have to do then?" Rob wanted to know what surgery would be like.

"If we have to fix it, and I'm not sure we will, it's an outpatient procedure, done with intravenous sedation and local anesthesia. Takes about an hour. I break it and put it back in place. No packing, just a plaster splint over the bridge to hold the bones in place. It comes off in a week. Tell you what. Let's check you next week before we make any decisions. What do you say?"

"Sounds like a plan, but I might have some problems with the court system. I just don't know what penalties I might be facing. The way the DA was talking, my lawyer thinks he might be trying to make an example of my case. This thing can really get out of hand. Jeez, I wasn't the least bit high. The accident was so freaky. I mean, why did the steering go out, and why did it happen when I got up the hill, not while I was still down in town?"

Mason seemed like a reasonably bright fellow. He didn't impress Tony as being irresponsible. Tony asked him, "How much did you actually smoke?"

"Honestly, my wife and I only had a couple hits before dinner, and we only had a couple glasses of wine during the entire meal. We were looking forward to that grass after we got home. The grass had been in the car, but after the accident the cops took it. They told us they found two joints, one partially smoked with Stephanie's lipstick on it. That should prove we smoked very little, but for some reason, the cops never found the other four grams that were in our glove compartment. They think we smoked it. I think one of the parking attendants probably grabbed some. How am I supposed to prove that? The burden of proof is supposed to be on the prosecution, but they're trying to put it on me. Meanwhile, the media is starting to pick up on this thing. You can't believe how many calls we're getting. It's a circus."

Tony just shook his head. This guy had problems much worse than a bump on the nose. "I don't think the police can tell how much you smoked based on blood or urine levels – at least not yet. I would think they would have to prove you're not telling the truth. I think it's more important that you were clinically sober. It's still a tough situation. Maybe you have a little luck left over. Anyway, let's plan on checking your nose in a week."

Tony ushered Rob out of the exam room and brought him to Joanna's desk. "One week, please."

"This just came for you," Joanna said, handing Tony a FedEx letter package.

While Tony opened the package and pulled out the letter, she issued an appointment card to Rob, who then turned and left.

"What the hell is this all about?" Tony was loud and annoyed.

"Dr. Ryan," Joanna said softly, "there's patients in the waiting room. They'll hear you. What's the matter?"

"It's a letter from the state medical board. They're conducting an investigation and they want copies of charts on these three patients. Do you recognize anything special about them?"

Joanna looked at the names in the letter but drew a blank. "I don't recall anyone complaining to me. I'll pull the charts."

"It says all three of these women have filed a grievance with the state medical board. Is it April first yet? This has got to be some kind of mistake."

Always trying to keep things calm, Joanna reasoned with Tony, saying, "You don't even know if this is an investigation about you. Let's pull the charts and review them first before you jump to any conclusions. By the way, Roger Felton's here. I put him in your office. You've got a few minutes, and I'll bring the charts in after he leaves."

When Tony walked into his office, Agent Felton was sitting in his chair behind his desk, facing the ocean view. Unaware of Tony, Felton tossed a silicone gel-filled breast implant in the air. He seemed to be quite at ease and enjoying himself.

"Agent Felton, what's up?"

Felton wasn't fazed, and Tony wasn't surprised he didn't jump up and apologize.

"So this is what you use in the breasts. They really feel natural. Cool stuff. Must be a lot of fun building boobs."

"Loads. What's the surprise you have for me?"

"Surprise? I just wanted to discuss our plans for the DPC."

"And what are our plans, Mr. Felton?"

"As I was telling you yesterday, we're going to have to go through all of our screening checks and try to find out who's contaminating the drugs."

"How do you know it's being done internally?"

"Frankly, I don't, but how else would you explain four heroin overdoses with all of the vials at ten times the normal concentration? And in the

Weissman murders, he was using cocaine laced with PCP. This has all been confirmed by the bureau. And so far it all links back to the DPC."

"PCP? How in the hell does PCP get slipped in there? I imagine you've got the staff rechecking all of the cocaine sources."

"Buchman requested that to be done, but I doubt we'll find anything unless the contamination was made at the pharmaceutical company," Felton said as he continued to rock in Tony's chair, oblivious of any social infraction he had committed.

Tony sat down on the couch across from his desk, forcing Felton to turn around and face him. "Couldn't the contamination have come after the purchase? What if someone added the PCP later?"

Felton rubbed his chin. "A little far-fetched, but until the investigation's complete, I suppose anything could have happened. We're going to plant some sample drugs — contaminated, high-concentration stuff like we've seen. We'll then monitor your screeners to see if they're really doing their job."

"What do you guys know about Weissman and his gun?" Tony asked.

"So far, that's the easy part. Weissman bought his gun a few months ago at Western Rifles and Guns. The bullets were all shot from his gun. No forced entry. What else is there to know?" Felton was starting to sound a little annoyed.

"I've heard Weissman was very much anti-gun, so why would he own one?"

"Look, gun sales went up nearly fifty percent the last few months. A lot of people are scared about this new liberal drug program. What makes you think Weissman wasn't one of them?"

"So what's the bottom line? Is there anyone or anything about the system that you see as culpable?"

"Who's at fault? Personally, I think the whole system sucks. I don't know if we'll find the responsible party. Have you heard the radio? On one station they're saying this is a right-wing conspiracy to teach the left a lesson. Who the hell knows? A lot of people are suggesting we close the program down before there's more violence."

Tony stood up, signaling to Felton that the time was up. "And what do you want to do?"

"If it were up to me, it'd be history. Frankly, working with Buchman, I get the feeling you've got too much personally and professionally at stake to be objective. But these aren't setbacks you're witnessing; they're disasters."

"I thought you had the authority to pull the plug."

Felton shook his head. "To put you in jail for obstruction, maybe. The real powers that be have let it be known that the program is to stay on track for the time being. I guess they want you to keep selling drugs for a while." Felton got up and made his way to the door.

"If the experiment is corrupt, why wouldn't they pull the plug?"

Felton turned back, adding, "God, you've got a great view. How do you get any work done?"

Tony looked at Felton, wondering if he would get a straight answer.

"They feel it's got to come from you," said Felton, his tone harshening slightly.

"They want me to call for an end of the experiment?" Tony held his emotions in check, not wanting to give any satisfaction to Felton.

"Yeah, otherwise I guess they want you to keep up the good work selling drugs. They want to make sure you've had an adequate time."

"For what?"

"For the public to hate you. I think they would have preferred it if Phillips ended the program, but under the circumstances you'll do. If you take a stand against the program, I don't think we'll ever see it attempted again."

"Mr. Felton, you may have found a point on which we agree," Tony said, catching the breast implant that Felton flung to him on the way out.

A moment later, Joanna brought the three charts into Tony's office.

All three patients were simple consultations for breast augmentation done within the last two months. The last one was done as recently as two weeks ago. Offhand, nothing in particular struck him about the routine charts. He looked at the names and his notes, but he couldn't remember the faces. All three women were single, one of them divorced, but there wasn't anything unusual that he could tie to their meeting.

"Why waste time beating yourself up?" he asked himself. He dialed the state medical board and promptly connected to a Mrs. Furston in the investigation department.

"Yes, Dr. Ryan, I am well aware of this case file, but it would be inappropriate to discuss it until we've been able to conduct an investigation. Once you send copies of the charts, we can start formulating a status sheet, and during your interview we'll be in a better position to advise you of your options."

Tony was not charmed by Mrs. Furston's bureaucratic indifference. He decided to badger her for the information he wanted now.

"Come on, Mrs. Furston. What difference does it make if you tell me what the allegations are? For all I know, they can be directed at some other doctor."

As though she was annoyed, which she most certainly was, and wanted retribution, she offered, "I can assure you it is not directed toward one of your colleagues."

"So it is something I've done, or at least I'm accused of doing. What in the world could merit an investigation? These women weren't even operated on." He was wearing her out.

"All three filed separate grievances claiming nonprofessional conduct."

"What?" Tony was aghast.

And to rub it in just a little more, she added, "Basically, physician sexual harassment. You're aware that the state finds that to be a very serious offense, aren't you?"

"This is absurd. I've been in practice more than fifteen years and have never had the slightest incident. How is this possible?"

"The medical board is investigating on your behalf as well. Although it's possible that the grievances are without merit, that's not our experience, but I assure you, you'll have a fair investigation."

"So what's next?" Tony was indignant, fighting hard not to start swearing at the emotionless bureaucrat. He was certain that she knew that her tone of voice, with its complete lack of emotion, was driving him nuts. She probably also knew how hard he was trying not to let her know it.

"Once the charts and complaints have been reviewed, you'll be contacted by one of the board members."

"And when can I expect such a visit?"

"Most likely by the middle of next month."

Tony was starting to lose his cool. "You've got to be kidding. Why so long? Or do you like to give the press lots of time to print the story? Once they print the allegations, I will have been tried and convicted by the public. This could ruin my practice. How do you guarantee this won't become public record?"

"I assure you, we are not interested in selling your story. We're here as your medical board to investigate the matter on your behalf as well as the complainants. Like I said, we'll be contacting you shortly. Goodbye." And she hung up.

Tony held the phone in his hand a few moments, looking blankly into the receiver. This has got to be a mistake, he thought. Who are these women? Surely if he'd done something off-color, he'd remember it – even one out of three.

Tony looked over the charts. Lucy Melendez, Diane Turner and Joyce Douglas. All single, one divorced. None of them listed a referral source. Big deal. Many of his patients didn't list referrals. They wanted privacy at all costs. And lately he'd done several breast consultations. He certainly remembered some of them, but in a fragmented way, and nothing stuck.

He knew for certain that there had been no improprieties. In his years of practice, he had never had any complaints registered with the state medical board. To be called about three complaints at once was unbelievable. If they hadn't named the patients, he would have thought they had the wrong doctor. He started thinking maybe there was some misunderstanding, something administrative on their part.

He buzzed Joanna on his intercom. "Do you remember any of these patients?"

"Sorry, Dr. Ryan, none of them scheduled, so I'm not really sure who's who. Is there anything I can do?"

"Just send copies of their charts to the medical board, then leave the charts on my desk. I'll look at them later."

He took a deep breath and let it out slowly, reminding himself that he had done nothing wrong and ultimately someone else had a problem. He had to get back to his patients and not drag this new baggage along the way.

Helen Gordon waited in exam room three.

"Hi, Helen. Boy, you're looking good," he exclaimed. He didn't give her time to respond or question the frown that was etched into his head.

"The swelling's gone down nicely," he said as he reached around her head and lifted her hair. "The scars are very neat and flat. You can barely see them, even back here where they are normally slowest to heal."

Helen's face lift had healed nicely. For a moment, he caught himself looking out the window at the church up the street while Helen was talking to him. She asked about the numbness in her face. He wasn't paying attention, but he heard the question in the back of his head.

He turned back to her, saying, "That's normal. You can expect the feeling to come back within the next few weeks, but sometimes it takes longer." Tony was momentarily struck with a vague feeling about one of the patients listed in the complaint. He put on a lousy smile, thanked Helen for coming in, and told her he'd like to check her again in five months unless she had any problems.

As the day wore on, Tony found himself on autopilot, handling the new consultations with charm and ease. He actually started to have fun again, chattering with his patients like they were old school chums. He sincerely liked his patients and enjoyed knowing about their lives.

Maggie Kramer, a fifty-two-year-old beauty, sat in the exam chair, already wearing a patient gown with a sheet draped over her legs when Tony walked into room three. Eight years ago, Tony had done a face lift on her and added some cheek implants as well. Because she had inherently pretty features, she could now pass for Linda Evans' sister.

"Hi, Maggie. You're looking good. What are you gowned up for?"

"Tony, dear, thanks to you, I'm seeing a younger man, and he wants to take me to Hawaii this summer. I've just got to tighten this belly. I've done thousands of sit-ups, but look." Maggie pulled up the gown, revealing a belly that had been the source of three children and now wrinkled slightly and drooped over her floral panties.

"Very cute." Tony reclined the exam chair and proceeded to examine her abdomen, checking for possible hernias, the position of the muscles and the redundancy of the skin.

"Did you hear about my ex?"

"I'm not sure. He's still practicing surgery, isn't he?"

"Oh, he's practicing all right. He should have been retiring, except that little tramp he married changed her mind about children, and now he's got two more. We've got a grandson older than his daughters."

"Yipes. He must be exhausted."

"Speaking of kids, what are you and Montana waiting for?"

"The new Neiman Marcus catalogue. I think Montana wants to order one."

"Wise guy. You better get busy."

"I'll do my best."

For the next ten minutes Tony explained the procedure. He sent her back to the front desk to get instructions and schedule a date. He went on to see his last patient in room three.

There was a new patient chart on the door. He walked in and greeted Allison Keyes – a lovely young women interested in breast enlargement.

"I have two sisters with perfect boobs like my mom. I got my father's breasts."

As he chuckled, Tony noticed the church outside the window. With the sun going down, the light bounced off the steeple and back-lit the cross like a Renaissance painting. He stared at the cross while Allison asked about implants. And then it came to him. Precisely at that moment he remembered the necklace with the cross of amber-colored stones.

Chapter 9

6:00 p.m., Monday, March 14

TONY SAT IN HIS office staring at the chart of Diane Turner. No referral, no work listing, nothing special — just that amber cross she wore around her neck. The amber cross he'd seen last night at Frascati's around the neck of a girl that sat with Emilio. No wonder she avoided Tony. She either hated him or was embarrassed.

He looked at everything on her chart. She had a birthday at the end of June.

"Scorpios make very good surgeons. And of course Cancers and Scorpios are both water signs and get along so well," she had told him.

Still, not unusual, especially in light of the number of patients that actually scheduled surgery because he was a Scorpio.

Her brown eyes seemed vivacious, not self-conscious like last night in the restaurant. Although physically attractive, with stylishly short brunette hair, Tony knew that after breast augmentation she'd be stunning.

What was she hiding? Emilio was his link to her. Maybe he could learn something from him so he placed a call to Frascati's.

"Dottoré, what can I do for you?" Emilio asked.

"Emilio, how well do you know Diane Turner?"

"She's a pretty girl. She was at the restaurant last night. You saw her. I'm more friendly with her girlfriend, but she's a sweet kid. I gave her your card a long time ago. She needs a little help up front. You know what I mean. She's pretty flat. She gets that done and she's a ten, no? Has she been in yet?"

Tony didn't want to say too much, certainly not to Emilio, the town crier. Otherwise everyone in town would know Tony was being investigated by the medical board. "I saw her a couple of weeks ago. I just wasn't sure if that was her last night. I would have thanked you, but she didn't list any referrals."

"Hey, you know how these girls are. One day they've got great breasts. A gift from God. They don't want anyone to know."

"I suppose. Anyway, thanks for the referral."

"Hey, what'd you expect? You're the finest cosmetic surgeon around. She'll look spectacular."

So much for that. Then Tony asked, "You wouldn't know what kind of work she does, do you?"

"Sure. She's one of those counselors for drug rehab. She works over there at Recovery West."

Bingo. Burton Wesley's Recovery West. Tony pulled out the phone book and looked up the number while Emilio finished his comments.

"Say, what night you want to come by for dinner?"

"Maybe I'll see you tomorrow. I'll call in advance. Thanks, Emilio." He hung up and stared at the phone. He should have known. He had to check and be sure, so he dialed the number.

An operator answered on the second ring, "Recovery West. May I help you?"

Tony held his breath.

"Hello, may I help you?"

He responded finally, "Yes, excuse me. I'm looking for Diane Turner."

"She's gone for the day, but if you like, I can transfer you to her voice mail."

"Thank you, that won't be necessary. I'll call tomorrow." Tony placed the receiver in the cradle and tapped his fingers nervously on the phone. Son of a bitch, he thought. Burton Wesley probably knew she had been referred for a consultation, got to her and coaxed her into setting him up. Good idea,

107

Tony thought. Let's get Dr. Ryan discredited, maybe some bad press, maybe a license suspension. That would make Tony look real good. It certainly wouldn't hurt Wesley's cause at all. Tony pulled out the other charts. One of the patients listed her work number with a real estate agency, Montecito Properties, Inc., while the other was a clerk at First Montecito Bank. It certainly was conceivable that Wesley knew people at those places.

Tony had the modest satisfaction of imagining that Diane Turner, and probably the other women, knew Burton Wesley. Tony cringed at the thought of his smirking face. They all deserved each other.

He looked at his watch for the first time since Joanna had checked out. It was approaching six. It would still be several hours before Montana landed in Rome, and he was anxious to talk with her. In the meantime, he just wanted to go home and disappear for a little while.

He packed his briefcase to leave the office. He heard a squeak from down the hall as the front door opened, and then he heard it shut.

He shouted, "Hello," thinking it might be a late delivery. There was no response. Tony closed his briefcase and wandered into the front office just as the front door closed. The office lights had been turned off except for the one he left on in his personal office. He walked back down the hall to get his briefcase when suddenly someone opened the door to the second exam room and walked silhouetted right into his path. Tony stopped mid-stride within inches of banging into the man. Tony may have been startled, but the man in the dark-blue cleaning crew outfit was so surprised that he dropped the trashcan he planned to empty, spilling most of its contents on the floor.

Tony bent down to help. "Oh, man. Sorry, Pete, I didn't mean to frighten you. I thought maybe there was a delivery man out front."

Pete, the man in charge of the cleaning crew, held his chest while his heart raced. "Dios mio, I thought you were gone, Dr. Tony. I just was picking up the trash. Ooh, you scared me to death." He exhaled a deep sigh and then smiled, not quite ready to laugh at the incident.

"I thought you guys vacuumed first."

Pete corrected him, "Oh, no, first trash, then vacuum. Vacuum last, always."

Tony went back to his office, gathered his things as Pete finished, and left through the front door. He heard the bolt click as Pete locked the door behind him, not wanting any more scares.

When Tony stepped out into the hallway, it was already dark. He suspected the cleaning crew had shut off the lights for the evening, having been told by the landlord to conserve energy, a euphemism for keeping the electric bill down. It was annoying to leave after hours and have to make your way around the barely visible surroundings. Tony regarded it as just another inconvenience in his day. The red exit sign provided enough glow to guide him down the hallway. He stood by the elevator and waited. He heard it making its way up the shaft, and then it stopped. He waited, even pushed the button again, but it didn't start up again. He was not surprised. The elevator had seen better days, and it wasn't the first time Tony had had to find his way down the stairwell. He started to exit by the stairwell next to the elevator, opening the door and then changing his mind, opting for the stairwell at the rear of the hall, which led directly to his car. As he turned away from the closing door, he was fairly certain he heard the sound of a door slam a couple of flights below. The cleaning crew, he figured. He shrugged and walked down the dark hallway in the other direction.

Passing through the rear door, he skipped down the stairs, nearing the first floor landing before continuing on to the garage. Then he heard the door slam two floors above. No one had been on the floor with him other than Pete cleaning in his office. Suddenly he realized someone might be following him. The stairwell would not be a wise place to hold a conference. He realized that his casual jaunt down to the car might now be a chase. He didn't worry about being paranoid. Caution ruled — someone was pursuing him. When he heard the door slam two floors above, he knew that someone must have purposely stopped the elevator and waited for him in the stairwell. They must have heard the door open and shut, and when he didn't show up, they set out after him.

Tony stopped at the first floor landing and exited, taking the hallway out to the street. He didn't need to continue down to the garage, where he might be stuck without a quick exit route. The crowded sidewalks of State Street offered instant safety.

As he left the building, he felt a momentary sense of relief. He crossed

State Street, dodging between a couple of cars, and tried to walk along casually, melting into the crowd. He ducked into the doorway of a local coffeehouse. This time he thanked God they had been popping up all over the place. He turned around from his little hiding spot long enough to see someone walk out the front door. In the dimming night light he could see a man in a tan sports jacket with dark slacks. His hair was slicked back, maybe with a ponytail, and he wore sunglasses. The guy looked so East Coast he might as well have worn a neon sign with "I 'heart' New York." From his present distance, Tony couldn't make out any other details.

The man looked from side to side, but Tony remained out of sight. The man seemed to dismiss the situation casually and smiled, then turned and walked away. For a nanosecond, Tony thought maybe he had run away from a sweepstakes award – but not today. Not with what had been happening the last few days. It was more than the feeling that spring was in the air. Tony knew this was his warning. If Wesley planned to play hardball, he did a hell of a job. Until today, Tony had never thought he was ever a threat to anyone. Now he knew someone was bugged. He felt it. Someone wanted Tony to stay out of their way.

Tony followed the man as he walked a couple of blocks down State Street and then turned to his right. Tony didn't dare get close. The man walked up to a blue Firebird and unlocked the door. But before he entered, another man, taller, though similar in build and facial characteristics (at least from fifty yards), approached. They shared a few words before he got into the car and drove away. The second man headed in Tony's direction, and then farther away down State Street. He got into what appeared to be a brown unmarked patrol car.

A small Irish pub, Kitty O'Brien's, stood nearby on the corner. Tony walked in and ordered a pint of Guinness at the bar. As he took a sip, he made his way to the window and stood there for a while to make sure he wasn't having any unexpected company. After five minutes, Tony figured the man wasn't coming back, but he wasn't ready to go back to his car. He pulled out his phone and made a call. He hoped Jimmy McVee worked late. He needed someone he could trust.

The desk sergeant answered the phone, saying, "Daniels, Police Department."

"Could I please talk with Detective McVee."

"I'm not sure he's in. Let me check. Who's calling?"

"Tell him Tony." He didn't want any more people to know he called the police station. He sincerely hoped he only felt paranoid and that had nothing to worry about. He contemplated his next move. He hoped McVee would have some answers.

The phone came alive. "McVee."

Relieved to hear him, he responded, "Jimmy, it's Tony Ryan. I think someone's trying to intimidate me, and right now it's working."

"What's up, Doc? Who's messing with you?"

Just then Tony realized he wasn't sure how much he wanted Jimmy to know, but he was stuck and needed advice. "I think someone came to my office, after it was all locked up, purposely to harm me." He recounted the events that had just transpired.

"And another thing, the guy he met left in a brown unmarked patrol car. What's going on? I'm not sure what to do."

"Look, I planned on leaving soon, so it might as well be now. Where are you?" McVee said matter-of-fact, like a cop, but still comforting, like a friend.

"I'm at Kitty O'Brien's, across the street from my building."

"Good. I'll see you in a few minutes. I'll meet you and we'll check out your car."

"Check out my car?"

"I'll explain when I see you."

"Okay. Thanks." Tony hung up and slipped back into the bar and waited by the window. He hoped these long days were not becoming a habit. He just wanted to go home and be with his dogs. He counted on the housekeeper, Silvia, to feed and walk them. She knew to take care of the boys if he were late coming home. He sipped slowly on the dark brew. It wasn't his favorite, but he needed the luck of the Irish right about now.

Jimmy McVee walked into the pub within fifteen minutes. "Well, now, top of the day to you, Tony Ryan." Tony stood, shook hands and pushed over the pint of Guinness he had ordered for him a few minutes earlier. "Ahh, but what a welcome sight. Now, lad, tell me about the boogeyman."

"Thanks for coming over. I wish I knew who the boogeyman was, but I don't. Let me tell you, a few too many things have happened, and in too short a time." Tony then recounted the story about the medical board investigation — how one of the girls worked as a counselor for Recovery West, Burt Wesley's organization; how so much animosity existed between the two; and how Wesley always sniped at him about his position on drugs. He wrapped it up with the man he ultimately followed down State Street to the blue Firebird and the meeting with the man in the unmarked patrol vehicle.

"You've been busy. If it wasn't for the fact that you're the director of this experiment, I don't think I'd be too cautious, but…" He made a conciliatory gesture to let him know this was the way things were.

Then McVee asked, "You sure it was an unmarked car? Did you get the plates?"

"From where I stood I couldn't read the plates, but I'm pretty sure it belonged to the department. What other car looks like that? Anyway, what's this stuff about checking my car?"

McVee sipped on his Guinness and looked out the window. Under other circumstances it would have been a nice time to share a drink with a good buddy. "I had to run a check on a stolen vehicle, so I stopped by the impound lot and met with Ron Sewell, our mechanic. Anyway, he had the Mason car on the rack, doing the forensics for Ramsey's file. I tell you, it's the most amazing thing that those kids are still alive. The car's trashed except for the passenger compartment."

Tony relaxed a bit more with Jimmy McVee present, and he slowly nursed his beer while McVee took another sip between sentences.

"So I said, 'I don't suppose you could make anything out of this mess.' Sewell raises the car on the rack and shines a light at the bottom of the chassis. All I see is a bunch of engine stuff. He holds the light steady, and then I see he's pointing at a hole. A hole. He says, 'Yep, that's it. A nice hole right in the power steering compartment.' So I asked if that didn't happen during the tumble. He tells me it looks like it was a small explosion because of the way the metal's been uniformly frayed. A blunt object would have given a different kind of penetrating wound."

"So he thinks someone tampered with the car?"

"Looks that way, or else something exploded off the engine block into the power steering compartment."

Tony chimed in, saying, "Then this favors Mason's contention that he experienced a sudden loss of control."

"Yeah, it does. So I pulled the Mason file and added Sewell's report. I left a note for Ramsey, of course, so he can have it back tomorrow and finish his report for the DA."

"So you think they'll drop the case?"

McVee shook his head affirmatively while taking another chug on the stout. "Anyway, you can see why we might want to take a look at your car, especially if someone could have been tinkering around in the garage."

"I can't believe these last few days. I wish we could have a do-over. Let me tell you something, too. This Agent Felton gives me the willies. Do you think he's a straight player?"

"He's FBI. Those guys are usually top of the heap, but stranger things have happened. No one's exempt from their potential corruptions. Remember that cop case we had a few years back where they busted the Los Angeles County sheriff's deputies for skimming drug money? They convicted more than two-dozen deputies and family members. Their code of silence had lasted years. Most of the deputies had years of experience as part of an elite anti-narcotics force."

"It's got to be awfully tempting staring at those huge piles of cash during a drug bust. How does anyone avoid the temptation? I mean, at the least you could pocket a few grand and no one would know the difference."

McVee added, "Yeah, but you would. But who's kidding who? Just look around at the way some of these cops live. There's more than a few with new power boats in the driveway and huge entertainment centers in their homes. And if you ask, you'll find that an awful lot of cops did extremely well in the stock market or some such investment. I admit I'm no fan of your experiment, but even the best cops have moments of personal or financial weakness, so if this helps keep the good cops honest, you know, keeps them from being tempted, then maybe it's a good thing."

"Well, Felton seems intent on turning our organization inside out. He's so much as implied that we can't do effective quality control. I mean, how in the world would PCP get into our cocaine vials?"

"How is not so important. The fact is, someone's tampering with the drugs. So now you have these formerly illegal substances that can be dangerous. Any number of people, crazy or sane, could want to mess up the program. Could be some nut that just wants to cause trouble, like one of those computer hackers. You even said your organizational committee was always aware of that."

"Okay, granted, but how do you account for this Weissman guy, who's essentially on top of the world, and from what I'm told, very much pro gun control. How do you account for his murder/suicide?"

"Doc, there's a lot of people who have no business buying weapons. Obviously, Weissman was one of those, but we checked him out. Hey, he's registered, he paid cash for his toy, but he just didn't know how to use it."

"Apparently he knew how to use it," Tony noted, "but he didn't know when."

"Yeah, I guess that's the big problem with new gun owners." He finished his beer. "Come on. Let's go check your car."

They walked back up the street in a light spring breeze chilled by the ocean as the pastel sky darkened. By the contented look on McVee's face, Tony knew the answer before he asked, "Do you ever miss Boston? Ever think about going back?"

"Not really. I used to like the Celtics, the Red Sox, the pizza. Good pizza. They say it's the water. Who knows? It's kind of a small big city – lots of great Irish pubs and places to hang out. I knew everyone, but, hey, Santa Barbara is a great town. It's so easy living here day to day. If I get homesick, I can go visit, just like every other Joe that moved here from somewhere else. I know one thing. Sally loves this place. She couldn't stand the winters, and besides, my life with the police force wore her down. Look around you. This is the place to be."

They walked down into the mostly empty subterranean garage. Tony's car was parked at the far side from the entrance, near the far stairwell, where he had planned to exit only an hour ago. As they approached Tony's black XK8, McVee shot him a glance. "That's your car? Not too flashy or anything."

"I have a delicate ego."

"Yeah," McVee pulled on his chin, "well, I guess in your business you've got an image to maintain."

"According to my wife, I need more than the car."

They stood in front of the car and McVee stuck out his hand, saying, "Keys, please."

He opened the door, then popped the hood, pulled out a penlight and started looking around.

Tony looked over his shoulder, brushing up against the detective a couple of times. After the second time, McVee looked back at Tony and let him know he was intruding.

"Excuse me," Tony said as he backed up.

McVee kept looking around, saying, "This might not be the best time to get intimate."

"Maybe I shouldn't be standing in the garage at all."

"Hey, wait a second." McVee got down on his knees and groaned as he turned over on his back, slowly wiggling his way under the car.

"There better be no oil leaks under this expensive jalopy." McVee remained in place for a few moments, then exclaimed, "Holy shit. I found something, and I don't think it's a standard part." McVee slid his right hand into his back pocket and ferreted out a handkerchief. Then Tony watched as he slid back out with a neat little package wrapped by his handkerchief. "Christ, will you look at this? Pretty sophisticated stuff. I'll bet the Masons had one just like it."

"What is it?"

"It's a magnetic explosive. Not a big bomb, but something that will do damage to your car. I pulled it off the power steering reservoir. Here, hold on to this by the handkerchief, and be careful. There's a nice print right there. Grease is great for prints. Oh, and don't play with it. When I get back to the station, I'll have the prints checked."

Tony reluctantly held the device while McVee looked inside the car. "Nice interior," he commented as he probed about. "Hey, Tony, you planning on a few hits now, or gonna wait 'til you get home?" McVee held up a little plastic bag by the tip of a corner. It was filled with grass.

Tony hadn't really clued in when he asked, "Where'd that come from?"

McVee wasn't too certain now. "Why don't you tell me? I found it in your glove compartment."

"Don't sound so accusatory. First of all, it's not mine, but secondly, there's nothing illegal about having it."

McVee stood there shaking his head and added, "Unless, of course, you're driving under the influence, wipe out on the ride home or hit another car. Dead or alive, this will still hit the press, especially with your nice little stash of marijuana. Not too good for your reputation, don't you think?"

"Not too good for the program," Tony added.

McVee placed the bag gently on the device Tony held, then took them both. "Who knows? Maybe we'll find some prints. They better not be yours."

"I wouldn't worry about it," Tony added.

McVee started to walk away, stopped, then placed the device in his left hand and pulled Tony's keys out of his pocket. "Here, you'll need these," and he tossed the keys to Tony. "I think it's safe for you to go home. I'll be in touch."

"So what do you think? I'm not paranoid, am I? Someone's really trying to set me up. The others were set up, too," Tony said as he climbed into his car.

"There's definitely something sour about all of this. Mason looks like a set-up. Obviously, someone got into the heroin at the DPC, but there's really no explanation for the Phillips murder. Go home and sit tight. Let me check this stuff out, and I'll get back to you. Hopefully we'll find something soon."

"Well, come on then. I'll drive you back to your car at least."

McVee smiled obliquely, nodded his head and held up his prizes. "I've pressed my luck as it is, Doc. Just do me one little favor."

"Yeah, sure, Jimmy. Name it."

"Wait 'til I clear the garage before you start the engine."

Involuntarily, the key slipped from Tony's grasp as he was aiming to put it in the ignition. He thought about it for a moment, and before he bolted from the car, he heard McVee laughing.

McVee shook his head and just said, "See ya later, Tony." He was still laughing as he left the garage.

Tony put the key back into the ignition, held his breath and turned the key. The car revved up like always. He headed home. Finally. Home, sweet home. Even without Montana, at least he would have a few moments of peace before this all started up again in the morning. As he drove up the hill to their house, he pictured the explosive ripping into his power steering, with him then losing control and flipping out like Rob Mason. He wouldn't have been so lucky in his convertible.

He punched the garage door opener, proceeded up the driveway and parked next to Montana's Range Rover. He thought it might be a good time to switch cars for a while and get another parking space at the office.

Chapter 10

7:00 p.m., Monday, March 14

MEANWHILE, MCVEE DROVE BACK to the Spanish-style station on Figueroa. The device he had harvested from the Jaguar sat in a box in his trunk. He must have thought about it going off a dozen times. Even though he suspected the device not to be that powerful, he still felt relieved to pull into the station parking lot in one piece.

With the magnetic explosive in hand, he walked into the station. In spite of its diminutive size, he was sure the entire force would see it the moment he stepped into the station. He went directly to the crime lab and instructed Theodore Franklin, the criminologist on duty, to dust the device and the baggy for prints. "Be careful with this thing. It's some kind of explosive, but I don't think it'll go off down here."

The tech looked up at McVee, incredulous, saying, "You want me to dust an active bomb for prints? Are you serious?"

"Yeah, it probably won't go off, and you'll probably be working here tomorrow. Lift some prints and run it down as fast as you can, I'll call Sewell and get him over here to pick it up. You can do the baggie afterward."

Not exactly responding to the challenge, but knowing he had to get cracking, the tech pulled out his print kit and got to work. McVee could have used the phone on the desk next to the tech, but just in case, he strolled across the room to a phone farther away from the device.

"Hey, Sewell, it's Jimmy McVee. Better swing by the lab. I pulled a magnetic device off the belly of a car this evening. I want you to check it out for me. I wonder if this might be the kind of thing that did the damage on the Mason car."

He then dialed home to let Sally know he was running late. "I should be home in an hour or so. I've got to finish with this Mason file right after I get done with Sewell in the lab. I pulled some kind of explosive off Tony Ryan's car. We're checking it now."

"Why don't you just finish in the lab and bring the file home with you? Don't forget to pick up a nice chardonnay for dinner, too."

"Okay, Sallie, I'll make it snappy." He said before hanging up.

Five minutes later, Ron Sewell, in his dark-gray grease-stained lab coat, entered the room excited to examine McVee's recent discovery.

The criminologist completed the exam of the device, and the baggie, and, as it turned out, equally exciting to him, he lifted several prints from each. "I've got some good prints here," Franklin announced. "I can work with these, but I suggest you photograph that little bomb of yours before you blow us all up. Evidence needs to be properly logged." The tech took off to fix the prints and run them through the computer. With the advanced technology he'd be able to get a print match within minutes. There were actually more prints archived than Social Security numbers.

Sewell slipped on a pair of latex gloves and examined the device.

"I found it under Doc Ryan's car in his garage. I drove over here with it in my trunk. I'm guessing it's an explosive, but I don't really know, and I don't know what ignites the thing," McVee explained.

"It's an explosive all right. The detonating device is inside this unit here," Sewell said, pointing to a small compartment. He pulled a small flat screwdriver from his pocket, slipped it into the compartment and carefully pried it open, exposing a series of computer chips and a tiny meter. "Check this out."

McVee leaned over his shoulder, and Sewell held the screwdriver at the number 300.

"This is an altimeter set at three hundred meters. See the metric units there?" He pointed to some spot that McVee couldn't really see. "If you want to see this thing explode, we can do it right away, but I've got an idea."

McVee could tell that Sewell was excited about playing with his new toy. "Why don't we just get the photos and explode it in one of our protective bomb units?"

"Precisely, but let me show you how."

McVee waited while Sewell got the photos and then walked the device outside into the backyard of the station. He picked out one of the heavy lead-and-steel compartments they used for detonating explosives and dragged it over to a nearby flagpole whose flag had already been lowered.

"Now, we're at fifteen meters above sea level, and that pole goes up nearly thirty meters, so I'm going to reset this thing for forty meters. That ought to do the trick." Sewell carefully readjusted the meter, then placed the unit in the heavy compartment and secured it shut. He freed up the rope from the flagpole and secured it to the compartment.

Up until then McVee had thought Sewell simply planned to dispose of the explosive in the regulation manner. "Are you out of your mind? How do you know that thing won't go off? You can't pull that up the flagpole."

"Relax. This isn't a nuclear bomb. This thing's got the same kind of power as an air hammer. It's a little popper," Sewell reassured him.

"You spend too much time on the Internet."

"Okay, let's stand back and see what happens."

McVee and Sewell got behind a retaining wall and tugged on the ropes and hoisted the little tank into the air. One of the lab techs held a video camera to record the demonstration. Although there were lights in the yard, the compartment ascended into a darker sky. Between the two of them and the pulley system on the pole, the compartment rose fairly easily.

When the thing was halfway up the flagpole, McVee started to wonder if this was one of the stupidest things he'd ever done. "If this thing gives a little pop, like you say, we might not even feel it. Is that right?" McVee asked.

"Just keep pulling. We'll know." Sewell seemed to know what to expect.

Then, about three quarters of the way up the pole, there was a loud pop and a brilliant yellow flash that caught them by surprise, even though Sewell had predicted it. The compartment swayed but stayed intact. Not exactly fireworks, but a fine display of altimeter technology and a waste of a perfectly good computer chip.

"Holy Jesus," McVee exclaimed. "Little popper? That was an explosion."

Sewell shrugged innocently.

"That damn thing blew right on cue. It's a good thing the station's not in the hills. Otherwise I'd have blown a hole in my trunk. Hell, I'd have blown up the whole damn car. Mason must have had a hell of a jolt when that thing went off."

"Apparently," was all Sewell said.

"I must be nuts listening to you. Anyway, thanks for the demo. I'm going to check on the prints."

The criminologist waited for McVee with a report. "Here you go. I've got a match."

McVee reached out to accept the report.

"Jeez, Detective, you've got grease all over your hands."

"So? I'll wash them. Give me the report." He held the report and read aloud. "Michael Cirrelo, prior for aggravated assault, 1986. FBI note: seen at Gambino family functions, rumored 'troubleshooter' for hire." He held up the now grease-smudged report. "Nice job, Teddy. This is a good start. Do you have some clean copies?"

The tech shot him a look. "Give me a couple minutes and I'll get a couple fresh copies. I've got to retrieve it off the computer."

"Yeah, good. I'll run down to the locker and clean up. I'll be right back."

Not quite a country club, but a lot neater and cleaner than precinct lockers he'd been used to in Boston. Compared to the Boston force, Santa Barbara's police were treated to rather cushy amenities. McVee opened his locker with his greasy paws, dropped the smudged report on a shelf and carefully slipped off his jacket without soiling it. He dropped it on a hook and frowned to himself, looking at all the dust and dirt on the shoulders. "Jeez, I'm a walking pigpen," he said under his breath.

After a good scrub and a little freshening, he returned to his locker, dusted off his jacket, put it on, slammed his locker shut and returned to the lab.

"You look a little better," Franklin noted as he handed over a couple of fresh copies of the report.

"Yeah, thanks. Sewell lives in that stuff. He'd never notice if someone was walking around with crap on his face. Sally will appreciate it."

He checked his watch on his way back up to his desk. Not yet seven-thirty. He gave his wife a quick call. "I should be leaving soon. I got a little hung up here with Sewell exploding that bomb I pulled off the doc's car." He listened a moment and responded, "I just want to go over the prints we got with Frank, and then I'll leave, pick up the wine and should be home by eight."

McVee walked over to Ramsey's desk, where he still worked on his own reports.

"Hey, Jimmy, where's that Mason report? I need to make a few entries."

"Oh, I guess you talked to Sewell, then," McVee replied.

"Sewell? No, why?"

McVee looked at Ramsey and hesitated a moment, surprised he hadn't heard. "Sewell thinks the Mason crash wasn't an accident."

"I'll check it out with him and make the update. Have you seen the file?" Ramsey seemed in a hurry.

"You can do it tomorrow. Sewell's gone home. Anyway, I checked it out this afternoon. It's sitting in my car, and I've already got Sewell's report, so don't sweat it. I'll bring it back tomorrow and you can finish it yourself. I'll let you call the DA and fill them in so they can drop the case."

"You're sure about this?"

Something about the way Ramsey persisted bothered McVee, but he couldn't quite figure it out. "In the meantime, can you check out a guy named Michael Cirrelo? Get a complete profile analysis on him." McVee handed him the brief note and retreated to his own desk.

Ramsey looked at the paper, got up, followed him and asked, "Who the hell is Michael Cirrelo?"

"I've heard he might be in town, and he's supposed to have some major connections, but I don't know who he's working for or what he does. See if the name means anything."

"Why would his name mean anything?" Ramsey looked on as McVee casually neatened the files on his desk. "How did you tap into this info?"

"I suppose you didn't hear our little explosion in the back?"

"What explosion?" Ramsey said, looking at him quizzically.

McVee had to get moving. He looked at his watch. "Okay, listen. I found some type of explosive device on Dr. Ryan's car, probably the same kind of thing that tripped up Mason's machine. Also, someone, probably this Cirrelo guy, planted a bag of marijuana in the doc's car. We picked up his prints on both." McVee quickly flipped through some of the correspondence on his desk, most of which he threw into the wastebasket.

He looked up at Ramsey, saying, "I've got to pick up some wine before dinner. If you give that report to Chesney, I bet he'll have a profile ready in no time. I'm sure you'll know all about this guy by tomorrow morning. See you."

McVee pulled out of the parking lot and turned right. Two blocks down from the station he turned left and then headed for the hills. There was enough traffic on the streets that he didn't notice the blue Firebird following at a comfortable distance behind him.

The village shopping center was only a few blocks away. McVee smiled to himself, happy he remembered to stop for the wine. "Just get a nice Chardonnay," he said to himself, remembering how Sally had admonished him earlier.

He pulled into the parking lot and headed toward Delanie's Wines and Spirits. Crowded with shoppers, good parking spaces were sparse, but McVee found an open slot fairly close to the store.

He looked through a whole wall of white wine. Chardonnay, Schmardonnay, he mumbled to himself. He had trouble making up his mind but finally settled on a bottle of ZD, because he remembered Sally once saying how much she liked it. This should work, he thought as he paid the cashier.

McVee bounced back to the car with the wine in hand. He pulled his key from his right pocket and slid it into the door. A twist to the right and the door was unlocked. The van parked next to him didn't leave much room, forcing him to squeeze into the car. At the moment before he slipped in, he sensed that someone had come up behind him, and he turned sharply to his left. He saw nothing but the van. And quickly, another glance to the right failed to verify any suspicions. He finally slithered in and carefully cradled the wine near the file on the front seat next to him. Without looking, he reached to close the car door and gave a slight tug. It met with some resistance, and he turned directly into the barrel of an unregistered 9mm semiautomatic with a silencer. He reached for his chest piece, but there never had a chance. A single shot between the eyes robbed Sally McVee of her best friend. Jimmy McVee's head rocked back and then propelled forward as the bullet exited the back of his head. He slumped forward up against the steering wheel. The man in the tan sports jacket reached a gloved hand into McVee's jacket pocket and removed his wallet. He pulled out the cash and left the wallet behind.

It was so quickly and routinely accomplished that as he casually strolled back to his car, not a single head turned among the few patrons at the shopping center. The blue Firebird made its way out of the parking lot and turned back onto the street. It blended into traffic and was gone.

Ramsey hated night duty. He'd get antsy hanging around waiting for a call. An occasional burglary or an assault would force him into action, but other than this last weekend's bonanza, there usually wasn't much to do. Just as well, he thought. He could use a break from the hectic activities of the last seventy-two hours. The Michael Cirrelo note sat on his desk. If Fred Chesney ever completed a profile analysis, Ramsey would decide when to submit it. For some reason, he thought it wasn't too urgent. He seemed bored and spent time cleaning the debris from his desk, now and then chatting with some of the night people. On one occasion he nonchalantly checked with the front desk to see if anything had been reported.

Nearly twenty minutes had gone by before the owner of a van got into his car and noticed a body slumped over the wheel in the car next to his.

The phone rang on Ramsey's desk while he idly piled up paper clips. The duty officer reported a homicide in the village parking lot. Ramsey grabbed a large binder, a couple of pens and hit the road.

Several officers secured the crime scene as Ramsey arrived, but he was the first investigator with rank. He got out of his car with his investigator's binder in hand. The patrol cops had blocked off the area.

Ramsey started over to the scene. Herb Dawson, one of the officers, approached Ramsey. "Hey, Dawson, before I get too deep into this, should I call McVee? Are there any drugs involved?"

"Sir, you won't believe this, but it's McVee, sir. McVee's been shot."

"Oh, my god. No, not Jimmy," Ramsey groaned, heading directly over to the car. He looked down at McVee and stood silently. He drew his binder to his lips as his eyes welled up. A crowd started forming while sirens audibly blared in the distance.

"Please, secure the crowd," he asked the officer nearest the car. Ramsey looked inside the car, saw the wallet, the wine, and the Mason file McVee had checked out. As the officer turned to the crowd, Ramsey reached over and in a casual move, without looking down, picked up Mason's file and slipped it into his binder. The investigation then proceeded in the usual manner.

Ramsey notified Callison, the chief of police, with a preliminary report. "Sir, it looks like Jimmy was shot in the course of a robbery. Nothing's missing other than his cash. I don't think he was targeted as a cop. His wallet had been rifled. We dusted for prints — the car, the wallet, anything — but nothing turned up. We've got the bullet, and of course we'll run it through ballistics. There were no witnesses or any reports of suspicious activity. This is terrible, just terrible."

After the preliminaries had been thoroughly conducted, the coroner finally removed McVee's body. The car was impounded and the area cleared. Ramsey had the dubious honor of driving to McVee's house to break the news to Sally.

Ramsey stood in the doorway as Sally answered. With his head slightly bowed, he primed her for what she had begun to expect and dread. He could see she knew. He had called on her before, once when McVee was banged up during a drug bust, but that was just a busted nose. This time it was different, and she clearly sensed it.

"What is it, Frank? Jimmy's dead this time. What happened?" she said as she ushered Ramsey into her home.

Ramsey looked up and just bobbed his head in affirmation. Sally wrapped her arms around him and cried. Ramsey gave her a hug and helped her over to the couch.

He left twenty minutes later, but not before a police escort arrived to take Sally to the morgue. As the police escort left with Sally, Ramsey sat in his car for a moment, staring at his binder. He picked it up and pulled the file out and checked it. The Mason file was intact, with the Sewell report not yet bound inside. He would have it back on McVee's desk, the last person to check it out, and the case would be closed without any extra fanfare.

Too hyped up from his day, Tony found it hard to concentrate. His mind kept darting over the recent events. He couldn't remember a time when so much had happened in such a short period. He felt like a little child who'd just gotten home from school with a list of things to tell his mom. He couldn't wait to bounce the day's events off Montana. She always provided a good ear and sound ideas for him to follow up on. Her perspective never failed to astonish him – vive la difference.

Tony decided to settle down with a novel he had started last week. He probably hadn't read more that five pages when he realized he was reading the same sentence over and over. He put down his book and flipped on the television. As long as he couldn't concentrate, he might as well not concentrate on TV. He played with the remote control, flipping from station to station, watching everything and watching nothing. He sipped his beer and then dozed off for a while. He slipped into a vivid dream. In his dream he could hear an announcer report the murder of a local law enforcement official. Then he felt a wetness on his belly that woke him up.

"Damn." Tony had fallen asleep with the beer on his lap, and it had started to spill. He plucked it up before it unloaded the remaining contents, and he set it on the table next to him.

The television droned on, but now the picture was slightly clearer. He watched a news report. They ran a videotape of a shopping center, with the coroner's car leaving the scene.

The reporter went on to say, "There are few details available, although we know an officer is dead. The dead officer is Detective James McVee, victim of a gunshot wound."

Tony blinked rapidly, clearing his eyes and becoming more alert. He couldn't believe what he'd heard. For a second, in his confusion, he thought maybe he had been dreaming, but the newscast continued.

The reporter rolled a taped interview with Ramsey. When asked for details, Ramsey simply replied, "Detective McVee was part of our family. An investigation is under way. His wallet was on the floor, no cash. It appears robbery may have been the motive."

"Oh, Jesus." Tony wasn't dreaming. "This can't be. How in the world?" The dogs looked up at Tony as he spoke aloud. Stunned, he felt like someone had played a bad prank on him. He couldn't believe it. He had been with McVee just a few hours ago.

Tony sat and stared at the set for a while, trying to collect his thoughts. According to Ramsey it appeared to be a random robbery and murder. What a coincidence that McVee, the liaison for the drug program, had turned up dead. Tony should have been dead tonight, and as far as he knew, maybe someone thought he was lying at the bottom of some ravine right now.

He had to talk with Ramsey. There's no way Ramsey would let anyone get away with McVee's murder. Tony had to make sure he knew what McVee had found in his car. What if McVee hadn't gotten the device checked out? At least Ramsey would be able to check for prints. Maybe they had the prints of the killer. Tony called the station. Ramsey was still there.

"This is Dr. Tony Ryan," he announced.

After a slight pause, Ramsey asked, "Yes, sir, what can I do for you?"

"I heard about Detective McVee just now on the news. I just thought you'd want to know that he'd been with me earlier. He found some kind of device on my car. He told me he was going to bring it in to check for fingerprints. You might want to check it out. I believe it might have something to do with his murder."

"I saw Jimmy before he left this evening, and he told me about the device. It turned out to be some magnetic thing mechanics use when they adjust the timing. Your mechanic probably inadvertently left on your car. I can assure you it didn't explode. Unfortunately, the only prints were grease smudges that we couldn't use. Not that it would have helped, except we'd be able to return it to the right mechanic."

"What about the bag of marijuana that he brought in? Were there prints on that?"

"Just a few, that we matched with yours. I made a call to Felton at the DPC. He says the computer shows you picked up ten grams earlier today."

"That's impossible. I never bought any grass. Someone planted it." Tony's voice started to rise. He wasn't sure if it was anger or panic, maybe a little of each – maybe a lot.

"Look, Doc, as far as I know, there's nothing illegal about buying marijuana these days. All the same, I hope you're not planning any trips in the next few days. I'd like to be able to talk with you more thoroughly. I think this might be a long investigation. Right now, all we've got is a bullet."

Ramsey was blunt and he sounded calm. Then he added, "McVee was part of our family. We'll find the SOB, I guarantee it. By the way, where were you around seven-forty-five this evening?"

"I was right here in my home."

"Okay. Look, I'll be in touch." With nothing left to say, he hung up.

Tony stood over the phone for a moment then slumped back into his chair. "Okay, bright boy, what's going on?" he asked himself. Even the dogs seemed to sense Tony's confusion. Critter walked over to the chair and stood up, putting his front feet on the cushion so that he was looking at Tony. "You want to come up?" Tony asked.

The dog stood there with an expression — a furrowed brow, head slightly tilted to the right — and then he barked.

"Okay, smarty pants, what am I missing?" Tony stared back at Critter, locked his eyes in concentration for a moment, and then jumped to his feet.

"I've got to get out of here. Jesus, the dogs are smarter than me." Tony cleaned up and gathered a few clothes and toiletries into a small bag. His thoughts became more focused. While he hurried along, he pictured a scene in North by Northwest. He didn't need someone to force him into a drunken stupor so he could drive his car off a cliff. He took a few deep breaths through his nose, the kind he would do whenever Montana got him into one of those yoga classes. "That son of a bitch Ramsey," Tony said to himself. Tony had seen the prints on the device. McVee had warned him not to mess it up. Why was Ramsey lying? Was Felton playing along? He wondered who would have bought the grass in Tony's name? – only someone who could get into the system.

Tony packed up his cellular phone and laptop computer and grabbed his briefcase. He did one last check of the house to make sure nothing was out of place and then said goodbye to the dogs. They'd be all right. Silvia would be back in the morning, and she'd know to stay with them until she heard from Tony. Well, at least they'd be fed and walked. He hated to leave them, but they'd be okay.

It had been less than ten minutes since his phone call to Ramsey, but he knew there wasn't much time. He got angrier thinking about Ramsey's comments. A mechanic's timing device. Was he nuts, making up a stupid story like that? Tony almost bought into it, too. He wanted to believe that Ramsey, whom he'd seen by McVee's side, was a good guy. He wanted to believe all the cops were good guys. Come on, boy, wake up and smell the coffee, he told himself. Why'd they make such an innocent the director of this drug program? Maybe because you are such an innocent, he thought. He put his stuff into the trunk of the Jaguar and pulled out of the garage.

He turned left and drove down the hill, then suddenly stopped. Come on, Tony; start thinking, he scolded himself. He hesitated a moment and turned the car around, went back up the hill, and drove a few houses past his and parked in a neighbor's driveway, hiding his car behind the well-groomed hedges. It was late, so Tony hoped no one would notice. He grabbed his cell phone, walked back toward his house and climbed to a well-hidden spot across the street, where he could observe any activity.

Tony started to understand what he needed to do. His first goal was to check out for a while. He called Joanna. As he recounted the events following the office hours, he could tell she was shaken but alert and ready to do what was necessary. She would have to cancel their cases and consultations. She could have Brenda take care of the post-operative patients in the meantime. If there were any problems, she could call Hank Tarbon, a capable surgeon who would be willing to help out in an emergency.

"I'll go back to the office now and get the patient phone numbers," Joanna volunteered. "It won't take me long to do that."

"No," Tony told her. "You'll have to wait until the morning. Keep the first patient waiting. Go through the motions of trying to contact me. After a couple of hours, apologize to the patient, explain there must have been an emergency and you are deeply concerned. Try to reschedule her and then call the police. Tell them I haven't reported in this morning and you've been unable to contact me or anyone who has seen me. They may or may not want to check it out, but hopefully that will keep Ramsey and company confused. Maybe they'll relax for a day or two and give me time to sort things out."

Joanna listened and took note. "Okay, Dr. Ryan, I'll do what you say. Are you going to be all right? What are you going to do?"

"Whatever I have to," he replied. Tony knew that wasn't the answer she was looking for, but it was the most he wanted to tell her. He didn't want to put her in a position where she knew too much.

"Please be careful, Dr. Ryan. I'm not anxious to be out of work."

"Yeah, don't worry. I'm not ready to retire. That's why I'm taking this little vacation right now. I'll be in touch." As they said their goodbyes, Tony heard the sound of an engine approaching.

He could barely make out the blue color of the car as it passed under a street light and pulled into his driveway. Tony recognized the man as he emerged from his car. It was the same fellow who had pursued him earlier. The dogs started barking. The guy walked over to the garage, shone a flashlight through the side door and then quickly retreated to his car.

Before he could back out of the driveway, another car pulled up, blocking his path. Tony recognized Ramsey as he got out of the car and confronted the man in front of him. For a moment Tony was relieved. Ramsey wasn't the problem. What luck, he thought. Ramsey was going to bust this guy, and Tony would find out what was going on. Tony started to get up and move toward the duo so he could assist Ramsey in testifying against the intruder. He hesitated just long enough to watch as Ramsey casually returned to his own car and left the scene. The blue Firebird simply went on its way.

Tony stared as they both drove off. He stood in the darkness several moments longer, gathering his thoughts. At least that's what he thought he was doing. He soon realized he was just too scared to leave the confines of darkness after what he had witnessed.

Finally he scurried back up the hill to his car. He got inside, feeling momentarily safe in his little hiding spot. Although he thought of going back home, he knew they'd be back to look for him. It was nearly a quarter to twelve. He decided to call Brenda.

Tony got hold of Brenda as she drifted off to the Letterman Show. He told her something serious had come up and he had to stay at her place for a while. "Are you kidding me? What about surgery tomorrow? What's this all about?"

"Look, Brenda. I'm not going to operate tomorrow. I'll explain it to you later. Just get your couch ready for a visitor. One more thing – I've got to hide my car in your garage. Is there room?"

"After you get here, I'll move my car over. There's plenty of room. I wish I knew what was going on."

"I'll tell you what. After I get there, we can have a pajama party, and I'll fill you in on the whole story."

"Oh, good, a pajama party and no surgery tomorrow. We can stay up all night and watch old movies, huh?"

"Not exactly. You still have to go in tomorrow morning. I'll see you in a little while. Bye." Tony hung up without waiting for a reply.

He thought about his problem-solving class back at UCLA. He tried working backward without unnecessary limiting constraints. He finally had to conclude that these random acts of violence were actually well orchestrated terrorist attacks. One thing was very clear — he had a major problem.

He thought again about going to the police, but all he needed was the wrong cop and he was dead. The whole department could be corrupt. There was no way of knowing, not with McVee gone. He should have been more scared than he was, but somehow he felt as if the answers were there. All the puzzle parts were present. Somehow he had to figure it out, but he would need some time. He hoped he could count on a day or two, but he knew that as soon as he surfaced he'd be a target again.

Tony thought about Montana and how much had happened since she'd left that morning. Thank God she's out of town, he thought. Italy should be safe enough. He was anxious to talk with her. What else could happen before she called in the morning? He let out an exasperated laugh at the thought.

Tony wasn't too excited about calling Spencer, not at three a.m.

Washington time, but he had no choice. He needed someone he could trust completely. Spencer definitely fit that category. And as a longtime network producer at the Pentagon, he had access to the serious power brokers in the Defense Department. Tony looked up the number.

Spencer had originally followed his father's footsteps into the Navy. Oddly, he never developed a particular fondness of sailing. It was just something you did to cross an ocean. As a kid, he was mostly interested in journalism. He ran the school newspaper throughout junior high and high school. When he accepted a spot at Annapolis, his father couldn't have been prouder. Spencer had carried on the McCade tradition with noble aplomb. His writing and reporting skills helped him carve a niche in the Navy. He became well recognized for his ability to take a story and truthfully convey it in the most positive light. He kept getting reassigned to officers higher up the ladder as his reporting impacted their careers favorably. When he finally gave up his sea legs for the stability of terra firma, he was recruited by several agencies. Uniquely comfortable with the military brass, understanding of their mind-set, yet able to report a story truthfully, he was heavily recruited by a number of news agencies. After a few warm-up years with a major network, he took a job with a young emerging network, Satellite News Service. Spencer had the foresight to see that the satellite networks were the future of communications in a global marketplace. And SNS knew that Spencer was a perfect connection to the complexities of the Defense Department. As the producer at the Pentagon, he had cultivated confidential alliances that he served well and which in turn provided him with the essential insights that kept him and SNS in the forefront of defense reporting.

He also knew who were the men of integrity. Tony punched in the number. After the third ring, he thought of hanging up just as a "hello" that was still asleep answered the phone. Under any other circumstance he would have apologized and let Spencer go back to sleep. Instead, he just apologized.

"Spencer, it's Tony Ryan. I'm really sorry to wake you."

"Tony?" There was a pause.

"Spencer!" Tony could hear the heavy breathing of his sleepy friend.

"Spencer, really, I've got to talk to you. There's some serious shit going on out here, and I need your help."

There was an audible yawn and a drawn-out sigh while Spencer gathered himself, sat up and checked his alarm clock for the time. "Tony, it's three o'clock in the morning. Are you okay?"

"So far I am. You're not going to believe what's going on. I need some outside help. I've already been tagged as an accident waiting to happen."

"What are you talking about?" Spencer didn't sound annoyed, just confused, so Tony cut to the chase. Tony proceeded to review the events of the day.

The first thing Spencer said was, "I bet you're glad Montana is out of town."

"Yeah, I wish I were in Italy, too. Look, the way I see it, Ramsey probably knows I'm on to him, but he's probably got control of McVee's information, the Mason file, and God knows what else. I don't feel real safe going to the police. I can file a report, but who knows where it will end up. I probably have a day or two to figure out what's going on.

"I'm going to go over to Brenda's. I can hide my car in her garage and hang out there for a few days. I'll try calling Montana through Gina. Montana has my pager number, and I'll bring my cell phone, so she can always find me if I'm not home. I need you to find some honest men for me."

Though Spencer was listening, at this hour of the night he was still not entirely tuned in. "I'm not sure how I can help you. What do you think I can do?"

"I'm not sure. Here's the way I see it. I think there are a lot of people who don't want to see this program work. I'm willing to bet there's been a cohesive effort to sabotage the entire program. I need to find out how deep it goes. We've got to break this ring, if it exists, or I'm dead, too. But I can't do it through the Santa Barbara Police Department because I don't know who the bad cops are. Ramsey might be the only problem child, but if I call for an investigation, I'll just be setting myself up again. Do you have any good buddies at the bureau?"

"There's some good guys over there. I've known Mark Hansen for years. He's sharp and honest."

"Good. See if you can get him to run some background checks for us."

"For us?" Spencer was laying the sarcasm on thick. "Is this really an 'us' thing? Nobody's trying to take my car off the road."

"Who are you going to visit in California after they bump me off? Clearly, I'm doing this for us. Find out if there's anything on Burton Wesley and his Recovery West institutes. He's the one that concerns me the most. I'm sure he wants to set me up, make me look bad, but I'm not sure he'd actually want to kill me. Look, you need to check on Frank Ramsey, and while you're at it, find out if Roger Felton, the FBI agent, is really such a fine chap. Oh, yeah, and supposedly Weissman bought his gun from Western Rifles and Guns, so we might want to check on this place as well. Find out what you can. Anything you can find you can send by e-mail, text or just call me on my cell phone."

"Okay, Tony, I'll see what I can do. Burton Wesley, Recovery West, Frank Ramsey, Roger Felton, and Western Rifles and Guns." Spencer was sincere. Tony could count on him. Before they hung up, Tony gave him his e-mail address, his cellular phone number and Brenda's home phone number.

He drove down his street and looked at every turn as the potential one where he could have lost control of his car. He got angrier as he drove through each curve in the road. "Who the hell do these people think they are?" he thought out loud.

Clearly, the stakes were much greater than he had thought when he had suggested the drug dealers had the most to lose by legalization. Tony then thought of a conversation he had had quite some time ago with one of his colleagues, an attorney. They were talking about an infamous knife slaying in L.A., and Tony asked if it could possibly be mob-related. His colleague said, "No way. To the mob, it's just business. You go in, take care of business and get out. It's not personal, it's business." Still, it didn't make him feel any better realizing he was in the middle of something that wasn't personal.

He approached Brenda's home. She lived in a townhouse with a two-car attached garage. Because the homes shared certain community amenities, they were considered condominiums, but they looked more like single houses.

When he arrived at Brenda's, she came out to her garage dressed in a large fluffy robe and teddy bear slippers.

"You didn't have to get all dressed up for me. Really," Tony smiled. "Nice shoes."

She went to get into her dark-gray Acura, saying, "I can't wait to hear this story."

She moved her car over and gave him room to park his Jag next to her car. Once inside the house, he explained what had happened.

"Look, I'm sorry for dragging you into this. Don't let anyone know I'm here and we should be okay. Are you all right?"

She sat there with her mouth open. "So much for our peaceful Santa Barbara. Whose idea was it to bring this drug program here in the first place?" She was more teasing than serious.

"For your information, I had nothing to do with it. I was recruited."

"You're usually a pretty lucky guy. Why'd they pick you?"

"Maybe I'm just innocent enough that I actually thought it was an honor." Tony began to sense that a lot of alternatives had been planned and thought out by more than just the organizational committee.

Brenda tensed, then added, "Are you sure no one knows you're here?"

"Just you and Spencer. I've got to trust somebody. Please don't tell me you're working for Wesley or Ramsey or God knows who." Tony paused a moment.

Brenda visibly scolded him for the suggestion.

"Sorry, I know that's offensive, but on the other hand, this day doesn't need any more surprises." They sat there quietly, realizing that this wouldn't be a long-lived moment of tranquility.

"What do you think the Boss Lady's doing?" Brenda asked.

It was past one in the morning, which meant Montana should have arrived. "She's probably having an espresso with Gina somewhere on Via Veneto. I figure it's a little after ten in the morning there."

Chapter 11

9:00 a.m., Tuesday, March 15

Looking across the street to the Villa Borghese from Gina's apartment, Montana watched a couple of morning joggers disappear into the park. Gina busied herself putting Montana's things away. Montana started to laugh.

"What's so funny?" Gina asked.

Montana had a wispy smile on her face and arched a brow in response to Gina. "Those joggers reminded me of the first time I ever came to Rome with Tony." It was a story she remembered fondly and enjoyed telling. "It was September. After flying all night, with a stopover in London, we got to Rome in the late afternoon. It was after six by the time we got into our room at the Excelsior. Tony collapsed in a heap on the bed, and I walked out of the closet with my jogging clothes on. He looked at me and said, 'Where are you going? We just got here.' I said, 'You mean where are we going?' Begrudgingly, he was at my side five minutes later as we went for a long run and he got his first tour of Rome. Ultimately, he was happy to have done it. We saw more of the city in an hour than most people see in a week. But the look on his face when he saw me in my jogging clothes was priceless. He likes to tell that story more than I do."

Gina gave a light-hearted laugh in response to Montana's story.

Nonetheless, it was easy to sense a weight of tension in Montana's face. "You look a little sad. You okay? Tony? He's okay? You miss your Tony?"

"I guess," she said, hesitating for barely a second. "It's kind of weird being here without him." Then she smiled brightly, adding, "But it'll be a lot easier going through the stores." It was wonderful to look out across the street to the park. The weather was delightful – warm and clear. Aside from being two levels above the street and commanding a nice view of the Borghese Gardens near the Porta Pinciana, Gina's apartment was charming. Neatly furnished, with modern appliances, the two bedroom apartment reflected Gina's immaculate tastes with photos and remembrances scattered about but not cluttered. Light filled the unit and in spite of its proximity to the street below, it remained fairly quiet.

Gina chimed in, "Che bella! I know you'll miss Tony, but we'll still have lots of fun. I can't wait to introduce you to some of my friends."

"I look forward to that. I'm glad we have a few days before the meeting. It'll be fun to do some shopping and play around." Montana nonetheless still sounded a little melancholy.

"Well, then. It's a beautiful day. Let's not waste it. We can start walking over to the shops now. You can buy me an espresso."

The atmosphere of Rome energized Montana. Instead of walking directly to the Spanish Steps straight down Via Pinciana, they strolled to the left down Via Veneto, one of Montana's favorite streets. The streets churned with people busy enjoying life. The abundant cafes along the street, like magnets, attracted the masses to celebrate. Santa Barbara, with its renewed Mediterranean style, had lots of charming outdoor cafes, but nothing compared to those in Rome. Rome, with all of its piazzas, had more places to hang out than any other city on earth.

The Piazza Trinita dei Monti, in front of the Hassler Hotel at the top of the Spanish Steps, bristled with activity. Well-dressed ladies blithely descended the steps en route to some of the finest shopping in Europe. The view from the top of the steps painted a collage of terra cotta, the colors of Rome. The steps took on their own life. A guitarist serenaded from his perch halfway down. An artist applied his strokes to a canvas on an easel set up on one of the plateaus. Vendors sold little trinkets here and there. At the bottom of the steps,

137

a generous gathering of grown-ups talked to each other while they watched their young children run around Bernini's Fountain of the Old Boat.

The vibrancy of the city was pervasive, awakening the inner Italian soul of Montana. Like schoolgirls playing hooky, all smiles and excited to be out on their own, they headed toward Via Condotti. This was Montana's candy store. She enjoyed the feeling, not quite goose bumps, but certainly a warm and tingling feeling as she looked to see so many of her favorite shops squeezed into such a charming area. Since it was too early for opening, they continued past Gucci, Ferragamo and a dozen other stores that Montana would normally have ventured into.

They stopped at a little trattoria, ordered some café latté and sat outside in the sun. Though still not warm, sitting directly in the sun felt quite comfortable. "People watching" in Rome was one of Montana's favorite spectator sports. Though anxious to explore her favorite stores, she savored the moment.

"God, I love this city. I know I must have lived here in another life. How do you feel about it, Gina? Do you think you're going to stay here?" she asked as she cradled her warm café latté in her hands.

"I have family, many friends here, but I mostly ran away from Emilio. I'm not sure where it's best for me. I too love Roma, but I must admit, some of my happiest times were in Santa Barbara. I had good friends there as well." Gina took a sip from her cup and looked at the people walking by.

"We just saw Emilio Sunday. I know he still loves you. He says you left because you were jealous of him catering to all of the women around the restaurant."

"That's Emilio's problem," Gina said indignantly. "He's got the problem with jealousy. But that's just an excuse. Emilio doesn't let you into his life. He's very private, so it's hard to know him. Okay for a few dates, but not for life. I can't believe he'd make up such a story."

"Maybe it's a macho thing. He doesn't want to admit why he lost you. I can tell one thing. You've been closer to him than anyone. I can't stand any of the women he's been seeing."

"Emilio was too mysterious for me. I never really got to be a part of his life. You know, he was there, but with his head, not his heart. Also, it's funny how he could be so jealous but expect me to accept all of his mystery."

"I don't think men deal very well with their personal problems. Maybe he just wasn't expressive, " offered Montana.

"No, I think there were things going on that he just didn't want me to know about." Gina gave a shrug and a half smile with her lips closed.

Montana pulled out the card Emilio had given her and flashed it to Gina. "Did you know Emilio's family owned this ceramic business in Rome?"

"I don't think he was ever directly involved with that business. I just don't know for sure," Gina said, shrugging begrudgingly. "Of course, he stocked his restaurant with all of their plates. He just buys them or has them ordered through Bertolini's. Do you know how expensive they are?"

"I just bought a vase from Bertolini's. Well, actually, I bought it at a silent auction. I don't think I would have even spent the fifteen hundred dollars that Bertolini wanted. Emilio got me the matching one for free. How can he do that?" Montana asked, sipping her latté.

"Who knows? Emilio kept so much to himself. Sometimes he'd throw out dozens of perfectly fine dishes. I'd say, 'Hey, what are you doing? These are perfect dishes,'" Gina said, leaning forward. "He'd look at me, grab a dish and wave it around. Then he'd say, 'Since when do you know so much about the restaurant business? This plate is no good.' Then he'd slam it to the ground and point, saying, 'You call that a perfect dish?' I'd just look at him like he was nuts. He was nuts. He'd throw them out like they were paper plates."

"Maybe he's just a perfectionist," Montana offered optimistically.

"I don't think so. Before I left last month, he quit throwing the plates around, but he still kept to himself. He's a strange man. I just can't be with someone who wants to know everything about my life but won't open up about his own."

Montana started to laugh. "Most women would be happy if they found a man who cared about their lives. A lot of men just want to talk about themselves."

Gina finished her espresso. "So when are you two going to have some little bambinos?" she asked, changing the subject.

"We've been talking about it. I think we're ready. Tony can't keep putting it off much longer. It'll happen. It's nothing we've worried about. Come on. Why don't you take me to Frascati Terrecotte?"

Of course they couldn't go straight there without passing a few stores on the way. Montana found herself a wonderful sweater from Krizia, some unique dog collars for her furry buddies and a blue dress shirt at Brioni for Tony.

A few blocks from their initial destination, Montana saw a floral patterned vase, smaller but quite similar to the one she just acquired at home. It sat in a window display with a seven-euro price tag.

"Hey, Gina, look at this."

Gina came walking over. "Yes? Oh, that's lovely. It looks a lot like the pottery I used to bring home to Emilio's."

"Am I reading this right? Is this seven-euro?" Montana figured out the conversion while Gina nodded her head in confirmation. "I can't believe it. That's about ten dollars. It's smaller, maybe half the size," she said with a shrug, "but it looks a lot like the vase I recently picked up at Bertolini's at home."

They walked inside the store, and Montana grabbed the vase and looked it over. "Pinto, VSM. That's the same inscription on the vase I bought. Ten dollars. My god, you should see the mark-up on the ones they sell at home. Do you know what this means?" she asked Gina, pointing to the inscription.

"I don't know. I never paid attention to any of that. Emilio, he'd say, 'Go to Bertolini, pick out a nice set with Alfredo.' I never paid for anything. Alfredo would just send Emilio the bill."

"I wonder if Emilio's cousin here has the dishes that go with this pattern. The mark-up can't be as high as in the States. God, are they ripping us off!"

They continued their little journey to Via Frattina 37. There wasn't much of a storefront. A small patina sign, simply labeled "Frascati Terrecotte," hung over the doorway. Simple exteriors with well-appointed interiors marked the norm for the retail outlets of the area. They went in.

Montana and Gina looked at each other. Far from a glorious showroom, stacks and stacks of ceramic dishes and pottery spread throughout the store. Many of the wares were on display. Toward the back there appeared to be row after row of boxes, probably awaiting shipment. The dim light made it difficult to examine the dishes. A young lady dressed in a plain tan cotton dress sat by a simple wooden desk near the front of the store. She barely raised her head when they entered. There appeared to be no one else in the shop. A light shone from behind a partly open door in the back of the store. Montana guessed it led to a small office.

The woman kept busy filing her nails while browsing through a magazine on her desk. Finally, she looked up and offered a simple "buon giorno" and asked if there was anything they were interested in seeing.

Gina said they were looking for some dishes for Montana. She described the dish Montana had seen in the States. She turned to Montana, asking, "What was it you said was written on the back?"

Montana replied, "It said Pinto, VSM."

The woman then got up and walked over to a large stack of ceramics on display and picked up one of the dishes. "Could this be it?"

Gina and Montana waded over to the ceramics. The dish was very similar to the one she had seen at Bertolini's. On the back was printed "Pinto, VSM." "Yes, that's it. Can you tell me how much it costs?"

"Oh, yes, the entire place setting is 150 euro."

Montana didn't have time to say anything. Gina looked shocked and said, "That's impossible. Are you sure that's not the price for the entire set?"

"Oh, no, signora, it is for each setting."

Gina seemed shocked. "Who would pay that much for those dishes?"

The woman then offered, "We don't sell many here at all. These are very popular in the States, so we send most of them abroad."

Montana then spotted a vase quite similar to the ones she had at home, though a little shorter, under two feet high. "Gina, look at this one. Do you like it? It's a lot like the one I got at home at Bertolini's."

"Si, che bella," Gina said, walking over to take a closer look. "Oh, yes, it's truly lovely."

"Is this 1100 euro? Isn't that over fifteen hundred dollars?" Montana wasn't sure she was reading the price right.

Gina looked on as the young saleswoman confirmed the price and added, "It's a beautiful piece, no?"

Montana looked at Gina, whose eyes clearly expressed her astonishment at the price. Or at least that's what Montana thought. Montana put the vase down and proceeded to wander around the store while Gina engaged the woman in some polite conversation. Montana could occasionally hear them mention Emilio and the Frascati name. Soon she waded all the way to the back of the store into an area where there were many boxes marked for shipping. Many of the small tags she saw indicated they were going to Bertolini's in Santa Barbara. A few of the boxes were still open. She leaned over and pulled out a vase just like the one she had seen on display.

Bent over, examining the vase, she was unaware of Ernesto Frascati, who now stood looming over her. His thick eyebrows arched, having caught Montana prying into his goods. He snapped in Italian at the woman at the front desk. Completely startled, Montana straightened up and lost her grasp on the vase. It actually flew from her hands. She quickly reached out and re-grasped it as Ernesto simultaneously made a dive for the vase. His hands landed directly on top of hers. His menacing glare had frightened her, though not as much as the holstered gun she spied when his sport coat opened.

"Signora, please. I'll take that. No one is permitted back here," he harshly admonished Montana in Italian as he then stripped the vase from her grasp before gently replacing it in its box.

"Excuse me?" Montana didn't understand but tried to regain her poise. Suddenly the woman and Gina came over to her.

"Ernesto," Gina called out, "this is my dear friend Montana Ryan. She's visiting from Santa Barbara. She and her husband are good friends of your cousin Emilio."

Ernesto, almost fatherly, turned the women around and ushered them back to the front of the store. "Well, Signora Ryan, it is my pleasure then. I am sorry to have frightened you."

"I was just admiring your ceramics. I thought the one in the box was even more brilliant than the one on the floor. Is it for sale?" Montana inquired, trying not to show her displeasure at Ernesto's harsh treatment.

"No, not that one. It has been selected for export. But it's not so special. It's nearly identical to the one on the floor."

"I just like the colors more. How about if we trade, then?"

Ernesto wanted to end the conversation. "I'm afraid that's not possible, but I'd be happy to offer you a generous family discount on anything you purchase. How long are you going to be in Roma?"

"About a week."

"Wonderful. Then I must take you and Gina to dinner one night. How about this Friday?" Ernesto seemed considerably more at ease.

Montana looked over to Gina, who smiled in the affirmative, and so she answered, "We'd be delighted, thank you."

"Very well, then. I'll call Gina, but let's plan on eight-thirty."

Montana lifted one of the place settings and inspected it. She held the plate out in the direction of Ernesto. "I just love your ceramics."

Proudly, Ernesto replied, "We think this is the finest in all Italia."

"This notation, 'Pinto, VSM,' I assume it's the manufacturer. Can you tell me if that's right?" She asked.

"Yes, Pinto is the factory, in Vietri sul Mare." Then changing the subject, he asked, "So, tell me, what brings you to Roma? Is it just to visit your friend Gina?"

"Although one hardly needs an excuse to come to Rome, I'm actually here representing our medical implant company at a cosmetic surgery conference. My husband has designed several facial implants. Gina's helping us to promote them as well."

He reached for Montana's hand and smiled, saying, "Wonderful. I wish you a prosperous trip then. If you'll excuse me, I must finish some office work right away. If you need anything, Gabriela here will help you." He turned and retreated to his office, closing the door behind him.

Montana continued to browse while Gina said a few words to Gabriela. Montana suspected she was ready to leave. How long could you look at dishes? Montana came back to the vase on display. "What do you think, Gina? Isn't it beautiful?"

"It's a work of art. Oh, but it's so expensive," she offered.

"I'm going to buy it," Montana exclaimed. She picked it up and carried it to Gabriela, who appeared more startled than Gina at Montana's intention to purchase it.

Montana took a credit card from her purse. Gabriela put the vase in a bag, handed it to Montana, and then proceeded to process the credit card.

Montana brushed her hair back with her left hand and then almost frantically said, "Oh, my earring, my earring is missing." Then turning to Gina, she said, "I think it fell off when I bent over to look at that vase." She motioned to the back. "I'll be right back," she said without waiting for a response. She quickly headed back to the forbidden zone with her package in tow.

Gabriela went back to work processing the credit card. Montana glanced back, then quickly removed the vase from the bag and swapped it with the one in the box.

"Oh, I found it," Montana declared with relief. While she pretended to fasten it to her ear, Gabriela glanced back only once.

The door to the back suddenly opened, and Ernesto stuck his head out, having heard Montana.

Montana continued her charade with the left earring, casually looked at Ernesto and simply said, "Dropped my earring. I found it." She smiled broadly, finished her little drama, added, "See you on Friday," and watched Ernesto slink back into his office.

Montana strolled to the front with her new vase in the bag, and she signed the printed voucher.

Gina thanked Gabriela for both of them, and the two women left.

Strolling toward the Spanish Steps, Montana seemed to pick up the pace. She and Gina ascended the crowded steps, with Montana holding on to her package. Halfway up the steps, Montana took a quick, curious look back over her shoulders. She was fairly certain that she had spotted Ernesto. She pulled Gina over to one of the artisans, trying to look more casual and still see if they were being followed. When she looked back, she saw no one.

Again they started up the steps. As they neared the top, Montana took one last peek behind her at the same time that a little boy, no more than four or five years-old, came darting down the steps right in front of her path. She nearly tripped right on top of him. Still, she lost her balance and fell to the side, her foot slipping on the next step. Bracing herself from the inevitable fall, she put out both of her hands, at which point the bag fell from her grasp. The vase seemed to innocuously slip from the bag, and before she or Gina could move toward it, they watched as it began to tumble down the stairs. It suffered a series of little chips on route to its glorious crash on the next plateau, where it shattered up against the wall.

The two women, with empty bag in hand, started to descend toward the broken pottery. A couple of police and several artisans were well on their way to the melee that ensued.

Someone shouted out, "Drogas, drogas." Montana stopped. She could see someone lifting up a plastic bag that appeared to have come from the vase. The police descended upon the man. Before he could explain and point up the steps, from where the vase had fallen, Gina grabbed Montana, and they climbed the final few steps to the top. Montana casually deposited the shopping bag in the nearest trashcan.

They finally entered Gina's apartment. All the way back, they'd kept looking over their shoulder, anticipating that the police — or worse, a Frascati member — would subdue them.

One look at Gina and Montana could see she was visibly shaken even after she closed the door to the apartment. "What's going on, Montana?"

"Now I know why he carries a gun."

"What are you talking about?"

"Ernesto had a gun. I saw it when he first confronted me. When I went to look for my earring, I switched vases. I had no idea. I just thought it was a prettier vase. You heard what he said; they're all the same. Except now we know there are special prizes in some of those boxes. Otherwise, do you really need a gun to sell dishes?" Montana paced across the room and stopped by the window to look out and scout the area. There were no sirens. No one was running after them.

"You don't think the police can trace it to us, do you?" Gina asked.

"Probably. It depends on how hard they try. I don't know if the police will investigate, but they're not our problem. Because if they do start looking about, you can bet they won't learn anything from Frascati's, but old cousin Ernie, he'll know. And he won't be too happy." Montana then thought and asked, "Where is this Vietri sul Mare?"

Gina looked at Montana but didn't seem to anticipate her intentions. "It's down past Amalfi. Really quite lovely."

"How long would it take us to drive there?"

"At least three hours. You want to go?" Gina asked.

"It might not be a bad idea. I think Ernesto Frascati's dealing drugs. It might be nice to see if he's the source or if he has partners down south."

"I know I never saw any drugs around Emilio. Of course he only had dishes. I don't think you could hide them in dishes, no?"

"But Bertolini's could sell them. You know, I always wondered how these places stayed in business. Maybe they import more than we know."

"Oh, my god. Do you think Emilio's selling drugs? That's why he's so secretive, no?"

"I don't know, but we've got to find this Pinto place. We've got to find out before we tell anyone."

"Then we go to Vietri Sul Mare."

"Good. We can be back on Friday at the latest, still in time for the conference."

They packed a few things and threw them into the trunk of Gina's white Alfa Romeo, stopping to buy some cheeses, a couple of baguettes, bottled water and some pastries. Montana wouldn't go anywhere with the risk of being hungry.

They put the top down and enjoyed the warm pre-spring weather. Montana spent most of the next two hours mostly quizzing Gina about Emilio.

"So if Emilio grew up in Rome, how did he come to the States?"

"The best I can understand," explained Gina, "is that he came when he was young and worked at a restaurant for his Uncle Giuseppe. I wouldn't know anything about Emilio if it hadn't been for the trip we took to New York. I met his Uncle Giuseppe and his Aunt Rosa. Rosa, she liked me, but I think she also felt sorry for me. She told me as much as I know about Emilio." Gina had plenty of time to recount the story to Montana.

"So he learned the business inside and out, and it didn't hurt being as charming as he was. At least he used to be quite charming."

"He still seems to be," Montana said, but she didn't need to remind Gina.

"Anyway, a wealthy Wall Street broker named Sid Goldstein talked him into coming to Santa Barbara to open his own restaurant. He helped introduce him to the right bankers and put together a deal with a handful of rich Santa Barbara investors."

"Emilio must do very well. I assume he owns the restaurant now," Montana said.

"Rosa told me he repaid his loan within five years, but most of the investors refused the buyout offer and wanted to keep a piece of the restaurant."

"So why didn't you guys get married? If it was a jealousy thing, you'd think one or both of you would have wanted to tie the knot."

"Believe it or not, we never talked about it. Though Rosa, when she met me, she just patted my hand, shook her head and said, 'Good luck.' She thought Emilio was more in love with making business than making bambinos. I think she's right."

Two-and-a-half hours later, the women flew past the turnoff to Naples and followed the road directly to Vietri sul Mare. Vesuvius rose on their left, with the summit barely visible through a dissipating mist. They decided that after their mission they would drive the Amalfi coast back to Positano to spend the night at the San Pietro, if possible. They quickly passed the remains of Pompeii on their left as they hurried down the highway. It was too easy to look at the ruins of decadent Roman life and start drawing parallels with modern times. Montana supported Tony and his views on drug decriminalization, but passing Pompeii just made her wonder if she might not be witness to a new cycle in a declining civilization. She hoped not.

As they continued down the road, leaving Pompeii behind, a smile crossed her face. "God, I can't believe what we're doing. We're driving through the most romantic country in the world in search of ceramics with drugs." She looked at Gina and apologized, saying, "I'm sorry for making you drive all this way just to see some dishes."

Gina smiled back, saying, "It's as good a reason as any, especially when no reason is needed. I'm glad we have the time together."

"This may be one of the dumbest things I've ever done," Montana added.

When they finally arrived at Vietri sul Mare, they were treated to spectacular views of the Golfo di Salerno. The sharp contrasts of the jagged cliffs terraced with scattered dwellings and bougainvillea and the Tyrrhenian blues far below were hypnotic.

They came upon the Solimene factory, another ceramics maker, by accident and asked about the location of Pinto. Gina then navigated the way to the factory without much difficulty. As they pulled into the cobblestone driveway, Montana marveled at how clean and modern the facility appeared. She expected to see something more in line with Talaquepaque in Mexico. They parked and walked in through the sales office. Samples were laid out on a row of shelves in a well-lit cabinet.

A neatly dressed couple, probably in their sixties, were browsing the sales room when Gina and Montana walked in. The first thing Montana heard was, "Oh, Simon?"

"Yes, Arleen?"

"I can't believe how cheap these wonderful pieces are. Can you believe we can get six sets for only fifty dollars? We should get some for the kids, too." The accent was Southern, but subtle, maybe North Carolina or Virginia. The woman was tall and slender, with ash-blond hair pulled back and secured with a wide red ribbon. She had an air of aristocracy with down-home friendliness. Her husband, tall and broad, with straight white hair, had a very pleasant, easy-going demeanor.

Montana knew in an instant that the ceramics were a bargain, nothing compared to the outrageous prices she had been quoted in Rome and Santa Barbara. She and Gina casually browsed about while the salesman helped the American couple. Montana picked up vases and turned them over, inspecting the labels and now shaking them to see if there were any loose compartments sheltering drugs.

As Gina neared the salesman, he turned and greeted her in Italian, telling her he would be available to help her shortly. She responded with a simple thank-you.

As the American couple completed their transaction, they requested that the dishes be delivered to their hotel, the San Pietro in Positano. The salesman indicated that it would be no problem.

Montana spotted the dish she had seen in Santa Barbara. "Hey, Gina, come over here and take a look at this."

Gina headed over to Montana, crossing paths with the American couple as they headed out the door.

Simon held the door open for his bossy wife as she coursed through, leading two helpers who carried the boxes of newly purchased dishes. Montana couldn't help but watch the scene. Simon paused a moment after his wife passed and politely smiled back at Montana before he turned and followed his wife out. He had a kind face, with a respectful and charming air about him.

Montana examined the dishes as Gina made her way over. They both handled the plates, turning them around, inspecting the labels, feeling around the edges. Montana had the presence to ask the salesman, "Are these seconds? Are they defective?"

Gina quickly translated, and the salesman's inquisitive appearance instantly became animated and defensive. "Of course not. These are all excellent dishes, the finest quality. This is one of our most popular patterns. They are all flawless."

Montana had to check on the price again. "How much does it cost?"

Gina echoed in Italian, "Quanto costa?"

"Costa 35 euro."

Montana looked over at Gina. She understood the 35 euro, but she had to be certain what that included. "That other couple said they spent fifty dollars on the set of dishes they bought. Ask him exactly what we get for 35 euro."

For the next minute Gina and the salesman had a lively little discussion concerning the dishes.

Montana looked on, eager to know just what Gina had found out.

Finally, Gina turned to Montana and said, " He said the price includes a full setting for six. That's plates, salad plates, soup bowls, cups and saucers." Then with a smile she almost laughed when she added, "Because he thinks we are so 'bella,' he is even including the large serving tray and the big salad bowl."

Montana couldn't believe it. "In Rome I could buy one dish. Here I can get the entire place setting for six. This is my kind of shopping."

"Ask him if he can show us some vases. I don't see any offhand."

The salesman led them to the back. Montana found several like the one she'd dropped down the Spanish Steps, and again their prices were a mere fraction of those she'd seen in Rome.

"Are there any others?" Montana asked.

"This is all we make in this factory," he told Gina in Italian.

Montana decided to buy the dishes and three of the vases. She certainly didn't need them, but she thought it might not hurt to bring the set home along with a receipt. She had other plans for the vases. She anxiously anticipated sharing the news with Tony — cheap ceramics, some with value added, waited in large piles at Frascati Terrecotte for shipment to Santa Barbara.

The salesman offered to send them to their hotel. "Where will you be staying?"

Gina hesitated, uncertain, and looked at Montana.

"Tell him we'll take them with us," Montana said.

After they completed the transaction, they waited for the dishes and the vases to be packed and brought to their car. They stepped outside into the parking area. The late afternoon sun was still quite warm.

"Those dishes are so cheap. The store in Rome probably gets them even cheaper than we did. Hey, that's quite a mark-up." Montana had a grin on her face. "Boy, did we track down the best deal or what?"

"So now what? What's the difference how much the dishes cost? Stores must do that all the time. They buy real cheap and export real high. That's a good profit, no?" Gina added.

"No kidding. Cousin Ernesto has a pretty good system, and so does your old boyfriend. They aren't using all of these dishes to export drugs. I've got a feeling that's a very small part of the deal. The mark-ups are so high, it's probably a very effective way of cleaning up drug money." The salesman came outside with another helper, carrying two boxes securely wrapped with twine and makeshift handles for carrying.

Gina opened the trunk and moved their luggage to make room for the ceramics. They thanked the men and left.

They followed the road down to the Amalfi coast and then began to wind their way up to Positano.

"Pull over there." Montana pointed to a secluded spot off the road.

Gina obliged and Montana proceeded to dig out the three vases.

"What are you doing?"

Montana picked up a large stone and slammed it into the bottom of one of the vases. The ceramic shattered into pieces.

"Nothing," she said.

She shattered the other two in the same manner.

"Nothing. Not a damn thing."

"You don't think they're going to sell you a vase with drugs, do you?"

"I just had to check. Still, I'm even more suspicious of Frascati's than before."

The coastal route was enchanting, if a bit dizzying. Gina handled the curves in the Alfa Romeo like Mario Andretti. Clinging to the hillside were houses whose foundations must have been set horizontally into the rock. What appeared to be sheer cliffs that rock climbers might find challenging were mere home sites laced with ladder-like stairs and occasional funiculars. The brilliant blue-greens of the ocean below provided the color that livened the shades of gray along the coast. The abundance of dwellings along the rugged terrain with difficult access to the beaches below gave proof of the value of an ocean view.

It was nearly four-thirty when Gina stopped the car in front of the San Pietro in Positano. It had been a few years since Montana and Tony had been there. It looked the same, romantic as ever. It felt strange to Montana to be there under the circumstances of an impromptu ceramic hunt. And now Montana was beginning to understand why Emilio's relationship with Gina was so secretive. Or was it something else? For all the years that Montana had known Emilio, he seemed genuinely successful, so why would he get mixed up in anything to do with drugs?

In spite of the slow time of year, there seemed to be plenty of activity in the hotel. Montana was relieved that there were available rooms. She signed in and handed her American Express card and passport to the gentleman at the front desk.

Montana and Gina followed the bellman to their room. As they entered the darkened room, the bellman quickly went straight to the window and drew the curtains open. The room immediately flooded with the light and brilliance of the Tyrrhenian Sea.

The exquisite antique furnishings of the room were eclipsed by the magnificence of the view outside. Flinging their shoulder bags on the desk in front of the French doors, both women automatically drifted to the outdoor patio and stood there, taking in the view. The hypnotic desire to search the jagged cliffs and the seascape below laid the foundation for the theory of the "happy hormone." Montana recalled how Tony believed that the things we enjoyed looking at made us happy. He believed there was probably some chemical reaction going on in the brain when we look at things we really enjoy, explaining our desire to look at beautiful landscapes, seascapes, sunsets, buildings or people. Gina and Montana barely heard the bellman when he asked if he could be of any further assistance. Then, realizing his presence, Montana stepped back into the room while Gina stood gazing. She found her purse next to an elegant candelabra sitting on the marble-covered desk. She reached into it, recovered five euro and handed it to the bellman. He politely thanked her and wished them a pleasant stay as he let himself out.

Tony finally found a comfortable position on Brenda's couch with his head propped on a pillow and his legs hanging over the other end. He didn't fall asleep until late into the night. His cellular phone rang. By the third ring he was finally coherent enough to flip it open.

"Hello."

"Where are you? What're you doing on the cell phone?" Montana questioned.

"I'm trying to have an affair with Brenda, but it's not working. She knows I'm married, and she made me sleep on the couch." It's never too early to be a smart aleck, he thought. He looked at his watch. It was after eight. Brenda was already gone.

"Go on," said Montana, waiting.

"Well, actually I'm hiding out at Brenda's house temporarily. Anyway, I hope it's temporary. Jimmy McVee was murdered last night."

"Oh, my god. Do they know who did it?"

"Actually, I think 'they' do know. The problem is, 'they,' the cops, might be in on it. That's partly why I'm here at Brenda's. Before McVee was killed, he had come to the office at my request. He found some type of explosive planted under my car. Before that, someone, probably the guy who planted the explosive, scared me right out of the office. Oh, and guess who's being investigated by the state medical board for apparent improprieties against his patients?"

"What in the world is going on?"

"I really think there's a serious, well-orchestrated effort going on to undermine the drug program. I think Leslie Phillips and I were set up and marked for elimination, but I think Jimmy found something out they didn't want him to know. Isn't this fun?"

"God, maybe I should come home." Montana offered.

"I feel better knowing you're in Rome right now. I've called Spencer, and hopefully he'll get me some FBI protection and…"

Montana interrupted, asking, "FBI protection? What about Agent Felton? He's FBI, isn't he?"

"I don't trust him. In fact, I think he helped set me up. Do you know that McVee found marijuana planted in my car? Stupid, innocent me. When I called Ramsey after I heard McVee was killed, he told me the marijuana was registered to me through the DPC. Felton provided the information. Would you trust Felton?"

"By the way, I'm not in Rome. I'm in Positano."

Tony ran his hands through his hair and then rubbed his brow, feeling the tension build. "What's another surprise or two?"

"This might be helpful. Gina and I found Emilio's cousin's shop. I bought a vase…"

Tony interrupted, "You bought another vase?"

"Just wait a minute and then you can yell at me. Anyway, it turns out the vase was just as expensive as at home at Bertolini's. In fact, the one I took was from a box labeled for shipping to Bertolini's. I wasn't supposed to take it, though, but I did, and on the way back to Gina's I tripped and dropped it down the Spanish Steps." Montana paused a moment.

Tony realized she was expecting one of his tirades, but he knew it wasn't worth it. Why should he care how much a stupid vase cost, or even if she broke the damn thing. He'd be lucky to survive just to get the bill. He almost started to laugh at the irony. "It's okay. Please continue."

"The vase tumbled down several stairs and crashed. Guess what came out of the broken pottery."

"I give up, but I hope it was a genie and you've still got a couple of wishes left."

"Drugs. A plastic bag filled with drugs," Montana said excitedly.

"So the Frascati family is exporting drugs. Emilio's got to know, doesn't he?" Tony didn't want to believe Emilio was involved. He was beginning to realize there was a party going on and he was the only one not invited.

"There's more to it. The reason we're in Positano is that I wanted to see the factory where the ceramics were made. I cracked a few vases open looking for drugs, but didn't find any."

"Do you really think they'd sell you a vase filled with thousands of dollars worth of drugs?"

"You never know. Anyway, what I did get was really cheap. Same quality, great stuff, but really cheap. I think they serve at least two other functions besides being nice place settings. They're a source for smuggling drugs and a neat way of laundering drug money."

Montana had done well. Tony smiled thinking about his spousal sleuth.

Then she added, "The boxes were so stacked up I bet they haven't been able to send any out for a while now. The program's probably cut into their business, don't you think?"

"I think you're brilliant. I also think Rick Santiago deserves a call. Maybe he can see what kind of money is passing through that business and a few others." Tony exhaled audibly and then added, "At least you're safe in Rome and no one suspects anything."

"I'm not sure about that. I thought I saw Ernesto Frascati watching us after we left." She then explained how she had switched vases in the store. "Montana, he knows. I guarantee it."

"What should I do?"

"First of all, you're probably safe in Positano, but if you do go back to Rome, you've got to stay with Doctor Della Torrini. I'll call Alberto and arrange it. You'll be safe staying with his family. Besides, I doubt the Frascatis want to chance drawing any attention to themselves."

Just then Tony heard a loud double click in his earpiece.

154

"Montana, did you hear that?" He asked.

"What?"

"I think someone may have tapped into our conversation."

"That's a little paranoid, don't you think?"

"Paranoid? I'd really be crazy if I wasn't being paranoid," Tony barked. "Somebody's listening. I don't think we should say too much more now, but I know you'll understand this. If anything goes wrong, or you have the slightest doubt about your safety, don't hang around. Don't tell anyone where you're going. Just get to a 'piece of heaven' and I'll find you. Let's not say anything else. Please be careful."

"You, too." And she hung up.

Tony was irritated that someone might have cut into their conversation, but it also bothered him that he didn't really say goodbye, or "I love you." Neither one of them said the magic words. Maybe he was superstitious, maybe just paranoid or stupid. He hoped it wouldn't be their last conversation.

Chapter 12

8:30 a.m., Tuesday, March 15

IT WAS NEARLY EIGHT-THIRTY. Tony expected Joanna would be calling shortly to let him know the state of affairs. Brenda would be leaving the office, but not for an hour or so. He couldn't go anywhere until Brenda came back with her car. He turned on his computer and looked up Rick Santiago's phone number.

Rick worked out of an office — maybe a cubicle, for all Tony knew — in the Treasury Department. Tony called him at his office. A central operator responded and directed his call to Rick. The phone rang through one time, and there was an abrupt and blunt response: "Santiago."

Tony could tell that working for the FDIC was a real joy. "Hey, Rick, it's Tony Ryan. I need some help. Pronto."

"Hey, Tony. What's the problem?"

Tony then gave him a rundown on the whole story, including how he had asked Spencer to see what he could find out. He was really stuck. He needed outside help with people he surely could trust.

"I told you drugs were bad news," Rick reprimanded.

"It's not the drugs that are going to kill me. It's the people who don't want this program to succeed. And that could be a lot of different people. With what Montana found out and some of the names of the businesses I suspect might be involved, could you find out their financial status for me?"

"Here's what I think I can do. Typically, I can get deposit and debit information. We might as well check out the bank records on a few of the players you mentioned." He grabbed a pencil and jotted down the names. "You've got Western Rifles and Guns, Bertolini's, Recovery West, and Frascati's Ristorante. Give me some names of unrelated businesses as well. That way we can have some controls to check out your hypothesis. What do you think?"

"Anything you can find out might be helpful. I admit I'm grasping for a clue." Tony gave Rick the names of a few other businesses. Tony hoped Rick could magically tell him the answer to the problem.

"Okay, I'm on it. I'm not sure this will help you, but if there's anything very abnormal, we can subpoena their records. Still, I doubt you'll learn much from that. How far back do you think we should go? Is a year okay?"

"I guess. Start with a year and we'll see what we find. I really appreciate this. I don't have much time." Tony gave him his e-mail, his cellular phone number and Brenda's phone number and told him he could leave messages there. He needed some breaks, quickly.

Tony hung up and sat back on the couch. He started to get up and head for the bathroom when the phone rang. Brenda's message played through, and then Joanna could be heard on the line. "Dr. Ryan, it all worked out as planned. I called the police department." At that point Tony picked up the receiver.

"Joanna, it's me. How did the patients take it?"

"They were pretty upset at first. After I told them I couldn't get in touch with you, even on your pager, they became genuinely concerned. Then I called the police. They've already sent someone to your house. I couldn't believe how quickly, either. They called back and said you weren't there. Silvia was there, with the dogs, but not you or your car. Of course Silvia called the office right away. She was really worried about you. I didn't tell her what was going on. I wanted to, but I didn't. I told her to hang in there and everything would probably turn out fine. I suggested that maybe some emergency had come up and I'd call her if I found out anything. She's a worrier, though."

"I'm glad you didn't say anything. It's tough, but it's best to keep her out of the loop. There's less at risk for her." Of course, Tony knew the police had been there once earlier. Still, he wanted to know if Ramsey was still involved. "Who was the cop they sent out?"

"I don't know, one of the officers in the field already. That's why they got back to me so quickly. The guy that called me seemed very nice. He said he was A.T. Cooper, an investigator with the department."

Tony grabbed a scratch pad off the table and jotted down A.T. Cooper. Then he asked, "Where's Brenda? Has she left the office yet?"

"She's finishing up. We still have the first patient here. Ron gave her a little sedation to calm her down when you were initially 'just late.' I didn't say anything to him, either. He's worried, too. I told him you're a survivor, so was sure we'd find out soon enough what's going on. So, Dr. Ryan, what's the plan? How long are you going to hang out at Brenda's? What should I do about the rest of the patients?"

"I'm not sure when I can come back, but I would have to do it soon. If I stay out too long, they'll know I'm in hiding and I'm on to them. If I come back in a day or two, there shouldn't be much concern. I'll figure it out – hopefully sooner than later. As for the patients, just do whatever you would do if you didn't know what was going on. You might consider rescheduling them for a day or two from now. Don't forget Dr. Tarbon. He'll help out if we get stuck." Anxious to get on with the business at hand, Tony nearly hung up. He caught himself almost neglecting to thank her, and so he said, "Hey, thanks. I knew I could count on you."

Next, Tony needed to find out what Spencer had accomplished. He should have found something out by now, thought Tony. He used Brenda's phone and dialed his number at the office. He picked it up after the first ring. "Spencer, any news yet?" he asked.

"Tony, I was just going to call you." A brisk tone of excitement ran in his voice. "Check your e-mail. I've got some news for you."

While Tony opened his laptop and got online, Spencer continued. "Okay, so Mark Hansen came through. He's one of the few guys who think the end of drug prohibition won't collapse the bureau. Anyway, he ran the check on Frank Ramsey. Are you online yet?"

"Yeah. Here we go." Tony scrolled through the material and came down to a photograph. "Holy shit," he exclaimed.

"I take it you're looking at the photo from Iraq from the first Gulf War."

"This is the same Ramsey that I saw on the tube last night at McVee's murder scene."

"Ramsey had one of those real cushy procurement jobs working out of Kuwait."

Then Tony jumped in, saying, "That guy in the back, on the left side of the photo. The one with the beard looks just like Felton. That's Felton, isn't it? Is this for real?"

"Yeah, Hansen wondered if you'd notice that. He knows Felton, but not that well. He's checked it out but hasn't gotten confirmation yet. So far, he seems to think its coincidence. Felton's been out on the West Coast, living in L.A., for the last five years, but this is the first time he's ever worked in the Santa Barbara area."

Tony read through the names that came with the photo. He paused a moment at the name Cooper. He looked at the picture listing Cooper in the back row, third from the left.

"This Cooper fellow in the back row. Do you see the guy?" Tony asked.

"I can't be sure, but he looks like the guy who drove off in the unmarked cop car yesterday. Also, Joanna just got a call from an A.T. Cooper, and McVee mentioned Cooper Sunday night when Montana and I were at Weissman's. I didn't see him that night, though."

"I'm sure it's the same Cooper. We've already checked. There's an Austin Trent Cooper working for the department as a detective. How many Coopers can there be?" Spencer then added, "These guys have been buddies for a while. Cooper and Ramsey worked together. They worked out of pretty plush headquarters in Kuwait City. These guys were into everything. They could get Beluga caviar or Stoli vodka. They kept all the brass quite happy. I'm sure they could get anything for anybody. They spent six months there. They handled all the top brass and dignitaries that came over. They made the time in Kuwait real comfortable for a lot of people. It's a good thing they finally got transferred out of there. Anyhow, they eventually were given honorable discharges, a few decorations and a lot of cushy offers from different members of the brass. It seems odd that they both got into criminology and found a nice spot with the Santa Barbara P.D. Ramsey originally came from Southern California, and Cooper hailed from up north."

So far, it sounded as if they were a couple of buddies who simply went into law enforcement together. If they were rogue cops, at least they shared a common background.

As Tony continued to scroll down, he also noticed something else. "Hey, look at this tidbit. Ramsey's a part-owner of Western Rifles and Guns."

Spencer jumped in quickly, "Yeah," he said, "everyone seemed to find that quite interesting. We know that's where Weissman reportedly bought his piece."

Tony wasn't terribly surprised, but this wasn't something he'd expected to hear. Spencer continued, "Guess who owns the lion's share of Western Rifles and Guns? – none other than the Frascati Company. Emilio is the principal, but there are several other investors on the list. Can you believe it?"

Tony was astounded. "Why would a restaurateur own a gun store?"

"It's big business," Spencer replied. "The place is loaded with Berettas. It should probably be called 'Spaghetti Western Rifles and Guns.' There's quite a few Smith and Wessons as well."

"Jeez, these guys are in business together. I'm not sure I get it. Perhaps Frascati brought Ramsey in as the 'credible cop.' Maybe Ramsey is supposed to make the place look good. Is Cooper tied in with the place, too?"

"Apparently not. Cooper has some investments of his own, primarily in property in Humboldt County. He's from Northern California, so it makes sense to some extent. Nonetheless, Hansen was blown away by the connection between Frascati and the gun shop, not to mention Ramsey and Cooper. He really flipped out when he found out that guy was Felton. Meanwhile, Emilio checks out clean. The family runs a ceramics business in Italy and does a lot of exporting."

"I know about the ceramic business." Tony then told Spencer about his earlier conversation with Montana.

Spencer hadn't known anything about Bertolini, but by now he didn't seem surprised. "There was nothing in Emilio's background that tied him in with Bertolini's. Montana may have hit the jackpot. What a neat way to clean up your money, let alone bring in a little supply of drugs. Who, besides Montana, would track down the factory? Talk about your serious shopper. It's not as though she simply went for a stroll through Rome."

"Is this enough to go on?" Tony asked.

"Actually," Spencer continued, "there might be a little more to it all. Frascati was a key backer in Senator Winston's re-election. He held one of the biggest fund-raisers at his restaurant. Every one of his employees donated the limit, obviously backed by Frascati. He's well connected when it comes to the Washington inner circle. He goes to all of those Republican Senatorial Inner Circle Programs and has many friends there. Turns out Burton Wesley shows up fairly prominently on the same list. He's made some very hefty contributions through Recovery West. Of course, that's no crime."

"So what else do you know about Wesley?"

"Not much. He's running three rehab centers and a multispecialty medical group, but there's nothing striking in his bio, except for his congressional record against legalizing drugs. He lives in Montecito and owns a nice-sized powerboat that he keeps in the yacht harbor. Otherwise, we don't know much about him."

Tony scrolled through Wesley's information as Spencer spoke. "So where do we go from here?"

"Hansen thinks you're in the game. McVee probably just knew too much. He thinks you're right — that someone, or some group most likely, wants to end the experiment in Santa Barbara, and eliminating you could be very helpful. They might have knocked off Leslie Phillips. And now, with Montana's information, I bet he's going to move on this right away."

The front door opened, and in walked Brenda. Tony had been spending a lot of time on her couch and on the phone. She slung her purse on the chair, along with her sweater, and continued to the kitchen in search of some coffee. Except for a simple glance, there was no interruption in his conversation with Spencer. "This is about the drug business, isn't it?"

Spencer cut in and added, "Hansen thinks so. At the very least, he thinks you've got some cops who'd like to end the program. But they're probably the tip of the iceberg. He wants to come out to the coast with a few of his crew. Based on your present time frame, you may need to be ready to cover your ass but quick. You're a target as soon as you resurface. You'll need help. You can trust Mark. I've got to get back to work. I'll keep you posted on any details with the bureau. Call me if you hear anything."

"Thanks, Spencer, thanks," Tony sincerely added before he hung up the phone.

Brenda walked over with a cup of hot chocolate for Tony. He could clearly smell the coffee she held in her own cup. It smelled perfect for the overcast gray day, but these days Tony couldn't drink it without bouncing off the walls. The office staff knew caffeine wasn't his drug.

"So, Doc, how many patients are you going to turn away before you come back?" Brenda, still in her scrubs, sat down in the deep tan cushioned chair with her legs crossed under her. She held her cup in two hands, savoring the warmth as well as the aroma.

Sipping the hot chocolate, Tony responded with a cockeyed smile. Sitting on her couch, still in his sweat pants and t-shirt, he would, on a normal day, be starting his second case by now. Instead, he had a new headquarters from which he was planning his future. Temporary as it was, he found solace in the safety he enjoyed. "One way or another, I'll be back in two days at the most. Right now, I have to make the cops think I'm out of the picture. Let them look for me a little bit. The fellows that want me out won't be too anxious to search. It will give me a little more time. Hopefully, when I re-emerge I'll be in a better position to defend myself. Look, I know this sounds like silly double-talk. I can picture Montana shaking her head and telling me I still talk in circles, but frankly I don't yet know what I'm going to do. I just know it's got to happen soon. Does that make any sense?"

Brenda sat there in the same position, bent her head down slowly and took a sip from her cup. "You'll work it out. I have confidence in you, Doc. Let me know what I can do."

"Thanks. I need your driver's license number, birth date, mother's maiden name and Social Security number." Tony took another sip of hot chocolate and started off to the shower.

"Wait a second. You're not getting me messed up in this business, are you?"

"No, no, I've got a hunch about something. I need to go out for a little while, and I'll have to borrow your car. I want to check out the Western Rifles and Guns store."

Chapter 13

5:00 p.m., Tuesday, March 15

Gina came waltzing out of the bathroom, refreshed, with only a towel wrapped around her head. Montana, already showered, relaxed on the terrace in a white terry cloth robe. She sat on a lounge chair sipping from a glass of Pinot Grigio as the sun dipped below the horizon. On the other side of that sunset, she knew Tony was starting to shape his day. Another woman might panic, but Montana said her silent prayers and knew things would work out. Tony was a survivor and she was, too. So with a sense of tranquility, perhaps encouraged by the wine, she rested on the terrace.

Gina poured a glass of wine from the bottle on the desk and then innocently sauntered out onto the terrace. Leaning up against the iron railing, she sipped from the glass in her left hand and let her head tilt back with her eyes shut, savoring the air and the wine. The balmy breeze felt like velvet caressing her body. She enjoyed the moment.

Montana looked over and saw her friend standing naked on the terrace. She thought of telling Gina to get covered up, but she said nothing. Instead, she watched as the light, soft and filtered with hues of amber and rose, poured over Gina's curves. Her friend had a gorgeous figure, full and voluptuous in a classic Italian sense. They glanced at each other and smiled softly, as if to acknowledge one another, enjoying their late afternoon retreat. As Montana leaned back, she spotted a man, maybe three balconies to her left, staring across to their terrace. She casually leaned back in her chair and, after finishing her sip of wine, wanted to speak, but said nothing. She turned her gaze toward the man. From her perspective, he appeared to be thirtyish, tan, with well-chiseled features and dark wavy hair. He wore a dark double-breasted blazer over an open-collar white shirt and gray slacks. He stood on the side of his balcony directly facing them. His hands were on the rail with the base of a half-filled champagne flute caught between the rail and his right hand. He wore no sunglasses, and though he may have caught Montana's glance, he kept his eyes focused on Gina. And why not? This left Montana on the verge of discomfort and yet she said nothing. She waited to see how Gina would react. This was Italy. Why make an issue over a little skin?

Montana watched as Gina slowly turned her gaze to the man. Her body remained up against the rail, just her head now turned to the left. She stared back. In her left hand, she held the wine up to her lips, looking straight into his eyes. Her arm now obscured the view of her breast. If he had been watching her body before, he now remained locked in concentration with her eyes. Gina parted her lips ever so slightly then tilted the glass so that the wine could barely traverse the edge. As she swallowed, she lowered the glass slowly, first across her full lower lip then seductively lower, revealing the silhouette of her breast. In spite of her nakedness, it still looked as though she were undressing for him. Montana no longer felt uncomfortable. She became voyeuristically intoxicated with the passion between two strangers. No one made any attempt to excuse themselves from an obviously awkward situation.

His eyes were not wandering; they were caressing and penetrating. Gina held her position steady. She inhaled slowly and deliberately. Then her body reacted with a visible contraction of her areola as her nipples stiffened. She had been touched, and her breathing became just a little deeper, with a barely visible quiver. Montana remained transfixed but could not imagine this telepathic love-making progressing much further. Gina reached her free right hand down over her thigh, where it drifted lightly toward the inside of her leg. She looked as if she were going to shield herself as her hand slowly glided up her thigh and ever so slowly seemed to caress the softness between her legs. Lingering barely a moment, her fingers, long and graceful, flowed over the surface, remaining long enough to steal the warmth of her sexuality. Montana and the man watched silently as her hand continued its journey upward, lightly brushing against her soft dark hairs, dragging its way across her flat belly before coming to rest upon the rail of the terrace.

Montana continued to watch and still said nothing, becoming increasingly aroused as the tension increased. Gina, naked in the waning glow of the setting sun, appeared seductively vulnerable. In the seconds that followed, the growing anticipation added a sense of excitement, but unless the man across the way was Tarzan, this escapade of passions would remain purely visual. Then, finally perhaps, the man lifted his glass and made a gesture of a toast to Gina. He took a sip from his glass, nodded his head and expressed the slightest closed-lip smile, then simply retreated back into his room.

For several moments the two women continued to stare at the now-vacated balcony until Montana finally broke the silence. "It doesn't look as if he's coming back. I think he's giving you a chance to get dressed now."

"He was quite disarming. I was hoping he might come back with just a towel around his head," Gina said, and then turned to her friend. The air had now cleared of lustful fantasies, supplanted by the devilishness of two schoolgirls engaged in their secret tryst. They shared a moment of levity as a response to the departed tension.

Montana then got up from her chair and pointed the way into the room, ushering her friend along. "Let's get dressed and go down for cocktails before dinner. I'm certain your new friend will be looking for you. Let's see how interested he is with your clothes on."

Now laughing aloud, Gina was almost ready to explode. "Yes, let's see," she said.

In the lounge they found a cozy table near a window. The lights along the coast now provided the visual entertainment. A pianist with a synthesizer played tunes that sounded more like a small ensemble than a single piano. Montana thought a simple piano might have been more charming, but the music was enjoyable all the same. She reached for the cocktail menu on the table at the same time that a waiter delivered two flutes of champagne.

"From the gentleman across the room. Please enjoy. Salute!" With that, the waiter straightened up and turned away. The man from the balcony was in direct view of Gina. Montana turned her head as he raised his glass in a polite gesture. This time he smiled broadly – an almost innocent smile. If he hadn't been so tanned, Montana could've sworn he was blushing a bit. Gina stood up, put her hands on her hips and smiled back. Finally, she put up her hand and signaled with her index finger for him to come over.

As he neared the table, it was clear that he was indeed a very handsome man. He extended his hand first to Montana. "Buona sera, signora. Il mio nome e Carlo Ferante."

Before Montana could respond, Gina spoke to him directly in Italian. saying, "This is my friend Montana," at which point Montana politely smiled. "She is from California. I am Gina, from Roma. It is nice to meet you with my clothes on. Thank you for the champagne."

"Perhaps, then, it would be best if I spoke in English," he offered with a warm Italian accent.

Montana spoke up, saying, "Please, won't you be seated," gesturing at an empty chair at the table.

Carlo was charming from the start. Looking at Montana, he said, "I should apologize for staring at your friend, but she was so beautiful, standing there like a goddess drenched by the colors of the fading sun. And then those eyes. I swear, it did not matter that her clothes were missing." He turned to Gina. They smiled broadly at each other. Montana hoped they wouldn't go back into that trance from earlier. Carlo got straight to the point, saying, "I would be the luckiest man in Positano if you would be my guests for dinner this evening."

Gina smiled back at Carlo and then looked to Montana for her approval. To which Montana said, "I think you have already been the luckiest man in Positano, but we should be delighted to dine with you." They all laughed, a warm good-natured laugh that allowed them to enter a new chapter in their encounter.

Dinner was delightful. Montana leaned back and savored the Barolo left in her wine glass. Carlo had been a charming dinner companion. The three had shared several stories and quite a few laughs. Carlo didn't really offer much about himself. When asked about his work, he politely mentioned that he was in international banking, adding, "Exciting for the bankers, but not worthy of dinner conversation." Now, toward the end of dinner, Gina had his undivided attention. Carlo enchanted her the easy way; he simply listened. Montana almost started to laugh out loud thinking about the myriad of arguments she had had with Tony about not listening. Over the years, Tony had finally succumbed, admitting he was a victim of a genetic defect. Of course, he would argue, most of the male population suffered from the same malady.

Carlo then turned to Montana, catching her during a reflective moment and announced, "Would you like to join us for cocktails and dancing? I know a place we can go. It's a private club nearby. We can walk."

Montana was on the verge of yawning. She didn't want to be rude, but this had been a long day. Part of her was raring to go, still on West Coast time, but most of her was exhausted. "That is very sweet of you, but I would prefer if you go without me. It's been a long day."

"Oh, Montana, are you sure?" Gina asked in an almost perfunctory manner.

It didn't matter. Montana couldn't wait to hit her pillow. "Have fun," she said as she stood, figuring this would be a good time to fade away back to her room. "I had a most enjoyable time. Thank you for a lovely evening, Carlo." Then smiling, she turned to Gina, saying, "You have your key. I won't wait up."

Carlo stood and politely offered his hand. "Buona notte, signora."

It was only a little after nine, but Montana gladly headed back to her room. There was a charming sitting area just off to the right of the hallway. It reminded her of the club floor at the Ritz-Carlton. The hotel kept a variety of wines and spirits there for its guests. Herb teas and a few different ports and brandies were on hand for the jet-lagers and insomniacs. Montana didn't need a thing off those shelves.

It felt so good to lay her head down on the pillow. When you get right down to it, one of life's greatest feelings is the simplest – that wonderful feeling of being able to lay down your tired body at the end of a long and busy day. Montana's sublime awareness of her pleasure barely lasted but a moment, for she quickly fell into deep REM sleep.

Gina was wide-awake and gleefully walking down the street from her hotel. A few blocks down, Carlo led Gina to a simple building with a single awning over the doorway. The building could have been the side of a warehouse. There were no distinctive markings or any attempts at architectural enhancements to the exterior. A single doorman stood outside. When they approached, he nodded to Carlo and simply said, "Buona sera" and held the door as they entered. Inside, the club belied its modest exterior. Most of the walls were mirrored and trimmed with chrome. Plush gray leather booths were sequestered around the room. A dance floor at the far end of the club was bathed in a collage of flashing strobes and colored lights. A few couples danced, but it was still early by Italian standards, and the club was just starting to fill. Even in the middle of the week, a steady influx of revelers was prepared to meld the night into dawn.

Carlo and Gina were escorted to a small table tucked into a private corner. Carlo said something to the maitre d', who then flagged a waiter. Within minutes the waiter poured from a bottle of Dom Perignon. Gina took a sip, slowly, staring back at Carlo as she had from the balcony. This time she was within reach. He placed his right hand behind her head, then drew her face to his and graced her cheek with a tender kiss. He looked directly into her eyes.

Two hours later, Gina was in Carlo's hotel room. Between the lights, the music and the champagne, she had become progressively aroused. Up to this moment, she had been consumed with increasing desire. She had savored the chase but was now dying to feel him inside of her. Her arms were wrapped around his waist, and her hands were pulling firmly as he slid between her legs.

The drinks at the club and the groping on the way back to the room were part of the foreplay. Carlo had undressed her slowly, spending lots of time kissing between her breasts, around her breasts, on her belly and finally working his way up toward her areola. She could barely stand it. Her thoughts had become focused completely on her left nipple. She could sense all of her sensuous energies mounting in her breast as Carlo teased his way toward his destination. She was both overwhelmed and relieved when he finally touched her areola and nipple with his tongue. He had mounted such a slow campaign that she was stunned by his intense passion. She remembered that this was how it had been early on with Emilio. How quickly that had faded, though, so that sex had become purely perfunctory and much too short. She remembered now, of all times, how Emilio had become less content with his daily life, and it showed in their lovemaking. Emilio had become firm and almost brutal, no longer making love to her, but simply using her to relieve some new kind of tension he could not or chose not to express.

Now, after Carlo's prolonged session of foreplay, she had been taken to the edge a half dozen times, but now, finally, she guided him in between her legs. Her grip was firm and insistent. She began to breathe more rapidly as he positioned to enter her. Her back arched slightly as she raised her hips to encourage and hasten his entry. He stayed just at her opening. In fact, she could feel him pull back slightly. He did this again and again. Each time he would enter an infinitesimal amount more, but not all the way. She could not believe the sensation. She no longer thought of Emilio. She no longer thought even of Carlo. Her whole being was centered at the point of their sexual contact. She was truly on fire and knew she would explode with an intense pleasure if he ever connected. Her lips parted slightly with her eyes half shut in her impending expectations of ecstasy. She pleaded with his deep brown eyes just as he finally penetrated – all the way this time. Finally, when he was deep inside of her, she felt that her sensations had been multiplied, and now, without him even sliding back and forth, with the pressure of his pelvis against her, she lost her breath momentarily as she was enveloped in a shattering orgasm. Gina involuntarily dug her nails firmly into Carlo's back as her head flung back and to the side as she let out a barely audible gasp. The moment was intense, and the pure sexuality of it caught Carlo as well. He stayed put, fearing any more motion just yet would send him over the edge as well. As Gina settled down, Carlo too regained his control and started a slow, methodical pumping, gently pressing his pelvis against hers. Their lips met and softly caressed, eventually parting to the urgency of their tongues. Gina's concentration shifted between their kisses and the rhythm of their lovemaking. The tension continued to mount. The friction, now of a different nature, became stronger and more compelling. Again Gina felt herself coming to the edge, but this time Carlo stayed with her step for step. Their eyes opened, and they remained mouth to mouth. Their mouths open, their breath intermittent, their tongues barely touching each other's lips, Carlo finally exploded in a consuming orgasm that sent him deep within Gina and shook his body with a convulsive fervor. This time Gina was set off by her lover's excitement, and she experienced another orgasm. Finally spent, with her circuits significantly overloaded, she collapsed in Carlo's arms and quickly fell into a deep sleep.

Carlo made certain she was fast asleep before he freed his arm from under her and slipped away.

Standing in the lounge, Simon Babcock poured hot water over a bag of chamomile tea. He had been having a hard time with jet lag since he'd arrived nearly a week ago. He was happy that he could go to the lounge for teas and snacks instead of sitting in his room while Arleen slept. The first night he woke up and flipped on the television. His wife nearly sprang out of bed as an Italian version of the Flintstones came roaring over the tube at three in the morning. After that, he simply got used to putting on his warm-ups and strolling over to the guest lounge, where the hotel kept hot water available for guests like Mr. Babcock. Unfortunately, this was becoming an uncomfortable ritual for Simon. He had been surprised when the first night out he met a couple of other guests who shared his dilemma. He found himself engaged in an enjoyable conversation for a couple of hours. However, the last two nights no one else had had trouble sleeping. There was a little more serenity in his early-morning adventure, but without a little conversation, the wee morning hours seemed to pass slowly. He hoped a little herb tea might relax him a little and allow him to go back to his room for a little more sleep. Simon finished preparing his tea and settled back into an overstuffed couch that faced one of the large picture windows looking out into the bay. It was so quiet he could faintly hear the lapping of the waters against the shore below. Through the window he saw a few twinkling lights, but mostly darkness, which made the window more of a mirror, simply reflecting him and the hallway behind him.

Just then he heard the faint sound of a door being shut. Footsteps resonated over the marble floor. Simon began to anticipate company. However, the footsteps seemed to end abruptly. Simon could hear the sound of a key being pushed into a lock. Since he had seen no one pass behind him through the reflection in the window, and there was no entrance from the outside down the hall, it seemed odd to him that someone would be playing musical rooms at this time. He shrugged his shoulders, raised a brow and thought, "Who knows? After all, this is Italy."

In her dream, Montana rode an elevator in the Bank of America building in San Francisco on her way to the Carnelian room to meet Tony for a drink. Several nondescript people gathered in the elevator as the doors closed. She could smell the Chanel cologne on the man behind her. She vaguely remembered a rather attractive young man in a navy blazer getting on the elevator with her. While everyone in the elevator politely kept their eyes focused on the floor indicator, she became increasingly aware of the man behind her, and then she could feel him. He was now leaning up against her body and lightly breathing on her neck. Then she felt a gentle kiss behind her ear. She did not turn around. Suddenly, she was aware of his hardness pressed up against her buttocks. He slowly hiked up her skirt in the back and his hand reached underneath and began to caress her thigh, rubbing softly and then reaching under the side band of her panties, deliberately pulling them down. Still she did not turn around. Everyone continued to look straight ahead as she became increasingly aroused. She began to realize that they would soon be at the top, and Tony would be waiting. She almost lost her footing as she felt his fingers slip between her legs and gently rub against the slight moistness, lingering, but definitely preparing to enter her. She inhaled deeply as though she knew her next response would be to gasp as he proceeded. Suddenly, the elevator stopped and the doors opened. Tony stood directly in front of her, and as she turned to face her seducer, there was no one. She turned back to Tony, and now he was gone. She suddenly awoke from a dream that had left her unfulfilled.

She sat up in bed. She could feel her heart racing from her dream, but now she was wide awake. She had napped for a few good hours, but her jet lag left her unable to go directly back to bed.

She looked at the next bed. It was empty. Good for Gina. She got out of bed and wrapped herself in the terry cloth robe and wandered out onto the terrace. There was a slight chill in the air, but it felt good against her brow. She stood there looking out into the starry darkness and a few of the lights of Positano as the sea lapped against the jagged shore below. She then heard the door open, so Gina must have finally come back to the room. But it remained quiet and no lights went on. When Montana turned around to check on Gina, she lost her breath, startled by Carlo, who stood directly behind her.

"Is Gina with you?" Montana asked, forcing the words out breathlessly.

"She's resting comfortably in my room. And how about you, signora? Are you no longer tired?" Carlo leered at Montana, but not in a sexual way.

He stepped toward her, and she suddenly realized that she had backed up against the railing. A moment's glance over her shoulder left her a little dizzy, realizing a mere railing separated her from a certainly fatal fall. Could Carlo be that someone Tony had spoken of, someone to look out for? Whatever his intentions, they were evil. Montana took a chance and tried to expose his male sexual weakness. "Is it my turn to enjoy the fruits of Italy?" she asked. Motivated by fear, she sensed these were the best words she could drum up. As she spoke, she reached for the cord to her robe and unfastened it.

It seemed to be working. For a moment, Carlo stopped his approach and cast his eyes down on Montana's hands as she began to open her robe. Montana reached out her arms toward his waist as he reached for her robe. They were a foot apart as Montana's robe opened, and she suddenly shoved her knee directly into his groin. Carlo doubled over in agony, falling back into the room through the open door. Montana ran directly out of her room with her robe still open.

Simon Babcock saw the reflection of a barefooted Montana running frantically down the hallway. She had not seen him, but she clearly looked frightened. Before Simon could get up, he heard a door slam. He then thought of the key entering the door moments earlier. Had someone broken into Montana's room? He ventured over to the hallway and clearly saw a tall dark-haired man. The man froze momentarily, staggered slightly, then turned around abruptly and hobbled back to what Simon assumed was his room.

Simon walked toward the lobby, looking for Montana. The lights were dim, and there was no one behind the reception desk. He stood by the desk and looked around. In the quiet he thought he heard someone breathing heavily from around the corner near the house phone. He walked over there and saw Montana crouched in the corner, speaking softly into the phone, trying to summon security to help her. Simon was caught in the shadows but continued to walk toward Montana.

Montana pleaded with security, "Please hurry. A man just came into my room. I think he wanted to kill me. Please." She got up and turned around, only to see a man approaching her from the shadows. She was so frightened she couldn't even scream. She looked for something to grab to defend herself with. As the man came out from the shadows, she recognized him as the man she had seen at Pinto. She was relieved.

"I'm sorry if I've frightened you, but I saw you running down the hallway a minute ago. There was a dark-haired man in the hallway. I assume you were running from him. Did he hurt you?"

"No, I'm okay, thank you. Did you see where he went?" Montana asked.

"He appeared injured and inebriated. He walked down the hall and went into a room."

"My god," Montana whispered pensively. She looked down, thinking then turned her eyes to Simon. "It was Carlo. He used Gina to get to me. I think he wanted to kill me. He probably had been drinking enough that I was able to land a lucky kick. Oh, Christ, he must have gotten Gina's key and let himself in."

"Judging by the way he walked off, I think your kick landed directly. I think he's probably going to go sleep it off. Excuse me," he said as he reached out his hand. Montana took it and with his assistance rose to her feet. "I'm Simon Babcock. I'm vacationing here with my wife, Arleen, who I'm sure you heard earlier." He made a gesture with his hand, opening and closing it rapidly, suggesting she was chatty.

As she brushed down her robe and secured the tie, she introduced herself. "I'm Montana Ryan."

"What makes you think he was trying to kill you?" Simon was now supporting Montana and leading her back toward the lounge.

Montana felt safe with Simon. She saw Tony in his eyes. It was an eerie experience, but it made her feel secure. "I was standing on the balcony when he entered my room unannounced and very quietly. He came directly at me. He had a strange, almost scared look in his eyes. He had me backed up to the railing. I really thought he was about to throw me over."

"But why, why would he do such a thing? The Italians are known to be rather amorous. Isn't it possible ... ?" He politely didn't finish the sentence, but the implication was clear.

"He may have entertained such thoughts, but I assure you that wasn't his main interest. My husband's a cosmetic surgeon in Santa Barbara. He's also the director of the western region legal drug program. You know, 'the experiment.' Apparently, he has inadvertently stumbled on to something that involves a criminal network. We're not even sure what it's all about, but someone is giving him a really hard time. I've made some contacts in Rome which might be causing some bother as well." Montana stood there in her robe looking at Simon. He must have wondered if she was for real or just nuts.

Finally, a hotel security man approached. Not much of an imposing figure, Montana thought, looking at the slightly built gentleman.

"Signora, what's the matter?"

"What about Gina? I've got to find her. What if she's in danger?" Montana said frantically to Simon.

"Who's Gina?"

"I was attacked by a man who has my friend in his room. Please, we have to check on her," Montana pleaded.

"This man, he's staying at the hotel?" the security man asked.

"Carlo, yes, his name is Carlo Ferante."

They walked back to the front desk, where the security man checked on the room location of Carlo Ferante. A few minutes later the three of them stood in front of the door to Carlo's room. He knocked on the door a few times and waited. It was quiet.

Montana looked up at Simon, worried and confused. He put his hand on her shoulder, clearly trying to reassure her. The security man took out his passkey, and before he could use it, the door opened.

Carlo stood at the open door with a towel wrapped around his waist.

The security man spoke to him in Italian and informed him of Montana's claims. Just then a very sleepy-looking Gina walked up in a robe behind Carlo.

"Montana, what's the matter?" Gina asked.

Carlo then turned back at Gina, saying, "She thinks I went to her room to kill her." Then he turned back to the security man and said in English, "I tell you she's crazy. I go to tell her, her friend's okay. Not to worry. She goes to take off her robe. I reach down to close it. This is not right. She's a married lady. Then, va-boom, she kicks me right in the balls. Lady, I'm sorry if I scared you, but you're dangerous."

"Montana?" Gina gasped.

The security man quickly apologized, and Carlo closed the door. "I think nobody got hurt, so let's go back to bed." He walked away, leaving Montana confused and alone with Simon Babcock.

He spoke first. "Arleen and I have a big suite. Maybe it'll be best if you gather your things and we move you over there for the evening. She and I are driving to Nice tomorrow. We can get you all sorted out in the morning." He quickly looked at his watch then added, "Which isn't all that far away."

"I'd like to ask a really big favor," Montana said. Simon looked at her and simply nodded his head a couple of times in affirmation, to which she responded, "Give me a ride to the South of France. Gina will be all right, but I've got to get out of Italy. Do you have room for me? I'd really appreciate it."

Simon ran his hand through his hair and casually rubbed the back of his head. Standing before him at three something in the morning was a beautiful woman asking for a ride to France. He knew he was going to help her, and he knew Arleen would be particularly happy to be involved. Still, there was something almost comical about the situation. With a fatherly smile, he said,

"We'd better get your things together and get going. I suspect if we get an early start, we may be gone before he gets up."

She and Simon went back to her room and quickly packed. Montana left a note for Gina telling her she had to leave and that she would call her later. She told her that the room had been paid for including another night if she wanted to stay and party, and not to worry about any other expenses. She would call her in Rome before the conference. She thanked her for the ride but said nothing more. Montana figured Gina had been used for more than sex. She was convinced Carlo set it up so he could get to Montana during the night. For now, the less Gina knew, the better for her. Hopefully there would be an appropriate time to tell her in the future. Hopefully there would be a future.

Chapter 14

10:00 a.m., Tuesday, March 15

TONY REFUSED TO ACCEPT his new role as a fugitive, and so he drove Brenda's Acura out toward Sportsman Field. He tried to control his anger and channel it into purposeful thought. On El Sueno Road, he turned into the lot of Western Rifles and Guns. He wore jeans and a sweatshirt and pulled a baseball cap over his head. This was his "good old boy" disguise. Not that he needed one. He was quite certain no one knew there him.

He walked into the store and started browsing. The store was neatly laid out, with a huge assortment of weapons. He wasn't comfortable, felt out of place, but tried to act nonchalant. As he eyed some pistols under a case, a salesman approached. He was a thin man wearing wire-rim glasses, a checkered shirt and cotton pants. He looked like a hardware salesman but could easily have worked at a library as well. He had a gentle demeanor and greeted Tony courteously. "How do you do? Is there something in particular I can help you with?"

"Actually, I've been thinking about getting a little protection for home." Tony looked up from the case, and the salesman nodded his head in affirmation as though to validate Tony's position. Tony went on, "This drug legalization thing's got me a little nervous. I don't need no drugged-out crazies messing around my home. I think it's just a matter of time before things get out of hand."

"Actually, you're not alone. They say crime's been down some with this new experiment, but we think there's going to be a turnaround as more and more people mess themselves up on drugs. For home protection, you're probably best off with a shotgun." This was so matter-of-fact to him, just as discussing surgery was for Tony.

"Well, that might be good for me, but I'm also interested in getting a gun for my girlfriend. I don't think she'd handle a shotgun too well," he offered.

"Maybe not, but we have several guns that she could handle. You ought to bring her in so we can talk to her and see what suits her best." This man was very polite and no-nonsense. Leaning over the case, he pointed out a few of the pistols that were popular. "We sell a lot of Berettas here. This one's a 92FS – a nine-millimeter semiautomatic for around five hundred. It's a good gun, packs a clip. It's a little aggressive for a lady, but if she's strong, she can handle it."

Tony stood there nodding, getting a firsthand lesson he had never really thought of getting before. The salesman then continued. "This Smith and Wesson .38 is actually a good little gun for home protection. It's easily concealed, so the cops like it. Good stopping power for someone in a jam. It runs around three-forty, so it's pretty popular. She really needs to get a feel for the gun. Ideally, get over to the range and see how it feels to fire it."

"That's probably fine for her," Tony said, pointing at the Smith and Wesson. "Is there any way I can buy the gun for her and have it registered to her?" He made the question sound innocent enough.

The salesman responded as though Tony wasn't completely off the wall. "Actually, it's not unusual for husbands and boyfriends to come in for protection for their wives and girlfriends but prefer not to buy the guns themselves. We just need to do a background check on her. She needs to come in, get fingerprinted and we run the check. The weapon's hers in three days."

"Jeez, what a hassle," Tony said, somewhat surprised. "I'll never get her in here. Is there any way of doing it without her? She's not really too excited about the idea. I know if she has the gun, then she'll go to the range and learn how to use it. But I can't get her to come in. I had some bankruptcy trouble, and I don't really want to go through the check process myself."

The salesman knew Tony was lying but seemed to understand his little euphemism. He bit his lower lip slightly and then rubbed the back of his head. "Well, I might be able to help you out. It depends."

Tony reached into his pocket and pulled out eight hundred dollars in cash. "Well, I figured it would probably cost me a few dollars for the gun as well as the security clearance. I can give you her name, address, Social Security number and anything else you need."

Staring at the cash, the salesman took some keys from his belt, and opened the case next to them and pulled out the Smith and Wesson .38. He placed it on the counter. "This is easy to load and has good trigger feel. There's not too much recoil, but she has to learn how to shoot it. At three-forty, it's a great price. We might be able to get by with the security match, but it will cost an extra three hundred. I need to go through the 'proper channels' to get a hold of her prints so I can get clearance for her. Once she's clear, we can gift-wrap it and you can take it to her. What do you think?"

"Sounds like a lot of money, but for her security, it's probably worth it." At that point Tony pulled out a card from his wallet with Brenda's background information on it. He gave it all, including her mother's maiden name. He then counted out six hundred dollars, put it down on the counter and reached into his wallet for another fifty. "How do I get you her fingerprints?"

"We work closely with the Santa Barbara P.D. It's not hard to access the DMV files for prints, if necessary. Then the police can run the background check and complete the file. If she has any problem, I won't be able to issue this weapon, you understand." Tony nodded while the salesman completed his comment. "In that case, I'll refund the money on the gun, but not the security fee. Understood?"

Tony then replied, "No problem. Brenda's clean. She's a good girl. I just want to make sure she has protection. There won't be any problem."

"Okay, then," he said, pulling a pad out and jotting down the information. "Here's a receipt for the gun. Come by in three days, next Monday or Tuesday, and we should be set."

Tony took the receipt, folded it and placed it in his wallet. "Thanks. I'll see you next week then." That was it. The transaction was made.

Tony drove back to Brenda's with his eyes looking in the rearview mirror more than straight ahead. He didn't need anyone following him back to Brenda's.

He was surprised that he would be able to get a weapon for someone else quite that easily. These guys wouldn't have any trouble getting Brenda's fingerprints and even her signature. Once done, it would look like Brenda had bought the weapon herself. Once he picked up the gun, anything that happened with it could potentially be linked to Brenda. If Tony shot someone and the weapon was recovered without his fingerprints, how would he be directly linked to the gun? Someone at the gun shop would have to identify him as the purchaser. That would be unlikely, because that person would then lose his license. He would probably just show a receipt and not offer any other knowledge about the transaction. Brenda, on the other hand, could find herself arrested for murder.

Tony understood that real criminals usually used untraceable items for committing crimes. It probably wouldn't be that difficult to find out that Tony had actually purchased the gun for Brenda. But, in this case, the police could have been complicit with the gun shop. It didn't seem farfetched that Ramsey received partial ownership in exchange for police favors. Nothing was too obvious, and as the salesman said, if she didn't check out, then no deal. So these guys were anxious to deal but didn't want to leave themselves at all vulnerable.

As Tony pulled into the garage, some of the nervous excitement from his gun shop encounter wore off. Suddenly the picture cleared up.

Tony burst through the front door seeking Brenda. She had taken back control of her couch from where she read the morning paper. "Weissman was murdered," he announced.

She looked up at him. "And how did you find this out?"

"Look, Weissman didn't like guns. This guy was coming into his prime. He wanted to have sex with those women, not murder them. Someone bought the gun and had it registered under his name. This thing had been planned. The gun was purchased for Weissman as though he had bought it himself.

They were all in it together. Whoever was behind thwarting the program had set up the purchase. The store salesman just wanted to make a sale. He didn't care where the piece went. But the cops, Ramsey in particular, facilitated the sale of the weapons."

"And how do you know this?" She began to sound like a teacher or a mother.

"I just bought you a gun. Oh, they have to check you out, but that won't be a problem. We'll have it by the end of the week."

"So how does that mean Weissman was murdered?"

"These guys all need the illegal drug trade to stay in business. The dealers, the gun stores, the rehab centers, even the cops all need illegal drugs around in order to flourish."

"Your implications sound good, but it still doesn't prove he didn't do it. By the way," his new roommate added, "call Spencer. You just missed him."

Tony got Spencer on the phone right away. His familiar voice was excited. "Guess who's coming to dinner," he said, "I hope you'll be able to entertain a few people. I'm coming out with Hansen and two of his best agents."

"How in the world did you get into this picture?" Tony couldn't see why Spencer was involved in this investigation.

He promptly told him. "Are you kidding? This may be one of the hottest news stories of the year. I've been with the network long enough that when I tell them something's big, they let me go. We'll call you when we get in. We'll be there sometime tonight and meet you at Brenda's."

This left Tony surprised and relieved at the same time. He couldn't hang out much longer without being spotted. If someone didn't come to his rescue soon, he wouldn't be any match for the "organization." "Frankly, Spence, I'm glad they believe this thing's serious enough to follow my lead. I'm not sure you want to get mixed up in this, though."

"Don't worry. I have no intention of getting mixed up in this. I'm strictly along for the ride in case there's a story to report. Believe me, I don't want any of your friends to know anything about me."

Brenda looked at Tony while he talked with Spencer. He couldn't wait to tell her about the meeting they would soon be having at her place. Then he realized he still hadn't told Spencer about the gun shop. When he finished, he waited for Spencer to chime in something like, "Oh, Hansen expected that." Instead the line was silent. "Hey, are you there?" Tony asked.

"I was just picturing your situation. You're sitting in the middle of a mess. It's one thing that there may be drug dealers who don't like the experiment. But you have gun stores, and police, and rehab centers, and God knows whom else wanting to pull the whole thing down. Then again," he said with a pause, "this just might be about some really bad cosmetic surgery."

"Thanks a lot. I'm sure I'll have a real belly laugh when I look back on this a year from now. I'll see you later." Tony smiled to himself at the good fortune of having such a good friend and then simply said, "Thank you. Have a good flight."

He hung up and looked over to Brenda to give her the good news. "Oh, dear," he sang out, tongue in cheek, "I'm having a little company over tonight. Not exactly a dinner party. Maybe light hors d'oeuvres. It's the Washington contingency."

Brenda looked at him a little fish-eyed. "Okay, what's up?"

"Spencer's coming to town with a few FBI guys. They've done some homework, and I just gave Spencer a little more fuel for the fire. They know I don't have a lot of time, and I need someone I can trust that can help. It's my best bet."

"They're not planning to sleep here, too, I hope?" Brenda had some obvious apprehension about his plans.

"It'll be okay. Ritz crackers and some cokes. I don't know. What do you think the bureau boys will like? Maybe it's not a bad idea to have a few things around while we meet."

"Don't worry, Tony. This won't be the Last Supper. I'll pick up a few things at the market."

"Oh, good. It'll be my turn to watch the couch while you're gone."

Chapter 15

11:30 a.m., Tuesday, March 15

BRENDA HADN'T BEEN GONE ten minutes when her phone rang. After the fourth ring, Tony heard Rick Santiago calling out, "Tony, pick up the phone."

Tony quickly retrieved the hand piece and asked, "What's up?"

"Great, you're there. Open up your e-mail. You've got to check this out." Rick was breathing quickly; it sounded like he'd been running.

"Where have you been? You sound out of breath," Tony asked.

"I am. I practically sprinted back from Secretary Vincent's office."

"The Secretary of the Treasury, Thomas Vincent?"

Still puffing, he replied, "None other."

"Okay, here you go." Tony's e-mail came on screen, and he clicked to the first entry. "Oh, Jeez, you sent it from Vincent's office. Are you crazy?"

"It's okay. You're also working for the government. I just couldn't send it from my terminal. Check it out. Look at those numbers."

Tony clicked on his e-mail and perused the information. R.J.'s Hardware came up first, with a month-to-month listing of deposits and debits for the last eighteen months — right up until yesterday's postings. Tony scrolled down the computer right through Pacific Garden's account, down to Bertolini's and finally to Recovery West.

Deposits for Bertolini's didn't seem terribly unusual. Over the last year, business had been recording monthly deposits in the neighborhood of $75,000 per month. He had no way of knowing whether that was significant. There were a couple of months where they brought in an excess of $100,000. In fact, in December, they must have really nailed down the holidays, as they recorded deposits of $135,000. January was a very slow month, recording less than $25,000. February was even slower, and March had yet to show any deposits. A year ago at this time the deposit activity had been twice as strong in January and February.

"Montana's right on target with this Bertolini store," Tony noted.

"What do you think of the other stuff?" Rick asked.

Again Tony scanned the reports. Pacific Garden had shown deposits averaging around $35,000 most of the previous year but had slowed down a bit in the fall and surged mildly in December and January. February registered one of its largest deposits in the last eighteen months. R.J.'s Hardware had done a more consistent business throughout the previous year, with a slight gain over the previous January and February.

"Pacific Garden and R.J.'s are holding steady, but look at Recovery West. Not a bad business. Most of its deposits were around $1.5 million. The first two months of this year, the deposits were barely $400,000."

Rick wasn't surprised. "Based on how you set up the program, you knew Wesley's rehab centers would take a hit."

Tony kept looking over the files. "So where's Frascati's account?"

Rick hesitated shortly. "Yeah, let me tell you about that one. First of all, it took me a while to find the account. It's with the First Montecito Bank. This is one of those small institutions loaded with old East Coast money. The board of directors is a who's who of blue-blood industrialists and retired politicians.

"Instead of letting me talk to a clerk, they give me the damn manager. This Margolis guy treated me like I just crashed some debutante's ball. I go through the explanation and can hear him pounding a keyboard. Then he says

'Oops, got a little glitch here. This account's got security coding, meaning no one can enter without a special pass code.'"

"Security coding for a restaurant? Isn't that rather peculiar?" asked Tony.

"That's what I wanted to know," Rick agreed, "but these bureaucrats love to toy with you. He had nothing to offer. Security codes are usually given to companies working on classified material."

"Top-secret cannelloni," Tony interrupted. "Must be a real threat to the country if the recipe gets out. Okay, so who's got the pass code?" Tony asked. "Is this it — all these numbers and SC6471G04?"

"Not exactly. That's the account number and the security code. In order to open the account, you need a special password to get in. The security code just tells us it was registered as number 6471, a general legislative request in 2004. Even on Vincent's computer I couldn't find the code. He did have a list, though, of sponsors for the individual codes. I assume if he needed to get in, he could subpoena the sponsor, but we sure can't."

Tony closed the laptop. "So who's the sponsor?"

"The original request was placed with Senator Winston, but he turned it over to Congresswoman Phillips. So one of three people can get you the information, and the one that would probably do it is dead."

"Obviously Emilio isn't going to let us in, nor would we want him to know. I don't know Winston well enough to ask him or trust him." Tony then thought of something. "If I can find Leslie's computer, maybe I can find the pass."

"Oh, man, Tony, do you think it's necessary?" Rick sounded concerned, and Tony appreciated it.

"I don't know. I just know something's very wrong, and there's a good chance I'll be dead before anyone finds out why. I've got to get into Leslie's computer. Do you know she sent me e-mail from Weissman's house the day she got killed?"

"So you think you can walk over to Weissman's, let yourself in and pick up her computer. I can assure you that computer has become the property of the FBI." Then Rick added, "Sorry, I didn't mean to rain on your parade."

"I don't think you did, but there might be another option. Rick, I might need your help again. Anyway, thanks for all of your work."

"Call me if you find anything. If we have to, we'll get a subpoena through the Treasury Department. Bueno suerte, amigo."

"Thanks, hombre. Hasta luego."

Ten minutes later Tony closed Brenda's front door and walked to the cab he had called. It was only a ten-minute ride to Leslie Phillips' condominium, but he'd be insane to drive his own car anywhere.

When he arrived, he found the neighborhood quiet with few cars on the street. He figured there'd be a fair amount of activity still going on. Perhaps the investigation was waning. He pressed the security button for her unit, and no one answered. He proceeded to buzz a couple of people before one of them finally let him in under the pretense that he needed to drop off a package.

Located in the rear of the complex, her townhouse unit had a nice view of the ocean from the top floor. There was a small garden patio and a balcony above it that led to her study.

Tony walked up to the front door, where he read a note advising that the unit was off limits because of an investigation in progress. The door was locked, but he rang the bell anyway, just in case someone was there. He then hopped a small fence and tried the sliding glass door that opened onto the patio. A security bolt held it firmly in place. No chance through there.

He backed up and looked at the balcony. There were a set of double French doors and a separate window that opened to a modest patio balcony bordered by a couple of ficus trees and several pots of impatiens.

Tony looked around and didn't see any neighbors. He hoped they were busy at work like he should've been. He moved a patio chair over, got up on it and reached the bottom edge of the balcony. He didn't have much to grip onto until he pulled himself up high enough that he could grasp a metal rail and pull himself up. He climbed over the rail and went straight to the doors. He didn't expect them to just open, but they did give a little. He checked the window and found it securely locked. He tugged on the doors again and saw that the stationary door was not firmly bolted at the top. He grabbed the knob and pulled with sufficient force that the door gave way, splintering the wood housing on the baseboard with a loud cracking sound. He didn't wait to see if anyone noticed, but instead quickly ducked into the house, closing and locking the doors behind him.

Tony had been to Leslie's place on several occasions while they were setting up the program. She lived very tastefully but certainly wasn't extravagant. Remains of dark smudges from the fingerprint powder could be seen all over the room. He wondered what the FBI or cops were dusting for. Was it a real investigation, or were they just trying to make it look real?

He carefully scoured her desk. Damn, she lived with that laptop computer. They were so quick and had so much capacity that few people needed stationary modules any more. She did have several peripherals, a power cord, a scanner, a printer, and some speakers. Gone was the external hard drive. Tony hoped he'd find a backup file.

Obviously someone had already been there. The desk was clean except for the print powder. He walked over to the bookshelf and found a number of disks. There were several CD programs for the computer, a number of movies and some personal items. He pulled out a few of the personal CDs and read the covers. "Recipes and Restaurants" and "Vacation Spots," he read to himself. He recalled when he had worked with her that she would back up her personal data on "Vacation Spots" and congressional information on "Recipes and Restaurants." When he asked about that, she told him it was "just in case." At that time, he figured "in case" she had been robbed, not murdered.

He grabbed both of the disks. He went downstairs and let himself out through the front door, walked two blocks down the street to a pay phone and called a cab.

Back at Brenda's, Tony set up his laptop. He opened up her files for Recipes and Restaurants. There were dozens of files for legislation, congressional records, contributions, committees, and so on. Tony looked at the code, SC6471G04, and tried the easy route, bringing up "FIND" then typing in the code and "enter." He watched the screen expectantly, but nothing came up.

Now the hard way. Well, maybe not too hard. He noticed a file titled "applications." He double-clicked and it was open. He found another file titled "2004." Double-click and bingo. He stared at a list of all the programs and applications that had been requested in 2004.

There it was. "Frascati - 2004." Double-click. The file opened with a synopsis of the application. Frascati's Restaurant requested financial security protection in March 2004. The request was approved by the Department of Agriculture. It cited problems with "unfair pricing from competitive produce and food supply companies." The restaurant claimed that it was suffering from anticompetitive pricing and that other neighboring restaurants were getting lower price benefits. The proposal was recommended by Senator Charles Winston and sponsored by Congresswoman Leslie Phillips. So where was this password he needed to get into the account? She had to have it, but where would she keep it? Clearly, Leslie cleverly kept a separate file for that information.

Tony found a file called "Constituent Info" and opened it. The subfiles were divided into regions. He opened "Santa Barbara" and found Frascati's. "Okay, maybe now we're cooking," Tony said to himself. He opened that file and found information on Emilio, the dates of fund-raisers, copies of thank-you letters, the number of employees and contributions made, but nothing about bank information. He closed the file and went back to the general menu again. All of the obvious files were devoid of the information he sought. Tony looked through the file names again, hoping something would have some meaning. There were dozens of files on financial and legislative programs. He couldn't go through every file looking for a clue. He thought maybe he should ask Rick to have a subpoena ordered, but suddenly he saw the file "Games."

"Damn, I can't believe I missed it," Tony said quite indignantly as he clicked open the Games file.

The file had a list of games, some of which Tony recognized. It seemed strange to find these in her file, but he figured it was just some light-hearted stuff for the staff. He dragged through the menu and highlighted the game Password. Then he said, "God, it's so obvious I can't believe it took so long to think of it." Tony opened up the file to Password, and instead of the popular word game coming up, another file with multiple listings developed. The categories included business, personal, national, state, local, and constituent. Tony held his breath and clicked away. It was scary to realize that so many serious passwords might actually be hidden in a meaningless "game" section.

On the other hand, this was a good place to hide the obvious without being suspected of hiding anything.

Tony went straight for the constituent file. Almost glaringly clear in the list of constituents was the name Frascati. He clicked open "Frascati" and read out the password command. He grabbed a pen and paper and jotted it down: pw\ef*1011sbc\89-1777\0948-28743.

Working backward, Tony figured he had the account number, then the bank number, and then the password. Actually, it was a fairly simple password. It was probably Emilio Frascati, star, 1011, maybe his birthday or something, then sbc for Santa Barbara, California. Simple enough for Emilio, but even a serious hacker would have better things to do than guess at this code.

Tony called Rick immediately. The phone rang through, and once again there was that familiar "Santiago." Thank God, Tony thought.

"Okay, Rick, I've got it. I've got the password. Can you open up the files with it?" Tony gave him the code.

"How much information do you want?" Rick asked.

"Let's start with January 2010 and work up to now. Look at the balance sheet for total deposits, total debits, and total gross."

"Stay on the line. I'll do this right now." Tony could hear him tapping on his keyboard.

"Okay, here we go. Jeez, we're in the wrong business. Look at this. They're bringing in $1.8 million with debits of $520,000. Wow, not a bad profit for the restaurant business. And just for January." Clicking away, he reported on February and then proceeded month to month. It was consistent. The cash flow was tremendous.

"In August, they recorded 2.1 million against a debit of $540,000. Hold on to your hat. I'm looking at January 2011. Debits were still $500,000, but the deposits came to only $650,000. February '05 is pretty much the same. Give me a second. I'll send you a copy."

Tony looked at his computer screen. The "you have mail" icon soon flashed on.

"Okay, open your e-mail. It should all be there. I think the FBI will find this interesting."

Tony stared at the information on his computer screen. "I'll be damned," he said. "February debits were $494,000, and the deposits were $540,000. They're spending the same amount as they always have, and now they're clearing roughly twenty percent. Up till now they were cleaning up. Then in the first two months of 2011 their deposits are less than a third of what they had been. Is there any question as to what's going on?"

"We see this all the time," Rick said rather calmly. "Money laundering."

Chapter 16

1:00 p.m., Tuesday, March 15

Tony sat there with his head in his hand, staring at the numbers on his computer screen, when Brenda's phone rang. "Dr. Ryan, it's Joanna. Please pick up if you're there."

He lifted the receiver mid-sentence. "What's up?"

She had a cross between urgency and curiosity in her voice. "I just had a call from Sally McVee. She wants to talk to you. I told her you weren't in and I didn't know what had happened to you. She simply said to have you call when you checked in for messages. I told her again that we hadn't heard from you. She seemed to ignore it, as if she knew that wasn't so, and said, 'Have him call me.' What do you think?"

"Give me her number. I'll find out what's going on." Tony jotted down the number and said goodbye to Joanna. He dialed her number. He wasn't looking forward to talking to Sally and worried about putting her in any jeopardy by contacting her directly. Jimmy must have told her something.

Tony felt his apprehension rising as the phone rang. He considered hanging up, but then heard a simple "Hello."

He responded, uncomfortably, "Hi, Sally. It's Tony Ryan."

She came right to the point. "Tony, I know Jimmy was set up. He called me to let me know he'd be late. He always called when he was late, so I wouldn't worry." She paused, but barely, not wanting to give in to her emotions. "He told me he had pulled some type of explosive device off of your car. That's why I knew you were probably okay. He needed to finish in the lab and then he would come home. He wanted to stay and work on the Mason file, but I told him to just bring it with him instead."

"God, Sally," Tony spoke softly, shrouded by a blanket of guilt, "I dragged Jimmy into this thing. He was helping me out. I can't tell you how bad I feel."

"You can't blame yourself. Jimmy would have gotten involved eventually. There's no way he would have gotten out of this unless he was just plain stupid or didn't care. That's not Jimmy."

"How do you know he was set up?" Tony asked.

"Frank Ramsey came by to break the news. He told me what they suspected, you know, that Jimmy had been robbed. They took his cash and left his wallet behind. 'Was there anything else in the car?' I asked. He says, 'Just a bottle of wine on the front seat.'" She took a deep breath, composed herself and continued. "I know he was bringing home the Mason file, but Ramsey never mentioned it. Jimmy never had more than thirty or forty dollars on him. After he bought the wine, what did the guy get — fifteen or twenty dollars? This wasn't a robbery."

Tony finally spoke up. "I've been thinking the same thing. I knew about the file. Apparently someone in the department wasn't too keen on Jimmy knowing that an explosive device was planted on my car and the Mason's car. There may be more we don't know. The big problem, though, is that Ramsey's in the thick of it."

"Are you certain? My god, Frank has been like a son to Jimmy. I can't believe it." Sally was almost angry at the suggestion.

"I'm sure Ramsey didn't pull any triggers, and he might not have given the order, but he's involved with a group of people who are trying to undermine the drug program."

"That damn drug program. Honestly, we'd be better off without it. At least Jimmy would still be here." Then her tone softened a little and she added, "I just hope you know what you're doing."

"Please, Sally, I assure you the drug program is not the problem. This is about business. There's an awful lot of money involved."

Then she added, "I know you're in trouble. I never really thought anything like this would happen to Jimmy in Santa Barbara. I was so relieved the day he accepted the position out here. I wanted to come here so badly. I really pushed for it." Her breathing got deeper, and Tony could hear her fighting back tears.

"It's okay, Sally. It's not your fault. Believe me, I feel guilty enough. But we're not the bad guys. Jimmy didn't deserve for things to end this way." He could feel his anger welling up. The audacity of these people to take lives that got in the way of their business. This was the very thing that had compelled Tony to fight for the decriminalization of drugs.

Sally began to release a few sobs. "Oh, God. Look, Tony. Now you've got me started. Do you know we've been together since high school? The girls are really shook up, but it will be better when we're together. They're coming out tomorrow." She paused again, took another deep breath, and before she said goodbye, Sally added, "Whatever you do, please be careful."

He leaned back on the now-familiar couch and looked at the ceiling. He looked toward the heavens and gave a little thanks that at least Montana was thousands of miles away from all this. He'd call her in the morning, but in the meantime, he was getting pretty antsy holed up like he was a suspect. Time for some fresh air, he thought, and so he put on some sweats and went for a run. With a baseball cap and silver Oakley sunglasses to give him cover, he would be inconspicuous in this land of runners.

The cool breeze off the ocean chilled him enough that he was glad to be wearing his sweats. He started slowly down Cabrillo, heading toward the zoo. He generally enjoyed this run. A few boats sailed out in the bay. A group of guys played volleyball in the sand. Several mothers and nannies watched their children playing on the jungle gym areas set up in the park. Life seemed pretty normal, and the Santa Barbara throng enjoyed it in its Southern California way.

As he ran past the zoo, he had to chuckle at the giraffes, remembering the one with the crooked neck that had recently died. He picked up his stride as he warmed up and finally felt at ease. He crossed on to the bike path around the lake by the bird refuge and stayed to the side out of the way of the occasional cyclist. As he came toward the curve where the trail started heading inland, he saw several patrol cars with lights flashing. He continued jogging closer to the apparent police activity. Then he saw another car, which he recognized as the brown unmarked car he had seen yesterday.

By the side of the hill, three or four officers combed through the thick brush. Another officer stood by the door of his car with a radio transmitter in hand.

Tony stopped jogging and walked over to the area, where a small crowd had gathered behind an area cordoned off with yellow caution tape. Then he saw the body of a woman, her skirt hiked up around her waist. She wore high heels, she had long shapely legs, and her black panties were clearly visible. Her arms flailed at her sides, with her head turned awkwardly to the right and arched back. There was an officer standing above the body, while a plainclothes cop knelt down by her side, his back facing the crowd.

Tony walked behind the crowd and to the side to get a better view.

The standing uniformed patrol officer then shouted out, "Hey, Coop, what a waste. This was a beautiful woman, no?"

The plainclothes cop lifted his head but made no comment.

"Sorry, A.T., I didn't mean to offend you," the patrol officer responded a little meekly, turning away.

Tony moved to get a better look at the victim. There appeared to be a trickle of blood running down the right side of her forehead. Lying down the way she was, he couldn't see her that well, but she looked familiar. Then he saw, wrapped around her neck off to the side above her right shoulder, a large amber cross. It was his patient, Diane Turner, one of the women who had lied to the medical board and charged him with misconduct.

Tony stood there almost in a trance when the detective, Cooper, stood up, brushed himself off and turned toward the crowd. He might have been ten feet away from Tony, and for but a moment, their eyes, both behind sunglasses, seemed to lock. Tony definitely recognized him from his photo and knew it was the second man he had seen yesterday. Thankfully, Tony went unrecognized, and Cooper merely continued on to his vehicle.

The coroner's van approached. An officer walked directly in front of Tony and put his arms up to separate the crowd while the coroner came forward with the stretcher behind.

Feeling a little safer behind his sunglasses and hat, Tony casually walked back to where Cooper stood talking with one of the patrolmen. He watched as Cooper held her purse open and perused the items.

"Who'd want to shoot such a fine-looking woman in the head?" the officer asked.

"Maybe she was married," Cooper sarcastically replied. "Hey, looky here. Dr. Tony Ryan." He pulled one of Tony's business cards from her purse. "It's got a note on it: 'Call Cal. Med Board re: unprof. conduct.' I know Ryan's office was looking for him. Maybe this is why they can't find him. We'll have to bring him in for questioning if he shows up."

Tony couldn't believe his ears. Someone had killed Diane Turner, and Cooper already found a way to implicate Tony.

He decided to move on. He resumed his run, heading back to Brenda's house. He started out slowly enough so as not to call any attention to himself. After a few minutes he picked up the pace, no longer running peacefully, but simply running scared, away from imminent danger. He just wanted a safe place to hide, and soon he was nearly sprinting. In the background he heard the siren of an approaching police car. He looked back and could see the lights flashing in the distance as the car quickly gained on him. He started to panic and involuntarily picked up his speed, knowing it was only a matter of seconds before he'd be stopped and questioned. Hell, he was going to be arrested, he knew it, charged with the murder of Diane Turner.

The sirens grew louder, almost coming to a crescendo in his head. His breathing became more labored, not from running so hard but from the panic that gripped him. Then the car pulled alongside of him, and he glanced toward it, only to find that both officers had their eyes straight-ahead, unconcerned with him as a jogging, drug-dealing murderer accused of unprofessional conduct. The car continued on, the sirens grew faint and Tony admonished himself to breathe more slowly and calm down. He wrestled his emotions to a draw, at one point even laughing, realizing that the cops might have pulled him over for simply trespassing on the bike path. He resumed a more comfortable pace, and by the time he got back to Brenda's he had a clearer vision of what he needed to do.

As he emerged from the shower, he heard the front door slam shut. He checked the bathroom clock, which read 1:17 p.m. He quickly dried off and threw on some jeans and a t-shirt. He poked his head into the kitchen, relieved to find Brenda unloading a pile of groceries.

"So what's the word, Doc? You want to rent a couple of movies while we're waiting for the good guys? I can whip up a mean bean dip."

"I've got another idea," Tony replied.

"I don't think I want to know."

"Come on. Grab your car keys. We've got to pay a little visit to Sally McVee, and if you're a real good girl, I'll take you to visit the police department."

On the way over to Sally McVee's, Tony explained everything he knew to Brenda.

"I'm really sorry for dragging you into this thing. I don't exactly have the Midas touch as of late, but I really need your help, and believe me, I appreciate it."

They slowly drove up the hill, passed the house on purpose to make sure it wasn't staked out with cop cars and then turned around and parked out in front by the curb.

He had brought Brenda along for moral support.

Tony rang the bell a few times before Sally got to it.

"Surprise, I'm back," Tony said, noticing the dark baggy circles under her eyes from crying, "and this time I brought my friend Brenda. Actually, she's my surgical assistant."

"Nice to meet you, Brenda," Sally said, cordially extending her hand. "Won't you come in?"

Sally led them into the living room. The furniture looked like it had lived its life in Boston during the Victorian era. A little faded in some areas, but put together with sturdy craftsmanship. A baby grand piano stood in one corner with a series of framed pictures decorating it. Tony walked over and looked at the photos.

"Who plays the piano?" he asked while admiring the family photos.

"Jimmy mostly tinkered. Both of our daughters took lessons."

Tony fixed his gaze on an old black-and-white photo of Jimmy and Sally with the two girls when they were preschoolers. He felt himself getting misty-eyed and then angry. There was a more recent picture of his daughters and grandchildren. "They really turned out very attractive, your two girls and their kids," he commented.

Sally walked over to the piano. She held up the recent photo. "We all met in Yosemite last summer. The grandkids had a great time with Jimmy, just like the girls used to when they were young. Deborah's still living back east outside of Boston, and Susan is married to her college sweetheart and living in Tucson." She smiled softly.

Tony changed the direction of the conversation. "Sally, was there anything that Jimmy told you about these investigations? Was he suspicious about any tampering with the drug program?"

"Not at all. He told me about your car, I think. I vaguely remember him saying something about he and Ron Sewell exploding the thing they found on your car. Also he said there were prints he needed to discuss with Frank Ramsey."

"I'd like to go down to the police station and look around for some of that information Jimmy had. I have to make sure it doesn't disappear, like the file might have. Do you have the keys to his desk or locker? If you give me a note, I'll go down and pick up all of his personal stuff. I don't think there's much they can do to me down at the station."

Moments later, Sally returned with the keys and a letter authorizing Tony to clear out Jimmy's personal belongings. "I hope you know what you're doing. Good luck," she said.

"Do you know what you're doing?" Brenda asked as she drove them down the hill to the police station.

"No, but it's definitely time to improvise."

They drove to the Santa Barbara Police Department and walked in together, unnoticed. That didn't stop Tony from looking at everyone he saw as if they were about to arrest him. Arrest him, he thought. That probably wouldn't be the worst that could happen.

They walked up to the duty officer, who happened to be a woman. Tony handed her Sally's note and studied her face as she read it. Her brown hair was pulled back into a ponytail. A hint of eye make-up accentuated her long lashes as she looked down to read the note. Though her uniform served to make her one of the team, her full figure could not be adequately concealed. She was a good-looking cop. She seemed genuinely concerned as she read the note from Sally. Her nametag read simply "Campbell."

She looked up and politely requested some identification. She looked at the photo on his driver's license and his name on the letter. "Mr. Ryan," she said, then cleared her throat in mock consternation, "or should I say Dr. Ryan?"

He knew that she knew about him. "Yes, it's Dr. Ryan."

"Well, do you know your office called earlier today reporting you missing? We're not supposed to file a missing-person report for forty-eight hours, but I've heard that several field officers have been actively seeking your whereabouts. Now you simply walk into the department to collect Detective McVee's belongings. Can I assume that you're all right and are no longer missing?"

"Oh, yes, absolutely. I went up the coast last night and had some car trouble. I coasted to a stop off the road and lost all power in my car, so my car phone was useless. I just slept in my car until morning. I had to hike miles to a station and buy another battery. I tried calling out, but the circuits were busy, so I figured my office staff would take care of everything while I got my car fixed."

She didn't seem to take the story too seriously, but it didn't matter. He hadn't done anything wrong. She excused herself to find another officer to accompany him on his mission.

Brenda looked at Tony obliquely, asking, "Okay, Dr. Watson, so what are you planning to find?"

"It depends on whether someone else has had a chance to go through his things. My guess is that everything will appear the way this Ramsey fellow wants it to look. Still, I've got to look. Maybe I can bump into this Sewell guy. Who knows?"

Officer Campbell came back with another cop. "This is Officer Hernandez. He'll take you down to the locker area and then to McVee's desk. You need to sign the log sheet here." She handed Tony a pen and pushed the clipboard with the log in his direction.

As he wrote his name and address, he froze momentarily. On the list, logged in at 10:42 a.m., was the name Diane Turner. Following her name, there was a simple entry æ "Possible witness, invest. Ramsey.'" Tony tried to maintain his composure, but it rattled his nerves to know Diane Turner's confidence in the police probably got her killed. Tony wondered if Wesley worked with the police.

He looked up and asked, "Because I don't want there to be any misunderstandings about anything I should retrieve from his locker, could we get another officer to go with us? You know, kind of an extra witness." He knew he was taking a chance being there at all, but at least with two officers it was less likely that he would be caught in a potentially isolated situation.

Officer Campbell saw one of the cops coming in from outside. Tony suspected she knew he was on his way to the locker room. She shouted out to him as he walked in, "Hey, A.T., you going downstairs?"

Tony turned around and saw A.T. Cooper, the same cop he had just seen out in the field two hours ago. "Yeah, what's up?"

The two men looked right at each other. Tony could tell that Cooper didn't recognize him by appearance. He had a casual air about him, clearly comfortable to be in his own environment. He barely looked up.

Then Campbell responded, "Dr. Ryan here has come to collect the belongings of Detective McVee, sir. Could you go down to the locker room with him and Hernandez?"

She might have thrown a bucket of cold water over him. His casual attitude had been put on alert. Even he was aware of the change, enough so that he tried to resume his casual demeanor. He then walked over to the front counter and came right up to Tony. Tony looked directly into his eyes. They were deeply set back, framed by a cheekbone prominence made harsher by the gaunt nature of his face. Tony wondered what he'd looked like as a kid.

"Too bad about McVee. The guys feel real bad about it. He was really well liked." He then saw Hernandez coming around to the side door and said, "I can take him down myself if you want."

Hernandez stopped momentarily and looked up. Tony responded, "Actually, I requested that at least two officers be present so we can accurately record the contents of the locker and his desk. Personally, I wouldn't mind if the whole force came down."

"Well, then, let's go check it out," Cooper said as he turned and pointed the way.

Tony wasn't very comfortable with the situation at hand, but how much trouble could he have in the middle of the police department? He turned to Brenda and said, "I'll be back in a couple of minutes."

He then followed Cooper and Hernandez down the hallway to a staircase. The stairway went halfway down to a landing and then made a U-turn leading them to a corridor, where they proceeded to a door on the left simply marked "Men's Locker Room." Hernandez used his magnetized ID, slipped it into the lock and opened the door. Tony expected a locker room like the ones in high school or an NYPD precinct from the movies. He should have remembered they were in Santa Barbara. The room was carpeted, clean, and professionally decorated. It looked like an upscale health club. Several officers were in the midst of changing and showering, either coming or leaving. He felt a little more at ease, thanks to the presence of multiple "witnesses." He followed Hernandez to a bank of lockers, where he stopped and pointed to number 47. A simple label, "McVee," could be seen right under the number. He pulled out the key that Sally had given him, unlocked the master lock, and opened the door.

As he opened the locker he saw a picture of Sally and Jimmy taken in Hawaii taped to the inside of the door. Jimmy loved Hawaii. He often talked about retiring to the Big Island, where he spoke about the absolutely incredible fishing off Kona. He always got into the same dumb argument with his fellow cops as to whether the fishing was better off Kona or Cabo San Lucas. Below that picture was one of each of his daughter's families. Tony recognized Deborah with her two sons and Susan and her daughter. Tony looked back at the officers. Hernandez bit his lip and gently shook his head. His eyes glazed over with the hint of a tear. Cooper, on the other hand, scanned the locker not appearing concerned with any personal memorabilia.

Tony reached in and started with the items on the top shelf. The first thing he pulled out was a grease-smudged page. Tony looked at it long enough to read the words "Print match — Michael Cirrelo." Cooper, looking over his shoulder, quickly removed the item from his grasp.

"This appears to be official police documentation. I'll have to take it," Cooper demanded.

Even Hernandez looked surprised by the harsh action.

Tony responded with control, "No problem. Mr. Hernandez, please log in "One official police document; print match — Michael Cirrelo."

"Excuse me," Cooper indignantly replied, "this is not a personal effect that needs to be logged in."

Tony stood firm, almost nose-to-nose with Cooper. "This is why I asked for two cops. I insist that everything we remove from this locker, whether I take it or not, is duly noted. I have no intentions of leaving here with or without belongings that are not accounted for. Officer Hernandez is simply logging these items into an official 'police' document."

Hernandez finally replied, "Sir, it's no problem. I don't mind."

Cooper had no option but to back down.

Tony picked through the other items and placed the personal ones in the tote bag he brought along. Nothing unusual. Simple toiletries, a couple of pens and a yellow writing pad. Cooper picked off the yellow pad before Tony could stow it. "There's writing on this pad. It should be turned over to the investigative team for evaluation," Cooper said matter-of-factly, and he set the pad to the side.

More curious to get his reaction than interested in an answer, Tony said, "I thought the murder was considered a robbery."

Cooper stayed quite composed, showed little emotion other than a slight disdain for Tony's presence, and offered, "Doctor, until it's fully investigated we can't ignore any information or possible evidence." He scratched his chin in a supercilious manner. "Who really knows what happened? Maybe McVee left us some answers."

Tony had an eerie feeling standing by the locker with a man he knew to have been complicit in Jimmy's murder. He most sincerely desired to bash him in the face. Instead, he turned his attention back to the locker, and they finished cleaning it out.

"Okay, if we're through, then I really need to run these items over to the crime lab." Cooper picked up the materials and took off.

Tony turned to Hernandez, saying, "How about his desk? Can I clean out his personal things now?"

He nodded and gestured to an exit door on the other side of the locker room. Tony followed him through a simple maze and back upstairs to a bank of desks. He walked him over to McVee's desk. Tony picked up one of the pictures of Jimmy and Sally and held it for a moment quietly before sharing it with Hernandez, who started to well up again, enough that he was uncomfortable and excused himself to take care of the paperwork in his hands.

In the brief moments of his absence, Tony looked through the desk. A small pile of files was neatly stacked on the left-hand corner. He quickly looked at the labels. About four or five down he saw one labeled "Mason, Robert." Clearly the file had been neatly returned to the desk. It appeared as if it had always been there. As he pulled the chart back a bit, he noticed a slight discoloration of the file. It had a very faint appearance of a brownish tint sprayed over the top of it, like droplets of grease or some type of residue. Without looking around, he tore off the top right corner of the chart and put it in his pocket. He quickly pushed the pile back together. By the time Hernandez had returned, he was back to collecting mementos.

"Do you know when they're planning the funeral?" Hernandez asked sincerely. Tony liked Hernandez. He seemed to be a genuine person who respected McVee and was clearly touched by him. Tony couldn't remember the last time there had been a homicide involving a member of the Santa Barbara Police Department.

"I don't know. I would think the department would probably contact Mrs. McVee. I suspect you might know before I do." Tony offered his hand. Hernandez took it and Tony said, "Thanks, Hernandez. Thanks for your time."

He walked out and found Brenda still talking with the duty officer.

"I'm not kidding. Liposuction is the easiest thing you can do," Brenda said. "And with your figure, what in the world are you doing behind this counter?" She smiled, reached into her purse and handed her a card. She caught up with Tony and smiled.

He looked down at her and asked, "Doing business?"

"It's a good thing somebody is," she quickly replied. "I'm beginning to think most people think you're just the head of this legal drug program. You got to get out there and let people know you have a regular job, too. Anyway, I think Officer Campbell wants to do her hips and thighs."

"Let's get over to the lab at Cottage Hospital. I've got to check something out," said Tony, thinking about the piece of the chart he had.

On the way over to the lab, he called Phil Stanton to ask him to stick around a few minutes. Stanton, the chief pathologist at Cottage, loved solving problems. He had spent several years working with Dr. Thomas Naguchi at Los Angeles County General Hospital. He had developed a reputation as a persistent no-nonsense pathologist. He would look for details that other competent experts would not consider. His competence was sometimes overwhelming, especially to the district attorney. Stanton often made cases difficult for the prosecution, not by intent but by his desire to find the truth. Stanton had saved a few innocent men from unnecessary incarceration when the DA had the cases all but locked up.

This chart had a slight tinge to it different from the others but similar to the grease smudged paper Cooper had removed in the locker room. He expected Stanton would confirm the substance. Brenda followed him down the hallway to the pathology lab. They walked into the pristine laboratory and found Phil in his office with his glasses on the table and his nose pressed to a microscope. He looked up and smiled, "Hi, Tony. Rarely see you around here anymore. I'm almost through here." He bent back over his scope and added, "Just finishing a review of a Moh's surgery. I've got to make sure the borders are clear. This sample looks good. It was a pretty aggressive basal cell carcinoma of the nose. Fred Jacobsen's been in the O.R. half the day chiseling this thing out. He's finally free and clear."

Brenda and Tony waited while he called in his report to Dr. Jacobsen. Then he put his glasses on and asked, "Well, what do you want me to look at?"

"Phil, I tore off this little piece of a police file. It had been sitting on

Detective McVee's desk in the middle of a pile. Unfortunately, McVee was murdered last night, and I think it has to do partly with this file. His wife told me he had picked up a file to bring home, but no files were found in his car."

Phil listened, but Tony didn't clearly register with him. He suggested, "Maybe he never brought the file with him. What would be such a big deal about a police file?"

Tony went on to explain, "Earlier in the day McVee uncovered some information that was contradictory to a police investigation. He was reviewing the chart and had information he wanted to add. I think there are other people in the department who don't want to see the file completed accurately. They'd like it to go back to its shelf. I need you to take a good look at this file cover. It has some kind of a stain on it. It's probably some residue from the auto lab, but I thought it wouldn't hurt to check. It looked different enough from the other charts on his desk. I'm pretty sure Jimmy had it with him and he did have some grease on his fingers. I don't know for sure what we're looking for. I'm just running out of time with this problem."

"Why didn't you just run the chart over to the police lab? They could have told you what you wanted to find out," Phil said. He still didn't understand why Tony was hassling over this file.

"Phil, I just don't know who to trust over there. I can guarantee there are some very disreputable persons among what must be a very fine force. Unfortunately, I don't know if it's two or twenty. And they're not going to let me in the lab, so I'd never know if they were telling me the truth. I didn't want to take any chances. Can you take a look?"

"Give me your sample. Let's start with the microscope." Phil took the small piece of the chart and slid it into place under the microscope. He peered into the lenses and then backed up and rotated around in his chair to some chemicals on the shelf behind him. He took a micro-pipette of a clear solution and dropped a microscopic amount onto a portion of the paper while looking through the lens. "Tony, take a look through the teaching lens."

Tony sat down on the chair across from him, adjusted the teaching arm on the microscope to his eye width and then looked into the lens. He needed a very slight adjustment to focus in on the specimen.

"Tony, being dry, it's difficult to tell what this is, but it doesn't have the emulsification or spreading properties of a petroleum product that you would expect from an auto lab. So I've placed some hydrogen peroxide on a tiny segment, and look what's happening."

Tony could see the reaction going on quite clearly and responded, "It's bubbling."

"Precisely. There is a peroxidase reaction, which means this sample is blood. If you like, we can harness some specimen and do typing or even a DNA spectrum. Of course, I'm not sure what we're looking for." Phil leaned back, waiting for Tony to fill him in.

Tony knew they would have to do further testing, but he was certain what the conclusion would be. "It will be Jimmy McVee's blood. He had the file with him last night when he was murdered. However, his wife was told of no such file. When he was shot, a very fine spray of blood probably landed on the file. Being nighttime, that went unnoticed. Wanting to remove the chart from possible investigation, the first investigating officer placed the chart back into McVee's desk pile. Since it had been checked out to McVee, it would have to be returned to his possession. If it remained in the car, it would surely lead an investigation team to a bad cop. The best bet would be to innocently lose the file back into the pile on his desk. His blood on the chart proves it was in his possession at the time of the murder and that it was improperly removed from the scene of the crime. Where do we go from here?"

Phil looked stunned. "Congratulations, Sherlock. I can run a blood typing on this specimen. If McVee was ever hospitalized, we might have some information on him."

"I know he was here at least several years ago. I saw him in the emergency room for a nasal fracture. I doubt you would have any blood typing from that visit, though." Nonetheless, Tony was still anxious to see what Phil could turn up.

He watched as Phil pounded on the computer keyboard and brought up the files on Jimmy McVee. As he scanned through them, he found an admission four years ago for questionable hematemesis. Apparently, according to the history, he had an upset stomach at home and vomited. He reported to the emergency physician that it looked like there was blood in it. The E.R.

doc, on the presumption of a possible bleeding ulcer or esophageal varices, ordered a round of lab tests, including blood type. McVee was A-negative, probably the least common type. Phil looked up at Tony and said, "This should be fairly straightforward. Give me five minutes and let me pull a sample for a simple blood typing."

Tony nodded as Phil got up and took the sample back into the lab. Brenda remained quiet. By now she had come to realize how deep the problems were, not just for Tony, but for the drug legalization program.

When Phil came walking back with a bounce in his step and nodding his head at the same time, Tony knew they had a match. "A-negative. So what will you do now?" he asked.

"Hopefully, they'll leave those charts on the desk for a while. At least long enough for the FBI to get hold of them." Tony looked at his watch. It was after three. Spencer would be arriving in a few hours. "Thanks, Phil. I've got a feeling you'll be hearing something soon. I hope it's good."

As Brenda pulled out of the hospital parking lot, Tony got an idea. "As long as I've blown my cover, why don't we head over to the DPC and see what's going on? I don't think anyone's going to just shoot me. They might blow up the car, but I doubt they'd shoot me."

"Oh, great. Just what I want to do is get blown up with you."

"When we get to the DPC, we'll leave the car with security. I think they're still on our side," Tony shrugged as Brenda gave him one of her "you better not be messing with me" looks.

They parked the car right next to the entrance of the DPC. The security guard started to signal them to move it, but stopped abruptly as soon as he recognized Tony. Tony spoke very cordially and explained their problem and concern. Besides, this would be a short meeting.

They went into the DPC. Tony flashed his security pass and led Brenda to the secured employee entrance. He swiped his badge, punched in his security code and entered with Brenda. They signed in with the security officer. As Brenda stood signing her name after she surrendered her license, the obvious occurred to Tony. Security was good. It was highly unlikely that someone had broken into the DPC from the outside to contaminate their product. And he still strongly doubted that any inside connection could be responsible for contaminating the product.

Brenda followed him to his office. Buchman, like a fixture, sat behind the desk working the computer.

Buchman looked up — startled, relieved and then concerned — all within two or three seconds. "Dr. Ryan, I'm glad it's you. I was afraid something had happened to you. Joanna said they couldn't find you. We've got some problems. Pretty big problems."

"What a surprise." Tony said, his manner appeared calm, condescending perhaps, but calm. "Now, Mr. Buchman, what else can be going wrong?"

"Mr. Felton, or rather FBI Agent Felton, has been all over the place. He's sent random samples to the FBI lab in Washington. They've found three cocaine samples contaminated with PCP." Buchman was a little frantic.

"Only three samples. I would have thought he'd find more. Must not be working very hard."

Buchman sat there, curious, with his head turned slightly at an angle.

"You look like my dog, Sunny, when I ask him a question. Must be a universal look," Tony said as he glanced over his shoulder at the computer. Then he asked, "Anything on the surveillance tapes?"

"Actually," Buchman said as his demeanor seemed to brighten a little, "we went over all of the lab cameras, and the place is clean."

"Could someone in the lab have altered the drugs off camera?" Tony inquired.

Buchman shrugged. "It's possible but highly unlikely. Everything's calibrated and all labels are computer-generated."

"Good. Maybe they won't be so quick to shut us down if we check out clean internally."

"Not just internally. We went over all of the tapes inside the rest of the building, the parking lot, the whole thing," Buchman continued. "About the only incident, if you could call it that, occurred when a couple of patrons bumped into each other."

"That's it?"

"Yeah. One guy leaving, the other coming in. Although one of them was one of the overdose victims. Anyway, even Felton dismissed it as a polite little bump and run."

"Let's take a look," Tony requested.

Buchman proceeded to bring the data up on the computer. Tony leaned over his shoulder and watched.

"You see," Buchman said as he froze the picture with Ralston starting to exit and the man in the tan sports coat striding in the opposite direction, "just a polite little mishap. The guy would have been luckier if the vial had broken when he dropped it."

Tony shook his head so slightly Buchman didn't notice. "The guy's as good as David Copperfield," Tony remarked, recognizing the same man who had come to his office yesterday. "So where's Felton now?"

"You missed him by five minutes. He planned on stopping by First Montecito Bank and then had a meeting later with the police department. Do you think they'll close us down?" Buchman was genuinely concerned for more than his own job.

"Well, there's enough of them trying to find a way to do it, aren't there?" Tony walked back toward the door. Then something struck him. "Where's Felton staying? Maybe I should pay him a little visit."

"He's staying on Burt Wesley's boat."

Tony was astounded. "You've got to be kidding."

"It's supposed to be really nice. A fifty-three-foot something with a flybridge. The *Reco West*. Strange name. Felton's been telling me all about it, even offered to take me out. He says he knows Wesley from way back."

"I know that boat. It's a major piece of hardware. Hang in there, Jeffrey," said Tony, starting for the door. "Keep the faith."

Moments later, Brenda drove Tony down to the yacht harbor.

"I don't get it, Doc. You think you're James Bond now, or what? What do you think you're going to find on that boat?" Brenda hoped Tony wasn't getting too carried away.

"Well, actually, I'd like to find Felton. Maybe he might like to have tea with me. He could tell me how he knows Cooper and Ramsey, and maybe he wants to take me for a cruise around the bay in Burt Wesley's boat."

Once they got to the yacht harbor, someone directed them to where

Wesley docked his boat. Tony and Brenda strolled down the dock and easily found the boat. They stood facing the stern, which read "Reco West."

A neighboring boat owner came walking by and politely asked, "You a friend of Dr. Wesley's?"

"You might say so," Tony answered, adding, "I'm looking for the fellow who's staying on his boat."

"Boat? That's not just a boat; it's a Monte Fino Flybridge Cruiser. He's got a great layout in there, too."

"What's a flybridge?" Brenda quipped. "That thing up there?"

"Right," the neighbor confirmed. "You get quite a view from up there, but you can drive the boat from below as well. Hope you find your man. See you."

As the man walked off, Tony headed for the boat. "Where are you going?" Brenda demanded.

"I'm not really sure. Maybe I'll get lucky." Tony hopped onto the craft and looked around. The Monte Fino was pretty well locked up. He looked through the windows and could barely make out a stack of papers on the table inside the cabin. He walked toward the bow and played with the forward hatch. After a little coaxing, he freed it up, and it opened.

Tony crawled headfirst in through the hatch, landing in the forward stateroom on top of a quilted queen bed. The neighbor was right. This wasn't a boat; this was someone's bedroom, complete with cherry wood cabinetry, fine fixtures and plush carpet. Jeez, Tony thought, Wesley did all right milking the addicts into recovery or whatever he did. A little envy, perhaps, but Tony shrugged it off and continued exploring. There were a couple of small closets and a nice-sized chrome-and-mirrored head off to the left, or starboard, or whichever nautical term he was supposed to be thinking in. He opened the door and walked up to the galley. He flipped through the papers on the table, but nothing struck a chord. He went back into the stateroom, closing the door behind him. He looked in the bathroom and just found an array of toiletries. However, in the closet, he found a large brown leather briefcase.

Tony pulled it out, placed it on the bed and snapped it open. It was filled with cash. There were hundred-dollar bills packed into bundles of five thousand. Tony riffled through the bundles, quickly counting off fifteen.

Directly under the cash was a large plastic bag sealed shut and labeled "Evidence." Inside was a videodisk. Also inside the case were a number of dark pharmaceutical bottles. They were stoppered but appeared empty and unlabeled. There were a few small vials held together with a rubber band. Again, there were no labels to tell Tony what they were. He slipped one of the vials out of the group and pried the rubber lid off. White powder. He sealed the vial and grabbed a couple of other samples from the case and buried them in his pocket. He wasn't about to do any taste tests just because he'd seen it in the movies. Just as he picked up some papers, he heard the engines start up. Quickly, he closed the briefcase and replaced it in the closet just as the boat pulled out, stumbling slightly before he regained his balance.

He crept over to the window, looked out and saw Brenda standing on the dock as the boat pulled out of the harbor.

Tony looked for a hiding spot. Except for a few women's articles, the other closet was empty. Rather than plant himself in there, he decided to crack the stateroom door and take a peak. Felton must have launched the boat from the flybridge.

He was relieved that there was no one in the galley. He went back into the stateroom and waited, occasionally sneaking a peek to see where they were headed. Hopefully, Felton had planned a late-afternoon cruise and would soon pull the boat into port. Tony figured he could sneak out when Felton showered or left the boat for dinner.

After several minutes, he realized they were headed toward an oilrig. Tony was afraid to even peek out of the window for fear someone might be watching from the rig. Having never actually been on one, he couldn't get over the enormity of the oilrig as they got closer.

Felton pulled the boat up alongside the rig. Tony heard someone calling for a line. A moment later the boat was secured and the engines were cut. Tony peaked out through the stateroom doors in time to see a pair of trousered legs start down the stairs from the flybridge. He then quickly retreated to the empty closet, from where he heard Felton enter the room and apparently snap open the briefcase. Moments later, he heard it snap shut again. He could hear Felton exit, first from the room and then off the boat onto the rig.

Tony started to walk out through the stateroom to see if he could hear what was going on. He eyed the briefcase and then opened it. It looked like Felton had removed nearly half the money.

Tony slipped out the back listening for sounds. It was quiet and no one was in sight. There was a steel ladder leading at least twenty feet up on to the rig. Tony quietly ascended the ladder. The oilrig looked like a giant Erector set with a platform way above him.

Except for some muffled sounds from above, it was quiet, suggesting this was a deserted rig. He continued to climb after Felton. As he got to the top, he slowly looked around but saw no one. He looked down to see the boat far below him, gently bobbing in the water. He heard Felton's voice and then another voice coming from an office several yards to the left. He silently moved down toward the office, stopping by an open window. He braced himself near the ledge and listened.

"Where's Cirrelo?" Felton asked.

"Mikey's playing tourist this afternoon. He asked me to meet you. I assume you've planted the drugs. So where's the money?" The man had a thick, deep voice, definitely East Coast.

"Yeah, the PCP's planted. Here's thirty-five grand. Let's get it done this time." A chair scraped along the ground, like he was going to leave.

"Hey, wait," the man shouted. "Cirrelo said you'd be delivering the whole seventy-five. What gives?"

"The old man decided to hold on to it until the job's done like it should have been in the first place," Felton said sternly, even annoyed.

"You saying we didn't do our job? Frascati never said to kill him. He said to make it look like a DUI, an accident, plant some drugs. We did that. We set him up real good. It could have killed him, but Frascati didn't want that."

"That's not what the old man wanted. He hates Ryan, and he's still around." Felton became increasingly irritated.

"Cirrelo told me they reported the guy missing. I figured his car went off the road, over the edge. I don't know how he got out. Maybe he's got an ejection seat."

"He didn't go off any cliff. The damn explosive was removed by one of the cops before he ever got in the car."

"All I know is we did our job. Frascati gave us the orders. I can't help it if the big boss decides he wants him dead now."

The boat banged up against the rig. It made fairly loud echo as the sound reverberated through the steel rig.

Felton quickly asked, "Are you alone, Salinski?"

Salinski responded, "I was wondering the same thing about you."

The two men then got up and made their way to the front door and out of the office. They looked right and left, seeing nothing. They then walked toward the edge of the platform and peered over the safety line, looking down below, where they saw the boat bob again and clang into the side of the rig.

Felton turned and started to head back. "Shit, you should have secured the boat better. Wesley's not going to like me bringing his boat back with dings in the side."

Heading back to the office, Salinski said to Felton, "I wouldn't worry about it."

Just before the two men had emerged from the office, Tony had lowered himself over the side of the platform and clung to one of the pipes under the walkway. There was nowhere else to hide. He hung there silently while the two men checked the deserted area. Fortunately, they turned back to the office without seeing him directly below their feet, because he couldn't hang on much longer. Still, he was glad he hadn't taken down his ugly chin-up bar. He hoisted himself back onto the platform and decided he'd better get back to the boat before they spotted him.

In the office, Salinski picked up his money and went through it again. He scratched the back of his head and looked at Felton. "I need the rest of the dough now. We won't have time to come around to the celebration party after this thing goes down. We want to be out of here before the blood dries."

"Look, I want to get out of here as much as you do. If you don't get lazy, you'll have no trouble getting this thing done tomorrow. Like I told you, Ryan's been to the police station today, so he'll be back in the office tomorrow. You'll get your chance to do it right then. The other forty will be waiting for you on your way out of town. The old man will let you know where," Felton said as he turned and left.

Tony waited in the stateroom. He heard footsteps on the upper deck, and then the engine started up. It idled for a while without moving, and then he heard Felton come down through the galley. He quickly hid in the vacant closet. The door to the stateroom opened, and he heard Felton move about the room, grab something and fling it on the bed. He heard the clicks of briefcase locks as they were opened. And within seconds he heard the footsteps exiting the room.

He waited, trying not to make a sound, afraid he might leave his hiding spot only to slip into Felton's grasp. When enough time had passed and there were no other sounds in the room, he slipped out of his hiding spot, where he found the briefcase on the bed, open and relieved of the rest of the money. The vials remained, as did the videodisk in the plastic bag. Tony picked up the plastic bag and read the label on the DVD: "Weissman 3/11/11." He took the bag with the disk and slipped it inside his shirt. The boat lurched forward, and Tony stumbled before he caught his balance. Tony walked over to the port side of the boat and looked out the window. Surprisingly, the boat now headed away from the docks. This didn't make sense.

Tony ventured out through the galley. He could see the oilrig fading in the distance as the boat moved farther away. He started toward the back of the boat, avoiding the stairs to the flybridge. He stepped up on the ledge of the stern, planning to climb up from behind to catch a glimpse of Felton, when the boat took a hit from the side by a swell. The sudden jolt sent Tony tumbling backward, turning to face the sudden impact of the cool sea. As he fell, he just managed to catch on to the guardrail and hold on while his feet slipped to the side and hung like a pennant in the breeze, just inches over the water. He took a deep breath and for the second time that day managed to hoist himself up, this time back into the craft.

He caught his breath. He felt the spray of the ocean and then something warmer than ocean spray. He looked down and saw something red spraying lightly against the back of the boat. He made his way over to the stairs and cautiously poked his head up through the opening to the flybridge.

Felton sat in the captain's chair and rested up against the wheel. Just then the boat was hit by another swell, but this time Tony kept a strong grasp on the ledge of the stairwell. Felton, however, was tossed like a rag doll right off the seat and onto the flybridge floor. His body fell with a thud, landing on his left shoulder within two feet of the stairwell, and his head whipped loosely directly at Tony. Tony reflexively jumped back as he saw Felton's opened eyes blankly staring from a head that had been sliced through the neck. Tony now saw where the red spray he had seen on the back of the boat barely a minute ago had originated. A trail of blood had pooled behind the captain's seat.

Tony gathered himself together and climbed up to the controls. He grabbed on to the wheel intending to turn the boat around when he spotted a box with blinking red numbers within the instrument panel. He didn't recognize it as a marine instrument, and it was positioned on the far side of the panel under an enclosure that he couldn't reach. The numbers continued flashing: 19, 18, 17, 16. He had seen enough. He turned around and grabbed a life jacket off the seat. He stepped up onto the cushioned area on the back of the flybridge and jumped off the starboard side, away from the speeding boat. It seemed like he remained in the air for several seconds before he finally hit the water feet first. The jolt caused him to momentarily lose the life jacket.

He came to the surface, looked right, then left, took two strokes and then with relief grabbed on to the jacket. He turned and watched the boat as it continued its course, by now more than a hundred yards away from him. Suddenly it occurred to him that he had just jumped off a perfectly good boat. Was he crazy? He was now five or six miles away from the shore with only a life vest. He looked at the shore and began to secure the life jacket. The boat zoomed away. Tony couldn't see it very well from his perspective, but he heard it explode. The first explosion made a sudden pop, but came a second explosion, this one even larger, as the fuel tanks got into the act and the ocean shook. Tony looked on in horror and then had the presence of mind to remove the partially secured vest and place it over his head while he waited for any possible debris to land. Hopefully, if such a missile was launched, the vest might shield his most vital organ.

When it seemed safe, he secured the life vest. He swam for several minutes, soon growing tired of the taste of saltwater. How did these people swim the Ironman races? The taste of the ocean bothered him more than the swimming, he thought.

Tony rested a moment and looked up to shore. A solitary vessel moved in his direction. He figured the Coast Guard would be on its way at any minute. As the vessel got closer, he recognized it as a fishing craft. As the craft neared to within fifty yards, he could clearly see Brenda standing on board along with Jackson Rhineholt. The sixtyish Rhineholt leaned up against a boom, looking ever his crusty old self. But he had also been one of Tony's favorite patients – at the moment, his favorite patient of all time.

As they got closer to Tony, Brenda called out, "Do you want a lift, or are you out for the exercise?"

Jackson Rhineholt acted a lot more sensibly. He simply threw Tony a float on a line. Tony swam to the float and they pulled him in.

As he came up the ladder, Rhineholt grabbed him securely and wrapped a thick towel around him. "That ain't much of a wet suit. This time of year the water's still too cold to go swimming without a good wet suit."

Brenda laughed out loud while Tony smiled and shivered.

"Say, Doctor Ryan, you want to take a look at my nose while you're here? Since you fixed it, I'm breathing fine. The missus don't complain about me snoring, and I'm sleeping like a baby." Rhineholt held his nose up to Tony as Brenda stood next to him.

Tony wrapped his wet arms around Brenda and Rhineholt and pulled them together. "I am so glad to see you two. I can't thank you enough." He gave Brenda and then Rhineholt a kiss on the cheek.

Old Jackson wasn't too sure about the good doctor. "We better move out of here before the Coast Guard decides they might want to question us," he said.

On the way back to Brenda's, Tony sat in an old mechanic's jumpsuit Jackson had found for him. The thing smelled like someone had died in it, but at least it was dry. He was fortunate Jackson even had anything. Otherwise he'd be wearing just a towel. His wet clothes sat in a plastic bag in the trunk.

He had managed to hold on to the vials and the DVD, which had fortunately remained dry in the plastic bag.

"There's some guy named Cirrelo who's been hired to kill me," Tony said to Brenda. "It's the name I saw on the print check I pulled from McVee's locker."

"That means some of those cops are probably working with Cirrelo. Obviously Felton was working with them," Brenda surmised.

"Can you believe Emilio Frascati set me up?" Tony still didn't want to believe it himself. "And there's some other bigwig who's pulling his strings."

"Don't worry," Brenda said. "If anyone finds you wearing that thing, they'll think you're already dead." Brenda opened both car windows, saying, "My poor car's gonna stink."

"If I survive this thing, I'll have it cleaned for you. If I don't, ask Montana to take it out of my life insurance."

Chapter 17

8:00 p.m., Tuesday, March 15

TONY STOOD IN THE doorway of Brenda's house, squinting through the peephole. Having showered and changed, he looked and smelled a lot better. On the other side of the door he saw Spencer, who looked roundly warped through the peephole.

"Sound the bugles. The cavalry's arrived," Tony grinned as he alerted Brenda.

Although he rarely saw Spencer more than a couple of times a year, he was one of Tony's best friends. He opened the door and greeted him with a warm hug. Ironic that Tony stood there hugging Spencer, as he had never been that affectionate with his friends, but Spencer was his hugging friend. The first time they met, Tony rolled on the floor with laughter as Spencer told of his recent weekend with an all-male encounter group in the woods. They were supposed to be coming to terms with those deep hidden emotions, the kinds women easily deal with and men easily suppress. Tony and Spencer had an instant chemistry. By the time they had finished dinner at a wonderful restaurant in D.C., they had bonded. At that time, they went to shake hands, and Tony proceeded to give him a big hug and a kiss on the cheek. He thanked Spencer for attending the encounter weekend because it had made it easier for him to deal with his hidden feelings. Now there were no hidden feelings, only relief as Spencer and his three FBI friends strode through the door.

None of them came out of central casting or were in stereotypical costume. One agent wore a charcoal Armani suit with a black t-shirt, probably silk. He looked very chic under the circumstances, but he didn't look like a tough FBI agent. He had a sweet, kind face, an engaging smile, and an even dark-brown complexion. Tony stood a couple of inches taller and hoped this guy's suit hid a muscular frame, because he didn't scare anyone by his appearance. He was a very good-looking guy, and Tony wasn't the only one to notice him. Tony smiled as he sensed Brenda's stare crossing his path from the other side of the room.

Another of the agents wore a Fila warm-up outfit and Nike running shoes. He was about five-nine, slightly stocky in build, with wavy, dirty blonde hair. He carried a black leather briefcase. He may have been in his late forties, but he looked like he had been an athlete. His nose looked like it might have caught a fist or two along the way. He had a very pleasant smile and looked at ease as he walked into Brenda's house. Tony assumed this was probably Mark Hansen.

A female agent rounded out the pack. Tony figured her to be in her late twenties or early thirties. At around five-six, she had dark, straight, shoulder-length hair parted to the side, with a clip holding back a section on the right. She had big brown eyes and full lips that needed no lipstick. Dressed neatly in her blue jeans and crew-neck brown sweater, she didn't need any help from Tony. She too carried a briefcase.

Tony started the introductions with Brenda. "Spencer," he said, "let me introduce you to Brenda Williams. I think you've met before, but it's been a couple of years." He turned to the contingency standing in the hallway and added, "Group, this young lady, my trusty surgical assistant, has graciously provided us her home as our central headquarters."

Spencer smiled and said hello to Brenda. Then he pointed in the direction of the agents and asked, "Mark, why don't you make the introductions?" He pointed back to Tony and said, "Of course, guys, this is our illustrious Dr. Ryan. Tony Ryan, director of the experiment and former cosmetic surgeon."

With Spencer's introduction, the Armani-clad agent walked over, stuck out his hand to Tony and said, "It's a pleasure to meet you, Dr. Ryan. I'm Mark Hansen."

Tony shook his hand and simply said, "Tony. To my friends it's Tony. And if you guys aren't my friends, I'm in worse trouble than I thought. Thanks for coming."

"Well, then, Tony," and Spencer began, pausing to look over to Brenda, then politely adding, "and Brenda, let me make the introductions. This is Special Agent Jonathan Singer." The fellow in the Fila outfit stepped forward and shook Tony's hand and gave him a courteous nod hello. He then walked over to Brenda and did the same. "Johnny's been with the bureau quite a while. He's seen about as much of the drug game as anyone. He knows the line on most of the major players. In fact, he's pretty sure we can trace your group back to the Sandoval family in Bolivia. Anyway, we both came up from Quantico longer ago than I care to remember."

Hansen then nodded to the other agent, and she walked forward toward Tony. "Dr. Ryan, I mean Tony, this is Special Agent Linda Cortez. Linda is second-generation Cuban, but she tells me she still knows how to speak Spanish." Hansen smiled, not sarcastically, but rather affectionately, and added, "She's a real sharp agent." Tony shook hands with her. She had a confident look in her brown eyes that reminded him of Montana. She walked over to greet Brenda.

While the howdy-dos were taking place, Tony looked over to Spencer and commented, "So much for stereotyping. I would picture you three in G.Q. or Glamour quicker than the cover of FBI Weekly, if there were such a thing. Anyway, I'm glad you're here. I hope we're going to be able to resolve a few things."

"That's what we're here for, Tony," Hansen quickly reassured. "Our initial goal is to establish the foundation for the apparent conspiracy and find out who all the players are. If all of our assumptions are right, then we'll have to set up some kind of trap. That may or may not be too easy. We suspect the outside pressure may be great enough to force their hand here in Santa Barbara. At any rate, rest assured we have plenty of back-up. I'm running this thing as a special-permission request because it's so sensitive. I appreciate your concerns about internal leaks and outside contacts with the bureau, so I've kept this effort strictly confidential. Only one superior knows we're here and has authorized this investigation. Maybe Johnny ought to call Felton and get him over here for a debriefing."

"I think I can save you a call," Tony injected.

"How so?" Singer asked as they gathered around Tony.

"Well, first of all, if Felton could tell you, he probably wouldn't want you to know that he helped plant contaminants in our labs. I found these vials in his briefcase. Here, you can have them. I suspect they'll probably test positive for PCP, but that's just my guess." Tony handed the vials over to Hansen.

"He probably wouldn't want to tell you that some guy named Cirrelo and his buddy Salinski have been poisoning some of the DPC clients. He probably wouldn't want to tell you about his connections with Cooper or Ramsey. But most of all, he definitely wouldn't want to tell you that he got Burton Wesley's Monte Fino Cruiser blown up after Salinski slit his throat trying to cheat him out of an extra forty thousand dollars. Yeah, I'm sure he didn't want that to happen."

"Whoa, you've been busy. What else do you know?" Hansen was genuinely excited by Tony's revelation.

Tony went over to the table by the couch and retrieved a DVD. "I found this in Felton's briefcase," he said as he handed it to Hansen.

"Weissman 3/11/05," Hansen read aloud. "Brenda, you got a VCR for our viewing pleasure?"

Moments later the six of them sat uncomfortably watching what amounted to a porno film. Weissman obviously set the whole thing so no one knew they were being filmed. Hansen fast-forwarded through some rather steamy scenes until finally the trio fell asleep, with Weissman in the middle.

While the tape of the sleeping group continued at fast speed, Tony observed, "Unless they took it earlier, no one got up for any cocaine. I saw them take a few hits on the grass, but no coke."

Two men suddenly appeared on each side of the bed. Hansen slowed the speed back to normal. The man on the left had a gun in his right hand, reached over Weissman and pulled the trigger, unloading a loud blast into the back of Phillips' head. With barely a second passing, he blasted the back of the head of the woman nearest to him before she could move. The audience of six audibly gasped at the violent horror of seeing two lives extinguished. They could only imagine the fright and confusion Weissman felt when he jumped up after awaking from the explosions while still clearly disoriented from his drug-assisted slumber. The film suddenly went to black.

Hansen spoke the obvious. "Well, at least this dispels the investigative report that Weissman committed the murders. I'd say it also implicates the gun shop."

"You figure that's Cirrelo and Salinski?" Tony asked.

"Unfortunately, you can't identify them on the tape, but it would be the most logical conclusion. These guys are serious pros. I think maybe we should sit down and start comparing notes. Let's go over the whole program and see what we've got."

For the next hour and a half, Tony retraced all of the information he knew, starting with the episodes over the weekend. The three agents and Spencer jotted down notes on yellow legal pads. Brenda kept everyone well fed and watered. More than once Tony watched her make eye contact with Hansen. Hansen returned her gaze, at first courteously, but later it seemed he caught on and became as interested in Brenda as she was in him. During one portion of Tony's recital, he actually paused and started over. He didn't want Hansen to miss anything while he and Brenda made goo-goo eyes during one of their brief and subtle flirtatious interludes. Tony might have been alarmed, but instead he laughed to himself because he found it comical and charming.

As Tony pored over the situation, he watched the agents for visual clues as to their perceptions. Hansen, aside from the occasional ocular diversion with Brenda, stayed right on top of the situation. He'd periodically interrupt Tony to focus on details he might have glossed over. When Tony pulled out the e-mail from Rick Santiago and the figures he'd found on Phillips' computer disk, he mentioned the changes in deposits for Bertolini's, Frascati's, and Recovery West. Hansen asked to see the quotes on the other businesses as well. Tony found his inquiry methodical and thorough rather than doubting or suspicious.

Cortez and Singer asked very few questions. They dutifully stuck to their yellow pads, giving barely a hint of their humanity. Later, Tony realized their quiet concentration was simply out of respect. They acutely appreciated Tony's precarious position. While they remained consummate professionals, Tony would have been satisfied with a little levity to occasionally break the tension. His sarcastic quips had no audience, so he just plugged away and they took notes.

"Well, you've got Emilio Frascati and Burton Wesley. One of these guys, maybe both, are powering your conspiracy," Hansen concluded.

"What about Senator Winston?" Spencer wondered aloud. "Do you think this thing goes back to Washington?"

Hansen shrugged. "I'm not sure we can go that deep. I suspect Winston might be a useful pawn, but I doubt if he's complicit in real criminal activities."

"This area is fairly well known," Singer added, "as a territory whose major supplier and boss was Luis Sandoval. There's at least one reason not to point a finger at him, though. We've got fairly strong assurance that the Sandoval family had been cooperating as a major supplier to the pharmaceutical companies. When you guys came up with your amnesty plan, it might have worked for the primary bosses. At least we thought it worked."

"I think those bastards are scum," said Linda. Tony nearly jumped back in his seat listening to her spout off about the cartel. "But those scum have more money than God. They're laughing now. If this thing works, they can start pulling their money from all their laundry accounts, and they don't have to be outlaws anymore."

Spencer sized it up by adding, "Maybe it's the middle men, you know, the ones doing distribution, laundering the money, getting the kickbacks, who have the most to lose."

"I'm sure you're right," Hansen said as he flipped through his notes, then turned and smiled at Brenda as she refilled his coffee cup. "Thanks, Brenda. That's great coffee."

She smiled back, "I'm glad you like it. It's a Kona blend I found in Hawaii."

Tony wondered if this constituted a first date. He hoped it didn't get too mushy.

Hansen then got back on track and added, "Someone's losing or about to lose a lot of money. These are people we never considered because they're not directly involved with drug dealing."

Tony looked around the room, and then commented to Spencer, "I feel like I'm in an episode of the Mod Squad all of a sudden." Then to everyone else he asked, "Okay, so who has the plan?"

Hansen then volunteered his thoughts. "I'm initially inclined to have you lay low for another day or so. This will give us time to get subpoenas and gather more data. We need to tighten up our investigation in order to make these allegations stick."

"I think there's a problem," Tony argued. "The police know I'm around, so I've got no choice. I have to go back to work tomorrow. If I don't show up, then Cooper and Ramsey will definitely know I'm on to them. Actually, they're kind of a weak link in this conspiracy, so they might get knocked off themselves. I think that's what happened to Felton. He might have been trying to cheat these guys out of a few bucks. You just can't get out of line with these guys. I'm telling you they have the swiftest judicial system around."

"He's got a point," Singer noted, directing his comment to Hansen. "Going back to work tomorrow would demonstrate his naiveté. They'll be wanting to move as soon as they have an opportunity."

"Well, then, I'm afraid we have no choice." Hansen said, looking at Tony. "You'll have to be the decoy."

Singer then put it very succinctly: "You might as well get it over."

Cortez looked down at her notes, and then concluded, "It'll be tomorrow. They know you're alive and well. They'll probably find out if you've shown up for work. As soon as you show up, the pressure will be on their men to finish the job. They can't take you out in the middle of the day, but they'll look for their spot, probably when you're alone."

Singer then added, "It's got to be tomorrow, or these guys will scatter. They don't know we're here. In two days, once Felton's reported missing, this place will be swarming with FBI agents. Once that happens, they'll all scatter and destroy evidence, and we'll have a tough time bringing this case together."

Tony felt his pulse quicken. He didn't need any coffee to keep him awake. He thought about some of the natural drugs that are within our bodies. In the scheme of things, some of them are as harmful as those you could presently get at the DPCs. His anticipated heart attack never occurred, and he calmed down as he listened to Singer suggest a plan to Hansen.

"Are you sure I have to be the decoy? Couldn't we use an inflatable doll?" Tony mused, hiding his true, terrified feelings.

"You got one that does liposuction?" Hansen countered. Everyone laughed, especially Brenda.

Oh, great, Tony thought. Now we're having fun. This time he wasn't too thrilled that it was at his expense.

Tony watched and listened as they detailed what was to them a fairly routine-sounding sting operation. Being the new kid on the team, he didn't think it was so routine. For a moment, he thought of the day his brother was killed. It didn't seem real then, either. Now he occupied the central position where he'd be surrounded by gun-toting cops and murderers. What a thrill.

The three agents bantered among themselves with the same casual assuredness Tony was used to hearing in his O.R. Vitalized in their element, they moved comfortably, formulating their plan until it was just right.

Even Spencer looked at Tony and softly offered, "I hope they know what they're doing."

"My, what a vote of confidence. I don't suppose you'd want to hang out with me tomorrow," Tony whispered back.

"Aren't you the one who likes to quote from The House of God that 'the patient's the one with the problem'?" Spencer then somberly added, "Good luck."

Chapter 18

7:00 a.m., Wednesday, March 16

Montana sat on the edge of the couch sipping a cup of coffee. She knew she couldn't expose the Babcocks to the uncertainties of taking her to Nice. She needed other plans. Perhaps she had overreacted to Carlo's presence last night, but when she thought of the look in his eyes, she knew with certainty that she had been accurate in her assessment.

Last night, she had followed Simon Babcock back to his suite. Once inside, she had leaned against the wall of the well-appointed living room, thankful to have found a safe haven. Her heart pounded, and she heard each beat deep inside her head. It took several minutes and several slow, deep breaths before she sufficiently calmed down.

She worried about Gina, but she'd looked fine last night. If only Carlo hadn't looked so menacing, she might have been able to write the whole thing off. Why take chances at this point?

Simon had been a doll to help her out. Would she, or could she, ever be that kind toward someone she didn't know? He offered to have housekeeping send in a rollaway bed, but Montana refused, content on the couch with the blanket and pillow he already had available.

She'd tossed and turned last night thinking about today's planned drive

226

to the French Riviera. Leaving Italy didn't bother her much, but she thought something about leaving with the Babcocks might not be that simple.

If Carlo had really tried to kill her, he'd be back. He'd probably be waiting for her. He had screwed up big by letting her get away last night. All she could figure was that Ernesto Frascati must have put a tail on her. There was no way this Carlo guy had acted on his own.

She could only conclude that the Babcocks would be in serious jeopardy by leaving with her. It would not only be dangerous, but completely irresponsible to take that risk.

Montana listened as she heard Simon explain to his wife, Arleen, about the events that eventually brought Montana to their room.

Arleen came bounding out of the bedroom, saying, "Oh, my dear, you must've been so frightened. By the way, I'm Arleen." She offered her hand.

Montana took it and responded, "Montana Ryan. I really appreciate your help."

"Don't mention it, dear. We'd be only more than happy to have you come along with us."

"That's so sweet of you, but I'm afraid I can't ask you to do it. It's just too dangerous. If I'm right, this was purely business and I was very lucky earlier." Montana took another sip of coffee and reaffirmed her position. "You two have done enough already. I can't leave with you."

Simon regarded the situation a moment longer, then added, "Well, I suppose we do have choices we need to make." Then, turning to Arleen, he said, "After all, darling, we did come on this trip for a vacation. Smuggling young women out of Italy was never on our itinerary." He cast a paternal smile Montana's way as if to say, "It'll be okay."

Arleen looked at both of them inquisitively, waiting for them to make a decision.

Since seven a.m. Carlo had waited impatiently, nervously tapping his fingers over the steering wheel of the white Maserati. A dark-haired male companion, Vito Tanzi, sat stoically in the passenger's seat, and they watched from behind sunglasses as the morning activity around the San Pietro bustled with the departure of guests and their luggage.

Carlo glanced at Vito. Vito didn't avert his gaze, offering a subtle message for Carlo to pay attention. Carlo didn't need another message. His Uncle Ernesto had already threatened to cut off his balls if he screwed up again. Carlo had been so proud of himself when his Uncle Ernesto had asked him to follow the two women leaving his store. Carlo managed to trail them down to Pinto and over to the San Pietro. He notified his uncle about Montana's transaction. Carlo had done well. After his uncle passed the information on to the States, the decision was made. Montana had to have an accident. Simply, she knew too much. Carlo had come close to pulling it off the night before, but close didn't count, and Ernesto summoned Vito Tanzi to ride along with Carlo. Vito was annoying him by sitting there like a big shot, and worse, acting like his baby sitter. Who needed this?

He looked at his watch again – eight-fifteen. The man who had seen him in the hallway last night emerged from the hotel with a woman — probably his wife, Carlo surmised. They proceeded alone directly to a gray Peugeot waiting at the hotel entrance. The bellman loaded their luggage into the trunk. The man handed him a tip as his wife got into the car. They both settled in, fastened their seat belts and unceremoniously drove away.

Two more cars left from the hotel. Then he saw her, and quickly, almost victoriously, Carlo pointed Montana out to Vito.

Montana walked out of the hotel simply dressed in jeans and a short-sleeved cashmere sweater. She quickly glanced around while the bellman summoned a taxi. Carlo smiled to himself, knowing this would be easy. He shouldn't have any trouble isolating the taxi. Once they stopped it, his friend would engage the driver while Carlo pulled Montana from the car. The whole thing would be staged as an argument between a man and his mistress. The driver, for his part, would know to back off and keep out of trouble. Montana would have little choice but to proceed with her captors and hope she'd be unharmed. Carlo would probably just hang on to her, using her as a bargaining chip or a major diversion in case there was any problem with Dr. Ryan back in the States. At least that's what he was told.

Carlo grinned as he watched the taxi come to a stop and the bellman approach the rear door to usher Montana into her trap. Another bellman emerged from the entry pulling a cart filled with luggage followed by several guests, whom he led to the area behind Montana's cab. Carlo raised his sunglasses and squinted to see the back of Montana's head as she scooted across the rear seat to the right side of the car. The bellman nodded to Montana and then leaned on the door, speaking to the taxi driver. Another taxi drove up at almost the same time as Montana's left the hotel.

Immediately, Carlo started the engine and put his car into gear. He purposely kept a respectful distance from the taxi, not really interested in stopping the car in the crowded town. The taxi drove through the main part of Positano, darting its way through the narrow streets. The morning traffic was enough to force the taxi to dart in and out between cars. Twice the taxi turned a corner and momentarily disappeared from Carlo's sight. However, Carlo proved adept behind the wheel and managed to maneuver his car through traffic, eventually regaining sight of the taxi. This taxi would have a tenacious escort.

Once the taxi left the confines of the town for the road south, Carlo easily followed behind. Based on their direction, Carlo assumed they were on their way to Naples. Carlo proceeded at a comfortable distance while his passenger sat quietly looking ahead.

Carlo broke the silence. "You want me to pull him over now?" he asked in Italian.

Vito, with eyes still ahead, replied, "No. Let him run a little. Let's get further away from town. I'll let you know when to take him."

Carlo knew he had botched the job last night. He cursed his overconfidence, which had allowed him a few too many glasses of champagne. He pictured Montana standing on her balcony, so vulnerable. When she started to undo her robe, he froze. He actually thought he could have sex with her, then throw her off the balcony. Damn American woman, thinks she's so smart.

He had hated saying goodbye to Gina so early in the morning. He wasn't sure if she believed his excuse about the sudden business matter that required his immediate attention. He took her number, begging to see her again in Rome. That part was true. He really got off on knowing he had bedded Emilio Frascati's former mistress.

Meanwhile, Ernesto Frascati was ready to choke him with his bare hands.

But shortly Carlo would be redeemed. Things might actually work out better today than if he had succeeded the night before.

The road south to Naples wound through the steep hillside. Carlo kept a respectable distance, with the taxi always in sight. The more isolated the better. There was no rush. His Maserati hugged the road, purring along like a leopard getting ready to overtake its prey.

Several miles down the road, Carlo glanced over at Vito. Before he could lose his patience, Vito, with his eyes trained straight ahead, simply nodded, giving the signal. Ahh, finally, Carlo thought, and he applied more force to the accelerator.

The Maserati lurched forward, gripping the asphalt while smoothly gliding from one turn to the next. The taxi accelerated in response to Carlo's encroaching maneuvers. Carlo smiled at the evasive driving as he continued the easy pursuit. This made it more of a sport.

Carlo brought the Maserati to within a few feet of the taxi, which seemed to be slowing, probably hoping he would pass. Instead, Carlo came right up behind him and stayed glued to his tail. Again the taxi slowed and moved to the right, but there was a sheer cliff only three feet away. Carlo figured he'd continue to prey on his nerves. It seemed to be working, as Carlo watched the driver frequently looking up into the rearview mirror.

The taxi suddenly drifted slightly over to the oncoming lane. Carlo started to brake as he watched the taxi cross directly into the path of an oncoming truck. The truck's horn blared and the taxi driver turned hard to the right. The panic turn tore the taxi from the path of the truck but then caused the car to swerve, fish-tailing so that the rear spun to the left and the bug-eyed, terrified driver was momentarily facing Carlo. The truck passed as the taxi braked hard and then slid backward across the left lane, miraculously stopping in the soft dirt and a row of hedges on the hillside on the left side of the road.

Carlo couldn't believe the luck of the taxi driver, who had ended up on the hillside instead of plummeting to a spectacular death. Carlo had braked immediately when he saw the taxi swerve, and he calmly brought his car to a well-controlled stop next to the taxi.

He and Vito got out of the car. Vito approached the driver while Carlo ran to the rear door to get Montana, who, following the impact, was sprawled face down across the rear seat. As Carlo opened the rear door, she pushed herself up. He reached in and grabbed her forcefully by the left arm, and she screamed. As he pulled her up, she turned and cursed at him in Italian, wildly gesturing with her hands.

Carlo, expressionless, let go of her and backed up. His eyes widened slightly with astonishment as he watched this woman he had never before seen. He stared at the woman. He moved her aside, looking throughout the taxi, hoping his eyes had betrayed him. Montana was nowhere to be found.

Beads of perspiration began forming over his brow as the panic set in. There would be no promotion. He looked over to Vito, who now knew they had been duped. Vito was not pleased.

Although her plans had been hastily made, they were well executed. Montana had handsomely paid one of the night maids to take a day trip to Naples. The taxi driver had been overcompensated as well. When the bellman brought out the luggage amidst the departing entourage, the night maid walked along behind the cart. She entered the cab ahead of Montana and slid across the back to the right side. Montana got in, but stayed low against the seat, completely out of sight. All Carlo saw was the back of the night maid's head, which appeared to be Montana's.

Taking advantage of the morning traffic, Montana bid her new friends goodbye during a stop in the middle of town. She peeked her head up to look for the Maserati. It was out of sight, temporarily delayed around the corner. She made her move, exiting the left rear door, running around the back of the car and then hiding behind a fruit stand. She held her breath. Within ten seconds, she saw the Maserati come from around the corner. The taxi started up again, and the Maserati continued its pursuit. Once the car was out of sight, Montana ran toward a set of stairs which took her up a walkway and out onto another street. She stood across from a church. She didn't notice the gray Peugeot coming out of the shaded spot less than a football field away. Suddenly the Babcocks were upon her.

"Going west, young lady?" Simon asked with a relieved smile on his face.

"Thank God" was all Montana had to say. She got into the car, and they drove to France. No matter the length of the drive, she was relieved to have avoided certain disaster.

When they arrived in Monte Carlo, the Babcocks suggested that she stay with them at the Hotel de Paris. It hadn't been easy for her to refuse Arleen Babcock, but Montana politely assured her that she had a place to stay. While the Babcocks checked, she made a phone call to a dear friend of hers and Tony's, Jean Pierre Levant. He practiced surgery in Nice had become one of their friends after spending time watching Tony operate.

"Jean Pierre, this is Montana Ryan."

The salutations then flowed back and forth until Montana finally asked her favor. "Please, Jean Pierre. I need you to register me into a hotel under your name. Someone tried to kill me last night in Positano. I don't want to leave any simple clues as to where I am."

He made the arrangements and had the hotel hold the room for her, registered in his name. He suggested she wait in the lobby or the bar of the Hotel de Paris while he arranged to pick her up.

Montana left her luggage with the bellman and headed for the bar. A glass of Montrachet would be welcome at the moment, she thought. She ordered the white wine and perched at the bar, waiting for Jean Pierre. An older gentleman, exquisitely dressed in a Brioni suit, approached her.

"You must be the one. You are divine. But you must dress if we are to go to the Casino," he addressed Montana, as though she had been sent for him.

Not understanding, she simply said, "Excuse me."

The man proceeded to kiss her on the back of the neck and place his hand on her thigh.

She jumped from her seat, spilling most of her drink. "Are you crazy? What do you think you're doing?"

Realizing his mistake, the man said, "Then you are not the one the concierge sent for me?"

Montana was ready to verbally unleash an attack upon the man when she also realized what he was saying. She almost felt sorry for his blunder and at the same time almost a little complimented. He called the bartender to refill her glass, left the money for the drink, apologized and left.

Ten minutes later, she noticed two men staring at her from across the room. One man was an employee of the hotel, possibly a concierge, while the other man appeared to be in his thirties, with short wavy dark hair, sporting a gray suit with a dark-blue dress shirt with an open collar. He turned to the hotel employee and said something, all the time looking in her direction. She turned her back on them but continued to watch them through the mirrored wall of the bar. The two men separated and walked away. She watched as the man in the suit headed for a bank of telephones.

By the time he had finished his call and come back to the bar, she was gone. Quickly he raced back into the lobby, looked around and then left through the main doors. He instinctively reached into his jacket pocket for his sunglasses, as the bright sun caused a lot of glare, but he had left them in the car. He shielded his eyes and squinted in search of her. He thought he saw her running up the street past Chanel.

Montana had expected Jean Pierre, not another family member from Italy. She couldn't stay there waiting for Jean Pierre. By the time he arrived, she'd be missing. After all she had been through, they had still managed to follow her. She didn't think he had seen her. She ducked into the Chanel store and watched from behind a rack of dresses. He headed up the street. He looked left and right, constantly scouring the crowd for a glimpse of her. He walked closer to Chanel, finally passing by, and thankfully continuing past the building. She finally breathed again. She walked over to a chair and sat down for a moment. She needed to get to a phone.

A saleslady politely escorted her to the sales area, where she could make a call. Montana thanked her and began to scramble through her purse for Jean Pierre's phone number. Suddenly a hand reached out from behind her. She immediately recognized the gray suit and the dark-blue sleeve of the dress shirt. She stiffened in her panic, thinking her only chance was to yell for help in the middle of Chanel. Before she could utter a sound, the man spoke.

"Mrs. Ryan, I am here for Jean Pierre." As he spoke, he simultaneously handed her Jean Pierre's card. His name was on it as well. It read "Raymond Broussard, Assistant de Circurgia."

Montana unraveled and sat down, relieved. "I expected Jean Pierre. I'm sorry. I assumed you worked for someone else."

"Yes," he said, smiling broadly, "I understand. Let's get your things." He offered his hand and added, "Jean Pierre has made all of the necessary arrangements."

Chapter 19

8:00 a.m., Wednesday, March 16

BRENDA AND MATS WAITED patiently for Tony in the operating room. The melody of a Mozart concerto provided a welcoming ambiance. The patient, Emily Sanders, lay on the table, already connected to monitors with an I.V. flowing. Although lightly sedated, she still recognized Tony, and he greeted her again with a warm grip of her hand and a smile. Mats still had no idea where he had been, and Brenda had to pretend that she had been kept in the dark as well. Ever the professional, Mats simply said good morning, not wanting to say anything alarming or confusing in the presence of a fairly alert patient. Mrs. Sanders had been prepped for a face lift and upper and lower blepharoplasty. Tony had already marked her in the exam room before leaving her with Brenda to escort into the operating room.

The operating room offered a comforting place for his return. Having earlier driven his Jaguar into the parking garage, he nervously looked in every direction, waiting for the unexpected. He tried to act casual as he pulled his briefcase from the trunk. With other office workers in the parking lot, he felt a little more secure knowing he wasn't alone, but he had the feeling his movements were being monitored. Although they had discussed the possibility that he could be ambushed, it was important that he conduct his usual routine and not tip his hand. The agents suspected that a serious confrontation wouldn't take place until Joanna had called the police to inform them of Tony's return to the office. The agents surmised that it would be a lot easier to eliminate Tony if there were no guesswork involved. He stood by the operating table in his safe haven.

Ron Matsuda proceeded to increase the intravenous sedation until Mrs. Sanders was comfortably asleep. Tony anesthetized her face with a diluted solution of xylocaine. Mrs. Sanders then let out a little yelp. Tony realized that he had not added any sodium bicarbonate to the anesthetic solution. The sodium bicarbonate neutralized the acidity of the solution in order to take the sting out of the injection. He caught Mats giving him a "What's up?" kind of stare, knowing this transgression wasn't expected from him. He drew up the solution and then went back to work, locking himself back into focus. Once adequate local anesthesia was given, the patient was draped and readied for the operation.

Mats finally found a safe time to ask, "What happened to you yesterday?"

Unfortunately, Tony hadn't prepared any adequate explanation. He looked over at Mats, conjured a few thoughts while Brenda assisted him in putting on his surgical gloves, and then told him, "I had a family emergency. I was called late the night before and had to go into L.A. to see my parents." Then he paused, thinking for a moment that it couldn't be health-related. That would bring a bad "eye," as Montana's granny used to say.

"Nothing terribly serious, as it turns out. Some personal financial stuff. I really thought I would be back for surgery yesterday morning, but my car stalled on the way back up PCH. My car phone wouldn't work, because I was in that dead cell area. I waited for a while and finally decided to hike to a gas station, which turned out to be seven or eight miles away. The whole thing was a nightmare. I called Silvia at home because of the dogs, and she was supposed to call the office, but she forgot. So today I found out Joanna had called in a missing-person report. Anyway, it's just one of those ridiculous stories that would never be bought in Hollywood. Let's get to work."

For the next three hours Tony calmly proceeded through the operation. Except for the lie he had told Mats, the rest of the morning was uneventful.

He actually forgot for a while that three FBI special agents were in town to watch his every move, anticipating when he would be expended by the adversary.

When he finished the operation with Mrs. Sanders, he went back to his office to change his clothes. Several messages had gathered since yesterday and earlier that morning. He wasn't in the mood to start returning calls. Meanwhile, it was nearly nine in the evening in Italy, so he put a call through to Montana. The front desk rang her room, and Gina quickly picked up the phone.

"Gina, it's Tony. Let me speak to Montana, please."

Her voice was a little frantic. "Tony, she left a note. She didn't say where she went, only that she had to leave."

"You weren't with her last night?"

"I met this man. You know, very attractive, and we stayed out late. I went with him back to his room. Montana, she came to the room very late with another man and hotel security. They want to know why Carlo, the man I'm with, goes into Montana's room. Montana says he came to attack her. He says she's crazy. She kicked him in the balls. This morning I get up and they're both gone."

"And you have no idea where she went?"

Gina, clearly upset by the circumstances, sounded as though she were on the verge of tears. "Oh, Tony, I don't know what to do. You don't think she could be with Carlo?"

"Take it easy, Gina. I don't think Montana would be with any man she kicked in the groin. Go back to Rome. I'm sure she'll call you soon." Tony tried to sound reassuring.

Gina didn't seem reassured. "How come she didn't tell me why she's leaving?"

"I think she wants to keep you out of trouble. I've got some serious problems, and she may, too. I think she'll be okay." Tony instinctively knew he was right, but still worried and hoped Montana had left Italy.

As he hung up, he looked down at the phone, staring at it like a prayer book, hoping Montana had managed to find her way out of Italy. He felt helpless knowing he couldn't protect her. He would have to rely on faith and so said a silent prayer.

Tony sat at his desk and quickly looked through yesterday's mail. His usual daily schedule was missing. He gathered up his messages and sifted through them. One in particular caught his eye. Frank Ramsey had called while he was in the O.R. and left a return number. Tony used the intercom to contact Joanna to find out the nature of the call.

"Yes, Dr. Ryan. I called the police department this morning to let them know you were back at the office. I told them you were unexpectedly called away on an emergency, as you told me to say. They then told me you were at the station late yesterday afternoon. They put me on hold for a while, and then Detective Ramsey came on the line asking to speak with you. I told him you were in surgery. He said no problem and left a message for you to call."

"Thanks, Joanna." Tony called the police department and asked for Ramsey.

He picked up the line. "Ramsey."

"Hello, this is Dr. Tony Ryan. I'm returning your call."

"Thanks, Doc. I see you're okay, back at the job. Everything under control?"

"How can I help you, Mr. Ramsey?" Tony replied curtly.

"I was wondering if you could tell me what transpired the other night when you and McVee got together. Remember, you told me you had a little meeting." Ramsey was fishing, but why? Tony wondered to himself.

Tony decided to tell him part of the story. "McVee was a patient, and subsequently we became friends. He met with me yesterday because one of my patients was involved in a recent car accident allegedly tied to marijuana use. McVee wanted to find out what I knew. He apparently was reviewing some information." Tony paused, wanting Ramsey to pick up his cue. He did.

"Do you remember what his concerns were?"

"McVee thought someone might have tampered with the Masons' car. He had more information about the investigation." Tony knew this was nothing new to Ramsey, but he was at his limit.

Then Ramsey added, "Did you ever call your mechanic and check out that timing device you said McVee found? Do you know anything about it?"

Tony didn't appreciate the line of questioning. He indignantly responded, "Of course not. I haven't had time to do your work."

"By the way, do you own a gun?"

Tony started to reply in the negative, but then held back to ask, "What difference does that make?"

"Well, if you did, I'd have to advise you of your rights and subsequently do a ballistics check on it." Ramsey spoke in an authoritative manner that Tony found annoying.

"Are you suggesting I might be a suspect in his murder?"

Ramsey backed off a little. "Look, Doc, I'm not saying anything. I've just got to investigate the whole case." And then he added, "Everyone knows you've been active in supporting this free drug thing. Jimmy, even though he was the police liaison, was really against it. We just have to check out all of the information. No offense. What time do you get done with patients? Maybe I can swing by."

"Hang on a moment. Let me check the schedule and see when I'm through with the last patient." Tony put the phone on hold, took a deep breath and blew it out slowly. All of a sudden, Ramsey sounded like a good cop, and it seemed a little confusing. He called Joanna on the intercom, and she informed him when he'd be finished. He picked up Ramsey's line again. "I'll probably be through between five-thirty and six. Why don't you swing by around then?"

"Fine, Doc. I'll be seeing you." Done with his business, he hung up.

Tony put the receiver down. He was pretty sure he was being set up, but for some reason it wasn't obvious. Ramsey sounded a little convincing.

Tony pulled out his wallet and called Mark Hansen on the cellular number Mark had given him. It rang twice and then he answered, "Hansen." Did everyone who worked in law enforcement answer the phone the same way, with their last names?

"Hello, Mark. It's Tony. I've just had an interesting conversation with Ramsey from the SBPD. Where are you guys?" he asked.

"Actually," he said with a slight chuckle, "we're having lunch over at Frascati's restaurant. What did Ramsey want?"

"Frascati's? Oh, jeez, what are you guys doing there?" Tony knew it was a dumb question as soon as he asked it.

"We're having lunch, I told you. What did Ramsey have to say?"

"He's coming over here after work today to ask me some questions about the McVee murder. What do you think?" Innocently, Tony half-expected him to say there was nothing to worry about.

"It's going down. Don't worry. Just conduct your normal routine, Doc. I assure you we'll be ready. I'll talk with you later." Anxious to get off the cellular phone, he cut it quick and hung up.

Tony wondered what had happened to Spencer. There was no way they were going to have Spencer hanging around with them. He decided not to worry about it. He had to finish his work and leave it to Hansen and his crew to save the day. Playing the decoy was not a welcoming thought. He had been more comfortable the previous day without the glaring exposure.

He went down the hall, grabbed an apple and checked on Mrs. Sanders. She rested comfortably in the recovery area, with her head wrapped in a soft bulky dressing and a cool gauze compress draped across her eyes. A blood-pressure monitor and pulse oximeter continued to monitor her stable vital signs. Tony picked up the compress and asked, "How are you feeling, Emily?"

"Not bad at all," she replied with a slightly drowsy drawl. Then she asked, "When can I go home? And when do I come back to see you?"

"You'll be able to leave in a few minutes. We're waiting for the driver from the post-op care facility. Brenda will take you down as soon as he's here. And I'll see you tomorrow. You'll feel more comfortable tomorrow once the dressing comes off." He laid the compress back across her eyes. "I'll talk with you later," he said, hoping it was true.

"Thanks, Tony. I'm sure you did a great job."

"You know it, Emily. You might not think it the next day or two, but you're going to look really good once you've healed." He patted her hand and walked off to the front desk to see how things stacked up for the afternoon.

Joanna sat behind her desk, talking on the phone. Tony listened as she talked to a prospective patient. "No, Dr. Ryan doesn't do it that way. He stopped using the vacuum machine for routine liposuction six or seven years ago. He does it with tiny cannulas and a very large syringe. When you come in for your consultation, he can show you the instruments and explain the procedure to you." She paused momentarily, looked up to see Tony standing there, and then turned back to her call. He didn't need to disrupt her. He just borrowed the appointment book to see what the afternoon schedule presented. He could understand why his schedule hadn't been put on his desk. Joanna had been busy rescheduling patients and trying to fit in most of the ones he had missed by not showing up the day before. He was going to be busy. Aside from his follow-up patients, he had a fair number of new consultations on the book. A few had already checked in and were waiting in the reception area.

Joanna finished her call, looked up at Tony and asked, "Are you ready?" He gave a reluctant nod.

His patients kept him hopping. Normally he would spend more time enjoying conversation with his patients, but today he had to get down to business and keep moving. By four o'clock he had seen more than fifteen patients, including four new consultations. Working at this frantic pace helped keep his mind off the more serious problem that awaited.

He walked over to exam room three and picked up the chart waiting for him. A new patient, Lydia Curtis, age thirty-two, possible rhinoplasty, waited to meet him. He walked into the room, closing the door behind him. He started on automatic, his head buried in the chart. "Good afternoon, Miss Curtis," he said, and then he looked up and saw Linda Cortez sitting in the exam chair.

He continued the charade, probably to soften his own tension. "Well, Miss Curtis, I see you've come all the way from the East Coast to have me work on your nose. I suspect the only problem with your nose is what you get it into. How's a nice girl like you working at a job like this?"

Linda stood up and walked over to the guest chair, where a black shoulder bag sat. She gave Tony a slight smile and got right to the business at hand. "Dr. Ryan, I've brought a few things we need to set you up with now." She walked over to the counter and started to remove a few items from her bag. Without turning around, she then told him, "I need you to take off your shirt."

She gave the orders, and Tony knew he had to do what she said. He started to remove his lab coat and quipped, "Your art of seduction is a little intimidating. Don't you have a more gentle approach?" He removed his tie and shirt while she spread out a few things on the counter. He felt a little strange standing there without his shirt on. It was definitely a case of instant role reversal. Of course, the fact that she was an attractive woman didn't make it any easier for him.

She tossed him a t-shirt. "Here, put this on first. It will make things more comfortable." He grabbed the t-shirt and threw it on. She then approached him with a light-blue vest. "Let's put this thing on. I'll give you a hand with the Velcro straps."

He knew this concealable vest had the specific purpose of keeping bullets out of his torso. It surprised him how light and thin it felt. "I thought bullet-proof vests were made out of lead or something."

Cortez responded, "Actually, this is the same material they use in your tennis racket, Kevlar. It's actually a lot stronger than steel. And, Dr. Ryan, you look great in blue."

He was relieved to find there was a human inside of her body. He was still concerned about the obvious. "What if they shoot me in the head?"

"Given the opportunity, that's probably what they'll prefer to do. You need to keep them at a bit of a distance. We're not planning to let you be alone with an assassin. This is just in case bullets start flying. We might as well take all precautions." Then she reached for a small microphone with a fairly long lead on it. She clipped it to the inside collar of his t-shirt and slipped the lead in through the collar. She reached up his shirt with her hand, pulled the lead out and connected it to a small transmitter. "Tuck this in around your belt. You'll get used to it, and it won't bother you after a while."

He put his shirt and tie back on and tucked everything into his pants. With his lab coat on top of everything, he felt a little bulky but didn't look any different.

Cortez then picked up a walkie-talkie and called into it. "Okay, he's jacketed and wired. Are you ready to run a sound test?" She listened for the affirmation and then asked Tony to count to ten. "Okay," she replied into her unit and then closed it. She looked directly at Tony. "We'll be monitoring the rest of your day. We want to see what Ramsey has to say, but we will be in position to move in if anyone confronts you. It will all be recorded."

"I'm relieved to know that whoever kills me will have their gunshots recorded by the FBI. Where will you guys be, and by the way, where's Spencer?"

"We'll be close by in the building. We all have monitors. Spencer will stay in our van. We're letting him monitor all the transmissions, but he has to stay put." She then gathered her things together and threw her bag back over her shoulder. "Thanks for the consultation, Dr. Ryan." She opened the door and was on her way.

Tony stood in the exam room for a few minutes getting used to the Kevlar vest while wondering what to expect next. It wouldn't be easy getting through the next few patients and keeping his mind on their concerns.

By five-thirty he found himself alone in an exam room with his last patient. Alicia Danville drove him nuts. "But, doctor, I want to make sure you know what I want." He wondered how he could know what she wanted when her perceptions seemed so mixed up. Having come to him after some inappropriate facial surgery had caused some minor disfigurement that seemed major in her mind, Tony accepted the task of repair. No matter how strongly he would admonish her to keep her face out of the mirror, she would be back helping him understand how he could continue to improve her appearance with just a little more cutting here or perhaps by grafting a little more fat there. At times, he would project her before and after photos on the computer so she could see the improvements they had accomplished. No matter. She would still request perfection. Even though he had been the one to help her, she was so wounded from her perceived errors in trusting other surgeons that she would be relentless in her consultations with him. He sincerely thought of blurting out that he was looking forward to a possible meeting with an assassin more than to another session with her. He did not say this, of course. He did the cowardly thing. He reassured her and asked her to come back in three months so they could re-evaluate how everything had healed and then decide if it would be appropriate to do any further work.

After saying goodbye to Mrs. Danville, he stopped by the front desk. Joanna called the exchange and prepared ready to leave. At twenty minutes to six, Detective Frank Ramsey walked alone through the door. Tony had never met him, but he figured he would be harsher-looking, more in line with his buddy Cooper. Thus, it surprised Tony to see the youthful-looking Ramsey, with his sandy blond hair and athletic build.

Ramsey came right up to the window where Tony stood. "Dr. Ryan, Frank Ramsey. Thanks for taking time to meet with me." He stuck his hand through the opening, and Tony shook it without the reservation he felt.

Joanna looked up to Tony. "Would you like me to stay?"

"Thanks, Joanna. That won't be necessary. Mr. Ramsey, come on in." He escorted Ramsey to his office, where Tony sat down behind his desk and Ramsey sat across from him.

Ramsey opened the yellow legal pad he carried with him and started jotting down notes as he asked questions. "Doc, how long did you know McVee?"

"About six years, I guess."

"Can you tell me what you talked about the day he saw you?"

"I don't mean to be impertinent, but what I told you on the phone is what went on."

Ramsey made his notes and, without looking up, asked, "Can you account for your whereabouts Tuesday evening?"

No need to lie. Tony offered, "Absolutely, I was exhausted. I went home. In fact, I heard about the murder on the late-night news."

Ramsey continued, "By now I'm sure you're aware that your office called, reporting you missing. Clearly you weren't missing, but if you weren't missing, where were you?"

"I had some personal problems I had to take care of. My parents called me from L.A. late that night, and I drove down around eleven-thirty. I tried to get back early, but I had some car trouble on PCH. By the time I got back, I got a call from Sally McVee and went down to the station to collect McVee's stuff. Joanna knew I was back but didn't call the department until this morning, when I told her she probably should call back. She didn't think it was necessary. Not only had I just been at the station, but I hadn't been gone long enough for the police to file a formal report. Anyway, no disrespect meant, detective, but I just lost a good friend, too. How is this line of questioning going to help your investigation?"

"It probably won't. But you do understand, as an investigator, I must make certain I do a complete job. I can't simply write this whole thing off for what it appears. Do you own a gun?"

"No."

"Maybe you ought to consider it. I can't tell you for sure, but if McVee's murder was anything other than random, then you could possibly be at risk. These are uncertain times. Well, Doc, I don't think there's much left to discuss. I'll keep you posted." He then got up and offered his hand. Tony shook it and walked him to the door.

What kind of crap was that he thought as he walked back to the front desk and looked over the calendar for tomorrow's schedule? The office door started to open, slowly, and then with a small commotion, as Pete and the cleaning crew proceeded to push their trash barrow and cleaning materials into the office. At that moment Tony happened to look up to see Detective Ramsey exit the building at the other end of the hallway through the rear stairwell. He could see his mop of blond hair in the doorway just before it closed. It seemed strange that he didn't leave from the front or go down by the elevator.

The cleaning crew, in their dark blue jumpsuits, was now at work in Tony's office. Tony decided to walk down the hallway and assess the exit route Ramsey had taken. He expected to find the door leading to the back jammed and readied for entrance. That being the case, he figured he could help the agents and get them positioned to pick up their potential assailant. He opened the door to the stairwell and listened for Ramsey. It was quiet, so he figured Ramsey had already made it out the door. He bounded down the stairs. Not untypical, a light was out over the landing between the third and second floor. He quickly turned the corner at the darkened landing, heading toward the second-floor exit. He was halfway down the stairwell when he saw what appeared to be a pile of trash and boxes left by the cleaning crew. In the dim light it wasn't clear, but before he continued down, he stopped. Approaching the piled debris, he leaned forward and saw a leg. Involuntarily holding his breath, he moved the boxes to the side. He could make out a female figure, lying face down dressed in one of the blue cleaning-crew jumpsuits. He felt a wave of panic as he reached down. He reached up to the person's neck, gently feeling for a pulse. Instead, he felt a warm silky fluid that had to be blood.

He bent down closer and turned the person over. Linda Cortez lay dead in the corner of the second-floor landing.

Tony could feel the perspiration bead on his forehead and spread across his chest as a parasympathetic response uncontrollably swept his body. He was anticipating the message he knew he had to send via his transmitter. Linda's jumpsuit had been unzipped all the way down in front. He felt around her ears and then looked down around her waist. A piece of duct tape had been partly torn from the inside of her waistband. There was no sign of her transmitter or her earpiece receiver.

He didn't have time to mourn. The son of a bitch was in the office building and must have picked up a receiver/transmitter set for himself. For certain, Tony could no longer transmit solely to the agents. He couldn't let on about Cortez. He thought about leaving the building and making a run for it. He looked at Cortez lying in a small pool of blood, and the anger swelled inside him. He took a slow, deep breath through his nose, said an internal prayer and then strengthened his resolve.

There was plenty he didn't know about the assassin, but he took stock of his advantages. Tony knew he had a receiver, that he was in the building and that Cortez was dead. The assassin wouldn't know Tony knew any of these things. Tony then reached down and patted Cortez's side. Her gun was still in her harness. Perhaps the assassin didn't think of it, or it was of no use to him, but Tony removed it and tucked it in his pants under his white coat.

He replaced the boxes around her, trying to reset the scene before he cautiously started back upstairs. He wondered if Hansen and Singer were positioned to help him. Without an earpiece, he had to hope for the best. He wasn't feeling especially hopeful at the moment. He couldn't afford to be solely dependent on his agents. He opened the hallway door slowly. The door to his office opened as one of the cleaning crew wheeled the trash barrow out. He hoped that no move would be made around the cleaning crew. Although Tony suspected he was being watched, he thought he'd confirm his position. He softly but purposefully spoke for transmission. "The cleaning crew's still here. Ramsey left a short time ago. Everything seems quiet enough. I have some paperwork to finish in my office, and I'll leave shortly."

He hustled back down the hallway, pulled his keys out, nervously, trying hard not to jangle them, and let himself in through the private entrance. He then did a walk through the entire office suite while the cleaning crew finished up. He half expected to find someone hiding behind each exam table or in every closet. He found nothing.

The last of the cleaning crew walked out the door. They usually came back to vacuum after they'd finished the other offices on the floor. Tony sat alone in his office. It was time to make a communication. "Okay, Cortez, I hope you've got this place secured. You can get me out of here in a little while." He hoped the other two agents were still okay and that they might clue in that Cortez was out of action. Meanwhile, he sat like a target in the Eames chair behind his desk.

He got up and turned the high-backed chair around to face the window. He left the light on in his office and exited the room with the door partly opened. He then walked down the hall and proceeded to turn off all the lights. He found a spot in the reception area from where he could hide and yet watch the door. He didn't know how long he'd be waiting, but he decided to give one more message. "Linda, I'll meet you by the elevator in the garage. One or two minutes. Just finishing this last article."

Within moments, the door opened. He held his breath, expecting someone dark and ominous-looking. Instead, he saw another of the cleaning crew in his blue jumpsuit come walking in with a vacuum. The guy found a plug in the reception area and turned on the vacuum cleaner. He didn't bother to turn on the lights. He ran the vacuum back and forth a couple of times before he walked away, leaving it running.

The dim light made it too hard for Tony to clearly identify him. But Tony knew his purpose. Michael Cirrelo walked through the reception area and went straight down the hall toward Tony's office. As he walked down the hall, the light of Tony's office silhouetted him. Tony could see his slicked-back ponytail and recognized him. Now he knew his name – Cirrelo, and he recalled Felton and Salinski's conversation and the print ID in McVee's locker.

As Cirrelo drew his weapon, he proceeded to sneak quietly into Tony's office. Tony heard two shots coming out of a silencer and then "What the fuck?" Cirrelo came bounding out of the office, heading down the hallway.

He moved with heavy footsteps, deliberate and purposeful, definitely on the hunt. Tony wondered who Cirrelo and his partner worked for, a private concern or maybe a government agency. Or both. It didn't matter. The guy wanted to kill Tony.

Cirrelo then walked past the secretarial area back toward the reception area and the vacuum cleaner. He tucked his gun back into a chest holster under his jumpsuit. Tony stood quietly behind the shelter of the filing cabinet, his hand resting on the .38 in his waistband, and contemplated pulling the gun.

Just as Cirrelo reached for the vacuum, the door opened and another blue-suited man came in through the door. He thought it might be Singer. Tony wrapped his hand around the gun, anticipating that Singer would come to his rescue.

Then he spoke. "Is it done?" He had a deep, throaty voice that Tony easily identified as Salinski's. It definitely had not been Singer, but he had similar stocky proportions and was at least several inches shorter than Cirrelo.

Cirrelo turned off the vacuum and spoke. "He's not here. I must have just missed him." Tony couldn't imagine how they'd gotten past Hansen or Singer. They must have come in through the back, encountered Linda Cortez and then found their way to the cleaning-crew area on the ground floor. It wouldn't have been hard to grab a couple of outfits out of the stockroom and then be on their way. The crew was rather lax and always seemed to have several people scattered about, with multiple offices being cleaned at the same time.

So now he had two guys sent to do the job. And if Cortez was any indication, the agents and the assassins dressed alike.

For an instant, Tony thought about coming out shooting, but he told himself he'd probably blow out the couch and they'd take him out with a chuckle. He waited. He felt himself tremble with fear, but his anger seemed to keep him balanced.

Then he heard Cirrelo say, "Come on. We'll take the back way down to the garage. He said he'd take the elevator down to meet Linda Cortez. He probably thinks she's waiting for him."

"Good. Let's get it done already."

Cirrelo and Salinski walked out. Before the door closed, the light in the hallway allowed Tony to make out the earpiece receiver on Cirrelo's head. Tony worried that Cirrelo could hear his heart beating through his chest. He listened for their footsteps as they headed down the corridor. He then went back to the private exit. He listened for any activity but heard nothing. He walked back to the secretarial area and made another broadcast. "Hey, Cortez. Come on out. I'm waiting for you down in the garage." Then he realized this might not be such a good set-up for Hansen, wherever he was. Tony realized there was more to worry about. For all he knew, Hansen and Singer could easily be dead, too. Without an earpiece, Tony was the ultimate decoy. All he could do was transmit. He thanked God for his timing in seeing Ramsey leave.

He figured his stalkers would be down the back stairwell looking for him in the parking lot. He walked out of his office into the dimly lit hallway and headed for the elevator. Guessing that they were looking into the garage by now, he didn't want to keep them wondering. "Hey, Cortez, this isn't funny," he said into the mike. Then for a good measure, he tried sounding a little more upset. "Damn," he said almost under his breath, "I'm not into hide and seek. I'm taking the elevator back to the third floor. I'll meet you at my office." He pushed the button to summon the elevator. He hoped it would come up empty. Mostly, he hoped his stalkers would see that the elevator had returned to the third floor.

Tony began to turn back for the cover of his office when he felt a hand suddenly reach out and grab him around the face, covering his mouth. He couldn't have let out a chirp if he'd wanted to. With his heart stuck in his throat, he didn't have time to wonder how they were going to kill him. Another hand grabbed him on the shoulder and spun him around. With a frantic expression frozen in place, he turned to stare straight into the eyes of Hansen. Before his expression thawed or he could even let out a sigh, he lifted his fingers to his lips to signal Hansen not to say anything. Tony grabbed a pen from his pocket and started to write on a prescription pad. "There are two guys here. Cortez is dead, and they have her receiver. I took her gun."

He expected to see shock in Hansen's eyes. Instead, he saw a steely resolve. Hansen quickly grabbed Tony by the arm and led him back toward his office. He then spoke, but not for Tony. "Singer, I'll meet you in the garage. We'll secure the area. Cortez, meet the doc at his office." Tony knew what he wanted.

At the office, Tony unlocked the door. He turned on the light, and then Hansen pulled him back out by the sleeve before he could go in, and the door shut automatically. They backed down the hall, turning around a corner and hiding in a doorway that opened to the men's room. From their vantage point they would be able to see anyone going by en route from the back door to his office.

They looked at each other and waited, wanting to speak, but knowing the importance of absolute control and silence. They heard the back exit door open. Tony listened, but it was impossible to tell whether it was one or two sets of footsteps lightly treading across the industrial-carpeted hallway. He looked to Hansen for some kind of signal, but he just motioned Tony back. He now had his weapon ready.

Tony heard two distant shots from downstairs. For a moment, he felt a sense of elation, thinking Singer must have killed one of the intruders, but then he watched as Hansen's expression suddenly changed. His eyes closed tightly, and visible pain swept across his brow for but a moment. Tony read his expression and knew they had gotten to Singer, whose own shots were probably errant.

When Cirrelo's partner walked down to Tony's office, Tony figured that he was alone and not being shadowed. Hansen started his pursuit, with Tony ready to follow from behind. Hansen quickly turned to him and stuck out his arm, signaling him to stay. And then he looked at Tony and softly shook his head with his lips slightly pulled in, confirming what Tony suspected — that Singer had been killed. Now there were two on each side. Two professional hit men and an FBI agent and a doctor. Not a very good match-up, Tony thought.

Hansen's eyes seemed to fire up. They both heard the door to Tony's office open. Hansen then came out of the safety of their shadow hideaway and didn't wait this time. He turned the corner, and while the door to Tony's office was closing, he quickly pushed it open and fired three times directly at Cirrelo's partner. He caught him by surprise just as he entered the office.

Salinski seemed to voluntarily turn around. He raised his gun, and Hansen, realizing that he might have had a vest on, fired a fourth time, sending a bullet into Salinski's head.

The back door down the hall suddenly opened, and a hail of bullets sparked through the hallway. Hansen dove to the floor, rolling to his side. Tony thought he had been hit, but Hansen quickly rolled to his left and sent a volley of fire back in the direction from which the shots had come. Tony remained standing off to the side, out of the fray. Hansen tried to back up and find cover while bullets still flew in the darkened hallway. Tony readied his finger over the trigger of Cortez' .38 and got down low. Up until now, they had not spoken to each other, communicating with their eyes and simple gestures. Tony spoke into the microphone, "Oh, Christ, they got Singer in the garage, and Cortez is dead on the second landing. I'm coming up the back. Hansen. Hansen, are you okay? I'm coming up the rear stairwell."

Luckily, Hansen picked up the cue. "No, Tony, stay back. Don't come up this way. He's by the door."

The shots stopped. Tony never fired his weapon. Cirrelo went out the back looking for Tony. Hansen took a deep breath, got to his feet and came around to the safety of Tony's corner. Again, no words were exchanged, but Hansen gave Tony a nod of appreciation for controlling the present assault. Tony then signaled with his head for Hansen to follow him out the front.

They went quickly down a flight of stairs.

"Hansen, I'm on the second floor. I can hear him coming down the stairwell. I'm heading toward the front. Damn. Maybe he'll think I went down to the garage."

Hansen said nothing as they scampered down the front stairwell. Tony continued the charade by adding, "There's a ladies' room at the end of the hall. It's open. I'm going in there. I'll wait for you." Tony then looked over to Hansen and gave a nod as they stood on the second-floor foyer near the restrooms.

Tony checked the ladies' room door to make sure it was open. Damn, it was locked. He reached for his keys and started to fumble looking for the right one. It was a larger key than his others, with a dome-shaped top. It seemed to take forever to finally fit it into the lock. Tony unlocked the door, freed the bolt and opened the door to turn on the light. He let the door shut and then scurried back to the cover by the plants around the corner, where Hansen stood with pistol drawn. Their position in the darkened hall allowed them to see the restrooms without being seen. Tony nodded to Hansen, pointed to him and made a gesture, a shooting motion with his hand, in the direction of Hansen's leg.

"Tony, stay put. I'm down, can't move my leg. I'll call for back-up."

Tony replied, "Hurry up, man. I'll hide out here." Within seconds they could hear the back door open and soon saw Cirrelo come around the corner. The hallway was empty. Tony knew the cleaning crew, having finished Tony's floor a while ago, had already left for the evening. Tony and Hansen could see Cirrelo as he checked from side to side and surveyed the scene. A faint light shone from under the door to the ladies' room. He approached and slowly reached for the doorknob. The door was unlocked, presumably with Tony inside. They waited for him to make his move. He quietly pushed on the door and proceeded into the restroom. Hansen and Tony came down the hall and stood back behind the corner of the restroom exit.

They heard Cirrelo kicking in doors and cursing. Hansen positioned Tony low and signaled him to point the revolver at the door. Hansen went to the opposite side. Tony watched as the blue-suited thug emerged from the restroom. Everything happened so quickly, but perhaps because of its intensity it appeared to Tony in slow motion.

Cirrelo clearly looked confused and didn't have time to change his response as Hansen blindsided him with a direct blow to his head and a nearly simultaneous disabling blow to his right arm so that his gun fell free across the hall. The guy turned reflexively and blocked Hansen's next blow, landing an elbow high into Hansen's chest. Hansen didn't seem prepared for what was to come. He took a step back and reached for his gun, but Cirrelo sent a violent kick into Hansen's midsection, not only knocking Hansen back against the wall, but also knocking the gun from his possession.

Tony held the .38 steady, but didn't dare fire for fear of hitting Hansen. Cirrelo moved in and positioned himself to land another kick. This time Hansen anticipated correctly and moved deftly, blocking up and then planting a kick near Cirrelo's groin, just missing his target. Cirrelo adjusted and came at

Hansen with a flurry of sharp jabs. Hansen couldn't recover quickly enough. He made an attempt to block, but Cirrelo adjusted and Hansen couldn't regain an offensive posture.

Hansen tried to slide to his left and retrieve his gun. Cirrelo stepped back, and it looked like he was going to the opposite direction to get his gun, but then he whirled around, landing a kick that caught Hansen chest high and sent him back several steps. With the advantage, Cirrelo turned and went for his gun while Hansen tried to recover.

Tony had no choice. He fired, striking Cirrelo in the chest. Cirrelo turned and dropped to the floor. Tony ran over to Hansen. Hansen recovered enough to move toward his gun.

"Are you okay?" Tony said as he looked at the bloodied face of Mark Hansen.

Hansen, with gun in hand, managed to stand as Tony approached. Tony was reaching out for Hansen's face to check his wounds when Hansen violently pulled Tony forward, tripping him and pulling him face first to the ground. Tony, bewildered, found himself falling to the floor as he heard two shots.

Cirrelo, protected by a vest, had barely been grazed and had managed to retrieve his pistol. Hansen couldn't take another chance with this expert killer. He fired off two shots before Cirrelo raised his gun. This time Cirrelo went down with fatal head wounds.

Tony lay still. It took him a moment to realize he hadn't been shot. He looked up to see Hansen still standing. He raised himself on unsteady legs and turned to witness the dead Cirrelo. Turning to Hansen, Tony sighed with relief, and they exchanged silent glances that proclaimed survival, victory and thanks. He then put his arm around Hansen's shoulder, both in affection and in support, as they started down the hall.

"Spencer, can you hear me?" Hansen waited momentarily, adjusting his headset.

"Yeah, the doc and I are okay. Listen, call the bureau chief and let him know about Singer and Cortez. We're going to need back-up and federal warrants for the arrest of Wesley, Frascati, Ramsey and Cooper." They stood over Cirrelo for a moment.

"Oh, and Spencer, have them meet us at the office. Then call the paramedics and report the shootings at the building. I want more people here before the cops start filtering in. You'll have to call the police, but tell them you think Dr. Ryan's been shot." Again pausing and then slightly rolling his eyes, he said, "Yeah, you can come over."

Chapter 20

7:00 p.m., Wednesday, March 16

BY SEVEN P.M. THE place was swarming with the crew from the Santa Barbara Fire Department. They arrived first, followed by a local news team and then patrol officers of the Santa Barbara Police Department. This time the chief of the department, Leonard Callison, personally attended. He had been notified directly from the Washington bureau that the feds were present and involved, and that they were dealing with a federal crime. Callison played poker on Thursday night, and it was rare for his routine to be disrupted by more than an occasional inquiry about procedural matters from the station. Now he found himself at a scene at a medical office building where two FBI agents and a couple of hired assassins lay dead.

Callison arrived moments before two of his chief investigators, Frank Ramsey and A.T. Cooper, pulled their unmarked vehicle alongside Callison's car. They sprang quickly out of their car, surprised to find the chief standing next to his car. They conferred with him, and at their insistence Callison remained streetside, directing the general flow of traffic and gathering information as it filtered down. They preferred he stay out of the fray for the moment until they were certain everything had been secured. Callison didn't hesitate to agree. He could coordinate efforts just fine from the curb.

Michael Cirrelo lay dead in a pool of blood on the second floor while the police secured the building. There seemed to be a cooperative effort under way to investigate the crime scene and collect evidence. As planned, the paramedics arrived on the scene before the police. This clearly caught Ramsey by surprise and definitely perturbed him. Cooper tagged alongside and just kept looking over to Ramsey for a signal.

When Ramsey strode off the elevator on the third floor, he encountered Hansen. He would have drawn a weapon on him had it not been for the paramedics who were busy treating him. Although he soon expected a contingency of federal agents, Hansen would have to keep Ramsey occupied and off guard for a while.

"What's going on here? Who are you?" asked Ramsey, who appeared agitated but tried to sound in control.

Safely surrounded by two firemen, Hansen turned and offered his identification. "FBI, I'm Agent Mark Hansen. Are you with the police?"

Ramsey did the appropriate thing and showed his ID. "Frank Ramsey, investigator for the Santa Barbara PD. This is Detective Cooper." Cooper held his ID open for viewing. "We got a call that Dr. Ryan had been shot. What are you guys doing here?"

"Well, Mr. Ramsey and Mr. Cooper, we've got a federal criminal case here." The crowd of firefighters dispersed.

Ramsey asked, "Where's the body?" nonchalantly referring to Spencer's call.

Hansen walked back toward Tony's office as Ramsey and Cooper followed. They turned to his office and saw the body face down, but they were several feet away, unable to see who it was. "Poor Doc," Ramsey uttered without a hint of sincerity. "Do you know who did this?"

"Yes," Hansen stated simply.

Cooper looked over to Ramsey, waiting for some explanation from Hansen.

Hansen then asked, "Do you have any idea who this is?" If that didn't bewilder them enough, they froze where they stood as Spencer and Tony came walking out of Tony's office into the reception area.

"Hey, Detective Ramsey. And Cooper. I see you've met Agent Hansen,"

Tony said, adding, "The feds will be here in thirty or forty minutes. We just got off the phone with them. They left from L.A. ten minutes ago via an Air Force chopper."

It appeared that the two detectives needed to make a retreat. Ramsey actually backed up toward the door at the sight of Tony. He looked over to Hansen and asked, "So what's the score? Who's been shot?"

"Two/two. I've got two dead agents and two dead perps. Could you provide any information as to who they are? We'd like to know why someone's trying to murder Dr. Ryan. Maybe you can look at the one on the second floor. His name is Michael Cirrelo. We know these guys weren't working on their own. Any ideas?"

Ramsey maintained his composure, but the continuous clicking of his ballpoint pen signaled his uneasiness. He seemed to contemplate the question, looking in the direction of Cooper as though he hadn't a clue.

Hansen wanted to see him squirm. Tony would have preferred physical torture. These guys couldn't leave well enough alone. Money had become a drug they didn't want to give up, no matter whose life was at stake. Worse, they were the law. They held the power from the inside.

"How would I know? We'll be glad to help you with the investigation, though." Ramsey looked again at Cooper.

Tony then suggested, "Detective Cooper, as I recall, we found that sheet of paper in McVee's locker. Remember, the one you took from me. You know, the print identification for Michael Cirrelo, the one smudged with grease. I assume you told Ramsey about it."

The two detectives looked uncomfortably at each other.

Ramsey tried to downplay it. "We get print reports all the time. Maybe McVee was on to something. We'll have to check it out."

"You wouldn't happen to know anyone in the community interested in silencing Dr. Ryan, would you?" Hansen gave it another shot.

"Of course not. What are you getting at?" replied Ramsey, his apprehension mounting.

Hansen, perhaps sensing a change in demeanor, continued his discussion. "Well, we didn't just happen to show up. Somebody informed us that Dr. Ryan was in imminent danger. Normally, I suspect the police would have known that. You don't think someone inside the department has access to that kind of information, do you?"

Maybe because Tony knew what they knew, he read more into it, but Ramsey seemed to give Cooper an accusatory and questioning look.

Cooper remained poised yet quiet, furrowed his brow slightly and shot a glance to Ramsey. He might as well have told him, "Don't even think about it."

Ramsey rubbed his chin, still assessing the situation. He then looked at Hansen and simply said, "We need to get to work."

Cooper seemed to sense the difficult situation they were in and finally spoke to Ramsey. "Let's give a preliminary report to the chief. He'd probably like to come up here and meet Agent Hansen and assess the situation for himself."

They left by the elevator. As it descended, Hansen pulled out his agency-registered radio. He went on frequency with the response team. "Your two suspects, Ramsey and Cooper, will be exiting momentarily. Hold your positions until I signal."

They watched from the third floor as Ramsey and Cooper approached Chief Callison. They exchanged a few words, and then Callison headed for the building. Ramsey and Cooper got into their car. Hansen spoke a few words into his radio transmitter as Ramsey started to back up from the curb. Suddenly, like a steel curtain, four cars approached from two directions and blocked Ramsey and Cooper's exit. Callison, almost at the entrance to the building, turned around in complete bewilderment but made no move. Eight federal agents jumped out of their cars with weapons drawn and trained directly at Ramsey and Cooper. For several moments even the activity in the building ceased as the agents froze in position. Tony felt himself holding his breath during the momentary silent standoff. Over a loudspeaker one of the agents ordered them out of their car. Five very long seconds went by before the doors of the car opened and both walked out with their hands high above their heads. In a swarm, the agents swiftly approached and almost instantly had the two men handcuffed, frisked, stripped of their weapons, read their rights and then seated in separate cars.

Chief Callison came off the elevator on the third floor with three federal agents. "What in the world is going on here? Do you fellows have any idea who you've just arrested? Those are two of my top investigators. Who's in charge here?"

It actually amused Tony to see the chief so upset. Hansen stepped up, and before he responded to Callison, he shook hands with the lead agent. They just smiled at one another. "Stan Goldberg, this is Dr. Tony Ryan and Spencer McCade." Turning to Tony and Spencer, he said, "Stan is the main man in L.A. We're from the same graduating class."

"Who are you?" Callison interrupted.

Hansen explained to the dumbfounded Callison, and the investigation proceeded, with agents and police working cooperatively. Tony led Hansen and Spencer back into his private bathroom to clean up while he went to his desk to make a call. Tony's senses started to rebound as he shook off the numbing effect of his experience.

As Spencer emerged cleaned and polished, Tony stood up after hanging up the phone.

"So did you get a hold of her?" Spencer asked.

"No, that's not something I can safely do just yet, but I did talk to my buddy Jean Pierre. You might remember him — the doctor who came to visit me from France. We all had dinner together when you were out here. It was a few years ago. Anyway, he's seen that she's safely tucked away in a room under his name. I don't think anyone will find her."

They left Tony's personal office and walked out through the reception area, passing by the body still in his entryway. Tony shook his head. It could easily have been him, but instead his only real problem would be to replace the carpeting and patch a few holes.

He wondered how many holes in his psyche would need patching, for in this moment of victory, he was keenly aware that McVee, Phillips, Cortez and Singer would be impossible to replace, not to mention the poor people who had been used as pawns in the effort to dismantle the program. And yet he realized that the experiment was by no means a proven success. He looked at his good friend Spencer. He simply shook his head. All that male sensitivity stuff, and none of them really wanted to deal with the tragedy at hand. At least not verbally. At least not then.

Chapter 21

9:00 p.m., Wednesday, March 15

TONY AND SPENCER, LUCKY to have found seats in the crowded restaurant, sat at the bar sipping Chianti. They occupied a couple of stools at one corner. Tony sat with his back to the restaurant, leaning on the bar, wondering why he had convinced Hansen to let him and Spencer go in on their own. He told Hansen this would be the safest way to bring Emilio out, maybe even get a confession through the transmitter he still wore. Tony also wanted to see the expression on Emilio's face when Emilio saw he was still alive.

Spencer sat on the other side of the corner with a greater view of the restaurant. The light had been dimmed enough to enhance appearances, but Spencer could still adequately survey the surroundings. Frascati's restaurant on this Wednesday night flowed with a healthy following of its devotees. The lively chatter of the evening made it difficult to hear the barely audible background vocals of Tony Bennett.

Tony had a sport coat on over his shirt, which was still snugly filled by the protective vest. As he sipped the wine, he tried to relax, wanting to savor a few minutes of calm before pursuing what was bound to complete a memorable odyssey. The crowd around the bar thickened. A couple of ladies moved uncomfortably close to Tony and Spencer. Tony turned and asked if they would like his seat as they continued squeezing next to him. They thanked him but gave him a fish-eyed look when he took his drink and moved to stand on the other side of Spencer, as though he found their subtle flirtations offensive. He had a better view of the restaurant. Still adjusting to the light, he looked from booth to booth, trying to find Emilio.

"By the way, guess what the feds found while you and Hansen cleaned up back at your office."

Tony stopped looking for a moment and faced Spencer. "What?" he asked.

"They got warrants and raided the police department. Among other things, they turned up a copy of the videotape from Weissman's house. The one we saw. Found it in Cooper's locker along with that print ID sheet you saw. They also talked with the mechanic, Sewell. He confirmed McVee found an explosive device on your car and sent a memo to Ramsey. He says they blew the thing up in the courtyard." Spencer took another sip of wine.

"Good. After we killed Cirrelo, I wasn't sure there would be enough evidence against Cooper or Ramsey outside of my testimony. In fact, I wouldn't be surprised if they can't get a ballistics match with the bullet that killed Cortez. We ought to be able to put them away. What a price for a little peace, no?"

"Yeah, it's expensive, but maybe you've finally won the battle." Spencer patted him on the shoulder.

Tony, still looking for Emilio, contemplated his win. Then he added, "Maybe it's a victory for the program. I hope so. When we planned this thing, we went through several contingencies, trying to think of everything. We knew a lot of people didn't want it to succeed, but clearly we didn't focus on the right ones."

Tony continued, "Also, to be honest, I've always wanted the program to work. I've always thought it was for the best. You know that. But for a while it became a personal issue even beyond my brother's death. I think I believed some of the media hype. It's as though I had to prove the experiment was right; otherwise my entire character would be trashed. Any semblance of a good name would have been meaningless. I'd be history, even as a cosmetic surgeon. Yet, really, all I've ever wanted to do was run this experiment to see if it works. I don't need this for my ego."

"We all know that," Spencer said, using his comforting tone. "That's the great thing about having you run this program. You didn't need to. I'm surprised you did it at all, even with your history. Your benefit is marginal, while you had everything to lose. But hey, you're coming out on top. At least in this round."

"Hey, Spencer, I think he's over there." Tony gestured across the room.

Emilio wasn't in his usual location, but as Tony scanned the booths, he noticed the familiar face of an attractive young lady with shoulder-length dirty-blond hair. She wore the same bright red lipstick and a similar pair of large decorative earrings he had remembered seeing during her consultation a few weeks ago. He recognized her as one of the women who had filed a complaint with the state medical board. Seeing her, he still recalled little about the consultation, other than telling her that he thought her B cup breasts were well shaped and didn't require augmentation. He doubted there could have been grounds for a complaint. Obviously, Emilio Frascati had been the one to orchestrate these complaints.

She sat in a booth facing Tony. He couldn't make out whom she was sitting with, but there appeared to be at least two other people in her booth. A man with his back to Tony could have been Emilio, but he couldn't see well enough to tell.

Tony took another sip from his glass, more for ceremony and less for strength, and then tapped Spencer on the arm. "I think Emilio is sitting over there. There's a girl in the booth that came in for a consultation. She's one of the women who filed a complaint with the state medical board. It's such bullshit, the way I've been set up, yet they could potentially revoke my license. I saw Diane Turner in that same booth only two nights ago. It's a good thing we arrested Ramsey and Cooper, or they probably would have found some way of charging me with her murder. Anyway, I'm going to walk over for a visit. Keep an eye on me."

Walking through the aisles of the restaurant, Tony felt uncomfortably out of place. He had never been one to table-hop and schmooze with the crowd. It just wasn't his style. As he closed in on the people at the table, he saw Emilio was indeed seated with his back to him. Two women, in animated conversation, shared his booth. "I've spotted Emilio and am approaching," he said, speaking softly yet directly toward his transmitter, fairly sure no one in the restaurant was paying any attention.

Tony purposely walked over and placed his hand on Emilio's shoulder, giving him a firm squeeze. On other occasions it might have been affectionate, but Tony had a point to make. Tonight he figured Emilio had no expectations of seeing him, at least not standing with his hand on his shoulder. Emilio didn't jump, nor did he remove his gaze from the ladies, probably to show a sophisticated ennui for the sake of appearance. But when Tony said, "Hello, Emilio. I wanted to thank you personally for your referrals," Emilio turned much too abruptly unable to hide his astonishment. Then instantly he caught himself and turned on his casual charm.

"Why, if it isn't the famous Dr. Ryan. And where is that lovely creature Montana? Is she in Rome yet?" Not waiting for an answer, he continued from his seat, "Tony, may I present my guests, Cynthia and Barbara. Ladies, this is Dr. Anthony Ryan, Santa Barbara's illustrious cosmetic surgeon." Cynthia was an attractive brunette, seated in the middle, whom Tony had never seen before. She clearly had no idea as to the situation. On the other hand, Barbara's demeanor changed dramatically from the vivacious expression she had worn moments ago.

"My brother was engaged to a girl named Cynthia," Tony said. It didn't hurt remembering Paul at the moment.

"And for what referrals are you thanking me?"

"Well, for starters, Barbara here, and then poor Diane Turner. Gee, Emilio, you don't think Barbara could end up like Diane, do you? Did Diane do something very bad? Is that why she was killed?" Tony knew Emilio would try to play him for the fool, but Barbara appeared genuinely concerned, and her expression revealed she might actually be frightened.

"Tony, are you feeling okay? What in the world are you talking about?" Emilio stood his ground. Deny, deny, deny, thought Tony.

But Barbara became unglued before Tony's eyes. He decided to work on her a little. "Do you realize the penalty for declaring false accusations, let alone the potential losses you might incur from a civil suit for defamation of character? I hope you have very good counsel. I do. My attorneys are preparing the court case now. I don't intend to give up my practice and my good name without compensation."

Emilio tried to interrupt, saying, "Tony, if you have some problem."

Tony kept talking to Barbara, ignoring Emilio. "Listen, you can think anything you want, but I know Diane Turner is dead. I saw her myself. She also lodged false complaints against me. Do you think I would be telling you she's dead if I killed her? Unlikely. On the other hand, you know you lied about me, as did Diane. Could there possibly be someone who wouldn't want that information to accidentally leak out, and that person might even want to make me look like a killer?"

Emilio was now signaling for one of his security men. Barbara was frantic, looking at Emilio for support.

As the security man started past the bar, Spencer walked from the bar and backed into him, not quite spilling his drink, but causing enough of a commotion that even Tony turned around for a moment.

"Emilio, what's going on?" asked Barbara. "I thought you told me there wouldn't be any problems." Now she was on the verge of tears, saying, "How come this is happening?"

Tony could tell she was scared for herself and had no idea what really went on with Emilio's business.

Emilio tried to assure her. "I have no idea what Dr. Ryan is talking about. Now please, Doctor, will you kindly leave and allow me to salvage what remains of this evening?"

But Barbara had panicked. "Is Diane really dead? Did you know about that?" she asked Emilio.

Tony felt a sudden sharp jolt as a hand caught him firmly in the back and then grabbed his right wrist and pulled it up behind his back. The security man had broken free from Spencer and now had Tony in a bouncer's lock. He spun him around, pointing him toward the doorway. Tony felt every eye in the place following him as the security man roughly pushed him along toward the doorway. He tried not to resist, but his arm ached from the pressure. Out of view of the patrons inside, Emilio's security pushed him through the front door. Almost upon exiting, three FBI agents confronted the security man with their guns drawn. The agents rapidly dispensed of him without a struggle.

Tony walked back into the restaurant and right up to Emilio. He was clearly trying to hush up Barbara. She saw him coming, became quiet and stared directly at him.

Emilio turned around and saw Tony standing less than ten feet away. Provoked, he shot up out of his booth and approached Tony, face to face. "What the hell are you doing in this place?" Smart enough to know Tony didn't wrestle his big bouncer for the opportunity to come back in, he changed his tone quickly, saying, "Look, Tony, I've liked you and Montana all these years, but you can't come into my business and start disrupting everything." Emilio started to show some sweat along his brow and temples. It was the first sign that he was truly worried.

"It's over, Emilio," Tony said softly yet deliberately straight to his face. "You don't deserve it, but I came in here to get you, to save your restaurant, your employees and your patrons the embarrassment. The FBI is waiting for you outside. It's over." In that moment, Tony could see the fire in Emilio's eyes start to dim. "Cirrelo and his buddy are dead, and so are two FBI agents. I don't have to tell you where that puts you. Ramsey and Cooper have been arrested as well. It's your choice how you leave."

Emilio looked around helplessly. He may have been surrounded by his personal security, but there was no fighting his way out. He tried once more with words. "Tony, all I do is run a restaurant. All these people you're talking about mean nothing to me. I don't have a clue what you're talking about."

"Then you shouldn't have any trouble defending yourself," Tony said. He looked at Emilio, bit the inside of his cheek and shook his head. It wasn't something he wanted to believe, even now. It was sad and pathetic. "It looks like money was your worst drug. You had a good enough business, Emilio. Why couldn't you have just stayed legit?"

Emilio knew it was over and finally responded, "I couldn't. You have no idea how much money is on the line with your crazy experiment. It's deep. The organization is really deep. I just couldn't back out, even though I wanted to."

"So you were willing to have me killed?" Tony still couldn't believe it.

"No, not killed. I set you up. That's true. I just wanted to get you out of the picture, not kill you."

"For some reason I believe you. Then why were they trying to kill me?" Tony asked.

"Someone went over my head. There's an organization. You probably know of the Sandovals in Bolivia. I don't think they want to keep playing anymore, but there's others who do. I wouldn't play it their way. This thing got out of hand. They thought the experiment would be over within a week if you were eliminated, especially if it looked drug-related," Emilio continued. "So much money was being lost, and they didn't want Sandoval to walk away leaving them out. They put the screws to everyone."

"Who is 'they'? What's Burt Wesley's role? Is he the 'old man' Salinski referred to?"

Emilio stopped. He realized Tony didn't have all of the answers. Even Tony realized Emilio's best chance at a reduced sentence came from what he knew. He offered, "Sandoval pulls the strings. I don't know who else plays in the middle."

Tony knew he was lying. It would probably take a good defense attorney and some well-structured dealing to coax this information out of Emilio. Nonetheless, Tony still had questions and persisted. "What happened to Diane Turner?"

"A beautiful girl. You know, she really wanted that operation. I guaranteed her there would be no problems. I had her believing we were actually doing something to help you. You know, get you out of the flack. She went to her car one night and saw Cirrelo coming up from under a car. She also went to that charity affair and recognized Cirrelo talking with one of the bosses. She got too involved and went to the cops, realizing that this guy tampered with the Mason car. She was a kind person, so she went to the cops. It was easier for them to eliminate her."

He started walking out with Tony. A few faces looked up, but most people kept to themselves, conspicuously avoiding eye contact with them. They slowly trekked through the restaurant. This would be the last time Emilio would see the institution he had created. Tony wondered how much success was attributed to drug money. Perhaps he financed the restaurant with the money. Tony wondered if the restaurant would remain open. He hoped Emilio's foibles wouldn't automatically penalize the honest restaurant crew he had employed. Had it not been for a few breaks, Emilio and his network might have brought down the entire experiment. It was hard to imagine how this overtly congenial host had been the co-producer of so much violence.

They walked past his beloved bar. So many times Emilio could be found there, entertaining late into the night, himself behind the bar, freely pouring grappa for his friends. Reaching the entryway, he turned around, saying, "Just one moment," and he surveyed his restaurant for a last time. Without turning his head, he said, "It was business, just business."

An FBI agent quickly slapped a set of handcuffs on Emilio's wrists and led him away. Tony stared, wishing he hadn't been so close to Emilio all these years. Part of him felt sorry for the decent part of Emilio, wherever it was. Before he could get too melancholy about the past, Mark Hansen bounded up to the entrance with news for Tony and Spencer.

"Okay, fellows, we managed to track down Wesley and make the arrest. They tell me he's infuriated and vehemently denies any involvement with criminal activity."

"I'd expect as much," Tony responded, "but I'm not one of his biggest fans." Then he softened his stand and said something he didn't expect. "I hate to admit it, but he had legitimate reasons to be upset about the drop in his business. Maybe he's telling the truth." He hesitated, looked at Spencer and added, "God, did I just say that?"

Spencer then noted, "If that's the case, what was Felton doing on his boat?"

"I have a little trouble believing that's just coincidental myself," Hansen added. "At any rate, none of us think Wesley's the main organizer behind this. There may be quite a few characters we need to track down."

"I'm sure one of the cops or Emilio will be only too happy to name names," Tony suggested. "How else can they expect to reduce their sentences?"

Hansen then clarified the problem. "You're definitely right, but don't expect to see that happen right away. These guys will be meeting with their attorneys, and it will take some time before they actually strike a deal. By

267

then, it's quite possible that Mr. X, or a whole bunch of Mr. Xs, will be living in other countries."

"So what do you do?" Tony asked.

"We'll pester the hell out of those guys. We'll pull everyone's records and do a thorough investigation." Hansen sounded confident, adding, "We'll find dozens of people involved in this organization, I assure you."

Tony and Spencer participated in the preliminary investigation and debriefing for another two hours. When they finally left, it was ten-thirty.

They drove to Tony's house to spend the evening while Hansen ultimately found his way back to Brenda's. Tony pulled into his garage, feeling safe at his own home for the first time in two days. A man should feel safe in his own home.

Hearing no barking, Tony asked, "Hey, where are the dogs?"

"Silvia probably took them home since she hadn't heard from you," Spencer pointed out.

They walked into the dark house. Tony turned on the lights and did a quick survey to assure himself that no one had ransacked the house or done anything terrible to the dogs. He turned on the lights to the backyard and walked outside, tripping over a garden hose and the metal sprinkler control rod on the way.

Spencer laughed out loud and helped Tony up, at the same time picking up the metal rod and presenting it to him. "Here you go, old fellow. You might need a little cane for assistance around the yard."

Tony brushed himself off, saying, "I ought to look where I'm going, but I do that more often than I'd care to admit. When I look at this view, I never pay attention to the things around me."

"God, it's tremendous," said Spencer, standing next to Tony.

"It's really quite pleasant out here, isn't it? I bet it's over seventy. Warm for this time of year," Tony said as they strolled over to couple of lounge chairs. After the weather report, Tony offered, "Why don't I grab a couple of beers? We can unwind out here for a little while."

"You've got my vote," Spencer said as he plopped himself into one of the lounge chairs and Tony dropped his impromptu cane by the side of the other.

His endogenous drugs, when put to the test, had kept him full steam ahead on red alert, but now as the engines had a chance to idle, most of that feeling had waned. With slight feelings of exhilaration being replaced by exhaustion, Tony felt the slightest nervous tingling in his arms as he retrieved the brews from the refrigerator.

Outside, they reclined in the lounge chairs and mostly looked at the clear starry sky while they sipped on the cold beer. They laughed and they toasted, and they let their eyes glaze over with tears that didn't quite roll down onto their cheeks.

"What are you going to do about Montana?" Spencer asked.

"I can't very well have her go back to Rome. I hope Hansen's able to get the Italians to go after Emilio's cousin. Maybe I'll have Jean Pierre get her a ticket for home." Tony reflected on the last few days and relaxed for the first time, knowing that Montana was in a safe place and he finally had a moment of tranquility.

"Buchman's goin' to go nuts when he hears all that's happened," Spencer said as he tilted his head back and guzzled down the remaining beer. It must have landed straight in his bladder because he promptly declared, "I've got to go to the bathroom. Let me go see if I remember where it's hidden."

Tony had nearly drifted to sleep in his relaxation when he heard the side gate slam and a man enter the backyard. He started to stand up, but a loud voice ordered, "Stay where you are, Dr. Ryan. Stay right in that chair."

From the confines of the shadows a bulky six-foot silhouetted figure emerged into the dim light of the backyard. And Tony didn't move, because he could clearly see a gleam of light reflecting off a pistol in the intruder's right hand.

As the man approached, those endogenous engines in Tony's system starting churning again. He strained to see who this character was, but he remained a dark silhouette.

"I assure you there's not much in the way of easy cash or jewelry around the house, but you're welcome to it," Tony said, trying to ameliorate the tense situation.

"I'm not interested in your property, Dr. Ryan." The man continued his slow march toward Tony. Something about the deliberate nature of each step

269

made Tony feel as if this guy savored the idea of holding Tony captive. Tony had been through enough. He didn't feel like squirming for some monster's pleasure.

A few more steps and the man came within ten feet of Tony. The light from the house shone well enough off his face that Tony could now see the whites of Gordon Welding's eyes.

"Mr. Welding, what are you doing? Are you okay?" Tony looked as confused as he sounded.

Welding smiled, a broad menacing grin that held Tony in check as much as the gun in his hand. "Oh, I assure you, Doctor, I'm feeling better by the second."

"Why me, Gordon? What's the problem? I'm sure if we talk about it we can find a better solution." Tony tried not to be condescending, but going into doctor mode often had that effect. He wished he were still wired, so everyone would know what he now knew. Gordon Welding, with all of his wealth and power, with his position as bank president and confidant to a U.S. senator, stood near the top of the feeding chain of drug dealers. He might not ever have taken a single drug, but he made millions off the drugs others took.

"You smug son of a bitch. I watched you on C-SPAN during those congressional hearings talk about the failed drug war and all the people it harmed. Look, you stupid jerk. If those idiots want to take drugs, we don't need the country condoning it. The way it was, we took their money and filtered it back into private industry. With your program, the government will just find more ways of wasting it."

Tony was aghast, but Welding, in his demented way, made sense. "So does that make you a liberal, conservative, or libertarian?" Tony asked. "And you're calling me smug? Crime's down, innocent people don't have to pay for someone else's habit. But I guess we're lucky to have Gordon Welding to invest our stolen property. Capitalism, maybe. Free enterprise? I don't think so."

"Frankly, Ryan, I don't care what you think anymore. Your smart-ass antics are getting old. When I told Winston to have you appointed as director of the program, I figured it would be fun watching you disintegrate. You made it tough, though. Smart or lucky, take your choice, I just don't care anymore."

"Come on. You know every FBI agent in the country will be looking for you. It's not worth it." Tony must have sounded like he was pleading, because Welding looked a little more satisfied.

Tony slowly stood up. He needed to get a little closer to the gun if he wanted a chance to disarm him. Welding backed up a step, and before Tony could make another move, Welding sent a powerful kick into his midsection, sending him back onto the lounge chair gasping.

Tony watched Welding approach while he fought for a breath of air. Welding, possessed with a rage whose only rationality lay in how he planned to delight himself by tormenting Tony, held the gun in his right hand and pulled a pair of handcuffs from his left pants pocket.

"Turn over on your stomach."

"Welding, this isn't going to help."

"When I get through with you this evening, the whole world will know what a disaster this experiment has been."

"Me? What are you talking about?" Tony still hadn't moved.

"Turn over, or I'll start our little game now." Welding pointed the gun at Tony's crotch. Tony reluctantly turned over on his stomach with his hands down off the sides of the chair, ready to push himself back if he had the chance.

"You still haven't told me about your plans," Tony said to Welding. Just keep him talking, Tony thought. Spencer, where the hell are you already?

Suddenly Tony gasped as he felt the weight of Welding's left knee in the small of his back. "I thought you might like to try a little coke and PCP, registered in your very own name, of course, Welding said. "First, I thought we might want to restrain you. You know how violent you can become and how I'll have no choice but to fight for my very own life. Self-defense, of course. Isn't it a shame how these drugs have ruined so many valuable lives?"

Welding reached down with his left hand. "Okay, Ryan, put that left arm behind your back now. Right hand, too."

Tony lifted his left arm slowly toward Welding. Glancing back over his right shoulder, he saw the gun in his extended right hand while he heard Welding momentarily fumble with the handcuffs, readying them for placement on Tony's left wrist. Tony couldn't wait any longer for Spencer.

With his right hand, he reached down by the side of the lounge, grabbed the metal rod and with the swiftest, firmest backhand he'd ever swung, delivered a blow sharply to Welding's forearm. He thought he heard a snap, and almost right after that he heard the sound of metal falling against the deck.

The blow knocked Welding off balance, and he fell to his left. Tony quickly rose to his feet but didn't see the gun right away.

Welding steadied himself on the ground and stood up like an injured grizzly bear. He looked down to his right. Tony caught the direction of his gaze and followed it to the gun. Welding lumbered toward the gun a step ahead of Tony, but Tony had the speed and just managed to kick the gun far into the bushes as the injured Welding reached for it with his left hand.

Behind him, Tony saw the light in the kitchen go on. He yelled out loud, "Spencer!"

Welding, in a rage, went after Tony, throwing the entire weight of his body into him, trying to wrestle him to the ground. His right arm was ineffectual, but he outweighed Tony by thirty or forty pounds.

Tony started to fall under Welding's weight but quickly stepped back, ducked into a crouch and pulled Welding forward, sending him sprawling on the ground. Welding snagged Tony around the ankles and tripped him, so that Tony landed directly in front of his swimming pool.

Before Tony could get out of the way, the lumbering bear tackled him chest high, and the two landed with a huge splash in the middle of the lap pool.

Tony rose to the surface and, standing up, momentarily spotted Spencer. Before he could make a sound, Welding wrapped his left arm around Tony's head in a furious headlock, pulled him back and submerged him.

Tony struggled to regain control but couldn't push off the bottom of the shallow pool with Welding dragging him backward. Tony took his right elbow and swung it through the water, landing a blow directly into Welding's groin. The grasp loosened, allowing Tony to gain his footing.

Before Welding could grab him again, Tony latched on to the injured right arm and torqued it between the wrist and elbow with all his might. Welding let out a howl that must have echoed into the canyon. Tony landed a punch directly into Welding's nose, sending the broad beast backward. Tony's rage had taken hold, and he delivered a rapid fury of punches into Welding's bloodied face until Welding's legs finally gave in and he fell backward, unconscious.

At that point he could have easily let Welding drown, but he hated him too much for all the misery he had caused.

"Spencer, throw me those cuffs."

Tony quickly secured the cuffs onto Welding's wrists and then dragged him to the side of the pool.

Spencer used the lifeline by the pool to secure a restraining noose around Welding's neck while Tony pulled himself out of the blood-tinged waters.

"By the way, I called 911," Spencer declared a bit sheepishly.

Tony's energy had been spent. "Better than the coroner, I suppose."

While the puddles formed around Tony's feet, the two buddies guarded their number-one assailant. They silently welcomed the sound of the approaching sirens.

Chapter 22

4:00 p.m., Friday, March 18

STANDING IN LINE AT the Hertz counter in Nice, Tony patiently waited while an American argued in English with the saleslady. It was refreshing. Tony may have been the only one in line not bothered by it. He welcomed this triviality as an invitation back to civilization. He reset his watch to just after four. It was Friday afternoon. The southern coast of France was bathed in a warm afternoon sun. The way the air felt and the way the coastline swept an arc around the bay reminded him of Santa Barbara. However, this coastline, the Côte d'Azur, had been built over many more generations and sparkled with yacht-filled slips and moorings as well as a dense collection of hotels and condominiums encroaching on the shoreline.

He slowly advanced in line. His single suitcase off to the side, he carried only the L.A. Times from the day before. Spencer had indeed nailed down one of the year's biggest exclusives. Not only did the network news feature the Santa Barbara stories, but Spencer's written report had also been chronicled through a multitude of syndications.

Leaving from Los Angeles on Thursday night had been no small task. Although he should have been physically exhausted, he felt rejuvenated by the anticipation of getting away and of simply surviving. He had been up most

274

of the night before being debriefed by the FBI. The cleaning crew worked in the office late into the night, mopping up as much as possible. A decorative throw rug was still needed to hide some of the deeper bloodstains that hadn't come out.

On three hours' sleep, he managed to hold it together well enough to make it through the morning's cases and see patients in the afternoon. He checked Rob Mason's nose one last time. It didn't need to be reset, and his case with the SBPD had been formally dropped. This helped add a little more closure to the events of the week.

Joanna had taken care of all of his travel arrangements and rescheduled the next week's cases. Brenda would check the post-op patients, and Dr. Tarbon agreed, once again, to cover for Tony.

He caught a commuter plane to Los Angeles and arrived with ample time before his scheduled departure. He had to politely beat back a few news crews at the airport, but he was in such a haze it didn't bother him. When he finally settled into his business-class seat, he didn't mind that the seat next to him wasn't occupied. He was in no mood for conversation. He melted into his soft cushioned seat, and the stress of the last several days finally began to shed. With paper in hand, Tony looked forward to putting his feet up and reviewing the story.

On the front page was a picture of Tony and Hansen, and then smaller pictures of Cortez and Singer. The caption read: Two FBI Agents Slain During Coup on Santa Barbara Experiment. Crime: FBI arrests expose branch of Bolivian cartel. By Spencer McCade, Satellite News Service. Santa Barbara.

The story covered in detail the events of the last week. When Tony read that Burton Wesley had been released for lack of evidence, he shrugged, realizing how sometime the obvious wasn't so obvious. He wondered if Wesley might not have wanted Welding and crew to succeed anyway. Sure he did, he thought, and there were many others who probably felt the same.

Tony admired the way Spencer had constructed the story. It made him a little uneasy reliving it in the press, but he felt comforted as Congressman Michael Delgado (D-El Paso, Texas) provided a summation. "We are relieved to find that the cause of the recent violence in Santa Barbara was not attributed to drug use and the experiment directly, but rather to the same nefarious element that we are rallying against — the criminal organization that profits at the expense of all of the citizenry. Perhaps now Leslie Phillips can rest peacefully, and Congress won't be so eager to abandon its experiment in Santa Barbara. We will follow its due course, learning from its mistakes, benefiting from its successes and improving our understanding as we go along."

Tony laid the paper on his lap and let his head fall back, exhausted but relieved. He remembered Jimmy McVee admonishing him for his stubborn position on the experiment, believing that Tony's ego got in the way. Tony knew McVee was partly right. It had become a fuzzy issue without clear boundaries. It concerned him that they did the right thing with regard to the experiment and held their course. Nonetheless, he had to admit it bothered him to think how the community would react if the experiment, and he with it, failed. He wanted to be a Howard Roark or a John Galt out of an Ayn Rand novel, but this was real life and he had so much to lose. Now that he could reflect on the situation, having stood his ground, it bothered him that he had succumbed to the weakness within. Why should he care what people thought about him? His ego was rock solid, or was it? He could withstand the scrutiny of his critics. But what if the critics won?

Such had been the luck of his life, he realized. Believing in himself, even when nobody else did. Believing he would become a doctor when his college counselor told him otherwise. Believing in his implant devices when he was told they couldn't be approved. Believing in the decriminalization of drugs long before it garnered any popularity. All of these things, and more, he realized, did not come without self-doubt. It may have been a weakness in his ego, or perhaps even a strength. It was okay, he realized. To be willing to fail was as important as the desire to win and inevitably necessary in order to achieve. Self-doubt was simply part of the process.

The experiment was by no means a success story. Tony was not yet a winner, but for now he had survived a very critical test.

Tony didn't have any problem finding his rental car, but on his way out he made a wrong turn. He went around the airport a second time before he found his way out to the main highway. He worked his way down the concrete corridor of the Promenade des Anglais. The warmth had drawn a number of people to the beaches. The atmosphere was safe and civilized. Tony toured past the Hotel Negresco and several other hotels and apartments. He slowed down as he turned left around the familiar bay with so many boats packed into the docks. He might have been driving into the scenery of an impressionist painting. The brilliant colors, the contrasts of old European buildings with new modern facilities, a line of salty fishing vessels bobbing gently in the same waters next to sparkling luxury craft, and the smell of fresh baguettes provoked not only his appetite but his fondest memories as Tony headed eastward along the French Riviera.

Coursing up the hill on the main road leading to St. Jean Cap-Ferrat, he let his memory flood with images of the first time he and Montana had come to this place. He started to laugh to himself. Again he could remember his jogging wife leading him on a tour of Cap-Ferrat, up and down through the pine-scented hills, through Bel Air on the beach. His workouts with Montana had earned him the calories they later enjoyed at Louis XV or Le Chevre d'Or. He could picture Montana, with a golden tan and her hair highlighted by the late afternoon sun, standing on the balcony of the Grand Hotel du Cap-Ferrat. The gardens of the hotel spread beneath her like a green carpet leading to the azure-blue waters of the Mediterranean. It was one of the few times he looked at his wife as a priceless piece of art and had the presence of mind to actually capture it on film.

Driving the final half-mile to the hotel, he grew anxiously excited to find Montana. They had not spoken. He did not want to take any chances of alerting anyone of his presence. This had been their agreed-upon point of rendezvous, should it be necessary. Clearly, plan B had gone into effect, and now he passed through the winding streets of St. Jean Cap-Ferrat, past the stately French homes. A man and his wife strolled with their cocker spaniel along the way. He felt safe, as if he was going home. He drove into the driveway through the high gates of the hotel and pulled up to the entrance.

The bellman took his bag, and he left him several francs as he wandered over to the front desk. The receptionist appeared, neatly dressed in a blue cotton suit with white trim. Her young and attractive appearance belied her most proper and cordial demeanor.

"Bonjour, Monsieur. Avez-vous une reservation?"

Tony knew what she had asked, but had plenty of time to practice his

French later. He presented his passport, saying in English, "I'm Dr. Tony Ryan and I'm here to meet Jean Pierre Levant. Can you please let him know I am here?"

"Actually, sir," she said in clear, slightly accented English, "Monsieur Levant is not here yet. He has a guest staying in his room."

"Good, then. You can send my things up to his room." That elicited a startled response, but Tony quickly added, "It's okay. His guest is expecting me as well."

She smiled courteously, replying, "Très bien, monsieur."

Tony then turned toward the marble hallway leading to the back stairs down to the gardens. He couldn't recall ever walking down this path without Montana. A few tables in the garden were occupied with late-afternoon revelers enjoying tea.

He continued down through the gardens, crossed the cobblestone road and entered the panoramic patio courtyard that led to the path down to the pool. From where he stood looking out at the sea from a few hundred feet above it, the pool area wasn't visible. Far below, it lay cut into the rocky surroundings of the natural cove. A funicular to his right led straight down the hill to the pool, but he chose to walk the winding path, savoring the soft breezes of the late afternoon.

It took a few minutes to reach the pool. He stood at its entrance, scanning the area. The deep-blue saltwater horizon pool melded perfectly into the Côte d'Azur. Were he not anxious to find Montana, he might have stood there for several minutes enjoying the pleasure of the view. To his left, a cream-colored tent framed by salmon pastels provided shelter for a charming outdoor restaurant and bar where a few people were enjoying cocktails and snacks. Montana was not among them. Tony scanned the area by the pool for sun worshipers. A few people lounged about, mostly in pairs. With the late afternoon sun fading, most of the loungers wore tops, so he didn't feel intrusive strolling around the deck.

Farther away from the pool, a terraced hill crept down toward the shore. One could easily find solace in the hidden recesses of the jagged coastline. Unlike the west coast of California, no large waves broke on the shore. Rather, the waters splashed softly against the jutting rock. Then he saw her. She was nestled in a large pullover sweatshirt bearing the hotel logo, hidden behind a pair of overlarge sunglasses, and her tan legs blithely graced the cushion of the chaise lounge. As she had done so many times over the years, she read a novel, resting the book on her lap. It must have been interesting. Engrossed in her story, she didn't notice Tony as he walked over to her spot. Several times he would have come within her line of vision, but the final approach took him toward her chair from behind. He had imagined the scenario several times coming over on the plane. They would spot each other from across the pool and with abandon come running into each other's arms. Now that the moment had arrived, he found comfort in knowing Montana was safe, even if his fairy-tale ending was a little off course.

As Montana turned the page of her novel, a hand reached out to steady her book from behind her chair. Tony's hand. She didn't flinch or jump out of her lounge. Instead, her graceful hand grabbed him gently on the wrist and pulled his hand close to her face, simply kissing him on the back of the hand and holding it against her cheek. In that moment Tony reunited with his other half. From his awkward position, kneeling at the rear and side of her lounge chair, he moved forward, and without speaking, lifted Montana as she swung her legs to his side. She stood, and they looked at each other, almost as if to survey for any damage and simultaneously affirm their transcendent spirit. The words were spoken with their eyes. Tony drew her closer. They kissed lightly at first, backed off for a moment to make certain their togetherness was for real, and then they kissed again, deeply. He then slid her head against his shoulder, holding her so close he wished they could fuse together. They had no desire to tempt the fates again. But they had, by fate, survived one of life's hazardous encounters and now stood together in their safe haven. Bathed in serenity, simply by standing together and breathing the same air, they were at home.

ACKNOWLEDGMENTS

Writing this book has been a very unusual undertaking. I began it in 1993 and completed the first draft a little more than a year later. My mother-in-law, Melva, heard my thoughts from the start and was the guinea pig who read the first draft. I think she was shocked that she liked it. Unfortunately, first novels do not have editors to tweak them into proper form, and so the first of many rewrites ensued. Boy, was I naive about the process.

I'd like to thank my wife, Saralee, who put up with a lot of hours spent in discussion, or at least listening to me self-discuss, where I was going with this story. She helped me over several bumps. Having a full-time job made it difficult to find adequate time to work on the novel, and so it got done at the expense to our time together, or often after everyone else in the house was asleep.

Next, I would like to thank Marion Rosenberg for initially taking on the book. She helped me with innumerable corrections, found me my first editor, and tested the waters for publication. Sherry Sonnett reviewed my story and gave me a lot of good ideas.

Matty Simmons read the story and suggested that it might work as a screenplay. Ultimately, I wrote a draft for a screenplay. I took a couple of weekend courses, read a few books, and off I went. Along the way, I met Leslie Kallen, who has been very supportive. She did me a favor and sent my book to Frank Weimann in New York. Kathy McCormack, who read it for Weimann, suggested that the book had potential and referred me to Ed Stackler to edit the content.

I believe this was my most significant and fortunate connection. Ed really helped me more than anyone else to improve the story. Ed not only supported me in the writing process, but also in many other areas that a first-time novelist encounters.

At Ed Stackler's suggestion, I found a copy editor, Sue Coffman — www. grammardoctor.com. This Southern lady left enough red ink on my novel to confirm my level of illiteracy. I can't imagine anyone more thorough.

Several other people have read the book during its evolution. In particular, my Aunt Marie and Jo Ann Davilla, have provided insight and encouragement. My dear friend, Mark Brender, provided me with a number of pertinent corrections. Beth Althofer pushed me along with a number of good ideas. Several others have been kind in their support — or at least their lack of degradation. Even my son, Sean, as a pre-schooler suggested that I needed a "boat" scene in the story.

In preparing the story, I used many reports from several newspapers, books, and periodicals. Nonetheless, Peter McWilliams' Ain't Nobody's Business — The Absurdity of Consensual Crimes, provided the greatest wealth of information. Once I read his book, I realized that ninety percent of the research had been done. Ironically, Peter McWilliams became the center of a court case that denied him access to marijuana — the drug he needed. What's absurd is that he recently died because he couldn't use medicinal marijuana to stimulate his appetite or control his nausea. I always hoped I could share my novel with him — instead I'm only able to offer posthumous gratitude.

When I was an undergraduate at UCLA, I took an engineering course called "Patterns of Problem Solving," taught by Moshe Rubinstein. (He's also authored a book by the same name and still teaches.) Not only did the course discuss various ways to solve problems, it emphasized the importance of avoiding unnecessary limiting constraints — something we need to do if we ever want to solve the problem of drugs or drug prohibition. I thought it appropriate to remember him in this book.

When I began work on this book (in 1993), I was forty years old. I had never personally experienced any of the drug-related violence that prompted me to consider the solution to the drug wars. In 1996, however, that all changed. While picking up a little necklace for my wife at our jeweler's, an armed robbery took place. I was handcuffed, robbed, and threatened with a gun to my head. I contemplated the possibility of my book being published posthumously. As if that wasn't bad enough, my wife, Saralee, was robbed of her watch and ring at gunpoint in daylight nearly one year later. Both crimes were clearly drug-related — not because the perpetrators were on drugs, but because they needed money to finance their drug deals. This was the very reason I took up writing this story, never thinking I would have two opportunities to see such behavior up close.

Finally, I want to acknowledge who I am, or perhaps who I am not. I am not interested in taking drugs. I am not interested in seeing people have their lives consumed by drugs. I am not some burnt-out hippie bent on renewing the drug culture of the '60s. I am a husband, a father, and a doctor. I'm a forty-eight-year-old baby boomer who probably shares similar thoughts with thousands (or millions) of others. I look forward to living a fairly normal life without more violence. I am optimistic that if enough people think about the present drug wars, we might at least initiate a national dialogue and consider alternative solutions. We deserve a more peaceful society.

Mark Berman practices cosmetic surgery in Santa Monica, California where he lives with his wife, Saralee, and his son, Sean. He's authored several medical articles and books on cosmetic surgery. This is his first novel.

CPSIA information can be obtained at www.ICGtesting.com
Printed in the USA
BVOW041101210213

313812BV00001B/3/P